It HAD to Be a *Duke*

THE LIARS' CLUB

VIVIENNE LORRET

AVON

An Imprint of HarperCollinsPublishers

IT HAD TO BE A DUKE. Copyright © 2023 by Vivienne Lorret. All rights reserved. Printed in the United States of America. No part of this book may be used or reproduced in any manner whatsoever without written permission except in the case of brief quotations embodied in critical articles and reviews. For information, address HarperCollins Publishers, 195 Broadway, New York, NY 10007.

First Avon Books mass market printing: November 2023

Print Edition ISBN: 978-0-06-314312-8
Digital Edition ISBN: 978-0-06-314313-5

Cover design by Amy Halperin
Cover illustration by Judy York
Cover images © Shutterstock

Avon, Avon & logo, and Avon Books & logo are registered trademarks of HarperCollins Publishers in the United States of America and other countries.

HarperCollins is a registered trademark of HarperCollins Publishers in the United States of America and other countries.

FIRST EDITION

23 24 25 26 27 BVGM 10 9 8 7 6 5 4 3 2 1

It Had to Be a Duke

"On second thought, it is rather amusing to see my enemy all wet."

Longhurst scrubbed a hand over his eyes, his jaw clenched. Straightening his waistcoat, he approached her, his stride cutting through the water. Then, reluctantly, he held out his hand. "No need to behave like a child."

"I thought I was feral. Now I'm a child?" She splashed him again, the need to aggravate him—to see that flash of cinders in his eyes—too strong to deny.

"Miss Hartley." His tone was low and forbidding. But she didn't care, and moved to splash him again. "Verity, I'm warning you."

Her breath caught.

It was the first time he'd used her given name. And yet, it seemed so familiar on his tongue as if he'd said it a dozen times. A hundred. It slid warmly inside her, curling low in the pit of her stomach like it belonged there. And it took everything inside her to keep from asking him to say it again.

"What do you plan to do once I'm standing?" she taunted with a wary glance down to his hand. "Throttle me? I promise that will not end well for you."

His eyes were blazing, fierce with intent. And he didn't wait for her to grasp his hand. Instead, he reached out, took her by the shoulders and lifted her.

"How dare y—"

He silenced the last syllable on a deep growl and crushed his mouth to hers.

By Vivienne Lorret

The Liars' Club
IT HAD TO BE A DUKE

The Mating Habits of Scoundrels Series
LORD HOLT TAKES A BRIDE
MY KIND OF EARL • THE WRONG MARQUESS
HOW TO STEAL A SCOUNDREL'S HEART
NEVER SEDUCE A DUKE

The Misadventures in Matchmaking Series
HOW TO FORGET A DUKE
TEN KISSES TO SCANDAL • THE ROGUE TO RUIN

The Season's Original Series
"The Duke's Christmas Wish"
(in ALL I WANT FOR CHRISTMAS IS A DUKE
and A CHRISTMAS TO REMEMBER)
THE DEBUTANTE IS MINE • THIS EARL IS ON FIRE
WHEN A MARQUESS LOVES A WOMAN
JUST ANOTHER VISCOUNT IN LOVE (novella)

The Rakes of Fallow Hall Series
THE ELUSIVE LORD EVERHART
THE DEVILISH MR. DANVERS
THE MADDENING LORD MONTWOOD

The Wallflower Wedding Series
TEMPTING MR. WEATHERSTONE (novella)
DARING MISS DANVERS • WINNING MISS WAKEFIELD
FINDING MISS MCFARLAND

To my parents and sisters, who've taught me so much about being human.
And to my sons, who've taught me that the most important thing in life is unconditional love.

Acknowledgments

Writing a book is a labor of love, and I'm so grateful that I can share it with you. But it wouldn't be possible without some very important people.

To my editor, Nicole, your smiley faces in the margins and helpful insights throughout the manuscript always make the second draft so much better than the first. Thank you for all these years we've had together.

To my agent, Stefanie, your inner strength and no-nonsense character have been an inspiration and a guidepost that keeps me pointed in the right direction. Thank you for the support you've given me.

To my amazing friends, JuLee and Tracy, you've practically used the jaws of life to get me out of my shell and into the world. I'm so thankful that you have my back. Sending lots of love your way.

To Amy Halperin, Judy York, and the entire Avon team, thank you for this jaw-dropping cover. The colors are stunning and the image captures the hero and heroine perfectly.

To Madelyn, Adam and Molly, thank you for being the wizards behind the curtain.

To my readers, thank you for reading my books and for sharing your love for romance with me.

You've all made this dream come true for me.

It HAD to Be a *Duke*

Chapter One

AT THE TIME, climbing out of the window seemed like the only practical option. In hindsight, however . . .

Verity Hartley wished she hadn't forgotten that Father had broken several rungs of the ivy-enshrouded trellis when playing Romeo to Mother's Juliet last week. Now she was hanging by her fingertips, her feet scurrying in midair.

And it was all her sisters' fault.

They had been rehearsing another play when she'd passed by the drawing room a moment ago. Through the open doorway, she'd glimpsed Honoria standing in the center of the room like a queen, crowned with a twist of golden hair, and ordering three of her admirers to position a chaise longue on the raised dais in the far corner.

"Slightly left of center stage, if you please. No, the *other* left, between the papier-mâché columns. Now, angle it just so. A bit more to the right. Back a sliver. And . . . *there*. Perfect." If there was one thing true about Honoria, it was that she always knew what she wanted.

Althea had been standing at the desk, her thick plait of mahogany hair falling carelessly over her shoulder as she scratched hasty amendments onto the pages of another script.

"I *must* have a third Fury to complete this scene. Otherwise, I might as well fashion the bellpull into a noose and save myself the indignity of failure." As the youngest at eighteen, Thea erred on the side of melodrama, forever complaining that her days on this mortal plane were trudging by endlessly without a modicum of excitement to stir her soul. "Where *is* our sister, by the by? Not even she could make a hash of this part."

And that was when Verity had decided to dash across the hall to the music room and through the open window.

Granted, it wasn't her most brilliant decision. But she would sooner wear a chemise fashioned from pinecones than be cajoled into another production.

Then again, she thought darting a glance two stories down past the hem of her olive skirts and sailing feet to the spiny juniper spire below, *death by way of impalement would be another option.*

She gulped and turned back to the trellis, redoubling her efforts. Though none of this would have been necessary if her sisters just understood. But that wish was futile.

The pair of them had been born with the famous Hartley silver tongues and flair for the dramatic. Whenever putting on a show for guests after dinner, they enthralled their audiences. With the delivery of a single impassioned word or a graceful faint onto a well-placed chaise longue, they could make an old termagant shed a tear and the most cynical ogre sigh like a lovelorn swain.

As for Verity, her performances were about as adept as those of a potted ficus. If said ficus had been left in a dark closet. Without water. For a year.

Which seemed like the length of time she'd been dangling against the side of the house like a sad scrap of forgotten bunting.

As she struggled to find a secure foothold, the slender wooden slats dug sharply into the cushion of her palms. She hissed, biting into her bottom lip, and briefly imagined her funeral.

Father would put on an excellent performance, clutching his heart and recounting the many embarrassing tales of her childhood as he often did for company. Mother would join him, walking sylphlike in expertly draped black silk and lean upon his arm, her voice poignantly breaking. And by the time they finished, there wouldn't be a dry eye in the chapel.

Truman, the eldest and her champion, would return from his latest voyage and stand stoically off to the side. Honoria would wear a veil, concealing her beauty out of a final act of courtesy from one sister to another. Thea would sniff at proper intervals, all the while taking notes to use in a future play. And Verity, in her coffin, would wish that she and her family could have understood each other before her untimely death—a fate likely to happen at any moment.

But then, just when she thought she could not hold on an instant longer, the toe of her left slipper finally found purchase.

She breathed a sigh of relief, her forehead resting against the ivy. And even if she should acquire an itchy rash from this intrepid escape, it would still be better than standing on a stage.

"Ah-ha! Caught you!"

Verity startled on a gasp. Her gaze jerked to the window above to find Honoria. "But how did you—"

"Know precisely where you would be?" A pair of pale brows arched beneath an artful spill of lustrous blonde curls as she peered over the white stone sill. "You've become far too predictable. Frankly, I'm disappointed. You're supposed to be the clever one."

"No. I'm the practical one and this was the only escape since the stairway was blocked by the servants carrying out the rugs for beating."

Honoria's bow-shaped mouth spread into a smug grin as her deep blue eyes glinted with wry amusement. "You forgot that father broke the trellis during our lesson on great performances last week, didn't you?"

After a moment, Verity offered a reluctant nod. "Yes."

"Well, now that I have you, I refuse to leave my perch until you come back inside. The tongue-twaddlers are here and Thea and I are outnumbered."

Tongue-twaddlers was a sobriquet given to Percival, Peter and Carlton Culpepper.

Years ago, Father had used their names as an enunciation exercise before a tutorial on delivering impassioned soliloquies and, from that point on, it had become part of their practice, too.

The Culpepper trio were sons of a local country gentleman, as well as hopeless suitors of Honoria and Thea. No matter how many times their proposals had been refused, they still came back to try again.

Percival had once vied for Verity's hand—likely having drawn the short straw—but his attentions were short-lived. She was, after all, the plain sister, teetering on the abyss of six and twenty. And it was an undisputed fact that men did not continue fruitless pursuits for the likes of her.

She had accepted this long ago when the beauty of her two younger sisters had often rendered onlookers thunderstruck. If their spectators were able to form words at all, the declarations were often spoken with awe and wonder. Then those gazes would drift to Verity and . . . discreetly fall away in obvious disappointment.

She referred to that as the *last grape* look. It was the look one gave to the squished violet globe at the bottom of the fruit bowl, after it had fallen from the stem and tumbled through the cracks between heaped oranges, pears and persimmons, left forgotten until an unsightly green fuzz formed on its skin.

Though, as far as Verity knew, *she* did not have an unsightly green fuzz on her skin. At least, not yet.

"I'm afraid I cannot participate. I need to . . ."

She paused, trying to think of something that was true enough. As a matter of principle, she abhorred deception and avoided it whenever possible.

". . . check the birdhouses," she announced at last, proud of herself. After all, she would eventually look in on their resident nesting fowl.

Honoria scoffed. "Abominable excuse! I refuse to tell our guests that you would rather stare at painted blocks of wood on pikes than be in their company."

"Then invent another. You know very well that I haven't any talent for pretext."

In truth, she was absolute rubbish at lying. Yet another characteristic she did not have in common with her family.

She was fairly certain she'd been left on the doorstep as an infant. And even though she loved them all dearly, there were days when she wondered if being raised by a pack of wolves might not have been preferable to a pack of would-be thespians.

As her sister glanced over her shoulder, Verity surreptitiously lowered down another few rungs, avoiding the broken ones in the center.

"Very well." Honoria plucked at the puffed sleeves of her periwinkle day dress and expelled a single sigh that skillfully delivered both her acceptance and weariness. "Thea and I will have to take turns with your lines. Though, I'm certain, the tongue-twaddlers won't notice. Puppies, the lot of them. They spend half the afternoon panting and wagging their tails, and the other half hoping that someone will throw a stick. But no matter how many times I tell them that I've been betrothed since birth to the long-lost Viscount Vandemere, they never listen. Therefore, one must conclude that men enjoy the torture of hopeless endeavors."

Oh, to have such problems, Verity thought. "Perhaps they don't believe that your fictitious viscount exists."

"He does too exist, even if only in theory. And why wouldn't they believe me? My recitation of the somber tale is ever flawless."

"And being a flirt doesn't hurt, I imagine."

Honoria flashed an unrepentant grin. "What other entertainment is there for a young woman in this humdrum hamlet? I simply make the best of the talents I possess. And I firmly believe that a woman must embrace her own individual gifts. If she is not unapologetically true to herself, then she'll have little to show for her life. And why are any of us here, if not to take center stage of our own lives?"

Verity shook her head. "If our father had been able to afford a proper Season for either of us, I've no doubt yours would have ended with the next Trojan War."

"One could only hope." Honoria issued an immodest shrug. "Although, I should prefer something other than a wooden horse. A fire-breathing dragon is more to my tastes."

"You should tell Thea. Perhaps she'll write one into the play."

"Doubtful. She is past her knights and dragons phase. But that reminds me . . . She mentioned something regarding our bucolic set requiring an air of authenticity. Oh dear. You don't think she would bring chickens into the drawing room again, do you?"

Verity paused in her descent and shuddered at the memory. The instant their father's wolfhounds had caught the scent, it became a scene of total carnage. Feathers and bits of whatnot everywhere.

"I would hope that she'd have learned her lesson. Although she has been rather besotted with the new piglets. We'd better check, just in case. I'll climb down and slip around to the kitchen garden."

"And I'll return to the parlor," Honoria agreed with a

nod. But before she dashed away, she leaned over the sill, eyes narrowed and finger pointed. "And don't think you can use this as an excuse to escape. I will find you. I know all your hiding places."

She rolled her eyes at the foundationless threat. Her sister didn't know everything.

Then Honoria lifted one finger. "There's the little garden near the crofter's cottage."

"A lucky guess," Verity declared, unbothered. After all, she certainly couldn't know about the—

"The one past the copse of trees and bramble beyond the dower house. Shall I go on?"

Verity's brow flattened. "Have you been following me?"

"Remember that eyepiece Truman sent me last Christmas? Well, you'd be surprised just how far one can see from the windows in the garret," Honoria said with a triumphant grin. "And besides, it isn't likely we'd ever find you locking yourself in a cupboard, now would we?"

"Why you little spy."

"See you in a trice." Her sister trilled her fingers in the air then flounced off.

Well, drat!

It became abundantly clear that she would need to find a new secret place to escape to whenever she was feeling closed in or pressured to perform. Though one usually followed the other.

The problem was, whenever she needed a moment to collect herself, she never lingered indoors. Ever since she'd been a child all her hiding places were outside. And apparently, any sister with determination, an eyepiece and access to a window would be able to spot her walking along the rolling hills for miles around.

However, her lack of privacy was an issue to be solved at a later time. For now, she needed to ensure that Thea didn't bring chaos into the house. Again.

Cautiously, she descended down the waterfall of ivy. She was almost past the partially open receiving parlor window on the first floor when she heard her mother's voice.

"Of course, I hope my daughters find contentment. I want their hearts to soar into the heavens and to see stars shining back at them whenever they look into their husband's eyes. But, as you know, the choice is not always ours, even if it should be," Mother said with an airy laugh.

Verity paused, wondering who her mother could be talking to. As far as she knew, there hadn't been any guests announced. And even though some of the villagers occasionally popped by unannounced, they were usually wanting to see Father.

Of course, it might have been the neighbors from down the hill, the dreaded Hunnicutts.

Their visits were always unexpected and unpleasant. They were also the most condescending, pompous and disagreeable people in all of Addlewick. Especially their daughter.

Nell Hunnicutt had been a thorn in her side since they were both in braids. And if Mother dared speak to Verity's archenemy in such a convivial manner, then she would be heartily offended.

"No truer words have been spoken," the mysterious visitor answered. "And I must say I have missed your romantic sensibilities, Roxana. My daughter and grandson see marriage as a task to be endured and believe I've turned into a sentimental old fool."

At once, Verity recognized the smooth, rounded tones of the other voice, but she was surprised to hear it coming from any room inside Hartley Hall. Countess Broadbent's family had not exactly been on speaking terms with her own since the great scandal.

Curious to discover the reason for this unprecedented

visit, she judiciously maneuvered to the other side of the trellis, just enough to peer inside the open window. After all, there was no harm in a little eavesdropping, was there? And besides, this would likely be the pinnacle of excitement she would have all month.

She was surprised to spot the two women playing cards on a piecrust table like old friends. Then again, her mother was renowned for her engaging nature.

A society column had once referred to Baroness Roxana Hartley as having an aura unfettered by time or the constraints of ordinary existence, her dark beauty as ethereal as midnight mist, and her voice as lovely as silken ribbons unfurling on a breeze.

The most that had ever been written about Verity was that her only memorable quality was her misfortune in being Baron Hartley's daughter, but was otherwise forgettable.

As for the countess, she appeared older, as one might expect in the seven years since she'd last been under this roof. Beneath a chignon of silver hair, her velum skin bore a delicate etching of age around her mouth and pale hazel eyes. But there was no frailness in her poised demeanor, nor any meanness in her fine-boned countenance. There never had been. She was stern and opinionated, to be sure, but never cruel. And Verity had always admired her.

Lady Broadbent pursed her lips as she considered the fan of cards in her hand. "But that does not answer the question of Verity. Presumably, you would wish her to marry first."

Marry? Why were they on the topic of marriage? And, more importantly, why was she the object of their discussion?

In the distance, she could hear the dogs barking at some disturbance and couldn't hear her mother's response. Craning her neck, she shuffled closer to the mezzanine window, her left slipper crunching down on a knot of desiccated ivy.

Roxana Hartley eased back against the quilting of a rose tufted chair and frowned. "At one time, perhaps. However, my eldest daughter isn't like the rest of us. She has always been a bit . . . reserved."

The last word was spoken with a sigh, as if that was the worst trait one could possess. Verity felt it hit in the center of her heart. It was one thing to know that she was a disappointment, but another altogether for her mother to acknowledge it openly.

"And what's worse," Mother continued, "I do believe, if given the chance, she would have settled for a mundane existence."

"Heaven forbid," Lady Broadbent tutted indulgently. "Back in my day, marrying for love was unheard of. If you were saddled with a man you could tolerate that was really saying something. But I waited for Pomeroy, much to my parent's disapproval. And when he finally came around, that made all the difference."

"Con and I were practically disowned when we eloped to Gretna Green. The rebellion of it only fueled our desire for each other. Such passion!" Mother flashed her famously impish grin, but then she sighed again. "I want that for my children, even Verity. Although, now it is surely too late."

Too late? Was her mother calling her *old* as well as *boring*? And what was "even Verity" supposed to mean?

"At least, she is not like one of the empty-headed ninnies vying for my grandson's attentions," the countess interjected. "I'm sorely afraid he'll make one of them his duchess and I'll have to endure lengthy teas and endless dinners where she tells me that her primary achievement that day was how well she wore a hat."

Mother laughed in response. "Well, if you're terribly worried about that, he could always marry—"

Verity never heard the end of that sentence. For, in that precise moment, the rung beneath her foot snapped.

Unprepared, she grabbed at a tangle of ivy, but slid down to the next rung. It snapped as well.

She teetered backward, off balance. Clawing at the trellis, she only just managed to grab hold. She breathed another sigh of relief. At least until . . .

The telltale screech of long nails heaving from the facade drew her alarmed attention.

Splendid, she thought, *and now I feel portly, too*— "*Oooooaaaauurhh!*" she screamed as the trellis detached from the top, falling away from the house in a backward arc.

This was it. The end of her unmarried, unremarkable life.

Screwing her eyes shut tight, she dangled by her fingertips, her legs swaying beneath her as she pictured the epitaph on her gravestone.

HERE LIES VERITY HARTLEY
BELOVED DAUGHTER AND SISTER
IN AN OTHERWISE LACKLUSTER EXISTENCE

Hearing the dogs nearby distracted her from being swallowed by the greedy jaws of death. Strange, but their *woofs* and *aroos* were *much* closer than she would have expected.

When she felt something brush against her hems, she dared to open one eye, then the other, only to see that she was barely twelve inches off the ground. Then she looked up. The trellis was bowing over her like the ruins of a bridge.

Oh. Apparently, she was not going to die today after all.

Letting go, she dropped smartly to the ground and dusted her hands together, reassuring the dogs with a friendly scratch behind the ears.

Her mother called out from the window. "Verity! Are you hurt?"

Stepping out from under the canopy of ivy, she offered a wave after pushing an errant hank of hair from her face. "Perfectly hale."

"You nearly gave me a heart seizure! I shall have nightmares for a month! Whatever were you doing?"

Eavesdropping, she thought. *Eavesdropping and learning that even you think my marital prospects are beyond hope.*

Not that Verity was hoping. It was just that she imagined her mother would be the last one to give up.

She said none of those things, of course. If nothing else, she was adept at biting her tongue. And she was saved from the effort of confessing that her old, boring self had been trying to avoid being center stage of a drama— *and just look how well that had gone*—when the wolfhounds began to growl.

Both Barrister and Serjeant-at-Arms, otherwise known as the Queen's Council, stood at her side, their focus on something behind her.

She turned, then found the last person in Addlewick that she would ever wish to see. And, of course, the snooty Miss Nell Hunnicutt had once again managed to catch her at her worst.

She was like a homing pigeon for disaster. Then again, that was likely shedding an unkind light on a species of clever birds.

On second thought, Nell Hunnicutt was more like a tick on the homing pigeon of disaster. A bloodthirsty tick. Who happened to be dressed in a puce walking costume and carrying a matching ruffled parasol.

"Yes, indeed. Whatever *were* you doing, Miss Hartley?" the Tick asked with a simpering laugh. "It seems that little has changed since I've been away. Why the last time I saw you, I believe you were on your hands and knees in a mud puddle."

Regrettably, that was true. She'd been visiting the village shops with her sisters when one of the clerks had bowled her over in an effort to present a fallen ribbon to Honoria. The most humiliating part was that he hadn't even realized what he'd done. Apparently, spinsterhood had made Verity invisible. But *fortunately*, Nell had been there, snickering at the entire production from inside her carriage.

"Then again, I suppose this"—Nell gestured to Verity's torn dress and disheveled hair with the tip of her parasol—"might be somewhat of an improvement. At least, you're on your feet."

"So good of you to remind me. And what delightful errand brings you to Hartley Hall?"

"One of pure altruism, I assure you. I thought I might check in on my poor neighbors and see if I could cheer you with the tales of my Season. It's the very least I can do to bring a bit of London to those who will likely never witness the splendor of town long enough to truly appreciate it. And I must say—"

"*Must you? Really?*" Verity muttered under her breath.

"—that I've never had so many exquisite gowns in all my life. But one needs more than can fit in a wardrobe when one is invited to so many glamorous events. I have worn out seven pairs of slippers. Seven! And the Season is at its zenith. Oh, and I've found the most divine milliner. She has the cleverest hand at hats, and gentlemen often remark about how well I wear them."

Verity was instantly reminded of the empty-headed ninnies vying for the hand of Lady Broadbent's grandson.

"Then surely you will be greatly missed by not being in town for all these parties, and should likely return at your earliest convenience."

"Quite so. But that is the crux of my current situation," the Tick said with a sniff of condescension. "You see, I have had three gentlemen ask for my hand. Three! And I needed a reprieve to consider my options. Of course, three suitors may not seem like many compared to all the country squires that have been competing for a place in your sister's stables for so long." She paused just long enough to infer a degree of unseemliness and Verity narrowed her eyes. "Of course, I mean no offense. I have the greatest admiration for Honoria. For all your family, in fact."

"Of course." Verity was *this close* to setting the dogs on her.

"Oh, how I wish you could have had a proper Season, then I could beg your counsel for I do not know who to choose. One was recently knighted. Another is a viscount. And—I'm saving the best for last—a marquess with an estate in Derbyshire."

"How lovely for you. But I'm afraid I cannot offer my counsel and my sisters are otherwise engaged, so you'll have to postpone your visit for another day." *Or never*, Verity thought as she leaned down to pet Barry's wiry fur. Then Serjie nudged his way under her arm, demanding attention.

The Tick clucked her tongue and studied the house, her eyes scanning each window. "Such a pity. Another reason I popped by is that my gardener thought he saw Lady Broadbent's carriage rumble down the lane. Her grandson, the duke, is in town, you know. I've even dined with him. Twice." She paused as if offering Verity the chance to be impressed. "But it is unlikely, is it not, that her ladyship would ever cross *your* threshold? The very idea is laughable, to be sure."

"Actually, the countess *is* here," Verity said, all too pleased to affirm the rumor and put a stopper in her neighbor's haughty laugh. "It appears as though some things have changed since you were away."

"Is that so?"

"It is, indeed."

Nell shifted and plucked at the ruffled trim of her glove. "And just what, pray tell, could have brought about this sudden reconciliation between families?"

Verity wasn't sure what possessed her—whether it was spite, a leftover rush of nerves from having survived the *trellis de morte*, or if it was simply a need to put Miss Hunnicutt in her place—but for the first time in her life she managed to tell a lie. A whopping good lie. And she knew it was exceptional because she felt tingles wash over her skin the instant she said it.

"Because her grandson, the Duke of Longhurst, and I are engaged to be married."

Chapter Two

～

MAGNUS WARRING, THE fifth Duke of Longhurst, sat in a London warehouse office across from Phineas Snow.

The Button King was one of the wealthiest tradesmen in all of England. He was part eagle and part bull, not only in temperament but in physical attributes. Beneath a widow's peak of iron gray hair with a shock of white at each temple, his wiry brows sat in a flat line over steely eyes as he studied the latest buttons stamped from the die.

"What military officer would allow this rubbish to sully his uniform? The surface is grainy and dull. Where is the luster? The attention to detail?" he asked his foreman who stared back at him in nervous stupefaction. "Well?"

"I dunno, sir. These were stamped and brought to you straightaway, as ordered."

"Quality buttons, Mr. Jones, are a symbol of a person's status. At one time, they were so valued that a man could settle all his debts by removing one from his coat. *One.* These are an embarrassment to that noble history." Snow tossed the brass disc into the felt-lined casket. It dropped onto the other cast-offs with a discordant *plink*. "The die is clearly flawed. Start again. And bring me the very first button stamped. I want perfection. Nothing else will do."

The worker left in haste, nearly tripping over his own feet along the way.

"That man's a button short, if you ask me," Snow grumbled under his breath. Then he turned to regard Magnus. "Now then, with that settled, on to the matter for which I called you here today—my daughter."

Any other man might have been intimidated beneath such scowling scrutiny, even if only to shift in his chair. But not him. There was nothing Snow could do or say that would rattle Magnus.

Even before he had succeeded to the title, he'd spent most of his life issuing that same look to other men across the desk in his father's study. His late father had tended to be too soft, too idealistic, too . . . irrational to attend estate matters. Ever pragmatic, even as a boy, Magnus had taken up the reins himself.

"I believe I've made my intentions toward Miss Snow clear," he said, matter-of-factly. "Our union would be advantageous for all parties—your future business growth and elevated place in society, and—"

"Anna's dowry transferred into your accounts," Snow concluded and held up a staying hand when Magnus opened his mouth to speak. "Neither of us are foolish romantics. You and I see the world as it is. Let us not insult the other's intelligence by pretending otherwise."

Magnus inclined his head. It didn't matter that he was a duke and that a union between their families would bring this middle-class man into the realm of the aristocracy, or that the dowry would ultimately secure the Longhurst estate for generations to come. Snow didn't care about such things. He was all bluster and business and Magnus respected that about him.

Sentiment was for fools.

"I did not make my fortune on the backs of other men. I made it through delivering an exemplary product that spoke for itself. You'll find no scandal lurking in the shadows of the Snow name either. I take particular pride in that fact, which"—he stabbed a beefy finger onto the desk blotter—"is the reason that none of Anna's suitors have come up to snuff."

Magnus waited a beat for Snow to add "Until you, that is" and then offer his hand across the desk to shake in a gentleman's agreement. The contracts would be signed later, a mere formality. He was certain that this meeting was simply a preliminary welcome to the button empire.

And if there was one thing that the Duke of Longhurst demanded in all his dealings, it was certainty.

He waited another beat and then another, the interminable lull filled with the unsyncopated *whump* and *clatter* of the workers at their stamping presses. But he soon realized those words were not coming.

Instead, Snow filled his barrel chest on a lungful of office air, tinged with various aromas from the tang of metal to the bitterness of creosote and the sweetness of pipe tobacco. "This afternoon, I received word of a recent development that linked your name to a daughter of a certain Baron Conchobar Erasmus Hartley. The very same Hartley who was involved in that ruinous scandal years ago. The one regarding that business with the—"

"I know all about that scandal," Magnus interrupted through clenched teeth, his fingers curling over the arms of the chair. The spindle-legged construction squawked in protest beneath his athletic frame. Across from him, a pair of keen gray eyes flicked down to the telltale white edges outlining his knuckles, and he forced himself to relax his grip. "There must be a mistake."

"Mistake, you say?" The Button King pursed his lips. "I've never liked that word. Either you are implying that I have taken something in error, or admitting that you have done so."

"Neither, I assure you, sir. There is no possible way

I would have anything to do with any member of that family."

"According to my information, you and Hartley's son went to university together."

"And whatever acquaintance we might have had was severed years ago with his father's involvement in that swindle and the subsequent loss of my father's fortune. There are certain misdeeds that one cannot forgive." And the very fact that Truman "Hawk" Hartley had neglected to warn him of his father's part in the scheme proved him to be a most dishonorable cad.

Snow pushed his chair back, the legs screeching sharply against the hardwood floor.

"You and I are of like mind," Snow said with a nod. He had a habit of standing with his thumbs tucked into the open sleeves of his tightly fitted waistcoat, his arms bent at the elbow like a pair of wings at rest. "Deficiency of character is unacceptable. Faults in one's actions—or perceived actions, as it were—must be eradicated with utmost expedience. As far as I can tell, your character does not lean toward ruinous behavior. In fact, considering the shambles of your estate earnings at the time you succeeded to the title, you might have made any number of those imprudent decisions your class is known for, such as gambling, borrowing against your estate, selling off parcels for a pittance only to find yourself worse off the following year. Instead, you rolled up your sleeves and worked your land with your tenants, producing profitable crops for the first time in decades. Frankly, I'm rather impressed," he said. "But not *too* impressed."

Knowing that resolving this misunderstanding would be his only chance to secure permission to marry Miss Snow, Magnus stood as well. "I will travel to Addlewick straightaway and correct the"—he paused—"confusion."

Then he turned sharply on his heel and left before the Button King decided to give him a definition of that word as well.

∽

MAGNUS SEETHED ALL the way to his town house. He did not know what Hartley was up to, but he was damned sure going to put a stop to it.

For the past seven years, he had worked hard to fill the deficit in his family coffers. Through the sweat off his own brow and calluses on his hands, he had done all he could to work the land, install an irrigation system for times of drought and help his tenants grow more lucrative crops. But last winter had been a hard one and spring had brought flooding. Whatever ground he'd gained would be washed away soon enough.

Therefore, he was going to do what any duke in his position would—marry an heiress.

But this ridiculous rumor that he was betrothed to the daughter of a liar, cheat and swindler could ruin everything.

Crossing the threshold, he gave orders to his manservant to pack a satchel, then broke the news to his mother.

As expected, Geraldine Warring, the Dowager Duchess of Longhurst, didn't take it well. Beneath a tight chignon of grizzled dark hair, her forehead furrowed with disbelief. But then, as the name of Hartley lingered in the room, stirring the coals of a hatred that would never be extinguished, her lips compressed into a thin line. "You must quiet the matter with utmost haste."

"I plan to, Mother."

"Everything depends upon it. Not only for the sake of the Longhurst estate, but for your brother."

As he attempted to stretch a pair of black gloves over the hands that had thickened over these years of laboring out of doors, he heard a faint tremor in her voice. With an alert glance, he saw the lower rims of her eyes turn red.

When their gazes met, she turned away quickly and began to fuss with a flower arrangement on the hall table.

She was such a hard woman on the outside, stern and remote in the way that circumstance had forced her to become. Women who married tenderhearted dreamers often had to be. However, when it came to her sons, the softer uncertain aspect of her nature slipped through the cracks of the sturdy walls that held her together.

Tossing the gloves aside, he laid a hand on her shoulder and pressed a kiss to her cheek in a show of compassion. Compassion which did not necessarily extend to his wayward younger brother, whose devil-may-care ways had been indulged more often than not by their father.

Rowan had been away these many years and had only written recently with a promise to come home . . . *if* the life that their father had once promised him was still obtainable.

For years, Magnus hadn't had word from him and assumed the worst. But then, a month ago, Mother received the letter. And now, in addition to needing Miss Snow's dowry to replenish the Longhurst coffers, he needed it in order to bring his intrepid brother home again and settled with a respectable living.

And yet, once again, Hartley's name crept out of the shadows and threatened to ruin it all.

"I will do everything within my power to resolve this unforeseen complication," Magnus assured her. "I promise."

She sniffed, blinking rapidly before she turned to nod up at him. "It's just that I haven't seen Rowan in so long and I want him—I want both of you—to have every chance at the life you are entitled to. I didn't marry your father for nothing."

Magnus knew little about entitlement. But he knew

about duty. And he knew enough about his brother that he doubted Rowan was after stability or security. He was likely running away from something far more dangerous. As usual.

But before Magnus could continue on the course of securing a future for the longevity of the Warring family, he needed to discover what the deuce Hartley was up to this time.

Chapter Three

༄

$\mathcal{A}$s FAR AS Verity was concerned, there was only one thing worse than the guilt felt after telling a convincing lie—having her mother and Lady Broadbent overhear it.

This meant that there was no way she could deny it. No way she could convince them that Nell Hunnicutt must have misunderstood. And no way to undo the strain her declaration would put on the already frayed relationship between houses.

It had been two days since the *Big Lie*. Two days of looking over her shoulder in fear of Nell returning and Verity knowing she would have to reinforce one lie with another. And who knew where that would lead? Descriptions of the Belgian lace in her imaginary trousseau? A map of her fictitious honeymoon trip? A list of names for the make-believe children she would have with a man she'd never actually met?

It was exhausting to think about. Soon she would be swallowed whole by the entire ordeal.

So, when a missive arrived with an invitation to tea at Swanscott Manor, Verity knew this was it. Her comeuppance. Time to pay the piper. If she had a hair shirt, she would have worn it.

Being short on medieval means of self-flagellation, however, she popped her head into Thea's chamber and agreed to take a part in the play instead.

"And just so you know," Verity added stoically, "the experience will likely kill me."

Unmoved by the prospect of her untimely demise, her sister grinned. "Look on the bright side. Your performance will likely kill the audience first. Either way, it should be entertaining."

After that *happy* encounter, Verity left Hartley Hall with a determined yet somber stride.

The rain had stopped several hours ago, but she wore the hood of her cloak pulled low over her head all the same. She did not deserve sunshine. Only mud puddles. And by the time she arrived for her presumed arraignment, her legs felt as leaden as if she were dragging a ball and chain by each ankle.

Much to her surprise, she was welcomed graciously into the countess's sitting room, where the walls were lined in flower-painted silk and the air perfumed by bright bouquets of hothouse flowers. But she refused to allow the cheerful surroundings to lift her spirits, and she steeled herself for the worst.

Haranguing would be involved, of course. Along with castigations, raised voices, finger pointing and, quite possibly, smelling salts.

Unable to bear the weight of suspense of what was to come, Verity started explaining the matter all over again before she'd taken two steps into the room. "I must apologize once more for involving your family in my own act of perjury, my lady. There is absolutely no excuse for what I have done. I cannot even lay the blame at the feet of Nell Hunnicutt, who has been a thorn in my side for most of my life, because I have plenty of faults of my own . . ."

Unfortunately, once those words started flowing, a torrent of confessions swiftly followed.

She couldn't stop herself from recounting every inadequacy. ". . . a potted ficus, if I'm to be honest . . ." Every embarrassment. ". . . and there I was on my hands and knees in the mud, and it was far from the first time . . ." Every well-intentioned but, ultimately, disastrous decision. ". . . then I was just hanging there with the dogs barking at my heels and the rest you know. But not a moment has gone by since, that I haven't wished I'd fallen on my head instead."

Lady Broadbent waited patiently for her to finish and shook her head. "Good gracious, girl! Did you think I summoned you here in order to flog you?"

"Well . . . something to that effect."

Turning, the countess rang the little silver bell sitting on the round table beside her. A maid appeared in the doorway at once. "The cat-o'-nine-tails, Adelaide, if you please." When the maid blinked in confusion, she added, "Oh, better make it tea and cake instead."

The maid curtsied and left them alone. Lady Broadbent gestured to the ivory damask settee, the corner of her mouth hitching in a grin.

"So, my lady did not call me here to chastise me?" Verity asked as she sank to the edge of the cushion.

Having been raised in a house where absolutely anything could happen at any moment—like chickens in the drawing room, or Father pretending that Mother had poisoned him at dinner and then performing a death scene—she preferred to understand the point of things whenever she could.

The countess ruffled the air with her fingertips and shook her head. "Nonsense, my dear girl. In your shoes, I might have done the same. In fact, I told a small fib or two in order to secure Lord Broadbent's attentions."

"Oh, but I wasn't trying to gain your grandson's attention. In fact, I'd rather he never knew. Is there any way that we could arrange that, do you think? To disavow the rumor before it has a chance to spread?"

"Rumors are rather feral creatures, I'm afraid. There really is no way of containing them once they are let loose."

Verity nodded glumly. She knew, from overhearing the servants gossiping in Hartley Hall, that her lie had already spread through the village faster than chicken feathers in the drawing room. There were people paying calls and sending word of congratulations who had rarely acknowledged her existence.

Then again, the villagers used any excuse to pay a call on Father in the hopes of being cast in one of his productions.

"My only consolation is that this lie cannot run wild for too much longer. The truth is bound to come out," Verity said.

And then everyone would look at her with pity just as they'd done after the bakery incident. Ugh. However, that was another nightmare altogether and she could only deal with one at a time.

"Perhaps," the dowager offered. "Though, it is my experience that people often invent their own truths."

Verity's father had said the same thing when she'd confessed. Conchobar Hartley believed that the truth and a lie were two sides of the same coin. If you spin it cleverly, it was impossible to tell which was which.

The thought sent a surge of panic through her. Her lie was bad enough. But it would be even worse if it took on a life of its own.

"The story is too outlandish for anyone with sense to believe. The very idea that any members of our families could ever have any sort of romantic involvement . . . well, it's almost Shakespearean. We're veritable Capulets and Montagues," she rambled, feeling a pang of envy toward Juliet and wishing she had a *happy dagger* to end her current misery. "And besides, I've never even met your grandson."

Lady Broadbent appeared neither alarmed nor concerned by her guest's outburst. She merely pursed her lips and offered a *Hmm* in a noncommittal fashion, the way that one might shrug one's shoulders. "Those trivialities rarely matter when there's a tantalizing tidbit of gossip to spread. Doubtless, there's another rumor abounding about how you met."

When the maid reappeared in that moment, tray in hand, Lady Broadbent inquired, "Tell me, Adelaide, have you heard any news regarding my grandson and Miss Hartley?"

"If I may be so bold, my lady," the maid began as she arranged the tea service on a low rosewood table. "I heard that Mr. Hartley, the miss's brother, introduced them years ago and they've been corresponding in secret ever since."

Lady Broadbent's brows arched with intrigue as she eyed Verity. "And passionate letters, no doubt."

"Oh, yes, my lady. Mrs. Rayburn at the post office says that she accidentally intercepted one a few months ago. The address was poorly written and she opened it by mistake, but it contained a lock of His Grace's hair as well as a poem he'd written about their love being forbidden since their families hated each other. It has sent many a heart aflutter."

Verity growled in frustration. Of all the dukes she might have mentioned, or even invented, why did it have to be him? And why wasn't anyone, other than herself, taking this seriously?

Flustered, she went to the box window, staring out at a neatly ordered world through nine panes. The three tiers were sky, horizon and garden. It would have been so simple to continue her life as she had always done if she'd just managed to keep her mouth shut in the vicinity of *the Tick*.

Verity had only seen the duke on a few occasions, years

ago, when he'd visited his grandmother and accompanied
her on jaunts to the village. But it had always been from a
distance. There'd been the throng of her sisters' admirers
to contend with, after all.

He'd also gone hunting with her brother. She'd seen
the pair of them from the window, riding off across the
meadow. But Truman had never brought friends to sup
with the family, for the obvious reason that said family
would inevitably embarrass him by staging an impromptu
production after—or heaven forbid, *during*—dinner.

"This tittle-tattle is ridiculous. After all, wouldn't a
man who wrote passionate letters be eager to visit the
hamlet where his beloved lived, not to mention his own
grandmother? Forgive me, my lady. But has everyone forgotten that he hasn't been here in ages?"

"As a matter of fact . . ." Lady Broadbent began.

But Verity didn't give her the chance to finish. She was
too incensed by the absolute lunacy of this entire ordeal.
"And I suppose it doesn't even matter that His Grace and
I have never been in the same place at the same time. Of
course not. Village folk would prefer to invent letters that
have never been written. My only consolation is that there
isn't a single person who can honestly state that the duke
and I have ever been standing in a room—"

A throat cleared from somewhere behind her and she
turned away from the window as the last word fell from
her lips.

"—together."

A man stood in the doorway. And not just any man
either.

No, no, no, no, no. It couldn't be, she thought as her
stomach flipped with dread and her heart started thudding
heavily beneath her breast.

Oh, but it was. The Duke of Longhurst was here!

Even though she'd only seen him from a distance, she

would know the coal black hair and proud set of those broad shoulders anywhere.

What she had never witnessed, however, was the muscle jumping along an angled jawline that was so hard-edged and unforgiving that it might have been cleaved from a slab of slate. His mouth was surely made of the same substance for all the welcome it possessed.

In this closer proximity, she noted that he had something of a swarthy appearance, his face tan and lean. Beneath heavy dark brows, a pair of light brown eyes glared intensely at her as if his skull contained the brazier fire that belonged in Honoria's Trojan dragon and he was prepared to burn a hole through his enemies.

And right now, *that* was Verity.

"As I was saying," the countess continued, "the reason I called you here today was because my grandson is visiting and I thought the two of you could settle a few matters. Magnus, I should like to introduce you to Miss Hartley. Verity, my grandson."

He issued a curt, perfunctory nod from the doorway, those eyes raking disdainfully down to her mud-speckled hem and back up again.

Part of her wondered if anyone smelled smoke in the air or if she was imagining things. Another part was glad he remained on the other side of the threshold and she could hold fast to her claim that they'd never been in the same room.

Swallowing down a rise of nerves, she curtsied on wobbly legs, her palms perspiring against her skirts. "Your Grace, I must apologize for bringing you into all of this. Please know that I never imagined that my insignificant little lie would ever reach your ears."

"Ah. Do you lie for your own amusement, then?" he asked, his voice low and gravelly. If dragons had ever spoken, she was certain they'd sounded just like that.

"Well, no. What I was trying to say . . ."

Her words trailed off as he arched a brow and she realized that he wasn't actually interested in the answer.

When he stepped into the room, she could have sworn she felt the quake of it beneath her slippers, jolting upward through the marrow of her bones.

Then again, he was a veritable beast of a man, powerfully built in a way that wasn't typical for a gentleman. At least, not the ones she'd met. Though, strangely enough it wasn't his size that made him intimidating, but the way he carried himself.

Beneath his tailored coat and trousers, he had a way of prowling, smooth and controlled like some sort of wild creature that might pounce the moment you looked away.

Verity didn't dare take her eyes off him. She didn't even move from her spot in front of the window.

He stopped by the mantel on the opposite side of the room, shoulders squared, arms crossed. "You will put an end to this nonsense at once. Tell everyone that you invented this betrothal and that there is nothing between us."

She had intended to do just that. After all, she had come here full of humility and remorse.

At least . . . until he spoke.

The instant he issued his command in that gruff, superior tone, she would sooner strip to her chemise and recite *Fordyce's Sermons* from the rooftop before she did his bidding!

Her hackles rose, her spine straight as a pike, and all contrition over her culpability in this matter evaporated. "How dare you imagine that you can order me about as if I were one of your servants! Though I should hope you'd have sense enough to treat the people who might spit in your teapot a bit better. As for me, I am still the daughter of a gentleman and if you want to ensure that everyone knows there's nothing between us . . . tell them yourself," she huffed. Then, remembering her hostess, she looked to the countess and said, "I beg your pardon, my lady. But it had to be said."

A small smile lifted the corner of Lady Broadbent's mouth. "You have a bit of fire in you, after all, Miss Hartley."

"She is a veritable shrew," the duke muttered.

Verity knew her sisters were far more outspoken than she had ever been, but no one had ever called them shrews. Clearly, labels such as those were reserved for plain women. But she refused to let the barb bother her.

Ignoring him, she continued speaking directly to the countess. "I am not usually so volatile. But I detest when a person makes rash judgments over appearances or circumstances about which they know nothing. If your grandson had bothered to speak to me in a cordial manner, he would know that I am equally upset by this turn of events."

"Events which *you* created," he growled, his hands fisted at his sides.

She clenched her teeth. "If I could have conjured the name of any other duke in all of England—nay, in all the world—I surely would have done so and saved myself a megrim."

"Then why not simply invent another? Say you spoke in error."

"Do you think I did not attempt that already? I listed the names of every duke I'd ever heard of and even a few I had not." The latter category had been soundalike variations on Longhurst, such as *Longwurst* and *Langerst*. A few others were just her muttering nonsensically. Until finally, and much to her mortifications, she'd said *Songburst*. Which had been greeted with a chorus of giggles and knowing grins.

"The servants only imagined that I was trying to protect our secret," she admitted in frustration. "Regrettably, I've always been rather dreadful at lying."

"And you expect me to believe that a member of the Hartley clan, a family known for spinning falsehoods that lead others to ruin, is unable to lie convincingly?"

She could have argued her point. And, oh, there was something about him that made her want to argue . . . perhaps even bare her claws and teeth . . . but instead, she took the sensible high road.

Gathering her composure on a deep breath, she said, "As long as we stay away from each other—"

"That won't be difficult," he interjected.

"—the rumor will disappear on its own." She narrowed her eyes. *Ooooh, that man!* She absolutely abhorred him. How her brother could have been friends with such a cretin was beyond her. "Forgive me, my lady, but I shall take my leave. Thank you for the generous invitation."

"My driver is at your disposal, my dear."

"Thank you, no," she said with a curtsy. "Walking will help alleviate the murderous compulsions I'm feeling toward your grandson at the moment."

She received a surprised laugh from her hostess as she marched out of the room without a backward glance to the duke. The only problem was, she was afraid this wasn't over. Not by a long shot.

❧

So that was the famed sister which his former acquaintance Mr. Hartley had regaled him of for years, extolling her cleverness and dry wit? Magnus could account for nothing of the sort. In fact, he had rarely been so incensed as when he watched her walk out the door.

There must have been something in the Hartley blood that brought out the worst in him.

"Another round and I'd thought I would have to ring

for a ewer of water and toss it on the pair of you. But she certainly held her own. I daresay, her eyes were hurling spears at you and her tongue was whip sharp," his grandmother said with a pleased chortle.

"Do not tell me that you admire that . . . that *creature*."

His grandmother's dove gray brows lifted as she pursed her lips. "She surprised me. Usually, she's such a quiet girl. But you know what they say, silent on the outside with a storm brewing on the inside."

He glowered at the window where she'd stood with the light silhouetting her plain brown hair and prim features. Her spear-hurling brown eyes were least remarkable of all. And when she was riled, the straight line of her shoulders stiffened and her slender arms gesticulated wildly.

One should never trust anyone so easily lured into fits of pique.

He couldn't remember the last time someone had dared speak to him in such a manner. "She didn't seem to have any trouble unleashing that tempest today."

"No, indeed. Perhaps it was simply time. Or perhaps she needed to meet someone disagreeable to bring it out of her."

"If I was disagreeable, the blame is hers alone. You don't know what she has cost me. I was this close"—he raised his thumb and forefinger—"to finally securing the deal with Mr. Snow when her outrageous lie put a damper on the entire affair."

His grandmother scoffed. "You speak of taking a wife as little more than a handshake. Have you no regard for the future mother of your children?"

Feeling the seams of his coat strain around his flexed bicep, he lowered his hand and regained control of his composure on a slow exhale.

"Certainty is all I require. And I am certain that Miss Snow is an accomplished young woman who will make a fine duchess, and her fortune will ensure the stability of the Longhurst line for many years to come."

"Be still my heart. Such poetry," Grandmother said dryly. "And what will Miss Snow think of the rumor that you have jilted another woman for her?"

"She will think nothing because that did not happen."

"Oh, but in the eyes of society that is precisely what will happen if you return to London without so much as a by-your-leave to Miss Hartley."

"Preposterous."

"I'm afraid not, Magnus. You see, this entire village has already invented a lengthy betrothal for the two of you, which began when you were still at university."

As his grandmother proceeded to explain the confounded rumors flying about, he was dumbstruck. Apparently, during the years that he'd been toiling on his own lands from dawn to dusk, he'd also been keeping a sweetheart? And while sweat had been pouring from his brow, his back breaking, he'd been composing love letters and sonnets? Ha!

"So you see," she continued, "the only way to truly extricate yourself from this ordeal and gain that certainty you require is to ensure that Miss Hartley ends the engagement."

"Then that is precisely what she will do this very day. I have far too much at stake to let this utter nonsense go on a moment longer."

When he took a step toward the door, his grandmother gave him a pitying look and shook her head. "It won't be that simple. With you showing up just minutes before the betrothal is canceled, it will only make people question. If a reason is not supplied, they will invent one themselves. Furthermore, since you do not visit often, the blame will likely be yours, which will leave you in no better position than you are now."

He considered this for a moment and, damn it all, she was right.

"Then what do you propose? That I marry a Hartley and let the family estate fall into utter ruin for the sake of these addlepated villagers?" He shuddered at the thought.

"Surely not. All I'm suggesting is that you spend a few days here. A week at most."

"A week!"

"Merely escort her to an assembly. A dinner. Visit the village shops with her on your arm and let them see for themselves how ill the two of you are suited. Then, in a sennight, Miss Hartley will release you of your obligation—"

"It is not *my* obligation," he cut in, tasting bitterness on his tongue. "And how do you even know that Miss Hartley will agree to this plan, hmm? After all, she is the one who embroiled me in this nonsense in the first place, risking my reputation as a man of honor and reason."

He could picture Phineas Snow, standing with his thumbs hooked in the pits of his waistcoat as he glowered with disapproval at the duke who did not *come up to snuff*. And then the fortune that Magnus needed to secure his family's future would be lost.

Starting again, seeking a new heiress to woo at this stage would take far too long. Much longer than he had.

"I know it is difficult to imagine at the moment," Grandmother continued kindly. "But Miss Hartley is a practical young woman who will see the sense in this plan. And, by the time it is over, neither of your reputations should be harmed in the least. In fact, it might even improve yours by making you more approachable. Society matrons and debutantes alike will see you in a kinder light. There's nothing a woman likes more than to imagine herself as the saving angel for a heartbroken man."

He grumbled at the foolishness of that last statement. As for the rest of it, he supposed a shred of logic could be found. That was little consolation, however. Because, once again, his future was in the hands of a Hartley. He knew from experience that was the worst of all fates.

Embittered, he stalked to the window, the air tinged with the faint, sweet aroma of honeysuckle. He drew in a deep breath and stared out at the blue sky, wishing there was a single rain cloud that might follow a certain conniving creature on her trek back to Hartley Hall.

But the cloud she deserved was nowhere in sight.

Thinking it best to come up with a strategy and to cool his temper, he decided to wait until tomorrow morning before riding over to Hartley Hall to make his proposal.

Chapter Four

ॐ

*T*HE FOLLOWING MORNING, Verity found a missive lying in wait on the foyer table. The folded edges were parted, the red scaling wax cracked, suggesting it had been read by another member of the family.

Out of mere curiosity, she picked it up. Then dropped it like a rancid potato.

An invitation, of all things! And worse, it was for a dinner party at the Hunnicutt's.

Oh, how she wished she could have held the card over a sconce flame, burned it to ash and pretend it never arrived. However, at least one other person beneath this roof had read it, making that an impossibility. Not only that, but knowing the scheming persistence of Mrs. Hunnicutt—the apple did not fall far from that particular tree, after all—she would only send another and another until it was accepted.

Nell's mother was the daughter of landed gentry who married a younger son and often joked that she wouldn't be too put out if her brother-in-law choked on a fishbone and left the viscountcy to her husband. But no one really thought she was jesting.

Nevertheless, Elaine Hunnicutt and her daughter would likely do anything to ensure that they could tell everyone about having a duke dine at their table . . . even hand deliver an invitation to him in order to ferret out any titillating gossip!

She could picture it—the Hunnicutts fawning over him, stroking Longhurst's already overinflated ego as he revealed the unvarnished truth, supplying Nell with enough fodder to lord over her for all eternity.

And all because of one, thoughtless little fib.

As the realization of the power that she'd simply handed over to her archenemy sank in, Verity's breaths became shallow, her lungs tight. The foyer walls seemed to crowd closer, pressing in on her.

Dashing outside, she drew in a huge gulp of air, hunched over with one hand propped against the portico column and the other braced against her knee.

This wasn't an unfamiliar sensation. By now, she knew that all she needed to conquer these episodes was to be out of doors. But, just to be on the safe side, she walked away from Hartley Hall and the dreaded invitation.

There was only one thing for her to do—head toward Swanscott Manor *before* the Hunnicutts could sink their fangs into Longhurst.

Unfortunately, that meant Verity would have to ask that irritating man not to reveal her lie. Though, after her dealings with him yesterday, she doubted he had one ounce of humanity in him. But it was the only hope she had.

Well, that *and* the hope that he'd already left for London.

If he hadn't, however, then perhaps she could try harder to express the contrition she'd intended yesterday before she'd lost her temper. At least, she could *if* . . . he wouldn't continue to be so disagreeable.

The dinner was in six days. The Tick left for London in seven.

One week. That was all she needed. Just one week of letting this lie run wild. Then, when the Tick was gone and too far away to snicker in her face, Verity would set everything to rights. Somehow.

"Surely a few more days shouldn't matter," she said to herself as she stepped over the stile along her familiar, well-worn path through meadow grass and thicket. "It would only be a small delay."

And yet, she had a sense that he would put up a fuss over every trifling detail. Longhurst seemed the sort of man who required control over all things and would throw a fit if he didn't get his way.

Essentially, he was a very large child.

Contemplating the likelihood that he would agree to this plan—*not very likely*—she turned onto the towpath by the river. Her footfalls on the hardpacked earth were muffled beneath the skirts of her petticoat and sprigged muslin, the air cool, dewy and fragrant with the budding perfume of spring and the chirruping songs of finches and pipets.

She'd been in such a hurry to escape the suffocating invitation that she hadn't bothered to don a bonnet. But after such a cloudy, wet spring, it felt good to have the sunshine on her face. She didn't even mind the chill that penetrated her fringed shawl.

Instead, she simply quickened her stride. After all, the sooner she was done with this encounter with the duke the better. And if he was already on his way back to London, it would be even better yet.

The thought brought a hopeful hop to her step as she neared the old white ash with a trunk as thick as a staircase and arms that hung heavily above her head and over the path.

As children, it had been a rite of passage to carve their initials near the knothole. But just as she drew close enough to skim her fingers over the timeworn letters, she heard a sound that made her pause.

It wasn't the call of the sparrows or starlings that usually nested here, but something else entirely.

Her eyes narrowed as she spotted the cat on the branch overhead. Even though she had a fondness for all animals, cats were her least favorite.

She preferred the wolfhounds, as well as the birds that lived in the painted houses in the garden. Each spring there were new gawping, fuzzy-headed arrivals and she could always cajole Father into adding another house. They had a veritable village now. And the last thing she wanted to do was to offer assistance to a predator.

However, when she heard the plaintive mewls from this orange-speckled cat, she couldn't ignore it. The poor thing was clearly stuck. He or she had obviously climbed too high.

Her ever-bendable heart went out to it. If anyone could understand the panic one felt when trapped and unable to escape, it was Verity.

As a child, before her parents had become baron and baroness and were still traveling with a small theatre troupe across the countryside, she had been at the mercy of an exacting governess who locked her in a closet whenever she failed to meet the arbitrary standards set before her. Which had been more often than not, especially after Truman had gone to school and wasn't there to stand up for her.

She shuddered at the memories that still haunted her, and looked up at the mewling creature with sympathy. It stared down at her imploringly, clearly begging for assistance.

"Come down, kitten. I won't hurt you," she crooned with soft encouragement. When that didn't work, she scratched the tree trunk and made kissing sounds.

The cat was not interested in the least. Which led her to one conclusion—he was obviously male.

So, she tried shaking the fringe of her shawl as further enticement. Serjie and Barry would have been mesmerized and eager to play. Then again, they were easily entertained. The cat, however, was not similarly impressed. In fact, the plaintive mewling only increased.

Well, she supposed her errand to Swanscott Manor could wait a few more minutes.

Without further delay, she hiked her skirts up to her knees—*How's this for decorum, Miss Gundersen?*—and set her foot on a protruding knot.

Boosting herself up, she reached the lowest branch. The bark was roughly grooved beneath her palms and solid enough for her to dig her fingertips into the deep furrows as she hugged the massive trunk.

On her ascent, she felt a little tug that caused her a small worry over the state of her dress. But it was only the barest snag of frayed thread on the hem. Nothing too severe. Though, after the trellis incident, she certainly wouldn't want to ruin a second dress this week.

Cautious with every foothold, she ascended higher, prodded onward by the constant helpless whimpers from the cat. "Fear not . . . I'm coming."

By the time she reached the overhanging branch, she was panting and winded. It had been a long while since she'd climbed a tree.

Her attempts to draw the cat to her resumed. She even wriggled her shawl like a snake, but only managed to earn a disdainful feline glower.

"Now," she murmured to herself, "how to get to the end of the branch?"

From the far end, the cat tilted its head, seeming to consider the options, but he offered no sound advice. Typical male.

The bark up here was smooth and slick with morning dew, telling her that she shouldn't dare try to stand and walk out there like a circus performer on a tightrope. Which left only one choice.

Spreading out her shawl in the hopes of protecting her dress, she leaned forward on her belly and scooted out on the thick branch.

Then she heard the telltale rip of fabric.

Looking down at the hem, she cringed. Even though it was an outdated fashion by seven years, harkening back to the days of capped sleeves and a slightly lower, less modest bodice, it was still one of her better dresses. She supposed she should be thankful that there were no gigot sleeves, frills or ruffles to contend with, or else she'd leave the tree decorated like a maypole.

But there was no point in stopping now, so she continued her course. And when she finally wormed her way to the cat, it was cleaning itself as if it didn't have a care in the world.

"Come here, kitten," she cajoled. "I won't hurt you."

In response, he turned suddenly and hissed, back arched. And as if that greeting wasn't bad enough, it darted out a paw and scratched her on the back of her hand.

"*Oww!*" she cried. Then, without a by-your-leave, it leaped over her head, pounced on her back with all four paws, scrambled over her and skittered down the tree.

Once on the ground, the little ingrate twitched his tail, then sauntered off.

"That is precisely why I never liked your kind!" she called after it, pressing the corner of her shawl to her smarting flesh. "See if I ever come to your rescue again, ungrateful little cur!"

Taking a moment, she considered the state of her dress. It wasn't too terrible. She could still walk to Swanscott Manor and present her argument. The real problem was in getting down from there.

Unfortunately, it looked like the only path was the very one she'd just taken.

Resting for a moment, she blew a fallen hank of hair from her eyes and looked out over the leafy edge of the branch.

Just beyond the river, she could see the mossy and weathered shingles of the chapel steeple. Their new vicar lived in the little brick house just around the bend, where an islet of rock and earth sat, topped with a copse of guelder rose shrubs that jutted up and redirected a slender arm of the river to form a shallow pool.

Truman used to take her fishing there when they were young.

Oh, how she missed her brother. He was the only one who truly understood her. Unfortunately, he'd been gone for a number of years on a merchant ship, trying to earn back his fortune and any possible future. She supposed it was too painful for him to return home and be reminded of the life he no longer had after the scandal.

That stupid scandal! She hated what it had done to her family.

She might have married if not for that. Then she never would have lied to Nell Hunnicutt and wouldn't be in this predicament.

Distracted from her thoughts, she noticed the new village vicar, the handsome Reverend Tobias, walking toward the very spot where she had fished long ago. Perhaps he was planning to do the same?

Then again, he didn't have a pole with him, unless it was resting on the other side of the log, where he was sitting to remove his shoes. So, he must intend to wade into the water. It wasn't unheard of. But if he chose to, he could catch plenty of fish just by standing on the shore and casting the line.

Idly, she observed him set his shoes off to the side and stand, stretching his arms above his head. Apparently, he wore no stockings. *Scandalous*, she thought with a grin.

She recalled the time when Althea had been young and asked, quite loudly, in church, "Papa, what does the vicar have beneath his robes?"

Her question had received a number of gasps, a few snickers, then utter silence. The elderly Father Wainwright had coughed, his face red as a beet as he tried not to laugh.

It was Mother who'd answered after clearing her throat. "Wings, dearest."

The service had recommenced, the old vicar stammering over a passage regarding angels.

But Thea had been disappointed. The only reason she'd asked was because, just before they'd set off for church, the nurse had confiscated the pencil and scraps of foolscap she'd stuffed into her stockings, stating, "When the vicar starts carrying scribbling paper in his robes on Sundays, then you can, too."

From that point on, all of Thea's dresses had been made with pockets and Father always burst out laughing whenever anyone mentioned the vicar's robes.

Verity smiled at the memory, her gaze unfocused on the figure across the river. At least, until . . . the reverend Tobias suddenly stripped out of his robe.

Off it flew, whipping over his head and landing in a heap on the grass. In that moment, Thea's question was foremost in her own mind. And the answer was . . . nothing. Nothing at all. Not a stitch. Not a single scrap of fabric. Just arms and legs and . . .

Verity swallowed.

She should probably avert her eyes. She most definitely shouldn't be looking curiously at the pale appendage resting amidst a tawny nest of hair between his thighs. It swayed back and forth like a mesmer's charm as he strode through the grass without care to the water's edge.

Dipping a toe into the river pool, he chafed his hands

together and then smacked himself on the chest a few times just before he plunged in. A breath stalled in her throat. And when he broke through the surface on a great gulp of air, she took one, too.

Heavens! He just stood there with the sun shining down on his dark golden head and with water sluicing down his body as he scrubbed beneath his arms and between his—

"What on earth am I doing?" she asked with incredulous self-reproach. "One does not peep through the leaves at one's vicar! This is shameful. Sinful, even!"

She shook her head, wondering what sort of penance she would have to perform. He was a man of the cloth. An undeniably handsome man of the cloth. But that didn't matter. She shouldn't know that he was hiding all of . . . *that* beneath his robes.

How would she ever look him in the eye on Sunday?

Though, thankfully this was Tuesday. There were plenty of days to forget all about this. So, one more small glance surely wouldn't—

The sudden thundering of horse hooves startled her.

Turning her head, she saw a rider fast approaching. And the last thing she wanted was to be caught in a tree.

She shimmied backward as quickly as she could. But her dress caught on one of the branches. Trying to tug it loose, she made the mistake of looking down.

All the way down.

The ground seemed to rush up at her as a swell of dizziness overtook her. Losing her balance, she teetered to one side. Her grip on the smooth branch faltered. She scratched and scrambled to find purchase, but her shawl thwarted every attempt.

In a last-hope effort to save herself, she hugged the branch and squeezed her eyes shut, only to feel herself slide . . . and slide . . . until she was hanging on to the underside like a drunken lemur.

The rider drew closer.

The pounding of the hooves thundered through the tree, threatening to shake her loose. And, what was worse— yes, there was something worse than being caught in a tree with a direct line of sight to the naked vicar—a sudden gust of wind brought her to the unfortunate conclusion that her dress was not around her legs where it ought to be.

Instead, the muslin was rucked around her hips. And the only thing between her bottom and all of creation was a pair of fine cambric drawers.

"Hold on," the rider called.

But the deep baritone sent a shiver of familiarity through her.

No. Oh, please, no. It couldn't be. It wasn't possible . . .

Verity dared to peep open one eye. Then she closed it immediately as dread coursed through her.

There was indeed something even worse than her current predicament. And that was seeing the Duke of Longhurst riding toward her.

Chapter Five

Oh, why hadn't she just ignored that blasted cat? Then she wouldn't be in this predicament.

Verity turned her head away from her fast-approaching adversary on horseback and glanced down to the ground again.

She was high, but—quite possibly—not too high?

The more practical side of her nature, which she vehemently chastised for not having been with her *before* she'd climbed the tree, told her that she could come out of this reasonably intact if she managed to drop down softly in the way that her brother had shown her when they were young. She might suffer a sprained ankle. But really, wasn't saving her neck—or *bottom*, in this case—worth it in the end?

Making her decision before it was too late, she stiffened the arms wrapped around the branch, locked her hands tightly about the wrists, unhooked one leg, then the other . . .

Oh, blast. That was a mistake. She heard another rip as the momentum swung her body with more force than she'd anticipated.

There wasn't any way she could hold on. Her arms were already slipping, legs whisking in the air.

"I've got you," the duke said.

In that same instant she felt a strong hand curve around her calf to the back of her knee, past her garter ribbons and the ruffle trim of her drawers to her—

"Don't you *daaaaaare*!" Her reprimand came out on a screech as her arms gave way and she fell.

And yet, she was *not* falling. Instead, she was being held securely, albeit awkwardly.

He was seated on his mount. Her arms were now wrapped around his head, his face smothered to her midriff, with her legs on either side of his hips and her knees bent with the tops of her feet against the tops of his thighs, and . . .

He was gripping her bottom. With *both* hands.

Though, he seemed to realize this at once and quickly adjusted his hold, sliding up to her waist as he lowered her down . . . directly onto the pommel!

With a yip, she lurched forward, nearly unseating him as she wrapped herself around him like the lemur she'd become.

His gruff grunt stirred the disheveled curls resting against the side of her neck, and a frisson of awareness trampled through her. All at once, her senses were inundated with the warmth and smoothness of his cheek against her own, the strength of his arms, the rapid thudding of their hearts beating in tandem, chest to chest.

She drew in a startled breath, her nostrils assailed by the scents of saddle leather, horse, male sweat and some spice she couldn't name.

"Your pommel," she said by way of explanation, her voice oddly husky. She swallowed, too embarrassed to meet his gaze. Then, untangling her fingers from his hair—which was thick, dark and slightly damp at the roots—she pressed her hands against his upper chest and eased back. But their hips were still inappropriately close. "You should probably . . . um . . . lower me to the ground."

His fingers flexed as if he did not entirely agree. But he

nodded, nonetheless, and took pains to ease her over the pommel and down to her feet.

While he dismounted, she shoved a fall of hair out of the way to look down at the ruins of her dress.

Drat! The snagged and soiled muslin was rent from hem to hip, revealing her petticoat beneath. Inanely, she clutched the two edges as if expecting the perspiration on her palms to fuse the fabric together. It did not.

Looking for her shawl, she found the blasted thing dangling from the branch and too far out of her reach. And when she looked back at the duke, she saw his swift perusal of her from hairline to hem as he assessed her predicament.

"Here. Take my coat," he said, already shrugging out of the garment. Reaching around her, he draped it over her shoulders, his low voice eliciting a peculiar shiver. "And allow me to escort you home."

The pleasing fragrance she'd noticed before clung to the superfine blue wool that fell to the middle of her thigh. The very same thighs that had been wrapped around him a moment ago, she thought, feeling her cheeks color. "There is no need."

"I insist. You've been through an ordeal and I cannot in good conscience leave you."

Longhurst was being awfully nice to her. Which was surprising after their heated exchange yesterday. It was almost as if he'd forgotten all about it. And she hadn't taken him for the forgetful or forgiving sort.

Whatever the reason, she hoped he would be this genial when she asked him her favor. Not to mention, she should probably stop ogling his broad shoulders. But it was rather difficult. There were miles and miles of them to ogle and they were accentuated so nicely by the fit of his waistcoat.

She blinked, forcing her gaze up to his. "Very well. I thank you for the offer."

"Excellent. Where do you live?" he asked as he proffered his arm.

Her brows furrowed. "In the . . . um . . . same house I've always lived in?"

It was only when he responded with a blank expression that she began to wonder if he didn't recognize her. Apparently, there was something worse than the *last grape* look. It was the *you're so forgettable that I don't even remember meeting you* look.

"Hartley Hall," she supplied. "The same house you used to call upon when you knew my brother."

He considered this for a moment, then nodded. "Ah. Then you must be the middle Hartley sister, Honoria."

"Hardly." She laughed. "And, pray, do not insult my sister by comparing us. I am Verity. We were introduced yesterday in your grandmother's parlor."

He shook his head at once, adamant. "You must be mistaken. The woman I met had brown hair and brown eyes. She was . . ."

"Plain?"

Frowning, he scrubbed a hand against the back of his neck, studying her with the intensity of one searching for a hairpin in a nest of pine needles. Then he pointed a finger at her. "You've altered your appearance. Applied rouge to your cheeks and lips."

"I have not." She straightened with a sniff of haughty indignance. "Are you accusing me of being vain?"

He continued as if he hadn't heard her. "Your hair is a different color—nay, colors, for there are shades from barley wheat to chestnut with strands of burnished gold and cornsilk . . ."

That was oddly specific. But were there?

As he spoke, she grabbed a hank of it from over her

shoulder and held it up to the light. It looked the same as it always had done, an unremarkable brown.

". . . and your eyes are different, too." His accusatory tone took on a grandiose edge as if he were ready to be crowned King of Spotting Deceptive Females. "They are not brown. They are a deep violet with a ring of umber around the center."

"I. Know," she countered, rolling her "not brown" eyes. "Did I accidentally kick you in the head or something?"

He stared at her. Hard. His gaze raked down her form, from the top of her tousled head to the bark-scuffed toes of her shoes, then slowly up the rip in her dress as if he were replaying the entire event in his mind. His hand tightened on the lead, the leather creaking under the pressure. His horse shifted.

"Aye. You must have done, for that is the only explanation. Either that"—his eyes slitted with suspicion—"or this is simply another one of your lies, which I'm more inclined to believe."

"I beg your pardon! You don't even know me."

"I know your kind well enough."

She growled, seething as she twisted to jam her arm into the sleeve. A thousand sharp retorts lined up on her tongue, but all she managed to utter was, "Oh, why don't you just fly back to London!"

"I would. Gladly. However, there is a certain matter we must discuss first. Here," he said impatiently as he assisted her with the overlarge garment. Then, as if for good measure, tugged the lapels closed. When that was complete, he took a step back. "You will tell everyone that you have released me from our betrothal because of a change of heart. *Your* change of heart, to be precise."

Her hackles rose. Was he actually ordering her?

"If you want out of this, then why don't you just announce to the entire village that I've made it all up?" *Oh, please don't announce to the entire village that I've made it all up.*

"Unfortunately, my grandmother brought up a salient point. Though it is altogether preposterous, should I end this farce, then I will appear the blackguard."

"And what should that matter?" she asked flippantly. "You are a duke. By title alone you can afford to have people think whatever they so choose."

"First of all, I abhor deceit. And second, I cannot afford to have my reputation as a gentleman and man of honor sullied. Before your untimely falsehood, I intended to take a wife whose father has a great deal of pride."

She hummed with intrigue. "So, in a sense, I'm holding your fate in the palm of my hand."

As soon as the words were out, she knew that was the wrong thing to say. He seemed to grow larger before her eyes, his countenance darkening as he loomed over her.

"Make no mistake," he growled, "if you refuse to cooperate, I will do whatever I must."

Verity didn't doubt it for a minute, but she wasn't about to be intimidated by a broody man. She had her own future to think about. And while it would give her great pleasure to keep him wondering if she would cooperate, she decided to be honest.

"Oh, settle your feathers," she said, standing her ground. "That is actually the reason I was headed toward Swanscott Manor this morning, to let you know that I will gladly tell everyone we didn't suit."

"Which will likely be the only truth to ever pass your lips."

Her mouth tightened. "I understand that we have met under somewhat strained circumstances, but do not make assumptions about me. Ask anyone and they will tell you that I'm dreadful at professing things that aren't true.

I don't know why my falsehood was believed this time. Whatever the reason, it matters not at this point. However, that brings me to a favor I should like to ask."

"You are hardly in a position to—"

"One week," she interrupted, holding up her index finger with only the top portion sticking out from the cuff of his sleeve. "All I'm asking for is one week of a pretend betrothal."

"Considering the trouble you've caused, why should I grant you a minute longer, let alone a sennight?"

Should she tell the humbling truth about this as well? Considering the fact that he'd already seen her at her worst, there was no pride to be gained by withholding it.

Therefore, on a deep breath, she said, "Because there is this horrid insect who takes great pleasure in reminding me of all my failings and I cannot bear to have her laugh in my face again. Her family is hosting a dinner on the eve of her return to London for the remainder of her Season. I simply want to survive that. When she is gone seven days from now, I will happily make an announcement releasing you. Then you will be free to marry your . . ."

"Miss Snow."

She nodded, briefly wondering what it was about this other woman that had captured his interest. Beauty? A biddable nature, perhaps? A willingness to overlook his argumentative and testy temperament?

Whatever it was, she hoped Miss Snow would knock him down a peg or two.

"Then do we have an agreement?" Verity extended her hand, watching as he considered her with a mixture of curiosity, speculation and distrust in the minted copper of his irises. But when he reached out, she made the mistake of adding, "After all, surely you could lie for a single week, if I can."

His hand lowered and he shook his head.

"Oh, come now, Longhurst. It's only seven days."

"I realize that," he said. "And, truth be told, I was going to agree to it regardless of your reasons, if only for the sake of appearances."

"Then I do not see the problem."

"Of course, *you* don't. But how can I willingly enter into an agreement which I know to be a deception? It goes against every fiber of my nature."

She wished she could be angry at his reasons, but she couldn't. And though it pained her to admit, she actually admired his deeply rooted sense of honor. It was just rather inconvenient for her.

"Very well," she said. It was only a matter of time before she would have to face the consequences of her own actions. She began to turn away.

"So, I will have to ask you to marry me."

She stopped dead in her tracks. "Did you just say . . . *marry me*?"

"Not to actually marry you, of course. Devil's teeth but that would be a trial. No, I mean only to ask you. Formally," he clarified. "Then, in one week's time, you will formally resign from our agreement. Unfortunately, that is the only solution I can see that will allow me to maintain any measure of honor and dignity."

"But it will still be a lie, all the same."

"Not for this week. I fully intend to treat you as I would if we were betrothed. Therefore"—his lungs expanded and contracted on a resigned breath—"Miss Hartley, for the next seven days, will you consent to be my betrothed?"

Her skin tingled. Why did her skin tingle? She did not want to tingle, or to have the fine hairs at her nape lift, or for gooseflesh to cascade down her arms.

She opened her mouth to respond, but her throat was unaccountably dry. So she just nodded.

His mouth flattened into a grim line. "Formally, if you please."

Irritation quickly subdued any of those unwanted sensations.

Clearing her throat, she looked up directly into his gaze and said, "Magnus Warring, Duke of Longhurst and most vexing man in all of England"—she flashed a grin when he growled—"I hereby accept your offer to be your betrothed for one week. Even if it kills both of us. Though, preferably you."

There seemed to be something happening to the corner of his mouth. It was lifting ever so slightly.

Was that a smirk? Did the man actually possess a sense of humor?

Hmm . . . she doubted it.

"I already regret this." He reached out to take her hand.

She obliged without thinking and instantly felt the shock of their skin connecting, the rasp of his calluses, the heat of his palm. Beneath her skirts, she could still feel the imprint from where he'd gripped her. Surely that wouldn't be the case if he had the proper, refined hands of a gentleman. Instead, he was rather rough around the edges in a way that she never imagined a man of his rank would be. Perhaps there was more to the stuffy duke than met the eye.

He released her abruptly and looked down at his hand as he closed it into a fist, his brow furrowing. Absently, he said, "Send the invitation to Swanscott Manor."

"No," she said, her voice edged with a note of alarm. "I mean, that isn't necessary. If they haven't sent one already, then there is absolutely no reason for you to return from London to attend a mere trifling dinner."

"I won't be in London. I'll be here."

"But . . . but whyever would you stay?"

He arched a dark brow. "Am I to leave my fate in the hands of the woman whose lie brought all this about? I think not."

Ooooh! That man!

She gritted her teeth. "I assure you, there is no need to linger. I will be more than happy to tell everyone how disagreeable you are without you needing to prove it."

"One week, Miss Hartley. And then everyone will see just who is disagreeable."

He swung up to his mount with the ease of a man born into the saddle. With the slight urging of his knee, the horse stepped beneath the ash branch and Longhurst plucked the shawl from its roost.

However, as he turned to hand it to her, he glanced across the river.

Verity cringed.

Through the cluster of the guelder rose on the islet, she could just make out a figure climbing from the water, a flash of pale skin, and then the darkness of the robe.

She colored as the duke looked at her.

Heaving out a great sigh, he handed her the shawl. "Why am I not surprised?"

"I don't know what you could possibly mean," she said, unable to meet his gaze as she hurriedly took the bundle.

"And that, Miss Hartley, would be another lie."

Before she could explain about the cat, he spurred his mount and rode off.

Of course, it didn't matter at all what he might think of her. Not a whit. In a week, he would be gone from her life and she was already looking forward to it.

∾⧽

IN THE MIDDLE of the night, Verity awoke in bed, her nightclothes damp with perspiration, heart thundering like a racehorse.

She'd just had a dream of a man bathing nude in the river. Only it wasn't the vicar. And before he'd stepped into the water, he hadn't stripped out of a clergyman's robes either. No, indeed.

With eyes that burned like bright coals in a brazier, Longhurst had held her gaze as he unbuttoned his waist-coat, untied his cravat and collar, and slowly peeled away every stitch of clothing he wore. Then he swaggered to-ward the riverbank, lifted his arms above his head and dove, swift as a seal beneath the ripple of slate gray water.

She'd scarcely been able to breathe as she waited for him to emerge. And he was under for so long that she feared something terrible had happened. So she'd stepped to the edge, her toes sinking into the cool grass and soft earth.

Suddenly, he broke the surface directly in front of her. His hand surrounded her ankle, climbed to her calf, to her knee and higher still . . .

Then he'd paused and looked up at her with something of a grin curled at the corner of his mouth. "I'm afraid I must demand the return of my garment, Miss Hartley."

Confused, she'd looked down at herself, at his hands parting the dark blue wool. And that was when she'd realized she wasn't wearing anything other than his coat.

The very same garment illuminated by a shaft of moon-light as it hung on the door of her wardrobe.

Chapter Six

ℐɴ ᴛʜᴇ ʙʀᴇᴀᴋꜰᴀꜱᴛ room of Swanscott Manor the following morning, a paper-wrapped parcel arrived for Magnus. Untying the string, he saw that it was his coat, neatly brushed and folded.

This did not surprise him. The note, however, did.

To the unduly skeptical *Duke of Longhurst,*
  Thank you for the loan of your coat. And, if you must know,
  I had been saving a cat.

                                Sincerely,
                                Miss Verity Hartley

He read the looping scrawl twice more. Each time, he could almost hear the haughty indignation in her tone.

Yesterday, he'd witnessed an array of emotions sweep across her countenance, from wide-eyed shock to furrowed confusion, from arched annoyance to taut reprimand. How she dared to level him with a glare while appearing so thoroughly disheveled and pink-cheeked with guilt was beyond him. The woman was utterly audacious.

"Pray, what has put a smile on your countenance this morning, my boy?"

Abruptly, he lowered the card and sent the coat upstairs to his valet. Then he stood as his grandmother passed through the oaken archway, her hand resting on the knob of her cane.

Stepping to her side, he proffered his arm. "I wear no smile, ma'am. Perhaps it is the haggard look of a man suffering from little sleep you are seeing instead."

She patted the top of his sleeve as he led her to the armchair at the opposite end of the oval walnut table. "You appeared to be reading something that pleased you. I thought it might have been a missive from your Miss Snow."

"What, this?" he asked when she glanced to the card in his other hand. He quickly tucked it against his palm, disliking the unfounded rise of guilt he felt in the pit of his stomach. "This is nothing."

And to prove it, he strode to the marble hearth, prepared to toss it into the fire. But as he held it to flames that licked hungrily over the three logs resting in the grate, the ink seemed to capture the light, inviting him to read the scrawl once more.

He shook his head. *Saving a cat, indeed.*

"Are you going out this morning? I thought I heard you ask after the carriage."

"I am, and I did," he said, crossing the room to the bay windows that overlooked the rose garden just beginning to bud with hints of pinks and reds. "I plan to escort Miss Hartley into the village for our initial public exhibition."

"*Initial?* That sounds suspiciously as though you plan future outings with her. And I was under the impression you saw no necessity in my suggestion."

He had never intended to give it a second thought. However, after hearing Miss Hartley's plan to cast an ill-favored light on him as a means to extricate herself from the debacle that she had caused, he decided to make it a little more difficult for her.

"No more than one or two will be required to prove

my point, I should think. After all, I must ensure that my reputation is in good standing when I return to London."

Yesterday, he had explained the bargain to his grandmother. Well, most of it. He'd omitted the part about the tree and the state of Miss Hartley's dress. Those particular details were hardly important. Certainly not to his grandmother. She was simply pleased to know that her own visit with her grandson would be extended.

Additionally, when he mentioned that, for the sake of honor, he'd made his week-long betrothal official, she'd said nothing. Hadn't even batted an eye. So, clearly, she saw the necessity of it as well. For that, he was immensely grateful. And yet, part of him wished she would have questioned him.

He had come up with several sound reasons behind his decision. Reasons that had all made perfect sense to him as he'd been standing by the river.

In the morning light, however—after having his encounter with Miss Hartley play again and again through his sleeping mind last night without his permission—he'd begun to harbor a kernel of doubt. He did not particularly want to think about how she'd tumbled into his arms, or the way her lithe body had wrapped around him in a crush of soft curves and the tantalizing fragrance of honeysuckle . . .

He swallowed. Even now, the memory prevented him any measure of peace. Then again, any man would have been unprepared for such an event. And, for that matter, what gently bred woman went around climbing trees of all things?

Agitated, he reached out to widen the space between the drapes only to realize that he still held that card in his hand.

Magnus stared down at it in bewilderment. He could have sworn he'd dropped it into the fire a moment ago. Clearly, his sleep-addled mind was playing tricks on him.

Vexed with himself, he crammed it into the inner breast pocket of his coat.

"Take the curricle," his grandmother said as she stirred her tea. "That way there won't be room for her to bring a maid who might overhear a conversation you'd rather not have bandied about in the village square."

He bristled, every hair on his body standing on end. "Surely, it would be improper to take Miss Hartley anywhere without a chaperone."

"My dear boy, Verity Hartley is of an age where a chaperone is no longer expected. Come now, you must have noticed that already."

The first meeting, perhaps. She had been plain and very much the spinster who had invented a fiancé in order to gain either attention or notoriety.

Yesterday, however, he had seen a different side of her altogether. And he was not left the better for the experience. In fact, the entire episode left him feeling rather cross.

If there was one thing Magnus Warring detested above all else, it was deception. And she *had* deceived him. There was no other way to explain the alteration in her appearance. Or, perhaps, she had purposely stood with her back to the window so that he could not obtain a fair impression of her during their introduction in this very house.

Either way, she was guilty of something. A great many somethings, would be his guess.

"You'd better go now while the weather holds," Grandmother said, her voice drawing him out of his windowpane musings.

With a blink he saw that not a single cloud dotted the blue sky over the trees and rolling hills that led to Hartley Hall in the distance. "I see nothing ominous."

"Ah, but I have a knee that kicks up a fuss whenever a storm is brewing."

His mouth quirked in a wry grin as he glanced over his shoulder at her. "I think your knee oracle might be imagining things."

"You'll see," she said, nodding with a distinct air of smugness, her hand resting on the brass knob of her cane.

BY THE TIME he reached Hartley Hall, there were only a few clouds gathering on the horizon. Nothing to be concerned about.

The only storm he knew of was brewing inside of him.

This would be the first time since the great swindle that he had stepped foot on the grounds of the Hartley demesne. The first time in the seven years since his father had died, humiliated and penniless.

I was certain this time would be different, were his father's dying words. They'd rasped over his ashen lips as he'd clutched Magnus's hand.

And his father had been certain because he had trusted a dissembler like Baron Hartley.

Taking in a deep breath, Magnus felt the iron shutters he'd carefully constructed years ago fall into place. Then he lifted his hand to the scrollwork door knocker and rapped twice.

When the door opened, he was greeted by the familiar visage of Mr. Mosely, the same large-beaked butler who had been employed here back when Magnus had not harbored such animosity toward all who resided beneath this roof.

But before Mosely could utter a syllable of inquiry, Magnus supplied, "The Duke of Longhurst for Miss Verity Hartley."

He wanted to hurry this along. The less time spent here, the better.

"Miss *Verity*, Your Grace?" the old butler asked, his

wiry gray eyebrows inching high toward a receding hairline.

Unaccustomed to having to repeat himself, he inclined his head sharply.

The butler bowed, quickly overcoming his apparent surprise. The nearby maids, however, remained agog beneath the ruffles of their caps, leaving the feather dusters in their grasps in want of occupation.

He wondered at the cause. After all, if there were widespread rumors regarding a secret betrothal between himself and the eldest daughter, why should they be surprised by his appearance?

"Would you care to wait in the parlor?" Mosely held out his hand to take his hat, but Magnus kept the black beaver brim in his grip and his boots rooted to the stone tile.

"I'll wait here."

As Mosely left the foyer, the whispers from maid to maid traveled up the mahogany banister, where polishing cloths distractedly rubbed the same spot on the railing and stunned sideways glances fell upon him. He kept his gaze fixed on the curved staircase, refusing to give in to the desire to clear his throat or to look over his shoulder for the time on the longcase clock.

His father had been a fidgeter when he was restless or anxious over the state of one of his speculations. Magnus had seen that as a measure of weakness, even childishness.

Leander Warring had dealt with problems that arose by dithering over them, until those problems grew so large in his mind that even the smallest inconvenience—such as a hole in the roof or a bill from the drapers—fell upon him like the weight of an immense boulder that he could never hope to lift.

And while his father would wring his hands in his bedchamber, woefully declaring a need to gather his composure for a moment—which usually turned into a day, a week, or a month—Magnus would set matters aright with swift decision.

He did not dither. Consequently, this resulted in a certain lack of patience, which usually set his teeth on edge as they were in that very moment.

In the direction of the upper hallway, there seemed to be a commotion afoot. He heard what sounded like furniture legs scraping against the floor, followed by the scurry of footsteps, then the creak and crack of doors opening and closing in rapid succession.

One feminine voice repeated a call of Verity's name as if unable to locate her. Another mentioned something regarding birdhouses. And a third wondered if she should write a character called *the duke* in her next production.

Yet, of the three voices he heard, none had the honeyed tone that would put an end to this interminable waiting.

Another minute ticked by before he heard the syncopated rhythm of sure footfalls coming from an adjacent corridor. He turned with expectation. Then regretted it at once.

Baron Hartley appeared, dressed for a morning ride in his green coat and buff breeches. His broad smile was set between deep fissures on either side of his mouth like a pair of double parentheses. A spray of wrinkles beside his eyes told Magnus that he must still have found reasons to smile, to be happy with his life. Therefore, clearly, he was unbothered by the fact that he'd ruined the lives of so many others.

In fact, the only mark of aging upon the spry and lanky man was in the copious strands of white threading his blond hair.

"Welcome, lad. Welcome," he said warmly, holding out his hand. When it was not taken, he wasn't deterred and cuffed Magnus on the shoulder. "'Tis good to see you. You look well. And I've heard great things about you since you and Truman were at university together. No finer boys than the two of you, that's for certain. Come into my study. We'll have a nip of brandy with our morning tea, hmm?"

Magnus straightened his spine, jaw clenched. "As you should well know, I am not here to pay a social call, but only for the pretense of one. Make no mistake, Lord Hartley, I would rather walk through hell shackled to the devil than stand beneath your roof. However, I am not a man who turns away when an unpleasant task falls upon his shoulders. Nor do I run from responsibility, even when not of my own making. I do what must be done as any gentleman worth his salt ought. And that, sir, is the sole reason I am here."

The one good thing that might be said of Hartley was that he didn't prevaricate or make excuses for his actions. He did not even flinch from the biting scorn in that rebuke. He stood there, taking every ounce of hatred and animosity fired at him and merely inclined his head.

"Your Grace," he said. Then he turned and walked away, his steps noticeably less sprightly than before.

Magnus gladly watched him go. Yet, part of him had wanted more—like the apology he'd never received, a word of explanation, something that might have made sense of the havoc that had been wreaked seven years ago—but he was left with nothing.

Just as his father had been.

On the other hand, Magnus would have refused to listen. There could be no apology, no word, no excuse, that could take away the agony and despair Hartley had caused. He was sure that nothing ever could.

His attention was diverted from those dark musings as someone approached from the back of the house.

The figure walked crisply toward him along the paneled hallway, where angled shafts of light poured from open doorways. Even though the hood of an olive cloak eclipsed her face in shadow, he recognized the proud set of those shoulders at once.

Until that moment, he didn't realize he'd been anticipating this, wondering and waiting to see if she would alter her appearance once more. Would she revert back to the plain creature he'd first met in his grandmother's parlor? Or would she be that tousled wood nymph that had fallen from a tree and into his arms?

As she neared, she lowered the hood to her shoulders and he beheld his answer.

Her hair was swept away from her face in a prim knot that made it difficult to pick apart the various hues he'd witnessed yesterday when it had been unbound and gilded by rays of sunlight. And yet, even though it appeared to be light brown from a distance, when she entered the rectangular glow from the transom window behind him, he caught sight of the mélange of lustrous strands of nut brown, gold and cornsilk all mingling together.

Her cheeks were tinged the palest pink from being in the cool, crisp air. He knew this because she brought with her the fragrance of fresh morning dew and the scent of honeysuckle not yet in bloom. As for her eyes, they were shaded by a thick fringe of chestnut lashes. However, it was not until she stopped nearly toe to toe with him, and glaring up into his countenance, that he was struck again by their startling color.

"Whatever are you doing here?" she demanded, but when he arched a brow at the impertinence in her tone, she added, "Your Grace."

Hearing the tapping of her toe, he allowed his gaze to travel down her cloak to the flash of jonquil muslin revealed between the part in the fabric, to the dark saturation of dew on her hems and to the muddied tip of her shoe. Then she cleared her throat, drawing his attention to the perturbed pursing of her lips.

"Are you always one to exhibit such ungoverned responses, Miss Hartley? You certainly are not hiding your displeasure at having an unwanted guest, or your impatience as you await my response. And I thought, perhaps, the wild creature I'd witnessed yesterday was an aberration. Apparently, you are quite feral the majority of the time."

"You didn't answer my question."

"And you didn't answer mine."

She huffed. "Very well. I am governing myself. If I weren't, I would be shoving you outside and bidding you farewell. As a matter of fact . . ."

Stepping around him, she jerked open the heavy door. But she did not evict him as threatened. Instead, she crossed the threshold herself and waited for him beside a column beneath the portico.

The instant he followed and closed the door behind him, she flung out her arm in an agitated fashion. "You shouldn't be here."

"There are a multitude of reasons which support that statement," he answered dryly. "However, I should like to know yours."

"First of all, you've put the servants in a frenzy. It's one thing for a rumor to exist in the ether, but quite another to have it appear on the doorstep. They'll never stop talking about the day *the duke came to pay a call*. And worse, it will become more dramatic with every retelling."

"Which is something you should have considered before you involved me in your falsehood."

"Well, you weren't supposed to find out now, were you?" She huffed again, having the gall to lay the blame at *his* feet. "And furthermore, I don't know if my brother ever told you this, but my family is rather . . . fanciful."

"Hawk—I mean, Truman, or Mr. Hartley, rather— mentioned it a time or two."

Magnus frowned. He didn't like accidentally referring to her brother in a familiar sense, as though they'd remained friends. They had not. There had been a complete severing of ties between them. *At least*, he thought with an inward groan, *until now*.

"Believe me, experiencing it is far different than simply hearing about it." She shook her head. "In any given moment, someone might sing their thoughts as if living in an opera, or gracefully deliquesce onto a nearby chair on a bored sigh. Father is forever quoting the lines of Shakespeare in order to instruct us on managing our lives. And Mother—who rules the roost here—is the worst of all. She has quite a determined romantic nature, much like a siren who lures the unwary into indeterminate fates."

"I fail to see why their inclinations should have anything to do with your current vexation at my paying a call. You did explain the matter to them, did you not?"

"Of course, I did. Not the bit about the formal proposal. That's only between us," she added quietly, abruptly absorbed with a stray thread on the seam of her cloak. "Nevertheless, having you show up at our door, especially when it must be unbearable to you, will only make my mother admire you for going along with this lie of mine."

This time, when she gazed up at him, there was no blame directed at him. Instead, her violet eyes turned soft like velvet, a sea of understanding in their depths.

An uncomfortable sensation stirred inside him, making *him* restless, making him want to shrug his shoulders or shift from one foot to the other.

But a self-respecting duke never succumbed to errant impulses. "It is only one week."

"For Roxana Hartley, love doesn't take that long. And

she has been waiting a very, very long time for a gentleman to pay a call on her spinster daughter. So she will get her hopes up. She will look for every possible goodness in your nature. She will find the oddest things about you handsome and clever. She will picture you seated in the drawing room with the family and think of what a perfect portrait that would make. And when you leave in one week, even though she knew it would happen, her heart will break. She will be listless for days. Father, in an attempt to show her that things could always be worse, will do an appalling job at comforting her, likely by reciting Romeo's final speech in the tomb. And I refuse to put my family through this."

"That is absurd," he said. "You're having a lark with me, and I am in no mood for it."

She issued a humorless laugh. "Absurd, hmm? I can guarantee that there are three Hartley women with their ears pressed to the door, listening to every word we say. Open it, if you don't believe me."

In that very instant, he heard the unmistakable scuttle and scurry of motion, a scrape against the other side of the door like a glass being withdrawn in haste. He wondered—should he lift the latch—would he find a farcical scene of her entire family in the foyer pretending they were all gathered by happenstance?

Turning his attention back to Verity, he was beginning to see her in a new light.

By all accounts, she was the sanest member of her family. In truth, her brother had said as much on a number of occasions. Which left Magnus to wonder, why hadn't she married some sensible fellow and freed herself from this bedlam?

He quickly dispelled the unwarranted curiosity. The answer did not matter to him in the least. "There is no sentiment between us, nor will there ever be. I care not what your family thinks or how they will fair when this ordeal is over. My sole concern is bringing this nonsense to a swift conclusion."

She closed her eyes and pinched the bridge of her nose between her thumb and forefinger. "Could you not simply go back to London and leave me to sort all this out?"

"Leave you to besmirch my reputation with your falsehoods and fabrications, you mean. Absolutely not."

When she lowered her hand, rosy impressions lingered briefly on either side of her nose from the pressure, and he had a peculiar impulse to reach out and smooth them away.

He shook his head firmly at the absurd notion, the command more to himself than to her.

But she took offense, squaring her shoulders. "I have no desire to invent any more untruths. My plan is to extricate us both from this as simply as possible."

"No. You would have the entire village believe that I am at fault. However, I cannot have Mr. Snow thinking that I caused the termination of your supposed affections by having an unreasonable and quarrelsome nature."

"You forgot callous, disdainful and onerous."

Ignoring the peevish jibe, he continued. "Therefore, the two of us will make a brief public appearance where I will act according to my true nature as a gentleman and you will act according to . . . your own."

"And just what is that supposed to mean?"

He issued a carefully controlled shrug. "If the shrew fits, madam."

She planted her hands on her hips, her eyes narrowing to slits. "*Oooh, you—*"

Abruptly, she stopped, brows lifting as if something had just occurred to her. "You don't remember much about the people living in this village, do you?"

"I remember well enough."

Her head tilted as she studied him, a glint of wry humor curling the corners of her mouth. He felt his first frisson of wariness at the sight. Just what was she thinking?

But before he could decipher an answer, she offered a succinct nod.

"Very well. I see that you are determined to have your way." Her gaze shifted to the waiting curricle. "And you intend for us to jaunt about in that contraption when there's a storm coming?"

"Don't tell me you have a soothsaying limb as well." When she stared at him blankly, he shook his head and pointed skyward. "There are only a handful of clouds above the tree line."

She flitted her fingers dismissively as if there was no correlation between storms and clouds. "The birds know that one is on the way."

"You talk . . . to birds?"

"Don't be silly. They were all chattering excitedly while hiding deep in the shrubs in the way they always do whenever a storm is coming. I just pay attention to the signs around me. It's the sensible thing to do."

"Ah," he said, marginally relieved that he wasn't dealing with a liar *and* a lunatic. "Fear not, I will return you well before a single drop of rain falls from the sky."

"And I will endeavor not to say *I told you so*. But first"—she moved to the door—"I shall take an umbrella."

The instant she lifted the latch and pushed, a trio of voices exclaimed an alarmed *oof!* The sound was immediately followed by muffled thuds. And he didn't need to glance inside to know that the eavesdroppers had just fallen into a heap of skirts and limbs on the floor.

He just turned and walked toward the curricle, wanting as little to do with the Hartley bedlam as possible.

When she came up beside him, using a furled black umbrella as a walking stick, she slid him a glance. "Bringing the villagers into this is a mistake. There's still time to change your mind and return to London."

"Because we are not well acquainted or are likely ever to be, I will repeat myself just this once. I shall see this through until I am satisfied with its conclusion."

He held out his hand to assist her into the curricle, waiting for her to accept. Waiting for her to acknowledge that this was the only way out of the tangled mess she had put them in.

Miss Hartley slid a glance to the recessed door beneath the portico and slid back to meet his unswerving gaze. "If you insist. But don't say I didn't warn you."

Then she laid her cool fingertips onto the warm flesh of his palm.

It would have been ridiculous to say that it took him by surprise. But a shock bolted through him all the same. His hand closed reflexively as if pinpricked by a static charge. It tingled underneath his skin, almost to the point of itching, if not for the relief provided by the soft pads of her fingertips.

Once she was seated, he released her and ignored the lingering sensation.

And yet, as he arranged his limbs next to hers into the curve of the snug seat and caught the alluring sweet perfume of honeysuckle rising warmly from her side, he wondered if it was too late to heed her warning.

Chapter Seven

As far as Verity was concerned, Longhurst deserved what was coming to him. So he wanted to show everyone how much of a gentleman he was? How impossible it would be for his own superior qualities to be at fault in their ultimate separation?

Well, he didn't know the villagers the way she did. And he certainly didn't know that their country manners would try the patience of a saint, let alone a smug stuffed-shirted duke.

But he was about to find out.

Not only that, but he didn't know that the reason the villagers had eschewed any sense of formality was because they were forever auditioning to be in one of Father's productions. And he encouraged them, providing advice, such as: *Let the muse take you . . . Unshackle your restraints . . . Allow your inner voice to speak and rail at the world . . .*

In her opinion, their inner voices were often too free. Today, however, she would welcome it if only to gloat over the duke. And she wouldn't have to wait long.

The first sign that Longhurst was in for a rude awakening began when a man on horseback rode up the lane. The rider and gray mare stopped at once. And beneath the brim of a brown beaver hat, Percival Culpepper gaped at them in stunned stupefaction.

Though he seemed to have recovered by the time they

passed by because he turned his mount around and dashed on toward town ahead of them at breakneck speed.

"We're in for it now," Verity muttered with a shake of her head. "By the time we reach the high street everyone will know we're coming, and we will be the center attraction as though the circus had come to town."

Longhurst issued an unconcerned flick of the ribbons, the horse clipping along. "You forget, Miss Hartley, I have driven down this lane on a number of occasions and never once was I ogled like a dancing bear."

"Oh, you were most definitely ogled *and* whispered about behind cupped hands. But because your title has earned you a degree of distinction and your stiff-shouldered demeanor has made you unapproachable, you were likely saved from the overfamiliar tendencies of the villagers." Feeling those very shoulders tense beside her, she added sweetly, "It wasn't meant as an insult. Merely an observation."

He issued a grunt of disbelief.

"You see," she continued, "my father has a more *every-man* nature, where the villagers feel as though they can talk to him about anything. Consequently, they also talk to, and about, all of us with the same familiarity. And since you are with me . . ."

"You believe that I have been brought down to your level."

It was her turn to stiffen. "I wouldn't phrase it like that."

"Of course, you wouldn't. That would suggest an ability to take responsibility for the fact that it was your untruthful nature that caused all of this." When she scoffed, he countered with, "It wasn't meant as an insult. Merely an observation."

She whipped a glare at him. "I'll have you know that I have never denied my own—"

"Devil's teeth!" he cursed, pulling hard on the reins.

The accident—or near accident—happened so fast, there wasn't even time to cry out in alarm.

Suddenly, there was a phaeton in front of them. It darted onto the lane just before the narrow turn toward the stone bridge leading to the high street.

Longhurst swerved to avoid the collision. Their well-heeled horse stopped with a jolt on the berm. She lurched forward. The duke's arm reflexively shot out as a cross brace. She gasped, anchored to her seat. And the phaeton slowly meandered around the bend as if nothing had occurred.

"Are you unharmed?" Longhurst asked.

"You may remove your hand," she said simultaneously.

His brow furrowed as his gaze searched her features for any sign of distress. Then his attention shifted lower and—

He abruptly dropped the hand that was cupping her entire right breast while his forearm had been squashing the left.

"I . . ." He didn't finish whatever he'd intended to say, but merely looked at his hand as if the appendage had suddenly sprouted at the end of his arm and he couldn't make sense of how it came to be. And in some strange, comical way, she completely understood.

There didn't seem to be words to describe how ridiculously bungled every single encounter with him had gone.

Yesterday he'd been gripping her bottom and today, her breast. She shuddered to think what tomorrow might bring.

But no, there wouldn't be a tomorrow. Because she was absolutely certain that he would leave for London directly after their morning jaunt.

"That driver spurred his horses on purpose," he muttered under his breath, urging their horse back onto the lane. "He looked directly at me."

Rearranging her cloak, she tried to ignore the warm imprint that seemed to linger on the pale flesh residing beneath the layers of wool, muslin, linen and cambric. Her cheeks felt as if she'd scrubbed them with hot coals.

"I don't doubt it at all," she said, keeping her face averted. "That was Peter Culpepper. He was driving his younger brother, Carlton, who'd sprained his ankle leaping from the drawing room stage the other day. Their elder brother was the rider on the horse who'd passed us. And they were likely on their way to pay a call on my sisters, but decided to slow us down instead."

"For what purpose?"

"So the entire village would know we're coming, of course. Being the first to deliver the latest on-dit will make them the heroes of the day. And they will strut about quite proudly for this accomplishment." Risking a sideways glance, she caught sight of his disbelieving expression. "It still isn't too late to turn back."

"The Duke of Longhurst does not 'turn back.'"

"But apparently, he does refer to himself in the third person, much like Julius Caesar in that eponymous play. 'Caesar should be a beast without a heart,'" she teased.

The Duke of Longhurst was not amused. His jaw clenched and there was a jagged vein protruding just above his temple. Oh dear.

If he couldn't learn to laugh at the absurdity of what had already transpired, he was surely going to lose his top by the time they arrived at the turnabout by the haberdashery.

Even though part of her wanted to gloat and smirk when this pompous man received the comeuppance he so desperately deserved, another more deeply ingrained part of her nature wanted to soothe any ruffled feathers.

That was the trouble with being the practical one in her family, because it also made her the mediator by default.

She did her best to solve squabbles between sisters as well as any discord among the maids. Of course, she preferred to avoid conflict and confrontation at all costs. However, since passions tended to run high beneath the Hartley roof, she was often called upon to intervene.

And the best method, she'd learned for dealing with a minor agitation, was to deflect and distract.

"Shall I try it, do you think? Verity Hartley does not like cabbages," she said with mock bluster, lowering her voice to imitate him. "Hmm . . . Doesn't quite possess the same authority, does it? Perhaps if you say it. Go on. It won't hurt, I promise."

Heaving out a taut breath, he spoke through gritted teeth. "If this is your attempt to distract me from the very reason I am here, driving behind a phaeton inching forward at a snail's pace, you needn't bother. I am perfectly capable of managing trifling annoyances."

He demonstrated this by flicking the reins in a pointlessly impatient gesture.

The lane was too narrow to pass the Culpeppers' conveyance, not unless he intended to mount the narrow pavement on either side and mow down all the basket toters and clerks who'd stepped out of the shops to gawk at the spectacle.

"Very well. But if you *manage* yourself any harder, then either the ribbons are going to disintegrate in your grip or that vein on your forehead will explode."

She didn't know why, but she had a strange compulsion to brush her fingertips over the jagged protrusion and smooth it away. Which was absurd. They hated each other. And besides, he would likely bite her if she so much as lifted a hand in his direction.

Turning, she faced forward as a sudden gust of wind pushed back the hood of her cloak. Her attention lifted to the bank of clouds that appeared above the rows of shingle-roofed shops, painting the sky in colors of dark gray and burnished silver.

Beside her, he darted a glance to the ominous canvas overhead, then down to where her hand drifted to the handle of her umbrella. "We will return in time."

Did he think that speaking the words in a commanding voice would force the weather to listen?

She thrummed her fingers on the crook just to taunt him. "We won't."

As he issued a responding growl, she spied the village's premier busybody bolting from the dressmaker's shop up ahead. Draped in a heap of lavender silk with pins still sticking out of her new frock, Elmira Horncastle gripped a handful of skirts and strode their way. Tenacious and jowly as a bulldog, she ignored the gale that threatened to steal her hat and simply lifted her arm to anchor it to her silvery carrot-colored hair.

That was when Verity recalled the village assembly that Mrs. Horncastle and her husband were hosting tomorrow evening. And it would be just like her to try to corner the duke into attending.

"Prepare yourself. We're entering the first gauntlet," Verity warned. "Oh, and you might wish to have a ready excuse regarding your plans for tomorrow evening."

"A duke does not—" He stopped at the sight of a smirk on her lips and cleared his throat. "One does not require excuses on hand if one is of a forthright nature. Only dissemblers store a cache of untruths to extricate themselves from situations. Though, I am hardly surprised such behavior is your first inclination."

She clearly understood the reason he hadn't married already. The arrogance fairly oozed from every pore. Such a *charming* man! And poor Miss Snow!

"Besides," he continued, "as I am unacquainted with these people, I have no intention of engaging in conversation. An occasional nod or a touch to the brim of my hat will suffice for my purpose."

"Fine. I just hope you enjoy dancing."

Her saccharine tone earned her a questioning glance, but before he could inquire, Mrs. Horncastle was upon them, bustling beside the crawling curricle.

"Hullo, Your Grace! You remember me, don't you? It's Mrs. Horncastle," she panted, her plump cheeks rosy as she splayed a hand over her matronly décolletage. "My nephew, Willie, used to scamper about on the village green after you. He's in Cheshire now with his wife and four wee ones. He was married in a lovely church, though not nearly as fine as our chapel, of course. And while we're on the topic of marriage, when will your wedding be?"

Verity saw the muscle in his jaw twitch.

The likelihood that he would recall the obscure acquaintance of a woman who was the aunt of a boy who'd occasionally played with him in his youth was slim. In polite society, a proper introduction would be warranted. However, Addlewick was about as far from polite society as one could imagine.

Biting her tongue on an *I told you so*—it was still early yet, after all—she slid him an innocent glance and sat demurely by his side. His responding glare kindled a warm amusement that brought a pleased smile to her lips.

He issued a curt nod and directed a rather murderous glower to the back of the phaeton. "The matter has not been discussed. I bid you good day."

Anyone else would have taken the hint. Oh, but not the dear, sweet, on-a-mission Mrs. Horncastle.

"Well, you must hold the wedding here. It is the very least you could do after keeping your betrothal a secret for so long, and for keeping Miss Hartley waiting." She tsked. "I'm sure she's quite cross with you, Your Grace. Doubtless, a strapping duke such as yourself desires an heir. Perhaps even a large family." Her gaze shifted, traveling over him with immodest appreciation. "A very large family."

"I beg your pardon, madam." The reproach in his voice rumbled like a thundercloud.

Verity stifled a giggle behind her fingertips.

Elmira issued an unconcerned shrug. "Oh, pooh. There's nothing to be embarrassed about. If there is one thing I've learned from playing Mistress Quickly on the stage—and to roaring acclaim, I might add—it is that one must eschew any discomfiture over certain topics. Besides, we are all of an age to speak frankly. And Miss Hartley isn't getting any younger."

The smile dissolved from Verity's lips.

He dared to arch a smug brow at her. "Come now, Miss Hartley. There is nothing to be embarrassed about. Not at your age."

"How kind of you to remind me, darling," she seethed sweetly. "Though, thankfully I'm not too decrepit to enjoy a lively assembly. Oh, how I wish the two of us could attend one before you return to London."

Those amber eyes flared as if he were a torchbearer and imagining her tied to a pyre in the village square.

Mrs. Horncastle beamed with excitement. "Well, it just so happens that my husband and I are hosting one tomorrow evening, Your Grace. What luck! And I demand that you give me your second dance at the assembly, directly following Miss Hartley's of course. Until tomorrow then."

"Regrettably, I am unable"—he paused briefly as she dashed off—"to attend."

At the sight of his confounded expression, Verity's pique at being called a shriveled old hag faded at once. "Fear not, Longhurst. You needn't feel obligated to offer your first dance to me. I'll be more than happy to share you with every woman in the village."

"I will not be attending that assembly."

She wasn't either, but she couldn't stop herself from adding, "And leave me acting the wallflower all evening? Quite unchivalrous of you. The villagers will quickly decide that I was wholly justified in ending our lengthy betrothal when they witness your cold and neglectful nature."

That vein looked positively Pompeian. She wondered if she should open the umbrella to save herself from the volcanic blast.

Longhurst growled and suddenly stopped the curricle. After lifting the brake, he tossed a coin to a clerk standing near a hitching post outside of one of the shops and said, "Tie my horse."

Then, without a single word to her, Longhurst stepped down and walked away.

Apparently, she'd pushed him too far. Even so, she hadn't expected him to simply leave her sitting alone in the curricle.

Straightening her spine, she forced herself not to look around at the faces in the crowd. It was better to pretend that this was a planned stop.

Regrettably, this would not be the first time she'd been left to suffer the indignity of being abandoned. Or even the second.

In truth, she had been unceremoniously deposited by two separate gentlemen in the past. The first had left her alone on a bench on a cold, drizzly day in Hyde Park shortly following the news of her father's scandal. And the second had left her in the baker's shop on this very street.

Given the circumstances, Verity supposed it was inevitable that the duke would do the same. She just hadn't imagined it would happen so soon . . . or so publicly. Again.

She swallowed down a rise of nerves. The gazes of a dozen villagers fell upon her like links of a heavy chain that shackled her to the life she'd always known. To the life of being overlooked and yet dissected. Of being compared and found wanting. Of being insignificant and forgettable.

Then, to make matters worse, it began to rain. One icy droplet pelted her face, then two, and soon five, then six . . .

She stopped counting.

Verity wasn't sure if only a few seconds had passed or if it had been minutes, but from someplace deep inside her, she gathered the courage to say that enough was enough.

She was no longer going to subject herself to this treatment. Nell Hunnicutt could laugh all the way to London for all she cared. But as of this moment, the fake betrothal was off!

Opening her umbrella, she started to stand and reached for the curved lip of the scallop-shaped curricle to steady herself. But the polished wood was wet and slick. In the same instant, a gust of wind pushed at her umbrella.

She slipped. And in the seconds that her body began tipping helplessly forward, she chastised herself for tempting the Fates. Did she actually think that being abandoned again would be the worst thing that could happen?

Oh, but there were many, *many* ways to thoroughly humiliate oneself. Such as nearly toppling into the gutter. In front of the entire town.

But then, out of nowhere, a familiar hand—strong and steady—stole around her waist, righting her and anchoring her to his side.

Relief washed through her as her gaze connected with Longhurst's.

"You're still here." The words tumbled out before she could stop them.

She flushed with embarrassment as his expression

promptly transformed from one of irritation to something far too perceptive.

"My apologies, Miss Hartley. I hope I did not keep you waiting too long."

His tone was convincingly sincere. Gentlemanly, even. But she wasn't fooled. It was clearly for the benefit of the few onlookers that remained out of doors. Many of the others had dispersed with the rain and were crowded behind misty shop front windows, rubbing circles in the glass to watch the production of *The Duke and the Spinster*.

She pretended that her slip of the tongue never happened. "Were we separated? I hadn't noticed."

"Liar," he said in a low whisper as he bent to her ear.

A shiver stole through her, even as her cheeks heated. But he gave her no opportunity to be embarrassed. He laid her hand on his sleeve, took hold of the umbrella and held it aloft until it was situated over the two of them. Then he began to walk briskly along the pavement. "I was detained by *Mr.* Horncastle, who invited me to shoot pheasants in the morning."

She glanced up to see if there was a look of pity on his countenance, but saw no trace of one. "And have you ever been introduced to Mr. Horncastle?"

"Apparently, I was six years old."

"Practically yesterday." She noticed a slight upward curl at the corner of his mouth. Yes, indeed, that was a smirk! Possibly proof that he wasn't such a pompous arse after all. "Do I dare say *I told you so* now, or shall I wait a little longer?"

His eyes lifted to the dark canopy that shielded only the two of them and he shook his head. "I honestly thought you were exaggerating."

"No," she said, biting down into the flesh of her bottom lip to keep from laughing at the incredulity in his voice.

"I've traveled through many villages in my life, but never once have I encountered such utter . . ."

"Insanity?"

"Aye," he said with vehemence.

They stared at each other, not quite laughing but agreeing for the first and, likely, *only* time. It seemed impossible that the ever-present antagonism could give way to this sudden truce.

Then again, she reminded herself, the reason for this unexpected camaraderie was likely a show for the sake of the villagers.

And yet, his eyes weren't so very intimidating, here, beneath their umbrella. In fact, they were quite nice. The pale amber almost served as a source of warmth. And he had strong, attractive features, too, his nose straight, his mouth . . .

She dragged her gaze away and tried to remember what they were saying. *Ah, yes. Insanity.*

"This looks like a good place to wait out the storm," he said.

She was grateful for the interruption from her wayward thoughts. At least, until he opened the white-glazed door and a bell tinkled overhead. Because the instant that the aroma of freshly baked bread assailed her, a sinking weight of dismay fell into the pit of her stomach.

The bakery. Why did it have to be the bakery?

The likely reason was that it was the farthest shop from where most of the villagers had congregated and was virtually empty. Even so, it was filled with the reminder of that day she'd been left standing there. Alone and forgotten.

Like a fool, she'd waited for more than an hour before she'd realized Percival wasn't coming back. Later, after she'd walked the four miles home, she discovered that he'd seen Honoria through the window and had completely forgotten Verity's existence. Then, there he was, having tea with Honoria, Mother and Althea as if nothing had happened.

Stepping inside the shop now, she hoped against hope that the baker was still making deliveries and wouldn't comment on it as he'd done for the past three years.

The remarks weren't meant to be cruel. Mr. Brown had a jovial nature and his jocular observations were usually accompanied with a belly laugh. In fact, most of the villagers—aside from Nell Hunnicutt—likely had the best of intentions when they remarked on her age, her unmarried status and the lonely years yawning before her.

But they often forgot where the road of good intentions led—directly to her own personal Hades.

After shaking off the umbrella, the duke stood beside her in the snug space. Both of them lingered in the entryway between baskets of quartern loaves and rolls that had been brought in from the rain.

In the ensuing silence, it was as though neither wanted to risk taking another step that could potentially lead to another awkward encounter and far too-familiar exchange. She read the truth of that thought in his wary glance around the empty shop before his brief survey returned to her. When she lowered her hood, his shoulders seemed to relax. Hers did the same.

Was it strange that she felt a sense of relief in this moment? That she actually found solace in the company of her enemy?

She didn't have time to come up with an answer.

"Good morrow," a cheerful voice chirruped from the back of the shop.

Verity and the duke instantly stepped farther apart. The backs of her legs jostled a basket and the subsequent patter of crusty rolls hitting the floor shattered the short-lived peace.

As they both bent to pick them up, she looked over to

the baker's wife, who was clapping flour from her hands, her round cheeks ruddy from the heat of the brick ovens. Recognition alighted in her eyes. Then an unmistakable flash of pity followed.

Splendid. Verity dropped her armful of bread back into the basket and quickly supplied, "We've only stepped in from out of the rain."

Before Mrs. Brown could do more than nod her head, the door opened behind them.

A man came in, walking backward across the threshold and slapping the water from his felt hat. "Just finished the last delivery before the sky opened. Cats and dogs, it is."

When the baker straightened and turned, his eyes widened on his two patrons. Then he grinned broadly.

"Well, if it ain't the bride- and groom-to-be. Stealing into my shop for a bit of privacy, hmm? What do you think, Bea?" he called out to his wife. "Should we disappear into the back room and leave these two lovebirds alone?"

"Henry," Mrs. Brown chided.

"We've only stepped in from out of the rain," Verity repeated inanely, her face toasty red.

"Ah, don't fret, Miss Hartley. Your secret is safe with us," he said with a wink. "And besides, at your age, there ain't no one to balk. When's the wedding to be? Soon, I should think."

Trying to hide her embarrassment, she drew in a breath and expelled it slowly, telling herself to be grateful that he hadn't given his usual advice about moldy bread. "I'm afraid His Grace and I haven't discussed it."

"Don't wait too long. A loaf of bread don't remain fresh forever, if you ken my meaning. Mold sets in after a spell."

Aaand there it is, she thought.

He chuckled, stepping farther into the shop and stopping beside Longhurst, who was regarding a rack of loaves as if he intended to turn it to ash with his glower. Then he turned that same dark look on the baker.

Mr. Brown drew back, clutching his wet felt to his chest. "Beg pardon, Your Grace. Don't mean no harm. It's only that I've known your Miss Hartley since she was no bigger than a sack of rye, and I have a regular pint at the pub with the ole baron. Casting me as Petruchio, he is." When this news failed to impress, he cleared his throat. "Needless to say, the happy news of his daughter finally marrying has the whole village in a dither."

"So, it would seem," Longhurst said tightly, that vein making a reappearance.

"Truth be told, most folks feared she'd die a spinster. Not me and the missus, of course," he added hastily when the duke's expression remained unchanged. "We knew she'd snag herself a fellow . . . eventually."

And with that happy thought, he bowed, mopped his brow, then headed toward the back room.

His wife shook her head apologetically. "Please, pay no attention to Henry, Your Grace. We're all just so pleased for Miss Hartley. It's about time, especially after . . . well . . . what happened before."

Verity wanted to sink into the crack in the floor and disappear forever. And even though Longhurst didn't glance her way, there was no mistaking the sudden alertness that emanated from him.

He was curious. Too curious. And the last thing she wanted to admit to her fake fiancé was that she'd been jilted in this very shop.

The moment for *I told you so* had most definitely passed. She could scarcely utter those words when she was under the quizzing glass instead.

Stepping forward, she slid her hand around his sleeve

and tugged him toward the door. "Drat! I completely forgot about a previous engagement this afternoon and—Oh, look! I think the rain has stopped."

It hadn't. In fact, the sky seemed more ominous than before. Thankfully, he didn't point that out but walked with her, keeping his thoughts to himself.

"I look forward to seeing the two of you at the assembly," Mrs. Brown said with a wave as the bell tinkled overhead.

And that was when Verity was determined to come down with a cold.

Her plan to allow his disagreeable nature to provide the perfect reason for the end of their betrothal had completely fallen apart. The duke could have been a veritable ogre for all the villagers seemed to care. They were just amazed that *any* man might take an interest in the spinster of Hartley Hall.

"I imagine that I have a brief window of opportunity to return you to your doorstep before these reprehensibly unforeseen clouds unleash their torrent," Longhurst said from beneath their umbrella, his long stride and secure hold forcing her to quicken her pace or else be dragged.

"The roads are well sloped. We should have no trouble." But this did not slow him. Struggling to keep up, she turned to chastise him but noted his clenched jaw and the vein returning for an encore. "If your pique has been caused by the weather—"

He gave her a scathing look that said, *The Duke of Longhurst does not allow such trifling matters to incite his irritation.*

"Then if it is the undesired invitation to the assembly, then you needn't attend. You are not obligated."

"Am I not?"

"You are a duke. Your title affords you the freedom to do what you will."

"It does, indeed. Which includes ensuring that my name is in good standing when I leave this wretched little hamlet."

"Well, that is your choice. But I don't see why you have to be so cross with me."

It took a few strides for him to answer. "Because you've made yourself a laughingstock with all this betrothal nonsense."

She bristled, even while knowing it was the truth. That she had indeed made herself a ridiculous spectacle. Verity Hartley—the spinster who'd caught a duke's fancy? Ha!

Still, she didn't need him to remind her. "Why should that matter to you?"

"I would think it should matter to you." He stopped and regarded the rain-slick leather upholstery of the curricle before he nudged the umbrella into her hand. Then he whipped out a handkerchief and began to ineffectively whisk away the water collecting in runnels along the seams as he continued. "And besides, I have a reputation to uphold for making sound decisions. I cannot have anyone believing that I would saddle myself with a woman who allowed others to consistently disrespect her."

When he faced her again, frustrated and clenching a soggy handkerchief in his fist as the drizzle pattered steadily on his hat, there was something else in his expression. It wasn't pity. There was too much hardness for it to be that. And it wasn't simply vexation, for she was well acquainted with that look already. This seemed almost as if he were angry. Not *at* her, but *for* her.

Then again, they hardly knew each other and she might be imagining things.

Deciding not to examine it further, she batted her lashes and smiled sweetly. "Remind me again. What were the words you said that captured my heart when you *saddled* yourself to me?"

"Get in the carriage, Miss Hartley."

"Ah, yes. They still make me all aflutter."

The muscle ticked in his jaw. "Get. In. The. Carriage."

"Fine," she huffed, putting the umbrella into his waiting hand. Then she unfastened the frog clasp at her throat and removed her cloak.

"What are you doing?"

Instead of explaining—which likely would have taken two whole seconds and irked the impossibly impatient man even more—she opened the garment and spread the damp outer wool over the seat, leaving the dry inner lining exposed. "There's no reason for the two of us to be soaked through."

He offered a curt nod, transferred the umbrella to her once more, then shrugged out of his own coat. "Here."

"How very gallant," she said peevishly as he wrapped it around her shoulders. It was warm against her skin and carried with it that fragrant combination of saddle leather, shaving soap and his earthy spice that curled snugly in her belly. She hated it. "You needn't put on such a thorough display for our audience. You'll ruin the speech I've prepared, listing all of your abominably callous traits."

"Pity, that," he said without a modicum of regret in the upward flick of his eyebrow. "But I have an ulterior motive. You see, this way you cannot claim an excuse by way of a cold tomorrow evening."

"*How did you*—I mean, I wasn't going to do anything of the sort."

"It's written all over your face. For a proficient liar, you certainly do not know how to disguise your thoughts."

In the entirety of her life no one had ever accused her of having expressive features. "Which I've been telling you all along."

A knowing gleam lit his gaze as he pulled the lapels closed. His close scrutiny made her pulse quicken in something akin to panic. For some reason she felt more exposed than she had when standing in front of him with a torn dress.

His eyes widened briefly as if he were recalling the same moment. Then, in a blink, he released her and stepped out from beneath the umbrella.

"Furthermore," he continued, handing her into the carriage, "you are the one who dragged me into this. If I can endure the next few days, then so can you. And that includes attending the assembly."

Dread filled her again, her thoughts distracted by the likelihood that the dance would be little more than standing in front of the villagers while they remarked on how pathetically old she was.

Not to mention, all the other secrets they might reveal to Longhurst. It was too much to bear.

She summoned a cough. "I really do think that I might—"

"If you are not in the assembly rooms tomorrow, I will drive to Hartley Hall and fetch you myself," he growled.

Of all the nerve! "And just what gives you the right to order me about?"

He spurred the horse and slid her a smug look. "Apparently, as a duke, my title affords me the freedom to do whatever I will."

Her eyes narrowed. *We'll just see about that.*

Chapter Eight

ᕫᕤᕬ

MAGNUS ONLY INTENDED to make a brief appearance at the assembly rooms. After all, it shouldn't take long to pay his respects to his hosts, engage in a single dance with Miss Hartley, then take his leave.

Instead, he'd been left to stand in the long, paneled room for over an hour. Though, it felt as if he'd endured eons of banal conversation with anyone who could utter a syllable—whether introduced to him or not—while he waited for Miss Hartley to appear.

As a matter of fact, her entire family was absent. This fact quickly became apparent to the entire village. He'd been assured by nearly every matron that his betrothed likely needed time to prepare in order to look her best, especially when standing beside her sisters.

He wasn't certain what that was supposed to mean, or why everyone kept saying it. Then again, it didn't matter to him. He just wanted this night to end.

Turning away from the revelers, he sent a glare through the window. The glass reflected his prison—the flaming sconces, the crush of bodies, the faces ruddy and sweating from the gathering heat.

If she doesn't arrive in five minutes, he thought darkly, *there will be hell to pay.*

However, just as he began to imagine the thorough tongue-lashing he would give her, the carriage bearing the faded Hartley crest appeared on the street. His shoulders relaxed marginally. He watched as each Hartley filed out, the baron handing down his wife and his daughters . . .

All but one.

Magnus gritted his teeth. *She didn't. She wouldn't dare!*

And yet, apparently, she had.

Wasting no time, he cut through the crowd and swept down the stairs to confront the clan of liars and deceivers.

But his mounting irritation stalled for a moment when he saw the baroness.

Roxana Hartley came toward him with the same beatific smile that he recalled from his youth when she had visited her son at university. She'd always been a famed beauty, moving with flowing, effortless grace as if dancing through every moment of her life. And if not for the barest of silver strands at the temples of her chestnut coiffure, she would have appeared as though age had never touched her.

However, it was not her poise or ageless beauty that stopped him from rudely demanding to know the whereabouts of Verity. It was the simple fact that he recalled her kindness and the heartfelt note she'd sent after the death of his father.

"Magnus, how good to see you again."

"And you, my lady." He inclined his head with courtly formality, offering her the manners he had withheld from her husband. "I see that your eldest daughter is not here."

"Quite true," she said without elaborating. Then as if the matter were concluded, she gestured to her two youngest. "However, I should like to introduce you to Honoria and Althea."

They curtsied and he bowed in turn, but immediately returned his attention to the baroness. "And Miss Verity?"

Her indigo gaze studied him for a moment as if expecting something else of him.

He realized that he was still being rather brusque, even for a duke. So, he gave her daughters more than a perfunctory glance. As he did, a recollection niggled at the back of his mind, of Truman complaining about the tedium of introducing his sisters to anyone due to all the fawning he'd had to endure afterward. If not for the fact that Magnus's own grandmother had mentioned witnessing similar occurrences, he would have wondered if it was an exaggeration.

They were pretty, to be sure, but nothing unworldly. Of the two, the elder was fair, the younger dark, and both resembling their mother in form and feature. Their absent sister was also represented in the general shape of the brow and eyes, all which were tilted up at the outer corners and gave the impression of mischievous tendencies. But neither possessed the perplexing, shifting color of Verity's irises. And, he believed, the eldest of the three was a bit taller.

Then again, he thought with renewed irritation, if she had bothered to attend, he would know for certain.

"A pleasure," he said, then returned his attention to the baroness once more.

Whatever findings came of her scrutiny must have satisfied her, for she smiled. "I'm afraid that Verity was struck with a megrim at the last minute and decided not to join us."

"She told me she'd stubbed her toe," the youngest interjected, only to be nudged by her sister. "Then again, with Verity, one can never tell. She could likely be at death's door and her countenance wouldn't offer so much as a flicker of animation. In fact, I once wrote her the perfect death scene and it was excruciating to watch. Afterward, I ripped the play to shreds and tossed it into the fire."

The other Miss Hartley stepped forward and laid a hand on her sister's shoulder. "Thea, I'm sure His Grace is not interested in the ash at the bottom of our grate. However"—she lifted her gaze to him—"if you are concerned for our sister's welfare, I would gladly deliver a message."

"Thank you, no. I should rather deliver the message myself when next we meet," he said, schooling his features. But inside, his temper flared.

Why that little pretender! He had absolutely no doubt that she was sitting at home and thinking how clever she was. Well, she could think again.

His attention shifted to the open door and the gray of twilight that blanketed the street. He wished there was a way to excuse himself from this *delightful* soiree and find the little imp so he could strangle her.

"Oh dear," Lady Hartley said with elegant dismay. "Until now, I had no idea that she'd injured her foot as well. I could never enjoy myself this evening while imagining her stumbling around in agony." She laid a hand on his sleeve. "I wonder if you might do us a favor, Magnus. If it wouldn't be too much trouble, might you call upon Verity this evening and inquire if she needs us to send a physician for her ailments?"

This seemed rather too convenient. And yet, he was not one to look a gift horse in the mouth. "If that is your wish, then I am your servant, ma'am."

"Splendid," she said with a pat, then looked over his shoulder to where her husband handed his hat and walking stick to a manservant at the door. "Ah, there you are, Con. Longhurst has kindly offered to look in on Verity for a moment. Would you like to join him? Perhaps take our carriage, for I'm sure that his is buried somewhere in that terrible queue out front."

Magnus had prepared himself for another encounter,

but it was clear in the way that Hartley stiffened that he had not. Or perhaps he did not relish the idea of being in close confines with someone who detested him for what he'd done.

Whatever the reason, Magnus was glad when Hartley declined with a shake of his head.

"His Grace may take our carriage," he said to his wife. "I needn't accompany him, however. He was always a young man of honor and I expect he is still much the same."

For most of his life, Magnus would have agreed that a man's character remained unchanged. Whatever lay at the core of a person stayed the same. And yet, Hartley had changed from the man he'd been.

Sadly, the lure of money changed many men. And it was likely that Magnus had seen Hartley through the blinders of youth, admiring the person who had seemed to possess all the qualities of a great man.

But that was long ago. And now he was stuck with his daughter to contend with.

❦

WITHIN A QUARTER of an hour and teeming with irritation, Magnus was at Hartley Hall once again. Though, having a decidedly different purpose than before made it easier to cross the threshold. And easier still to take the stairs to the library, where he was told she was resting.

Dismissing the maid that had ushered him, he waited outside the partially open door and took a steadying breath to calm the desire to charge in and rail at Miss Hartley for orchestrating this plot to make him look the fool.

The hinges made no sound as the door swung slowly inward. And he stood beneath the lintel with a clear view of his quarry.

She was settled into the corner of the settee, reading a

book, her slender legs stretched out across the cushions with her stockinged feet crossed at the ankle. The top one wiggled back and forth like a contented puppy's tail. The motion quickened as she licked the tip of her finger to turn the page and he wondered if she had reached a particularly exciting part of the story.

"Good book?"

She shrieked. The tome went flying from her fingertips. She bolted off the settee, eyes wide. Then, her face went pale as she blinked at the figure in the doorway.

"*Longhurst?*" she rasped, then nervously cleared her throat. "But . . . why are you here?"

"I am escorting you to the assembly." His gaze drifted over her disheveled appearance, from the thick plait of honeyed brown hair hanging over her shoulder and tied with a pink ribbon, to the skin of her throat exposed between parted frills of her unbuttoned collar, down her rumpled worsted skirt to the toes peeping out from beneath the ruffled hem. And by the time his eyes met hers again, he felt a self-satisfied tug at the corner of his mouth, pleased that he had caught her wholly unawares. "Though, you might wish to don a suitable frock first."

"I'm not going to the assembly. I have a"—she affected a pitiful sneeze—"a cold."

"I thought it was a megrim."

"Oh . . . um . . . that, too," she said, awkwardly pressing her fingertips to her temples and squinting. "And you need to leave. It is unseemly for us to be in the same room together when there is no one else at home."

Unconcerned, he prowled in. "We were in the same curricle together."

"That's different and you know it. We were in the open."

"The same way we were in the open with both of us seated on the same horse?"

When she blushed, her cheeks turned as rosy as her lips . . . just as they had been that day beneath the tree as he'd held her lithe, supple form in his arms and the earth had seemed to shift on its axis.

He hated that his thoughts kept returning to that moment. Hated that he could still feel the imprint of her body against his. Hated that he was oftentimes struck by errant impulses that were not in his nature. And hated that this week was not over yet.

But he would be damned if he would leave this house without her.

"Well, no. Not exactly. But that was brief and unintentional. And you really must stop"—she held out her hand, halting his progress for the moment—"before my reputation is ruined."

"You didn't seem to be too concerned for *my* reputation when you involved me in your scheme. Besides, the door is open and your servants are still wandering the halls. Not only that, but your parents know I'm here," he added, starting toward her again. "And furthermore, you and I both know this was a paltry attempt to leave me looking the fool. But all you have accomplished is to draw unflattering attention to yourself. So, I'll have no more of your excuses. You are coming to the assembly with me."

"I'm not going to be ordered about by you."

"There happens to be a rather unsavory rumor that states I am to be your husband. Therefore, by all accounts, I have every right to order you about."

"I would never have you for a husband."

"A little late for that epiphany, I should think." He arched a brow and took another step, and another.

She set her hands on her hips and leveled him with a glare. Which might have been intimidating if she were the prim and plain Miss Hartley, and not this tousled wildling.

It was strange, but seeing her like this compelled him to draw nearer. Demanded it. He wasn't certain of the reason. Though, perhaps, he was driven by an internal knowledge that he and he alone could tame her.

"If you take one more step, I'll scream."

"And if you do, I'll—"

His hands lifted. And he had every intention of taking her by the shoulders and silencing any further argument. He even saw the method flash across his mind: a kiss. A hard, penetrating kiss that would match the heavy thudding of his pulse.

Though, until that instant, he hadn't even known his heart was drumming with such ferocity. That the blood teeming through his veins was simmering. Fevered. That every instinct told him to grab, to devour, to . . . slake.

The realization stopped him in his tracks, barely a step apart from her as if iron bars suddenly shot up from the floor between them.

A ragged breath caught in his throat. That was when Magnus knew he was wrong.

He wasn't drawn to her out of a need to tame *her*. For some inexplicable reason, she had unleashed something wild inside of *him*.

She hiked her chin. "You'll what?"

His arms lowered, his fingers flexing toward his palms at the taunt in her voice, at the challenge flaring in the eyes that he wished were still brown. He wanted them to be plain and ordinary, not this unfathomable color. It irritated him that he was snared every time he looked into them.

And for the first time, he didn't feel wholly in control. No, he felt like a caged bear, capable of anything if she came too close.

Confused by this disturbing awareness, he turned on his heel and stalked away from her.

But on the threshold, he paused, his hand curling around the door frame as he looked over his shoulder. "Ten minutes, Miss Hartley. That is how long I will be in the carriage. If you keep me waiting again, I will come back for you, and I will not be responsible for my actions."

And the most frightening thing of all, he was telling the truth.

Chapter Nine

$\mathcal{V}$ERITY SAT ACROSS from him in the carriage with a huff of annoyance. And that sound was the only utterance she would give him this night.

Longhurst didn't deserve her conversation. Not that he noticed. He didn't even bother to look at her when the footman handed her in, but merely rapped against the hood with his ungentlemanly large hand.

Then they were off, riding together in tense silence, occupying opposite benches, facing opposite windows, both gazing toward the dark indigo blanket that had immersed them into night.

She was grateful for the silence. It provided her more time to imagine all the ways she would like to murder him.

Doubtless, he was imagining the same. Tension rolled off him in waves, so palpable that she could almost taste it in the air. She most certainly could see it in the way he held himself, his hands fisted at his sides, jaw hard as granite, posture taut as a coiled spring as if, at any moment, he could seize her by the shoulders and do whatever he'd had in mind in the parlor a short while ago.

Which had likely been strangulation. She'd pictured doing the same to him, only to realize that her hands would never fit around his thick neck. That was the trouble with murdering brawny dukes, she supposed. It certainly limited one's options.

When the carriage drew to a stop, she heard him expel

a weighty breath, like a prisoner escaping gaol. The sound grated on her nerves.

Then the blackguard had the gall to stand on the pavement and present his open palm to hand her down as if they didn't hate each other to the very marrow. She refused to accept. After all, he was only being polite for the sake of their audience of drivers, groomsmen, tigers and whoever might have been looking down from the windows above.

Verity would like to say that she descended from the carriage as regal as a queen and left him standing alone on the pavement without giving him a backward glance.

Unfortunately, ungainliness reared its ugly head at the worst possible moment.

Just as she rejected his proffered hand with a haughty sniff, her heel caught on the very edge of the step. She slipped. Her sniff came out as a snort, making her sound like a surprised piglet. And she stumbled. Or would have done, if not for him.

Longhurst rescued her, yet again. His hold was secure, his touch far gentler than his impatient growl as he steadied her at his side. Then he set her hand firmly on his sleeve, but said nothing. Neither did she. And when they entered the assembly rooms, they remained stiff at each other's sides.

Thankfully, there was no need to talk when their hostess bustled up to greet them.

Mrs. Horncastle ushered them through the archway, chattering in a rapid succession of words as if required to use them all. "Ah, there you are, Miss Hartley, looking fine in your dress. I'm sure His Grace would agree that the small delay was much worth the wait. And while we normally never play a waltz at these country assemblies, Mr. Horncastle and I have decided to make an exception. Oh, yes, indeed. 'Tis a special occasion, after all and—Ah! He has cued the musicians already. Well, off with you now. No time to dally. Shoo! Shoo! We all want to see the two of you together . . ."

Verity found herself unceremoniously nudged—*shoved* was more like it—alongside the duke and onto the open floor just as the dancers around them began to step and turn, rotating in their direction.

The eager crowd pressed in behind them. She tried to retreat, but it was impossible.

Then, before she could think of what to do next, Longhurst took her in his arms and swept her into the dance.

Her vow of silence was broken on the gasp that fell from her lips.

Reflexively, her fingers curled around his palm as she misstepped in the first turn. *Drat!* Apparently, being filled with both righteous indignation *and* clumsiness at the same time did her no favors.

Embarrassed, she refused to meet his gaze. "I haven't waltzed with anyone other than my sisters in many years."

As soon as the words were out, she realized she'd just given him an open invitation to insult her. And since she was forever falling whenever he was near, she had made it easy for him.

But instead of saying anything about her lack of grace, he drew her closer. Shoring her frame against his own, he guided her into the next turn. And she matched him step for step, her memory of the dance quick to recover.

"You have not required the practice," he said.

Verity eyed him with suspicion, waiting for him to finish that statement with one of his usual parries. After all, he couldn't have meant it. Otherwise, he would have adjusted the space between them to a more proper distance. So he must have found fault with her. And it was surely unseemly to be held this close. Why, she could practically feel the buttons of his waistcoat!

And yet, he held her with such command, such utter assurance that it was difficult to object.

With her sisters, she was often the one who led, giving them the opportunity to further enhance their skills. After all, no one expected Verity to be asked to waltz.

She hated to admit it but, in Longhurst's arms, she felt graceful in a way that she never had before. They moved in perfect symmetry, his solid form guiding her through every turn, their limbs brushing and twining fluidly as if they were one.

At the thought, she felt flushed, giddy as they whirled and turned, the room a blur of color around them. At this swiftness, any misstep or slightest separation could send them on a collision course with another couple. The possibility of calamity, along with the certainty that he wouldn't permit such an event to happen, was all so thrilling!

It made her breathless. Not in a panicked sort of way, but in the flustered sort of way that reminded her of the dream she'd had of him. The confusing sensation made her want to . . . to feel more of his waistcoat buttons against her midriff.

He seemed to read her thoughts because he drew her the slightest degree closer. And when her gaze flew to his in silent query, he offered, "It is quite the crush."

His eyes held that same dark look she'd witnessed in the library, his pupils spreading like drops of ink on a blotter. And when they lowered to her parted lips, her flesh tingled.

She wet them distractedly. "The assembly hall is not usually so full. Though, I'm sure they are all here for you."

"Then that would be a shame," he said, "because our hostess was correct. The small delay was, indeed, worth the wait."

Her spine stiffened at once. He hadn't even looked at her until now and when he did, he seemed . . . well, not angry but some cousin of that emotion. "I was not begging for a compliment."

"No?"

"No," she answered flatly. "Though if I were vain enough to do so, I certainly wouldn't wish for you to pacify me with a regurgitation from Mrs. Horncastle. Not that it matters—the result of the delay, that is—for I wasn't aware that I had a choice in the matter. Ten minutes, you'd said. Then you looked as though you were ready to throttle me or something."

"*Or something*, indeed," she thought she heard him mutter.

But then he cleared his throat and said, "I apologize for my earlier behavior. It appears as though the antagonism between our families has had an unforeseen consequence. However, that is all behind me now."

"How fortunate for you. In the meantime, I am at the assembly in the dress that had the fewest wrinkles. My hair is in an untidy twist. I'm wearing two different slippers, and not a single piece of jewelry."

His gaze traveled over the loose tendrils of her hair, her heated cheeks, her lips—again—and then drifted down, darkening even more as he took in the bare expanse of her shoulders all the way to the bodice of her apricot satin.

It was a brief glance. But thorough. And she felt exposed, her pulse thick, her breaths shallow, skin drawing taut beneath her corset and chemise.

"Your throat requires no adornment," he said, his voice low, deeper. Almost hoarse. A tinge of red color slashed across his cheeks and the bridge of his nose. Then he swallowed and lifted his gaze before offering blandly, "And your ears are not pierced."

Though, he must have found fault with her lobes because his gaze dipped once more to them and a muscle ticked along his jaw. His loathing was so powerful that they nearly collided with the couple in front of them as the music stopped.

She felt the flesh between her brows pucker in confusion. Did he truly despise everything about her?

"Such flattery," she said testily as she curtsied to his bow. "It is a wonder that some debutante has not snatched you up yet."

"And I wonder why *you* have not married. None of this would be happening if you had."

Needless to say, she was only too happy when he delivered her to her waiting mother and sisters. Their required dance was over. At last.

※

MAGNUS WONDERED IF he was losing his mind. A man of his age and distinction did not forget himself over a glimpse of a woman's bare throat and earlobes!

And yet, he couldn't even recall the last steps of the dance because his mind had been filled with thoughts revolving around the exposed column of creamy skin, imagining it arching on a sigh of pleasure. And those lobes, those little unadorned morsels appeared soft as the flesh of a peach, and he wondered what they would feel like against his lips, between his teeth . . .

Utter madness!

Clearly, the strain of these past few days had caused him to imagine an unfounded attraction to her. Which, of course, he did not have. She was a Hartley, after all. Born into a family of liars and cheats. Everything he abhorred.

Only an undisciplined fool would allow his thoughts to entertain the ludicrous notion that he actually desired her.

Therefore, the instant he deposited Miss Hartley beside her mother, he was only too eager to leave this infernal assembly.

Unfortunately, his escape was thwarted by Mrs. Horncastle, who reminded him of their dance, then proceeded to murder six of his toes while extolling him with tales of her acclaim on the local stage.

Having done his duty, he delivered his partner to her husband, then turned to leave. His errant gaze swept past Miss Hartley long enough to note her smug smile. Vexing creature!

Pivoting sharply on his heel, he took one step, but was blockaded by two more women.

Mrs. Hunnicutt introduced herself and her daughter, telling him that they had dined together in London. Twice, apparently. He merely nodded, not recalling either woman. Although, their narrow faces and long noses did remind him of horses but without the large teeth.

Mrs. Hunnicutt tried to cajole him into dancing with her daughter. A polite refusal was on his lips. Or at least, it was . . . until he heard a derisive snort from nearby.

He was certain the sound came from Verity's quarter. Though, when he glanced at her, there was nothing in her expression to reveal her thoughts. Nothing other than those eyes and the flash of ire within their depths.

Feeling no qualms over fanning the flames of her irritation, he decided that one more dance wouldn't hurt. So he proffered his hand to Miss Hunnicutt and relished the loathing that Verity directed at him.

But his sense of satisfaction was short-lived when she lined up for the cotillion with another man. A man whom she must have known quite well because she smiled and laughed easily in his company. But Magnus refused to be distracted by the two of them as they bowed and turned and circled each other, their eyes locked.

"That's what I despise about our village assemblies," Miss Hunnicutt said, drawing his attention. She tutted disdainfully in the direction of Verity and her partner. "They'll simply let anyone through the doors. And Mr.

Bennet Lawson is little more than a hired hand, for I've seen him working with the horses. But they allow him to live in their dower cottage, if you can believe that."

He could. In his youth, Hawk had often told him of his father's propensity to welcome those who were down on their luck to live on the estate for a time until they were on their feet again. Magnus had marveled at this way of thinking. Admired it, even.

But now, knowing that Hartley was allowing some transient to dance with his daughter, he thought it was irresponsible.

Not that it mattered, Magnus reminded himself. She was only his temporary fiancée, not a permanent fixture. In five days, he would hardly think of her again.

In the meantime, however, he returned Miss Hunnicutt to her self-satisfied mother and noted that Verity was taking the floor with another man. So, he decided to stay for one more dance. And then one more after that when he saw Verity with Lawson again. Magnus, in turn, escorted Mrs. Brown, all the while ignoring the smiles his betrothed gave to the transient.

This game of tit for tat between himself and Verity continued for another hour. And although she never danced with Lawson again, she was never in want of a partner.

Magnus was fairly certain that he had met and danced with every woman in this hamlet and the surrounding county.

Then an unexpected reprieve came in the form of Althea Hartley when she requested his escort to the refreshment table. The punch was surprisingly palatable, far more so than the pallid lemonade and tepid green tea served at many soirees in London.

"It appears as though my sister will soon be available for another dance."

"I think not," he said, his gaze already on Verity across

the room as a young man approached. Though, recognizing him as the one who'd ridden past them on their way into the village yesterday, he narrowed his eyes.

"Oh, she won't dance with him. That's Percy Culpepper," the youngest Miss Hartley said as if that explained everything. "I don't blame her either. If he'd have left me standing alone in the center of town, for everyone to snigger at, I'd have killed him off in a play. And not one of those simple poisonings where he tips forward into his plate at dinner, but a vile, gruesome death. I'm thinking beheading. Perhaps disembowelment. Or both. Now, there's a thought."

Handing him her cup, she reached into a hidden placket on the side of her skirts, withdrawing a small leatherbound notebook and the stub of a black pencil.

As she scribbled, it was on the tip of Magnus's tongue to ask for more information. He tamped down the urge. Such things were none of his concern. And yet, he was curious enough to watch the spectacle on the other side of the room.

Mr. Culpepper bowed, extending his hand in invitation. For an instant, it seemed as though Thea was wrong because Verity nodded. But then she took a step and cringed.

At least, it might have been a cringe. Or a sudden attack of her nervous system. She hopped, leaning on one foot and then, oddly, on the other. Then she shook her head and pointed down to her feet.

"Pitiful performance," Thea groaned, rolling her eyes as Culpepper walked away from her sister. "The old 'I'm too injured to dance' excuse. She could have slapped him, at least. Now *that* would have been something to see." On a sigh, she briefly took her cup, drained the contents and handed it back to him. "I cannot watch this any longer."

Then, without another word, she walked away.

It would have been the perfect time for him to depart as well. He'd done his duty, after all.

But his attention returned to Verity as she hobbled around the corner toward the stairs, just as Culpepper took to the floor with another girl.

Planning to bid his inconvenient fiancée farewell on his way out, Magnus left the cups on the window ledge and followed her.

He found her sitting on the little bench down at the end of the hall from the stairs, a window open on the far wall. But he didn't think it was the cool evening breeze that made her skin pale. It was drained of the becoming blush she'd worn when they'd danced. And those uncanny irises had lost the challenging flare he was becoming accustomed to seeing.

"They're lining up for a country jig. Plenty of foot stomping for those so inclined," he quipped, expecting a sharp retort from her.

But she did not take the bait. "Kind of you, but no. I'm afraid I've sprained my ankle."

"Hmm. And which ankle was it, again? The right or the left? Or the right *and* the left?"

She slid him a glance, then winced, her lashes bunching together. "Was my performance that bad?"

"Well, I *wanted* to believe you," he hemmed and that earned him something of a smile. It was only a small upward tilt at one corner of her mouth, but it was . . . something. And before he knew what he was doing, he shooed her to one side of the bench and took his place on the other.

"Then you are too kind. I really am terrible at lying."

"Except for that one time," he reminded her, stretching his arm along the back of the bench.

They shared a wry look. "Oh, yes. Except for that."

Absently, he brushed the pad of his thumb against a burl in the wood just over her shoulder, so near that he could feel the warmth rising from her bared skin. His gaze drifted down the curve of her neck, along the graceful slope of her clavicle to the rounded protrusion of the acromion at the top of her shoulder joint. It was the size of a comfit and made his mouth water to think of pressing his lips—

Devil take it! He was doing it again.

"So tell me," he said, requiring a distraction, "why didn't you accidentally utter the name of Mr. Culpepper on that fateful day instead?"

She scrutinized him as he shifted on the bench, drawing his arm away from temptation. Then she issued a resigned sigh. "Thea told you, didn't she?"

"Not all of it. Mostly that he deserves a grisly demise on the stage."

"That would be too much fuss for something so trifling. The episode wouldn't even deserve a page of a script," she said and added a stiff shrug for good measure. "The curtain would open to the bakery. The narrator would then say, 'Once upon a time, the eldest Miss Hartley had thought that Mr. Culpepper might have wanted to offer for her. But one day, she was left standing alone in this very shop because he became so distracted by the sight of her sister walking on the pavement outside that he forgot the spinster completely. That was when she realized she had merely been a placeholder. And so, she walked home in the rain and found him having tea with her family and no one even thought of her at all.' End scene. Curtain falls. And there you have it."

She dusted her hands together and swallowed, pasting on an unconcerned smile. And he had to admit, her indifferent expression was rather convincing. She must have practiced a good deal over the years.

"I suppose this is where a dutiful fiancé would offer words of consolation."

"Likely so. Though it is fortunate that neither of us expects that of you. Wouldn't want you to strain something, after all."

"Kind of you to think of my health," he said, his bland tone in keeping with their disinterested banter. And yet, before he could rein in the words, he heard himself ask, "Is he the reason you never married?"

She attempted a light laugh, the forced sound tinny to the ear. "Oh, I don't know if I would have accepted. He practically fawns over Father. And I could never marry a man who admired my father too much or, with that said, regarded him too little. So that counts you out, as well," she teased. "After all, neither sycophant nor enemy would make a worthy husband."

He nodded thoughtfully. Even though she tried to make light of it, he could see the hurt. And in that instant, he recalled the odd thing she'd said yesterday.

You're still here.

Now he understood. And in that moment, he felt an urge to grab Mr. Culpepper by the scruff of his neck and escort him outside, by way of the window.

The thought surprised him. Why should he feel compelled to do anything of the sort for someone who carried the blood of the man he hated?

He shouldn't. After all, she was also the one who'd dragged him into this nonsense.

He rolled his shoulders to ward off the unwelcome stirring of protectiveness. "And this deserving victim in your sister's play did not even bother to escort you to this bench?"

"I sent him to fetch me a glass of punch. Though, considering our history, he likely forgot."

Knowing that was the truth since Culpepper was on

the dance floor with the other foot-stompers, he offered. "If you are thirsty, then I will—"

When he shifted to rise from the bench, she laid her hand on his knee. It was the barest brush of her fingertips and withdrawn at once, her cheeks coloring, and yet the warmth of the touch stayed, lingering like a cinder that was burning a hole through his black trousers, heating the flesh and blood beneath.

She cleared her throat, her gaze drifting to the hands now clasped in her lap. "Thank you, no. I don't need you to play the hero any more than you already have done. The only consolation in this entire mess is that it's almost over."

"Aye. At least, there's that."

That would have been the perfect moment for Magnus to stand and bid farewell. And yet, he suddenly found himself in no hurry to leave the stillness of this narrow corridor.

"I imagine you're relieved that there is only one dinner to endure before this is over," she said. "One more evening where we are cordial but otherwise indifferent to each other. Just one simple dinner, then our betrothal will—" She stopped and frowned. "Why are you shaking your head?"

"The dinner might not be as simple as you expect."

"And whyever not?"

"Well, I hate to be the bearer of bad news, but I overheard Mrs. Hunnicutt and her daughter speaking to your mother, and they asked if your family might be willing to provide the entertainment—"

"No."

"—for the evening."

"Please tell me that my mother saw through Mrs. Hunnicutt's obvious ploy to humiliate me and decided to do something truly altruistic by refusing to subject her own flesh and blood to ridicule."

"I'm afraid I cannot. Lady Hartley seemed most eager, in fact." He saw with some concern as Verity paled, an almost greenish cast to her skin. "Come now. The dinner won't be that bad."

"But it will. There will be . . . a play. I'm sure Thea is already writing it. And worse, I will be poked, prodded and cajoled until I am standing there, wooden and lifeless, in front of everyone. There will be no escape." She leaned forward, elbows propped on her knees, and buried her face in her hands. "Do you carry a boot knife?"

His brow furrowed at the odd question. "Why do you ask?"

"Because I want you to thrust it into my heart. Right here and now."

"Oh, don't be so dramatic."

She turned her head to look at him, those eyes beseeching. "That's the problem. I'm serious. I am completely unable to be dramatic. Standing on a stage is sheer torture. I suppose my only consolation is that it will only be a small dinner party."

"Well, actually . . ." he hemmed.

"She has invited the entire village, hasn't she."

"I wouldn't say the *entire* village."

He nearly laughed at her responding groan, but stopped himself.

A frown pulled at his mouth. Surely, he wasn't actually enjoying her company.

Damn. He realized his problem at once. His efforts to be a dutiful—though temporary—fiancé were making him forget just how ruthless and diabolical her father had been. Just how despicable her brother had been, even while claiming to be his friend.

But that stopped now.

Magnus would never allow himself to be drawn in by a Hartley again.

Chapter Ten

༄

$\mathcal{J}$T CERTAINLY FELT like the entire village was gathered in the Hunnicutt's ballroom.

Oh, why had she agreed to take part in one of Thea's plays?

But she knew the reason. It was her penance, of a sort. The only problem was, it was supposed to be a self-inflicted penance, not a pillory in the village square. Which was precisely what this felt like.

Every single sconce in the gilded room was ablaze, revealing the entire audience waiting for the play to begin. And worse, one long wall was adorned with mirrors, ultimately allowing Verity the ability to see every expression of distaste and disappointment at her performance. Twice.

Standing behind the partially closed door of the servant's passageway, she turned around, prepared to beg and plead with her sisters to read the lines for her. But she stopped when she saw them in the lamplight. They were smiling and laughing together, reciting their *Percival*, *Peter* and *Carlton Culpeppers*.

She hated the small twinge of jealousy that pinched her heart. It wasn't only that her sisters were inhumanly beautiful, or that they could enchant and mesmerize with a flash of a smile. They had something else. A spark. An inner shimmer of light.

They were bold, too, and unabashedly themselves without the smallest kernel of fear that they would ever be judged and found wanting, then cast aside like the scraps in yesterday's rubbish bin.

Yet, no matter how much she envied her enigmatic sisters, she was also glad that they would never know what that felt like.

Turning around to peer through the crack in the door, her panic swelled as her attention fell to Longhurst.

He was looking gravely striking in his dark superfine wool. Even so, she wished he wasn't here. It was bad enough that he'd seen her disheveled and tumbling from a tree, heard every villager remark on her age, in addition to learning of the day of her bakery humiliation. Did he truly need proof of her pathetic acting skills, too?

The thought caused her stomach to churn. She supposed she should be thankful that she hadn't been able to eat much of anything for these last four days. Instead, she had dined on dread for every meal.

"I cannot do this," she whispered to no one in particular. Her hands were shaking, cold and numb but also disconcertingly damp. She smoothed them down the skirt of her Grecian costume.

"Of course, you can, my little finch," her father said from behind her, his tone attempting to reassure her. "You are a Hartley. This is in your blood."

"Are you sure about that? I mean, if you found me on the doorstep and decided to keep it a secret all this time, I wouldn't be cross with you. I am old enough to hear the truth."

He set his hand on her shoulder, his blue gaze steady and true. "It was act four of *Antony and Cleopatra*. I was on stage and wishing that it was your mother lamenting over my corpse instead of Cedric Mooney, who hadn't shaved before the performance and had a very coarse beard. Roxana, who'd never missed a curtain call, had been tired and told me she would watch from the window of our room at the coaching inn. And as I was lying in state, I heard a sudden cry, a boisterous squalling that had me leaping up from my grave and tearing across the courtyard.

"Then there you were, red-faced and shouting at the world, 'I am a Hartley, hear me roar.'" He cupped her face. "You were born with something to say. So when you take that stage, remember that. Speak your own truth, daughter of mine, and you will be magnificent."

She tucked her chin as he pressed a kiss to her forehead. "But what if I'm . . . not?"

"All we can do is our best *and*—as Cleopatra said— 'make death proud to take us.'"

With a fond pat, he turned and went to speak with her sisters and their tenant, Mr. Lawson, who'd been cast in the lead role.

Unfortunately, leaving her with that line from Shakespeare did not instill her with any confidence. After all, Cleopatra had decided to kill herself with an asp shortly thereafter. *Happy thought.*

Frowning, she peered through the crack in the servant's door once more.

She had not seen Longhurst at all these past four days. There had been no surprise excursions to the village. No awkward encounters on the river path. Not even a missive declaring that he might have a matter of business to attend. Clearly, he felt that he had done his betrothal duty by escorting her to the assembly.

It was for the best, she supposed. Their association would end soon enough.

At the moment, he was seated in between his grandmother and Nell Hunnicutt. The Tick was likely euphoric with anticipation of Verity's abominable performance. And, of course, they had to be in the front row. That way, when she literally died on stage, she would fall at their feet in one final act of humiliation.

HERE LIES VERITY HARTLEY
BELOVED DAUGHTER AND SISTER
IF ONLY SHE COULD HAVE EXPIRED BEFORE
TAKING THE STAGE

❧

THE PLAY WAS called *A Mistake of Muses*, written and directed by Althea Hartley.

Magnus tried to summon mild interest. Though, to be honest, he was far more concerned with bringing this farce to an end. Not only the stage production, but this entire betrothal nonsense.

He thought that keeping his distance and not playing the dutiful fiancé over the past four days would subdue the peculiar, uncharacteristic thoughts and impulses that had plagued him of late.

He had been wrong.

These had been the longest, most sleep-deprived days of his life. The only way he could account for it was the fact that he had made the mistake of rendering a formal proposal. For the sake of his honor, he'd had to. And yet, that seemed to have cracked some sort of fissure in his logical mind where thoughts of her were able to breach past his defenses and invade like a horde of marauders.

This would not do. He wanted—no, *needed*—to return to London in order to put Verity Hartley and this ordeal out of his mind, once and for all.

A decided inhale flared his nostrils as he took hold of his watch fob and opened the brass casing with a flick of his thumb. Sensing his grandmother's curiosity in the way she leaned closer, he angled it for her to see the time before snapping the lid shut.

"It shouldn't be long now," he said, watching as footmen on either side of the room were snuffing the sconces one by one.

A snicker answered, but from Miss Hunnicutt, seated on his other side. "I pray that Your Grace does not expect much from this Hartley theatrical. They are entertaining, to be sure, but much in the way a court jester would be when tripping over his own bell-tipped shoes."

Magnus frowned. He was about to ask why she had been so determined to have them perform this evening if that were the case. But then the play began with a clash of swords as Lord Hartley and Mr. Lawson rushed onto the stage.

As they fought, the narrator, Roxana Hartley, stepped forward in her flowing costume and addressed the audience.

"These two venerable men," she said, gesturing to the players, "were once friends. But now they are fighting a duel over the right to court the one woman who is so beguiling, so thoroughly enchanting that she has ensnared both of their hearts." When she splayed a hand against her own bosom and flashed an unrepentant grin, the crowd laughed. Even Magnus felt the corner of his mouth twitch. "And she has promised herself to the victor of this battle, whoever he may be."

Then she withdrew into the character of the damsel, every gesture graceful and convincingly distressed. Some of the members of the audience began to shout out encouragement and support for their favorite as the sword fight continued.

Magnus begrudgingly admitted that it was well orchestrated. Both men displayed fine footwork, feints and parries. Yet, when Lawson was slain, many in the audience gasped. Not Magnus, of course. He thought Lawson deserved an untimely demise for attempting to seduce a woman who belonged to another. And as the curtain closed, he felt no compassion for the man left dying on the stage in a puddle of red silk.

The play could have ended as far as he was concerned, but there were two more acts to go.

The second act brought comedy.

As Lawson leaned on the hilt of his sword, clutching his mortal wound, he called out to the Furies for vengeance. However, in his delirium, he accidentally summoned the Muses instead.

Thea entered. Playing the part of the Muse Clio, she offered him the inspiration to study the history of sword fighting.

"What good is that knowledge, when I can no longer lift my own sword?" he asked, and the frustrated Clio exited the stage.

Honoria entered next. Playing Terpsichore, she swept in on a flawless pirouette, turning and twirling, and offered to teach him about dance.

"I can barely stand," Lawson railed. "Besides, what would be the point of dancing while my enemy still lives?"

Disappointed, Terpsichore left.

Then, full of wrath, the dying Lawson staggered forward, shouting to the heavens with one final plea.

That was when Verity entered, looking ethereal in white muslin, the dress gathered over one shoulder and leaving the other bare. The gauzy fabric clung to her form, cinched at the waist by a thin golden chain. Carrying a kithara, she personified her part as the Muse of love poetry, Erato.

And yet, her ghostly pale complexion was likely not due to an application of powder but rather of the dread she had mentioned when they'd last spoken.

Proof of that came when she tripped on the hem of her costume and accidentally stepped on Lawson's foot, dropping her kithara. He hissed and hunched forward. She lowered to pick up her instrument, then stood upright so quickly that she struck him on the chin.

Lawson staggered in earnest this time, and dropped to

the stage on a groan. She stared down at him, her cheeks flaming poppy red as the audience laughed.

"Not the most poised of the muses, is she, Your Grace?" Miss Hunnicutt snickered. "But fear not, I've seen her in a far worse state. In fact, she'd been climbing out of a window on the day she told me of your betrothal."

"*Climbing out*—" He broke off at the appearance of her smug grin.

Beside him, his grandmother cleared her throat. And Magnus straightened, containing himself.

Even so, that did not stop the immediate anger that had rifled through him, wondering if Verity made a habit of putting herself in danger.

Misinterpreting his abrupt silence for permission to continue, Miss Hunnicutt did just that. "Some might even say that she was saved a great deal of embarrassment by not having a real Season. She was only in town for less than a fortnight before it became patently clear that she didn't belong in proper society."

Waspish comments were common amongst the *ton* and rarely concerned him. Of course, if Verity had indeed been more than his temporary fiancée, he would have felt a need to come to her defense. He might have reminded this harpy that he had chosen Miss Hartley to become the Duchess of Longhurst, a longstanding and respectable title, and she would do well to remember that.

Whatever set-down he might have given, however, was rendered moot under the circumstances. And yet, he found himself wondering why Hartley's eldest daughter had not had a proper entrée into society. Instead, she'd been left to run wild in the country.

Or was the reason, perhaps, that she preferred the company of someone who lived nearby?

Magnus felt his jaw tighten as his gaze shifted to the man on the stage.

"I see you are most eager to assist me, Fury, and for that I am glad," Lawson said, making Verity's stumble seem scripted. It quieted the audience. Lying on the stage, he coughed and blindly reached out a hand for her. "Pray, what vengeance shall be wrought against those who have wronged me?"

"I know naught of vengeance, good sir," she said, her voice quavering as she kneeled beside him, gripping his hand like a lifeline.

This was no act. She was clearly in distress. And Magnus began to lean forward reflexively as if to . . . to *what*? To go to her aid? Absurd.

Reining in the impulse, he rooted himself to the chair and sat up straighter. This was a play, he reminded himself. Nothing more.

Even so, he could not help but notice that, in her fall, a few curling tendrils had escaped her topknot. They snaked down past her gilded laurel crown to rest along her throat and settle softly against the slender valley of creamy skin just above her clavicle.

He shifted marginally, forcing himself to look elsewhere. Though, for her sake, he wished she could leave the stage, set herself to rights, and not return until she was more . . . composed. He also wondered if he should signal a footman to open the windows. The ballroom was growing uncomfortably hot and humid on this drizzly spring evening.

On the stage, Lawson pleaded with the Muse he'd mistaken for a Fury. "Have you never burned with the need to bring swift justice down upon another's head?"

"*Burned?*" she asked, licking her trembling lips. She blinked at Lawson as if waiting for his prompt. When he gave none, she glanced offstage. It was clear that she'd forgotten her line.

Then, for reasons only known to her, her gaze alighted

on Magnus, beseeching in a way that stirred that unaccountable protectiveness. Without hesitation, he offered her a nod of encouragement. It was all he could do. Though, apparently, it was enough, for she continued.

"I . . . I know well of burning . . . with need and with p-passion." Her stammer brought on a few chuckles, but not from Magnus. He splayed his fingers, opening them like fans to cool his perspiring hands, pressing his palms to the tops of his thighs as she plodded onward, oblivious to the wayward and unwanted thoughts running rampant in his mind. "The best remedy is . . ."

"Poisoning?" Lawson's bloodthirsty character interjected. "Decapitation?"

"Poetry," the Muse announced with satisfaction, this time earning an anticipated laugh. Verity exhaled a sigh of relief.

Lawson groaned in agony and flung an arm over his eyes. "What good could come of a mere rhyme? They deserve to suffer for what they have done."

"Then what better way than to send her a verse that will burn for all eternity in her heart, where no other man will ever compare to the beloved author? And your rival's victory will sour, his love for her forever unrequited and tainted by jealousy."

Lawson uncovered his face, doubt gradually falling away. "Then with my dying breath, so be it."

The curtain closed. And with Erato finally gone from sight, Magnus let out the breath he didn't realize he'd been holding.

This was insanity! He was tempted to walk out and set off for London directly. In fact, he even turned toward his grandmother to state his intentions, but then the curtain opened again.

It was the third and final act, and he decided he could bear it with dignity. Besides, the Muses were gone.

Then, happily, Lawson's character died. And the revenge poem lived up to its promise, ensuring an untimely end for the characters played by Lord and Lady Hartley.

The family and their tenant were greeted with cheers at the final curtain call, with Thea taking an additional bow for having written the play.

"What did you think, Magnus?" his grandmother asked when, at last, they were able to walk away from the chattering Hunnicutts to take a turn about the room.

"Given the family, it is hardly surprising that they are all exceptional actors."

His grandmother blinked. "Surely, you don't mean *all*."

"Perhaps the youngest was not as seasoned as the rest, but otherwise . . ." He left the comment unfinished as he attempted to comprehend the reason for his grandmother's astonishment. "Do you disagree?"

Something flitted across her countenance, but she schooled her features too quickly for him to discern what it might have been. Then her lips pursed. "Not at all, my dear boy. And I thought Mr. Lawson's death scene in the second act was quite well done."

"He improvised too much," Magnus decided. "Although I am not an aficionado of the theatre, there is something to be said for subtlety. In his scene with Miss Hartley, I don't believe he released her hand at all. It was on the verge of being indecent."

His grandmother coughed. When he looked at her, she patted her own throat. "I could use a glass of claret."

"Then, I am your servant, ma'am."

"And if it wouldn't be too much trouble," she said, staying him with a hand on his sleeve, "could you fetch Miss Hartley for me? I should like to speak with her before the evening is over."

Dutifully, he inclined his head and went off in search of his quarry.

Magnus found Verity standing alone on the terrace, the crackle of torchlight glimmering off the damp tiles. Her back was to him with her hands resting on the stone balustrade. And she'd changed out of her costume, dressed, once more, in the gown of mastic satin she'd worn at dinner.

As with the theatre, he was not an expert in matters of fashion either. But he knew well enough that, on any other woman, such a brown would have appeared dull and drab. On her, however, the color enhanced the gilded cornsilk highlights threaded in her hair and made the bare expanse of her shoulders shimmer like a ray of moonlight.

"Please don't tell me you were thinking of climbing down the ivy," he said as he stepped out to join her. "Again."

Her brow arched as he stood at the rail beside her, her gaze drifting over his face to discern the intention of the comment. "It seems that someone's been telling tales."

"Miss Hunnicutt may have mentioned something in passing."

"Oh, I'd just wager she did," Miss Hartley grumbled. "Fear not, Longhurst, my climbing days are over."

"I'm sure the good Reverend Tobias will be glad to hear that."

She gasped, and an appalled laugh escaped her as she darted a glance over her shoulder to the empty doorway. Then she playfully swatted his forearm. "For the last time, I was saving a cat."

"So you say. But we both know the truth."

As he looked up at the stars peering through the moving bands of gray clouds, a smirk tugged at the corner of his mouth. A moment of companionable silence followed and he felt himself relax into it.

It was strange, this feeling. Especially after having been so tense of late. Then again, no one had ever accused him of having a particularly serene nature. It usually took him a long while before he was at ease with anyone.

He was a man of few close friends, but loyal to the ones he kept. And the very fact that he was standing there, beside a Hartley of all people, and feeling any measure of peace astonished him.

The realization did not sit well.

He swallowed down a rise of bitterness on the back of his tongue. It tasted like guilt and the betrayal of his own family name.

His mood abruptly darkened as he glanced down to the hand on his sleeve.

To say that he'd been unaware of her lingering touch would have been a lie. Even though it may have been an absent gesture, or proof that she felt a measure of ease in his company as well, it was not something that he could welcome. Ever.

Squaring his shoulders, he said, "I leave for London tomorrow."

At the pointed impatience in his tone, she followed his gaze. Her surprise was evident in the haste of her withdrawal, her cheeks coloring. And any manner of amiability between them faded at once.

"Yes, I know," she said, tartly. "I hardly need the reminder when I've been marking off the days all week."

He took no offense. In fact, he understood better than she likely imagined. "As have I."

"Well, if that's the reason you came out here, then you needn't have bothered."

She could have made a grand exit that would have served a dual purpose of putting him in his place and providing a means to extricate herself from their temporary betrothal. And he wanted her to go, to storm off in a huff and leave him there.

Then again, he could have left her. Or he could have explained that he'd merely been sent on an errand by his grandmother.

Frustratingly, neither of them moved.

He stared down at her stubborn profile, the jut of her chin, the graceful trill of her slender fingers against her elbow as she crossed her arms. He was acutely aware of where those fingers had been only seconds ago. The warm sensation still lingered on his arm.

This was absurd!

All this week, he should have been negotiating a contract with Mr. Snow, not agreeing to a temporary betrothal to a Hartley!

Why had he agreed? Damned if he knew. It seemed as though a completely different person had made that decision. And now he was someone else entirely.

"I'm glad that my friendship with your brother ended years ago," he said, nearing his wit's end. "I should have hated for us to be acquainted and forced to acknowledge each other's existence."

She whipped around to face him, eyes flashing. "Thankfully, neither of us need worry about that. In a scant few hours, this will all be over."

"And I shall be the better for it."

"No more than I, I assure you," she hissed.

They were standing toe-to-toe. He wasn't sure which one of them had moved or when he had taken her by the shoulders. At least, not until she said, "Unhand me."

The command was little more than vapor in the cool night air, a hoarse breath that melded with his own in the heated space between them.

It wasn't until that moment that he realized her shawl had slipped, giving way to the petal softness of her bare skin beneath his fingers and palms. And in the same moment, he also realized that his thumb was stroking that very skin in gentle sweeps.

Dumbfounded by his own actions, he simply stared at the back-and-forth motion, his flesh swarthy and labor-roughened, hers pale and perfect. The barest shade of pink emerged beneath his touch.

Then his gaze drifted to her parted lips, to the flush blooming on her cheeks and to the question suspended in those unfathomable eyes.

His unspoken answer startled him.

He released her at once. What the devil was he doing?

"My apologies." He took a step back, still unable to master his own breathing. "That was . . . ungentlemanly of me."

And because he could not trust himself to linger one second longer, he turned and left.

Chapter Eleven

❧

VERITY HATED THE Duke of Longhurst. He was the most maddening, vexing man she had ever had the misfortune to know.

So then why was she still having dreams about him? And the most disturbing thing of all was how utterly panicked they'd left her.

As she'd done in the six prior nights, she'd awoken with her heart racing and her skin damp with perspiration the instant she realized she was only one garment away from being wholly naked in front of him. And since she wasn't a simpleton, she could easily surmise the meaning of these confoundedly salacious dreams.

It wasn't as though she'd never wondered about men and what being married to one might have been like. After all, her mother wasn't the typical prim and proper society matron. Roxana Hartley was a passionate woman who firmly believed that women had every right to enjoy their marriages, in every possible way.

Though, it was rather unfortunate that she hadn't shied away from supplying her daughters with a bit too much information regarding the marriage bed and precisely how children came to be.

Because of that—along with a rather traumatizing sock puppet show with the bumbling, droopy and lisping Lord Flaccid, and his alter ego the suave, athletic and much taller Lord Turgid—Verity had decided that it wouldn't be altogether terrible to remain a spinster. Not only that, but the very notion of Percival Culpepper having either of those sock puppets beneath the fall of his trousers was not appealing. At all.

With Longhurst, on the other hand, she was unpardonably intrigued. Hence the dreams. Which were unsettling, yet somewhat . . . thrilling. But only to a small degree. Minute, really. Hardly anything. Surely, not enough to be concerned about. Or, at least, that's what she liked to tell herself.

Nevertheless, those dreams had shed some light on the third character in the play—Lady Content, who dressed in the petals of a flower, was preoccupied with the state of the weather and tended to fall into fits of convulsions when Lord Turgid was near.

As Verity had bathed her flushed skin with a square of flannel, dampened from cold water splashed into the basin, she finally understood why Lady Content was so concerned about becoming wet. Though, she was grateful that she hadn't suffered any peculiar convulsions. How dreadful!

Thankfully, Longhurst was leaving for London today and these peculiar dreams would go with him. They simply had to.

After she rang for her maid and Tally finagled her hair into a well-heeled knot at the crown of her head, Verity went down to breakfast.

Her mother and sisters were in the midst of chatting companionably about the play. While tuning out the mentions of the sword fight choreography, as well as her youngest sister grumbling crossly about the improvisations made to her script during the death scene, she went to the buffet and began lifting cloches and filling a blue-flowered derby dish by rote.

Dazedly, she sat down, having no idea what was even

on her plate. Her thoughts were too muddled about the dreams, what happened after the play, and how she would announce to the villagers that her temporary betrothal with the duke was over.

"*We simply didn't suit,*" she could say, holding her head high. "*It would never have worked between us. Our temperaments are too different . . .*"

But that wasn't entirely true. Both of them were of a sensible nature. They spoke frankly. Neither bothered to put on airs, as many did when courting.

Which was likely because they weren't courting. Never had been courting and never would be, she reminded herself.

He definitely had a more controlling nature than she. Though, considering his level of responsibility, with a dukedom, family, demesne and tenants to look after, it was no wonder.

But did he have to be so mercurial? Sometimes his moods shifted without warning as they had done last night on the terrace.

And yet, part of her understood this, too. Hadn't she also been oddly short-tempered with him on occasion? Testy? Agitated? He seemed to draw out her inner demons. Perhaps she did the same to him.

They were like flint and steel, each of them seemingly designed to abrade the other's nerves to the point of sparking. And all because of the scandal.

That alone was an irrefutable reason that she could cite for their separation. "*The rift between our families is simply too great.*"

She practiced the line inside her head, imagining the townspeople nodding. They would wait until she walked away before any mention of the swindle that had caused the downfall of many fortunes and her father's part in it.

Verity would have to apologize to her father privately,

for bringing this all to the surface again. She knew it was a painful topic for him.

As these thoughts turned and twisted in her mind, she became dimly aware of him walking into the breakfast room, and she turned her attention to the far end of the table.

"Good morrow, Fair Roxana," he said to his wife, his voice rakishly low as he lifted her hand and pressed a kiss to her knuckles. "How did you sleep? Not well I should think."

Mother grinned back with a saucy flick of her dark brows and pressed a kiss to his hand in turn. "As well you should know, my lord."

"I believe it was 'my lord and master' last eve."

"*Oh, please,*" Thea groaned. "We are trying to eat."

When the youngest reached out to nip sugar from the cone in the center of the table, Father snatched it away, just out of her reach. "Then let your parents' love sweeten your daily porridge."

"Then you would have my teeth rot from overabundance," she grumbled.

He chuckled and returned the dish before ruffling her unbound hair. Moving on to the buffet, he paused to press a kiss to the top of Honoria's head as she slurped her tea and perused the society pages.

Then he came to Verity and laid a hand on her shoulder. "Woolgathering, daughter? Or does thine toast offend thee?"

She blinked, her gaze unseeing at the triangle of toasted bread pinched between her thumb and forefinger.

Only now did she realize that her mind had been set adrift. It came as a shock to her that, for the past few moments, she'd been wondering what kind of husband Longhurst would make. Would he greet Miss Snow in the morning with roguish words and a kiss on her hand?

Would he look at her hungrily, his inky black pupils surrounded by a burning ring of copper . . . that same way he'd looked at Verity on the terrace and the night he'd found her in the library?

She shook her head. But no. Longhurst hadn't looked at her that way. It wasn't hunger that caused his eyes to darken, it was the thought of murder.

The only reason her mind was confused now was because of the dreams. Dreams that were already dissolving like slips of tissue paper on water. Reaching for them only caused the images to fall apart, leaving her with only fragments. And she hated that the prospect of losing them forever made her feel restless and panicked all over again.

"Neither," she answered on a shallow breath, pushing away from the table. "I've no appetite this morning. I think I'll go for a walk."

"Do you want to take the Queen's Council with you?" Father asked when she was already at the archway, calling attention to Thea who was surreptitiously giving the wolfhounds her bacon. When Mother tutted in disapproval, the youngest sat up straighter and blinked with owl-eyed innocence.

Feeding Barrister and Serjeant-at-Arms at the table was frowned upon. So, of course, they all did it, even Mother.

At the question posed to Verity, the dogs quirked their heads in her direction, ears perked.

"Not this time, boys," she said to them and their ears instantly drooped and they both issued a disgruntled groan. But it couldn't be helped.

There were times when she couldn't stand to be trapped inside a moment longer.

It wasn't until she was already away from the house that she realized she'd forgotten her shawl and bonnet. A chill morning breeze penetrating her pink muslin, her skin prickling with gooseflesh.

But she wasn't going back. She needed to be outside to calm the erratic beating of her heart and the unbearable tightness in her lungs.

Cutting through the side garden where the eight posts of her birdhouse village stood, she paused briefly to leave the crumbs from her toast behind, along with a stray thread from her hem to decorate one of the nests. She pursed her lips and called out to them with her usual chickadee trill. There was chirruping in response and she knew that the instant she stepped away from the bench, they would descend eagerly on the offerings.

Sometimes, she thought that if she were a bird, she would take flight and soar as high as she could go. Higher than the clouds and simply glide endlessly, wings spread wide, and finally be free of these spells she suffered.

She'd experienced these bouts of panic for most of her life. There was no mystery regarding when or why they'd begun. These episodes had started when she was six years old and at the mercy of a governess who'd liked to lock her in the closet.

Even so, it still bothered Verity whenever she became overwhelmed and couldn't control her own reactions to events or circumstances around her.

As she stepped over the stile, she drew in a lungful of fresh morning air, and the tight cincture around her lungs gradually loosened.

The brisk temperature, however, compelled her to quicken her steps. In fact, she was striding so fast by the time she entered the path by the river that she startled a cat. And not just any cat, but the *you made me climb onto a branch and get caught ogling the vicar* cat.

It hissed at her. She was tempted to hiss back, but settled for narrowing her eyes. Then it bared its tiny white fangs and darted around the curve of the towpath.

"Believe me, you're not my favorite creature either," she called after it.

As her footsteps followed the conniving ball of orange-spotted fur, she was surprised to see a man silhouetted in the morning light.

She stopped in her tracks, taking note of the figure of a man in a black riding coat and buckskin breeches, as he leaned against the trunk of the old ash tree. And it wasn't just any man either, but the one who'd invaded her dreams. The very last man she wanted to see after trying so hard not to think about him at all.

Longhurst. His name whispered across her mind, descending in a cascade of tingles over her skin before dropping heavily into the pit of her stomach.

Her hand splayed over her midriff to quell the disturbing sensation. Briefly, she contemplated turning back around at a run. But her legs were strangely rooted to the soft earth beneath her feet.

Seeing her in the same moment, he pushed away from the trunk and offered an absent pat to the horse tethered to a low branch and grazing over the tall grasses.

Then Longhurst walked toward her. A pulse began to rabbit beneath the vulnerable skin on the side of her throat, and all she could do was watch him grow closer. And closer.

His stride was purposeful, his mouth set in a grim line. The very same mouth that had nearly claimed hers in the dream an instant before she'd awoken. The memory caused her stomach to flip beneath her palm.

"Thought I'd find you here," he said by way of greeting.

She lowered her hand to her side and tried to adopt a posture of someone who hadn't been having salacious dreams about him all week. And considering her acting abilities, this meant she was likely giving her best impression of a potted ficus. "After last night, I thought you'd be well on your way to London."

"Soon."

He stopped in front of her, his alert gaze on where her fingertips plucked a stray thread dangling from the side seam of her skirt. Abruptly, she stilled that hand, reminded of his lecture a few days ago regarding exhibiting *ungoverned responses.*

Then his attention shot directly to the loose tendrils resting against her cheek before she was even aware they'd slipped free of the pins. She watched as a muscle ticked on the side of his jaw. And even though he said nothing, she heard his criticism all the same.

She swiped the hair behind her ear. "That doesn't explain why you're still here."

He turned and gestured in a wordless invitation to walk beside him on the towpath. She agreed with a curt nod.

After a few paces, he said, "I wanted to ensure that you still planned to end our betrothal formally and expeditiously. Time is of the essence."

"If you think that I have any desire whatsoever—"

"Before you rail at me," he interrupted, "know that I'm not casting doubt on your word. It's just . . . after last night, I didn't want to leave you with the impression that there was something unsettled between us."

She stiffened. "Last night, when you took hold of my arms and looked as though you had every intention of throttling me or hurling me over the railing?"

Confusion glanced across his countenance for the barest instant before he schooled his features. Then he cleared his throat. "Yes, of course. That is the moment to which I am referring."

"You really should manage your temper better."

"I never lose control of myself. Which is a lesson that you should employ in your own dealings."

"And just what is that supposed to mean?"

He glanced down to the agitated flick of her hands an instant before they perched on her hips, her arms akimbo. "Comportment, Miss Hartley. One should always maintain control over the desire to fidget. Such behavior only demonstrates a lack of mastery over one's own person."

And there it was—her daily scolding from the duke. Was nothing ever good enough for him? Other than Miss Snow, of course. She was likely perfect.

"You sound like my old governess," she said. "I knew there was a reason I didn't like you, aside from the obvious. And I'll have you know that, until you, I've never exhibited any unsavory manners."

"I find that hard to believe."

"Well, perhaps it's you and your overbearing arrogance that brings out the worst in me."

"Some would argue that having a deceitful nature is far worse."

"It was one lie. One!" she shouted, her finger upraised.

"And what about the night of the assembly when you'd told your family you had a cold? Or was it a megrim? No, I believe it was a stubbed toe."

"It might have all been true. Not that it would have mattered to you with the way you'd stormed into the library and practically carried me out over your shoulder."

"And the time you pretended we'd had a prior engagement in order to leave the bakery?"

"That wasn't a real lie," she argued. When his brows arched as if she had just proven his point, she huffed. "It hardly signifies. Besides, everyone has stretched the truth for innocent purposes. Such as, tactfully inventing a reason to leave a conversation without slighting the other party, telling a neighbor who shows up uninvited that you are delighted to see them, or if your sister asks—after cutting her own hair—if the fringe on her forehead is attractive."

A smirk lifted one corner of his mouth, vexing her to no end. "In other words, you have absolutely no morals and will say anything in order for people to like you."

"No." She frowned at the accusation, something sour niggling at her conscience. Ignoring it, she hiked her chin. "Ask me anything and I will tell you the truth."

"Very well. Did you see the vicar naked?"

She tripped.

He immediately steadied her with a firm hand at her elbow almost as if he'd expected her misstep.

It didn't escape her notice that his cutthroat question was rather quick. She narrowed her eyes in suspicion, even as her cheeks heated to the temperature of jam bubbling on the stove. Had he just orchestrated this entire conversation so that she would fall right into his trap?

He had, blast it all!

Brimming with irritation, she held her head high and confessed. "I did. There. Are you pleased? But it was an accident. I really was rescuing a—" She broke off and shot a glare at him. "And will you kindly cease smirking so triumphantly. It's quite rude."

"I'm only thinking that you are so full of excuses that I am waiting with bated breath over what you might declare next." He chuckled as she growled. "Did it ever occur to you that you needn't have looked?"

"Did it ever occur to you that I am a woman of six and twenty, or soon will be, and I might have been curious? For artistic purposes? After all, we don't have any museums in Addlewick and I never had the chance to tour them when I was in London. An appreciation of the human form is the very foundation of art and it inspires the imagination. For artistic purposes."

"You said that already."

"I know," she fired back on a huff, wondering if there was smoke rising from her cheeks yet.

He pursed his lips. "You seem rather embarrassed, Miss Hartley. I highly doubt you would have survived a tour through the museums without fainting."

"I'm not embarrassed or ashamed, just surprised at your lack of tact."

"And I'm surprised that you're even lying to yourself. The problem is greater than I feared."

She gritted her teeth, her molars grinding. "Ask me another question."

As soon as she saw the glimmer in his eyes, she knew taunting him was a mistake.

"So, tell me, Miss Hartley," he began, "in these moments of artistic inspiration, have you ever imagined—"

"Why are you so fixated on this topic?"

He shrugged innocently and yet he was clearly intent on one purpose. "Mere curiosity. I'm sure someone like you can understand about curiosity. Anyway, as I was saying . . . Have you imagined other nude male forms?"

"I don't see why this would be of any interest to you."

"If it is nothing to be ashamed of, as you claim, then there should be no issue. Unless, of course, it's someone you'd rather not admit. Like Mr. Culpepper, perhaps?"

She scoffed. "Hardly."

"Then who?"

Verity would rather die than answer. But she couldn't very well refuse, not when *she* had challenged him. She was the one claiming to tell the truth, after all. And besides, if she remained silent or begged him to change the subject, he would likely surmise the answer himself.

Turning, she marched to the edge of the river, her heart hammering, rushing in her ears far faster than this lazy current. The water was so calm and clear that she could see the ripples in the sand beneath the surface. She drew in a breath, summoning her courage to answer.

But he spoke first, goading her, looming beside her.

"Surely, a woman of nearly six and twenty with her thoughts on the arts would summon someone she was attracted to. Now who could that be, I wonder." Was it her imagination, or had his voice developed a rough edge? There was certainly a bite to his next words. "Another man in the village? A tenant, perhaps? A certain Mr. *Law*—"

"It was you. There! Are you satisfied? I pictured you naked," she admitted just to shut him up.

And it worked, too.

His lips parted on a breath and those burning cinder eyes bored down on her. But when he said nothing in response, her embarrassment turned to insecurity which turned to aggravation and before she knew it, her temper was starting to climb.

"It meant nothing. It was just a dream," she spat. "My lucid mind would never have the remotest inclination to conjure such an image."

Still, he remained silent and she interpreted that as judgment.

She advanced on him, taking the one step that separated them and hiking her chin. "And I suppose you're going to tell me that you've never been plagued by a thought, invading wholly uninvited into your mind, hmm?"

In the periphery of her vision, she saw his arms move, hands lifting as if he were going to take her by the shoulders again. This time, he would surely throttle her.

She moved without thinking. Reaching up, she put her hands against the solid wall of his chest and shoved him back as hard as she could.

But she forgot that they were standing on the verge of the riverbank . . .

The next thing she knew, he was falling backward. His eyes went wide the instant before he fell with a great splash.

She was in such shock that all she could do was stare. Had she really done that?

He came up sputtering. "Did you just . . . *push* me?"

Not even she could believe it. And yet, it felt sort of . . . good. Really good.

So much of the tension she'd been carrying all week suddenly had a physical outlet. Perhaps that's what she'd needed all along.

She batted her lashes demurely. "It seemed like the sensible thing to do."

"*Sensible?*" he ranted, angrily swiping the water from his face as he stood. "What woman in her right mind would— No! That is precisely it. You, Miss Hartley, are insane. Which is likely inherited. You have no sense of decorum. Hell, you're practically feral, climbing trees and whatnot, forever out of doors without proper attire, hair disheveled with strands in five hundred different hues, and don't even get me started on those changeable eyes of yours . . ."

As his list of all her failings faded to a grumble, she squared her shoulders. "Perhaps you're right. I might be a lunatic for all I know, because I think I've wanted to push you in the water since the day we met. I only wish I could push you in again."

She added a haughty *Ha!* for good measure.

His eyes slitted in her direction, the muscle ticking in his jaw. "Do you find this amusing?"

"As a matter of fact, I*iiiiiaaahhh*—"

Her defiant declaration came out on a shriek as she slipped down the wet bank, her arms windmilling. She fought for balance, but lost her footing and fell with a soggy splat. Flat on her bottom. In the river.

Longhurst threw back his head and roared with laughter.

The sound was so raw and gravelly that it seemed to abrade something inside her, itching just under her skin until all she wanted was to feel her hands on him again, pushing, shoving, gripping, curling them into fists . . .

Not liking the sensation in the least, she shoved at the water, cupping it in the way her brother had taught her and sent a huge splash in Longhurst's direction.

It hit him like a tidal wave, full in the face.

His amusement faded at once.

She snickered. "On second thought, it is rather amusing to see my enemy all wet."

Longhurst scrubbed a hand over his eyes, his jaw clenched. Straightening his waistcoat, he approached her, his stride cutting through the water. Then, reluctantly, he held out his hand. "No need to behave like a child."

"I thought I was feral. Now I'm a child?" She splashed him again, the need to aggravate him—to see that flash of cinders in his eyes—too strong to deny.

"Miss Hartley." His tone was low and forbidding. But she didn't care, and moved to splash him again. "Verity, I'm warning you."

Her breath caught.

It was the first time he'd used her given name. And yet, it seemed so familiar on his tongue as if he'd said it a dozen times. A hundred. It slid warmly inside her, curling low in the pit of her stomach like it belonged there. And it took everything inside her to keep from asking him to say it again.

"What do you plan to do once I'm standing?" she taunted with a wary glance down to his hand. "Throttle me? I promise that will not end well for you."

His eyes were blazing, fierce with intent. And he didn't wait for her to grasp his hand. Instead, he reached out, took her by the shoulders and lifted her.

"How dare y—"

He silenced the last syllable on a deep growl and crushed his mouth to hers.

She went utterly still.

This couldn't be happening. Was the Duke of Longhurst . . . kissing . . . her?

If he'd wanted to shush her—to stun her—then he'd succeeded. And yet as the lips of her enemy took thorough possession of her own and his spiky lashes lowered, she was starting to wonder if she'd broken him.

He was usually so stuffy. So disciplined. Even when vexed, he was still judiciously in control of himself. But this? This seemed more like the actions of a man who was half-wild, unleashed.

Her feet paddled for purchase, the tips of her shoes brushing the sandy bottom of the riverbed. But she didn't want to be left floundering when he came to his senses and released her. So she clutched the lapels of his coat, the current pushing at her skirts.

He shifted. But not to drop her. Instead, he anchored her to him, pulling her close in a shock of cold, damp fabric.

Did he realize that he was holding the spinster he despised against the hard length of his own body?

Likely not, because he continued to kiss her, his lips firm, smooth and demanding. And their clothes heated at once, wool and muslin steaming.

A pleasurable shiver trampled through her. As if he felt it, too, his fingers flexed in response and he hitched her higher. His hand encompassed the small of her back as he drew her against his warmth, fitting her securely, her soft curves meeting his hard planes.

A sound she'd never heard herself utter vibrated in her throat as her eyes drifted shut. It was like a purr and it compelled her to slide her palms and splayed fingers over the broad expanse of his chest, climbing upward to curve around his shoulders. But he seemed to understand the sound and answered in kind with another low growl.

He cupped her jaw. Angling her mouth beneath his own, he coaxed her into response after response as if this was the natural evolution of their argument. And somewhere along the way, she stopped caring about why he was kissing her and simply ... let him.

His tongue trailed slowly along the seam of her lips. It almost tickled. Her instinct was to nudge her closed mouth against his, and she did. But then his thumb brushed her chin, applying the barest pressure to urge her lips apart.

Then his tongue slipped inside to the inner softness, to the satiny flesh that only she had ever tasted.

She gasped at the intrusion, at the textured heat that sent a thrill tearing through her. It was like a crack of lightning inside her body, tingling over her skin from her scalp to her soles. Then something warm and liquid pooled in her middle, settling low and weighted against a new and heady pulse. And her hands found the nape of his neck, her fingers threading into the trimmed silken layers of his hair.

Their kiss suddenly altered. His tongue plundered inside, tasting her, caressing her, inviting her to parry. And she did. Oh, she most definitely did.

Her first touch was tentative, a shock of sensation that earned a gruff grunt of approval. The second was bolder, venturing deeper into the humid interior to find a contrast of sharp-edged teeth, pointed canines, and the exciting, supple texture of his flesh. She withdrew, taking the spiced taste of him into her own mouth, drinking him in on a hum of delight.

It wasn't long before she was eager for more. And she returned his kiss with the untamed passion he'd ignited.

Her body was thrumming, sliding against his as he cinched his arms around her, his fists gripping the back of her dress. Hard, hungry, noisy kisses that left her lightheaded and needing air, until . . .

He released her.

The kiss ended as unexpectedly as it had begun.

She swayed, her feet sinking into the sand and silt. He stared down at her with burning eyes that were almost all pupil, his lips damp, his brow furrowed in confusion. Then he cursed. A long string of inventive expletives that would have made Shakespeare take note.

Breathing hard, he raked an accusatory gaze over her disheveled hair, heated cheeks, swollen mouth, then dipped lower to her damp dress.

She looked down, too, abruptly aware of the thin pink muslin plastered to her form *and* the notable chill in the air. She crossed her arms over her breasts.

He swallowed and screwed his eyes shut, pinching the bridge of his nose. "I kissed you."

"Of that I am well aware," she answered tightly, embarrassment mounting at his obvious regret.

Distractedly, her gaze drifted to his lips. She could still feel the tingling pressure of them against her own. In fact, she could still feel the way her body had fit against his where his damp waistcoat molded over the broad muscles of his chest and the firm plane of his stomach. Still feel where their hips had met and a thick shape was outlined beneath the saturated buckskin of his breeches. And it was *no* sock puppet.

He cleared his throat and her gaze jerked guiltily back to his, reproach in his countenance. "You kissed me back."

"I know!" she said. "Do you think me an idiot?"

Although, truth be told, she had never been kissed like that. Then again, Percival Culpepper likely wouldn't have known how. Oh, but Longhurst certainly had, and that knowledge did nothing to cool her cheeks or her rising ire.

She set her hands on her hips. "And what business do you have kissing me when you have a fiancée waiting for you in London?"

"I am not engaged to her yet," he clarified as if that made all the difference. "Nevertheless, that does not excuse my actions. It may be little consolation, but I never intended to kiss you."

"*Flattering*," she muttered under her breath.

She turned to stalk away. Or tried to. Unfortunately, her half boots did not agree with this course. They were sunk securely. She nearly toppled into the water again, and would have done, if not for his unexpected assistance.

Taking a hard step toward her, he swept her up into the cradle of his arms as if she and all her drenched garments weighed nothing at all. Then he stalked out of the river.

However, the instant they reached the grasses of the bank, he set her on her feet and backed away as if she were a leper.

Chapter Twelve

ᘓᕲᣠ

Magnus paced the pathway like an animal. Which was precisely the way she made him feel, like a rabid beast. And he had been on the verge of devouring her. In the river!

Clearly, he had lost all sense of reason and control.

It must have been due to the pressure he'd been under. Perhaps the strain of his family's finances. Not to mention, his mother's desire to bring his wayward brother home no matter the cost, Snow's potential refusal, the temporary betrothal to his enemy's daughter, and a week spent in this barmy hamlet. It was more than any reasonable man could bear.

He raked a hand through his hair, tugging on the short layers. Perhaps the bite of pain would bring some sense.

It didn't. Because the instant he looked over at her, standing beneath the shade of a tree, her hair snaking down in spirals and her fingertips resting against her bee-stung lips, all he wanted to do was brush that hand aside and take her mouth again.

Now that he'd had a taste of her, he wanted to sink into her soft surrender, taste her sigh, feel her body wriggle to fit perfectly to—

Devil take it! He had to stop this unwanted craving!

"Why haven't you married?" It was more of a barked accusation than a question.

Her spine stiffened, and she lowered her hand to her

side, her eyes narrowing as he prowled back and forth in front of her. "Surely, the answer is quite obvious."

"I wouldn't be asking the question if it were, now would I? Unless"—he stopped pacing—"don't tell me you'd actually set your cap for that pea-wit, Culpepper?"

"No."

He waited for her to elaborate. When she didn't and merely lifted her stubborn chin, which drew his attention back to her mouth again, his aggravation mounted. "Mr. Lawson?"

"*Mister*—" She broke off in momentary confusion, but that was swiftly replaced with square-shouldered ire. "No."

"Then, was it your father's scandal keeping the callers away?"

"Not exactly," she crisply enunciated through clenched teeth.

"Well, if those aren't the reasons, then why?"

"Because I'm plain!" she shouted. "Men take one look at me and turn their gazes away in disappointment. There. Are you happy? Is my humiliation, from admitting it aloud, enough for you?"

It wasn't often, if ever, that Magnus was dumbstruck. However, for a moment, all he could do was stare. He tried to recall that first meeting when he had thought the same of her. But he couldn't. The memory was there, of course, but his mind had painted her differently in these past days.

She was a chimera, shifting and changing. And he felt as if he'd been taken in by her deception.

Yet, looking into those rusty violet eyes now, he saw that there was something beneath that anger. Something raw and fragile. He'd glimpsed it on a few occasions this week. And even though he'd done his best to ignore it, to tell himself that the matter was no concern of his, he couldn't any longer.

His own strict code of honor—ironically, the same one that had nearly been swept away in the river—would not let her go on without hearing the truth. After all, the likelihood that she would reveal her inner insecurities in a tirade to anyone else was rather slim. He'd practically goaded her into it. Therefore, it was his duty to set her straight.

"Verity, there is nothing plain about you. In fact, there's something altogether"—against his will, his wayward gaze roamed over the entire length of her, his pulse thickening, heating—"*not* plain. You're actually quite fetching."

He heard her breath catch. Saw her eyes widen with startlement, then almost as quickly narrow with suspicion.

She stiffened. "Now who's lying?"

"That would still be you, lying to yourself this time."

She frowned and looked away. "You needn't tease. Though, I blame myself for providing you the ammunition."

"Do I seem like a man given to doling out compliments for my own amusement?" He took a step toward her, shaking his head in self-mockery. "As much as it pains me to admit it, I am in earnest. It's those eyes of yours. They're rather intimidating and likely strike fear into the hearts of lesser mortals."

Her scrutiny returned to him, searching, dissecting and stubborn. "*Lesser mortals*, hmm? But not you. Somehow your compliment to me was also one to yourself."

"And, clearly, you are capable of finding a reason to argue over anything."

"Or perhaps I've never been in this situation and do not know how to react. Poking the bear seemed the most sensible rejoinder." She reached out to do just that, but he stayed her hand, encircling her wrist. Brushing off his rebuff, she arched a brow. "What? So, if you're inclined to kiss the stuffing out of me then that's perfectly acceptable? Yet, I cannot even poke you with the tip of my finger?"

"Correct," he said firmly.

But his gaze drifted to her mouth. Absently, he wondered—if he traced the wry curve at each corner, the cupid's bow in the center—would her flesh feel as velvety soft as it had beneath his own lips?

He shut his eyes briefly and expelled a breath, trying to regain control, to put the shutters in place. "What happened between us was a mistake. However, I take full blame."

"How magnanimous of you," she fired back. "Now, if you'll excuse me, I shall take my leave, and I'm sure you are eager to take yours. Miss Snow is expecting you, after all."

"Wait," he said, without knowing why precisely.

It was only when she shot an impatient glance down that he realized he was still holding her wrist.

He stared at it curiously. Why hadn't he released her? Why wasn't he doing so, even now? But more importantly, had he ever felt anything as soft and delicate as the pulse that fluttered beneath the stroking pad of his middle finger?

Then their gazes met.

At first, violet eyes mirrored his confusion. But then something altered. And suddenly, the ever-present ire that kindled between them, swiftly turned into a blaze of a different sort.

He wasn't certain which one of them moved. Though, it had to have been her because he wouldn't have given in to temptation twice. Would he? And yet, they came together in a swift collision as if still helpless against the pull of the river's current.

Magnus shored her against him, his kiss ardent, fevered and greedy. But he wasn't alone in this. He felt a surge of satisfaction when her hands found his nape as she rose up on her toes. The action lifted the supple weight of her breasts against his chest and fitted their bodies together like lock and key.

Then she licked into his mouth without any shyness, and a warm tremor rocked through him as he lost himself in the sweet taste of her tongue.

He took a step, two, and felt the bark of the tree brush the back of the hand he threaded through her silken hair. He should be shocked by his own actions. He should pull away.

Instead, he corralled her with his body, their torsos, hips and thighs aligning in a frenzy of pulses.

A mewl tore from her throat. His mouth descended down the smooth column to claim it at the source, his nostrils flaring on her honeysuckle scent. Why couldn't he get enough of her? She intoxicated him in ways he didn't understand, arching for him as he opened his mouth against the tender flutter.

"*Longhurst*," she rasped, the soft plea drawing him back to take her mouth again. After a scorching moment, she turned her face, pressing her cheek against his as their combined breaths raced to catch up with the hard thump ing beneath the cages of their ribs. "This cannot go on. We need to stop."

It was embarrassing how long it took for her words to sink in.

He felt drunk, his head hazy as her hands slid down his chest. He blinked at the barrier between them, her flushed cheeks and thoroughly kissed lips came into focus.

Hell and damnation, what was wrong with him? He lowered her to the ground and backed away, muttering epithets under his breath.

She huffed. "I would appreciate it if you wouldn't curse every time you've finished kissing me."

"Me? You're the one who started it this time."

"Well, you looked like you were going to again, and I wasn't about to let you waylay me like the first time. A coup de main seemed the only option."

Magnus opened his mouth to argue that she'd misinterpreted his intentions, but his conscience niggled at him. He would not add lying to his list of crimes this morning.

"I'll see you home." He turned to untether his horse, but she chose to ignore him and began to leave on her own.

"No, you will not."

He caught up with her in two strides. "You are shivering. The very least I could—"

"Stop," she commanded softly, raising a hand between them, her gaze imploring. "You have already done more than enough. As have I. Please, Magnus, I need to be the one who walks away, for the sake of my own dignity."

He wasn't sure if it was the *please*, the use of his given name or the naked honesty that swayed him but, in the end, he conceded with a nod.

Against every ounce of enmity that he justly harbored against the Hartleys, he was surprised to discover that he admired one of them as he watched her walk away, head held high.

Chapter Thirteen

～

WHEN VERITY BROKE the news that she'd had a change of heart about marrying the duke, word spread through the village faster than Father casting parts for a new play. The rumors and whispers began immediately, even when she wasn't quite out of earshot.

"It stands to reason. The families have been bitter enemies for years," she heard the milliner say to the clerk as she turned to leave the shop.

Her shoulders relaxed with relief. That was precisely the response for which she'd hoped.

"And there was a definite degree of coldness between those two," the clerk added.

Coldness? Um . . . well . . . not always.

Verity felt her cheeks heat as the door closed behind her, the memory of the kiss never far from her mind.

In fact, she continued to be so distracted by it that, later that week, she was nearly run down by the baker's cart.

He swerved in time, but cursed a blue streak when a basket of bread toppled out onto the dusty road. Scuttling over to help him, she heard him grumbling beneath his breath. "I'd forever wondered if that one was barmy. Now I'm sure of it. Walked right out in front of me and just look at this bleedin' mess!"

"My apologies, Mr. Brown. I wasn't thinking. Or rather I was thinking, but my thoughts were . . . well . . . elsewhere. Not that it matters," she said in a ramble as she gathered an armful of quartern loaves. "I'll gladly pay for any damage done."

He gave her a hard look and shook his head. "No need."

Grumpily, he loaded all the bread back in the cart. Then he slapped his hat against his thigh and mounted the narrow driver's bench. But before he set off, he turned to her, his brows beetled in confusion. "*Have* ye gone barmy, miss? I ken no other explanation. What better prospect for a spinster of your years to marry at all, let alone a duke?"

She bristled at the harsh reprimand.

He didn't give her a chance to answer. "And to think, I might have been baker to a duke and duchess. I was even plannin' a special weddin' loaf for you. But no more. You've ripped me heart plumb out of me chest."

His shoulders slumped on a sigh of disappointment. Then, with a snap of the reins, his cart began to trundle down the lane.

Verity had the peculiar impulse to apologize again. Truth be told, ever since the river, she imagined she'd gone a little barmy, too.

Then, the following morning after church, Mrs. Horncastle drew her aside, declaring a need to speak with her directly, woman to woman. She looked at Verity with sympathy and offered a pat of condolence. "His Grace is a strapping, virile man. No shame in being afeared of the marriage bed, even at your age."

Over Elmira's shoulder, Verity saw Reverend Tobias quickly look away, his lips pressing together as if subduing a laugh. Oh, the humiliation!

Verity had chosen to ignore the reminder of her long-in-the-tooth status and offered a polite nod before walking away and returning home.

Besides, it wasn't as though she could confess to being incredibly curious about the marriage bed and the male form, could she? Why then, she might as well have told everyone about spying on the naked reverend, or announcing that Longhurst had kissed her as if the world were coming to an end and the two of them were its only hope.

A strapping, virile man, indeed.

Even now that a week had gone by, she could feel the pressure of his lips as if they were still locked in that scandalous embrace.

Worst of all, her dreams had become all too vivid.

Needless to say, these visions no longer stopped when he was about to kiss her. However, they typically ended at the rather alarming appearance of a sock puppet.

"If you are too warm, Miss Hartley, then sit by the window," Lady Broadbent said the following Tuesday, startling her out of her scandalous reminiscence.

Verity's cheeks flamed with embarrassment when she realized that her woolgathering had been noticed by Longhurst's grandmother of all people. "I beg your pardon, my lady."

Though, thankfully, neither the countess nor her own mother knew her actual thoughts. Her sisters had also been invited to tea that afternoon, but they were presently touring the library of Swanscott Manor with an invitation to borrow as many books as they could carry.

The countess lifted her hand from the arm of the tufted parlor chair by the fire with an absent shooing motion. "There is a nice cool breeze on the far side of the room. It isn't as though you've interjected much into our conversation, after all. And this way your mother and I can talk more freely about you."

The reproof caused a twinge of guilt in Verity. She hadn't even realized that anyone had spoken to her.

As she rose from the settee to take her place by the window, Mother fleetingly squeezed her hand with maternal affection, but there was an impish glint in her eyes when she offered a long-suffering tsk to their hostess. "She has been like this all week. At first, I thought she may have come down with a cold after the day she'd slipped in the river and was wet through when she crossed the threshold."

"Is this necessary, Mother? I'm sure her ladyship would prefer a more interesting topic than the state of my clothes." Verity sat in the window nook and arranged her skirts, all too aware of the dowager eyeing her with interest.

"Nonsense, child. And you're too far away to interject your opinion," Lady Broadbent said to her, then turned her attention on Mother. "I'm simply riveted. Roxana, do go on."

Unfortunately, Mother did. "I might have summoned the doctor, but the flushed cheeks she suffers intermittently do not seem to be related to a fever. I have also heard her sigh on a number of occasions."

"A week, you say?" The countess hummed with intrigue, her brows inching higher as if the walls were papered with a silk calendar, and an enormous red circle surrounded the date that her grandson had left for London.

His absence was completely unrelated. Which Verity would have told them, if not for Honoria's return into the room after her tour of the library.

With a slender volume of poetry in her grasp, her sister crossed the room to share the nook. Sitting down, she adjusted the fan of her ruffled cerulean skirts. "What have I missed?"

"The inquisition," Verity grumbled.

"I heard that, Miss Hartley," their hostess said, her lips pursed to hide a grin. "Take care, or I shall not attempt to find a husband for you."

Verity balked. "*A husband?* But I have no interest whatsoever in marrying. I shall be perfectly content to manage my brother's house, when he returns."

That had been her plan for the past few years. Truman would make his fortune as a merchant sailor, return and build the house he'd been designing since before his dreams of becoming an architect were dashed after the scandal. And then she would live in his house until he decided to marry.

After that, she wasn't quite certain where she would live. Beneath a rock, perhaps?

Another shoo of fingers was the countess's response as she turned back to address Mother. "Then we shall center our attention on Miss Honoria for the moment. With her handsomeness, she could land a rich gentleman . . . *if* she would only set her mind on securing her future. A connection with the right family would be advantageous to everyone beneath your roof."

"She does know that I can hear her, does she not?" Honoria asked Verity in a stage whisper as loud as a hunting horn and received a nod. But instead of being bothered by the attention, she grinned. "If this were a play, we would be the Greek chorus."

Mother cleared her throat and slid a disapproving glance to her mischievous middle daughter. Then she turned back to the dowager. "She hasn't met the man who will sweep her off her feet quite yet."

Honoria snatched a doily from beneath a cut crystal vase of flowers on the escritoire and draped it over her head as if it were a veil that allowed her to speak privately to her audience. "And she is not holding her breath either."

"If you ask me," the dowager interjected archly, "she has grown spoiled by the attentions of gentlemen. And when her youth fades what will she have to show for it—a few pressed flowers, keepsakes and romantic poetry? Stuff and nonsense."

"Oh, but she very much likes the presents," the Greek chorus chimed in.

Mother ignored the comment. "I would prefer Honoria to find a man she will love with all her heart."

"As do I, Roxana. Just be sure that she doesn't intend to meet them *all* before she chooses the *one*. He may be dead by then."

Verity smothered a laugh behind her fingertips. The countess certainly had her sister pegged.

Even Mother laughed. "Olympia, your dry wit hasn't changed at all."

And yet, when Verity looked over, she saw Honoria's complexion turn pale. She covered her sister's hand and found that it was cold as winter frost. "What is it, dearest?"

"I don't know what you mean," Honoria said, her voice barely audible as she drew the doily from the crown of her head and offered a half shrug.

"The teasing clearly bothered you."

"Nonsense. It was all in good fun." She shook her head and slipped her hand free. And when Verity opened her mouth to ask again, Honoria silenced her with a stern look. "Truly. No harm done."

Even though the sisters were not all graced with poise and beauty, there was one thing they had in common—stubbornness. And Honoria might have had the lioness's share.

So, Verity left the topic alone for the time being and turned her attention back to the conversation between Lady Broadbent and Mother.

"My daughter calls me a sentimental old fool," the dowager said. "Geraldine believes I've become too preoccupied with matters of the heart. Though, perhaps I'd raised her to be rather pragmatic." She pursed her lips, her fingertips flitting in a shrug. "It is important for a woman to keep a level head, after all. But it isn't my fault she married a man given to impulsiveness, who ran from his duties. Regardless, that gave her no right to have allowed the responsibility of running an estate to fall upon her son's shoulders when he was so young. She raised Magnus to be hard and unfeeling. And now here we are."

Verity wondered what that meant. Was she unhappy that Magnus was marrying Miss Snow?

Mother issued a sigh of commiseration. "We do what we can to guide our children. Yet, in the end, they will follow their own path to wherever it may take them. All we can do is support them in whatever manner they will allow."

"How right you are. Which is why I've decided to go to London. I hope you'll forgive me, but that is the reason I've asked you to tea this afternoon. You see, I should like to take your eldest daughter with me. If you can spare her, that is."

Verity started. "Me? But why me?"

"That sounds like a lovely idea," Roxana answered, ignoring her. "You know, she never had a Season. That horrible scandal happened after only a fortnight."

"Mother, I'm far too old for a Season. I would be a laughingstock."

"Quite true," the dowager agreed without batting an eye.

At least someone was listening to her. Even so, Verity frowned, feeling positively ancient.

Lady Broadbent might have offered a smallish blink of surprise, or an *Ah, yes. I completely forgot your age. You look so young.* Instead, she continued with, "It would be unseemly to bring her out as if she were in her first bloom. However, I am in need of a traveling companion."

"Then I'm sure her ladyship would prefer to travel with someone more engaging like my sister," Verity said, knowing full well that Honoria would blossom exceptionally. Unlike herself, a haggard, desiccated wart of a flower, apparently.

"And be plagued by gentleman callers day and night? I should say not."

"Not to mention," Mother added, "my sister and her

husband sponsored Honoria for a Season, alongside your cousin, Daphne. You, my dear, have not had that opportunity."

"But then Daphne eloped with the colonel after only three months. There was hardly any time for Honoria to see the sights."

Beside her, Honoria laid her hand on hers. "You needn't be so adamant on my account. I don't even want to go. If you'll recall, I went to Paris last year with Daphne and the colonel and, to be honest, I've had my fill of travel for a time."

"And most importantly," Lady Broadbent said archly, "I did not ask your sister, Miss Hartley. You will be perfect for what I have in mind. And fear not, you will be compensated for your time with a new wardrobe more befitting your—"

Verity stiffened, waiting for another mention of her age. She wasn't quite six and twenty, not for weeks yet, but she felt as old as Methuselah.

"—place in society," the dowager concluded with a satisfied smile as if she was saying that a spinster's *place in society* was second only to the queen.

And even though Verity attempted to pawn off Thea next, the dowager would hear none of it. So, it was settled.

By the end of tea, all the arrangements were etched in stone. And Verity, whether she liked it or not, was traveling to London.

Though, she was certain that the flip in her stomach at the thought of seeing Longhurst again was nothing more than nerves.

Chapter Fourteen

❧

IT HAD BEEN ten days since Magnus had left Addlewick. Ten days since he'd lost all sense and reason and kissed the daughter of his enemy. Ten days since he'd experienced the most confounding, wit-scrambling moment in his life.

And he had thought about it again and again and—*devil take it*—again.

During those scorching moments, he'd forgotten himself. But he would never make such an error in judgment in the future.

After all, giving into impulse without careful consideration and certainty was the very thing that led a man to ruin and dragged his family down with him. His father had taught him that by example, many times over.

Which was the reason Magnus was sitting in a carriage outside a chained iron gate in a rather ominous part of London, the air pungent with brine and sewage this close to the wharf. And a thick coat of creosote covered every building, dwelling and street in a black film.

He was there to meet a man by the name of Fitzherbert Eugene about a steamship business—the same enterprise that had bankrupted his father.

However, unlike his father, who never would have hesitated to invest in this sort, or any sort, of speculation, Magnus had researched the entire endeavor in depth ever since receiving his first letter from Mr. Eugene.

The proposal was sound. Simply stated, it was a business venture to take over the ownership of the foundry, dry dock and business that had been used to swindle men out of their fortunes seven years ago. Only this time, it would be a real company, not a fiction created by a liar and cheat. And, more importantly, it would only be Magnus taking the risk.

He did not want anyone other than himself involved. If the business was going to suffer setbacks or failure, then only he would bear the brunt of it.

He had first met Eugene at the trial, shortly after the scandal had been brought to light. As an engineer fresh out of university, the unsuspecting Eugene had been hired to develop and oversee the machine works.

In fact, an entire factory crew had been hired. But it was later presumed that those positions had only been set in place to provide an air of authenticity. And, in the end, every investor and worker had lost everything.

After the trial, the young man had approached Magnus with condolences for the loss of his father. Then, with great humility, he'd asked for work. His willingness to do any job from field hand to footman had left an impression, and although Magnus could offer no employment, he had given him a few pounds to help him find a new start in America.

Then Eugene had written to him months ago, hoping to repay that debt.

He had learned that the ship used to lure in unsuspecting investors to the scheme had been dismantled but kept in a warehouse. And it was purely by happenstance that his current employer had met with a certain Mr. Modine who'd made his fortune in scrap metal and who owned the warehouse where the ship lay to rest in pieces.

So Eugene had contacted Magnus with an idea: What if it was possible to buy the warehouse and actually build the ship? To start the enterprise that was originally proposed?

Since he knew that a shipping empire had been a wish of the late Duke of Longhurst, he didn't believe it was fair to let it all go to scrap.

And it was true. Magnus's father had risked everything to bring his youngest son home.

Rowan Warring had been adrift for many years, falling into one scrape or another, leaving university and purchasing a commission in the military. There had even been rumors of darker dealings, but Magnus had always tried to handle those matters in order to keep Mother and Father from knowing.

But Father had found out. He'd even used Rowan as a reason to invest the bulk of their fortune on the speculation set in motion by Viscount Underhill and Baron Hartley.

When Magnus had confronted his father about it, he'd offered a flippant shrug. "This time, it will be different."

"You said the same thing about the silver mine, offering up an exorbitant sum for a hole in the ground that had been leached of every mineral years before," Magnus had said, trying to hold on to his temper. "I was nearly thrown out of university due to all the time I'd spent trying to set matters aright."

"But that's all in the past. This is our future. I aim to bring your brother home, and provide a solid, respectable occupation. We're building a family empire," he'd said, his eyes bright with childlike excitement.

It had always been that way. The thrill of the venture. The great leap before looking.

And when everything crashed to the ground, it was always the same. "Magnus, my boy, will you fix everything, just once more?"

But there had been nothing he could do. The coffers were bare and moneylenders were lining up in droves. He was unable to reassure his father, who had retreated into his rooms for weeks on end, refusing to come out.

Magnus had thought the episode would have been like all the others. But he'd been wrong.

After the inquest, Viscount Underhill had been charged with the sole blame for orchestrating the deal. A separate bank account had been discovered with a sum of four thousand pounds that Underhill could not account for and he'd dissolved into a babbling, slobbering mess at the trial. Even though the money recovered had been only a fraction of what investors had doled out, it had been sufficient evidence to convict him of the crime and sentence him to hanging. No one ever discovered where the rest of the money had gone.

But Magnus had his ideas.

He'd always believed that there had been a mastermind behind the entire plot, someone slick and wily who could easily deceive people into believing whatever he chose. Someone who'd built an entire life on his ability to spin a yarn with a silver tongue. Someone who had been in the center of it all from the beginning.

And it could have been no one other than Hartley.

Magnus was not alone in this belief either. However, there had been no evidence sufficient enough to make Hartley stand trial. So he'd gone free and was able to hide away from society in his little hamlet while others had lost everything.

And having known all this, for the life of him, Magnus still couldn't fathom why the control he prided himself on had seemingly drifted away on a slow river current in Addlewick when he'd taken Verity Hartley in his arms and kissed her soundly. *Twice.*

"Forgive me for my tardiness, Your Grace," Mr. Eugene announced as he suddenly appeared on the pavement outside the carriage window, startling Magnus out of his guilty reminiscences. "I know how valuable your time is. And I want to thank you for agreeing to meet me here."

Magnus inclined his head in response. After stepping out of the carriage, he walked beside the younger man through the creaking gate, over the uneven cobblestones and up to the battered black door.

Fitzherbert Eugene was a plain bookish man of slight build with a pair of crooked spectacles on his nose. At the moment, he was trying to manipulate the key into a rusty lock. "I know it doesn't appear very impressive. But you did say that you wanted to build this business over time and not spend money for appearance's sake."

"Just so," he agreed and willingly stepped through the doorway to examine the rest of the proposed London office.

"Fortunately, I was able to procure this building before anyone else. As luck would have it, the offices are still equipped with furniture and there won't be a need to purchase more."

Magnus liked the sound of that. Eugene understood that he wanted to be frugal. This was to be a family venture, and he hoped his brother would commit to his promise of making this his own. Or, at the very least, take over a portion of it.

After lighting a lantern, he surveyed the space with a critical eye. There were crates stacked here and there, tools scattered about. The absence of order tempted the fastidious side of his nature, and he was itching to roll up his sleeves and set everything to rights. Yet, for now, he simply continued his assessment.

Seeing the open area from that vantage point, all it really required was a thorough cleaning. The structure seemed solid with a foundation of stone.

"If you'll walk this way, sir," Eugene said as he crossed to a windowed enclosure along the far wall. Inside was an office space, still littered with papers and supplies that the previous tenants hadn't bothered to take. The younger man gestured to the drafting table where pages of a steam engine schematic were already laid out for inspection. "As I mentioned before, I studied mathematics in France alongside Brunel. Together we collaborated on this design, and if not for the fact that he is still recuperating from the unfortunate collapse of his father's tunnel, he would be here today." He drew in a breath and gestured to the plans with a grin of modest pride. "With this, we're going to revolutionize the world."

His excitement was almost contagious. Magnus found himself wanting to dive into this project without delay. But those were the traits of a man who acted rashly, someone like his father.

But he was not such a man. Never one to trust on faith alone, he had done his due diligence in researching Eugene, writing to that school in France and verifying that he was, indeed, a man of letters and had been admired by his professors.

Not only that, but together they had toured the foundry in Birmingham. They'd even gone to the offices in Bristol and examined the dry dock.

"I almost forgot. Here are the bills of sale you requested," Eugene said, reaching into his satchel and withdrawing a sheaf of papers. "The problem was, none of the previous owners had enough capital in the beginning. After Lord Underhill's trial, they thought they could buy in with a pittance and pick up where he left off, then make a tidy profit. They soon learned that building a ship isn't child's play. You cannot make it out of paper and sail it down the river. It requires laborers, a foundry, a machine works, timber . . ." He looked at him steadily. "But you understand all this, unlike the others. And you know that this venture requires all the pieces be put in place from the beginning. Which is precisely why the Longhurst Shipping Company will succeed."

Magnus resisted the ego stroking and combed through the bills of sale that had changed hands over the past few years for the foundry, the Bristol office and dry dock. As for the scrap metal magnate, Mr. Modine, he was willing to consider offers for the warehouse when he returned from the Orient.

Modine would be in London in six weeks, but only for a few days. Which meant that Magnus must marry Miss Snow by then in order to have the money he needed.

"Those are yours to peruse at your leisure," Eugene said, pushing his spectacles up the bridge of his nose with an ink-stained index finger. "I understand how difficult this all must be for you. And trust doesn't come easy to either of us after what happened."

Magnus nodded as he carefully straightened the papers, the heavy weight of the past falling on his shoulders like a shroud.

Eugene cleared his throat, his voice solemn when he continued. "I was present when your father—rest his soul—agreed to invest, but only if his youngest son would be guaranteed a position of importance in the shipping company. Of course, as a man of honor, I never imagined that it was all a ruse. That I had been working for a swindler and villain. Lord Underhill deceived so many of us, and never once apologized, not even on the day of his hanging."

During the trial, Magnus had learned that Viscount Underhill and Baron Hartley had been friends since their boyhoods. The viscount had been a guest many times at Hartley Hall. And even though Hartley had never been charged with a crime, there wasn't any possible way that he hadn't been part of the scheme all along.

"We were all deceived," Magnus offered.

"Which is the reason I sent that first letter to Your Grace. That, and to repay the kindness you bestowed on me. So when I learned about the warehouse and Mr. Modine's plan to sell it for scrap, I knew that this was my chance to settle our debt. My own conscience demanded it. I never leave things unfinished. And besides," he added, "I know I've designed an exceptional steam engine. Letting this opportunity go would be insupportable."

Magnus looked over the schematic thoughtfully. He liked the engineer. The man was plain spoken and possessed more integrity than many men he knew.

However, because being a duke demanded a certain level of caution, he was not one to trust anyone implicitly. "Has it been tested?"

"Of course, and it is magnificent, if I do say so myself," he said with a humble shrug. "Regrettably, it is still in Germany, awaiting word of your final decision. However, if it would set your mind at ease, we could travel there together."

Magnus had plans to see Mr. Snow that evening to broach the topic of his betrothal again. He had waited this past week and a half to ensure that there were no lingering rumors or doubts of his suitability.

But even if he could secure an agreement from Snow during the visit, there would still be a requisite number of weeks before the marriage could take place. In the meantime, the Button King would likely expect a future son-in-law to spend time courting his daughter.

Not only that, but Magnus could hardly spare the expense of a trip to Germany. He shook his head. "I'm afraid I have no time to travel."

"Time is of the essence, for both of us," he said, quickly rolling up the designs. "Which leads me to bring up the rather unsavory topic of payment, sir?"

"Yes, of course," Magnus said, reaching into the inner pocket of his coat. He handed over the envelope containing the thousand pounds, which was nearly every last shilling he currently possessed.

Eugene tucked it away into a satchel, appearing uncomfortable. "I truly wish I did not have to take such a deposit. As I mentioned in my letter, I lost everything to Lord Underhill as well, and I firmly believe that, in case Mr. Modine returns earlier than expected, this earnest money would be our only insurance against losing everything again." He hesitated. "Unless, you have changed your mind regarding other investors. In truth, when it is all said and done, the sum will be quite the burden to carry on your—"

"No one else," Magnus interrupted. He abhorred any speculation whatsoever. His father had done it all too often with no thought to owning up to the consequences. But there was absolutely no way that Magnus would ever ask someone else to share in that risk. "The responsibility is mine alone. I am doing this for the sake of my own family."

Mr. Eugene accepted this answer with a nod.

Magnus took another moment to look around the space and envision what it could be like, once it was finished and bustling with activity. He only hoped that his brother was indeed willing to put himself into this role. He wasn't certain of the answer. But he knew that Rowan's nature was not suited for the clergy. The structure of the military had not agreed with him either.

Father had believed that this was the only path for his youngest ne'er-do-well son. And it had been the one decision that Mother had supported without question.

Magnus wasn't certain any occupation would hold his brother's interest for long. Nevertheless, he would do whatever he could to honor the wishes of his parents. It was his duty, after all.

❧

Mr. Snow invited him to share a drink in his home at ten o'clock that evening. He claimed that business matters and his daughter's social calendar had left him so preoccupied that he hadn't been able to find time any sooner. But Magnus understood the delay for what it was—a lesson in power.

He didn't mind it. When a man felt the need to measure himself against another, it meant that there was something he admired or envied. Either possibility worked in Magnus's favor. Obviously, his title and position in society were still in the old eagle's sights. Which was a relief.

There was too much at stake. He didn't want the added worry that Snow would entertain the proposal of another aristocrat.

"Ah. Punctual as ever, Longhurst. I appreciate that in a man," Snow said the instant he crossed the threshold. "Whisky or cognac?"

After the day he'd had, there was only one drink for Magnus. "Whisky."

"Good. I never trust a man who prefers cognac," Snow said, not bothering to hide that the question had been some sort of test.

Apparently, Magnus had passed. One would think that examinations ended at university, but no. There were always men who walked around carrying an invisible chart of ambiguous standards for others to reach. Because he understood that, too, he didn't take offense.

Nevertheless, he was in no mood for a series of trials. He was impatient to have this matter settled once and for all.

At the sideboard, Snow poured two glasses, then crossed the room and handed one over without ceremony. Lifting his own in a toast, he said, "To the future."

Taking that as a good indication of what was to come,

Magnus saluted and tossed back the amber liquor. His jaw clenched on the burn, a sweetly charred flavor lingering on his tongue. "Excellent whisky."

"By now, I thought you'd have realized that I would only have the best," he said with an archly self-satisfied grin.

Magnus offered a polite nod. "Indeed, sir."

"I demand it in all things, especially for my daughter." Snow took the empty glasses and returned to the sideboard to pour two more. "You managed that situation in Lincolnshire with diplomacy. From what I hear, you did not once deny the claim made against you. Were I in your shoes, I'd have gone in all bluster, raging against the reprehensible falsehood aimed at me."

It would have been easy to admit that his initial introduction to Verity had been a close cousin to that. Magnus had been furious. Yet, in hindsight, he realized that he'd detested having his name linked to a Hartley more than the actual crime itself.

Assuming this was another test, he carefully considered his words as his host crossed the room and handed off his refreshed glass. "I might have done. But I did not believe that inflicting humiliation on Miss Hartley would have left either of our reputations in good standing. I am grateful that she is sensible to the ramifications wrought by her misguided tale."

"I should hardly use the word *sensible* to describe a woman who imagines herself to be betrothed to a duke. Then again, why not a prince? Or a king for that matter?" He chuckled.

The next swallow of whisky lingered bitterly at the back of Magnus's throat.

"From what I gather, the declaration was uttered after some degree of chaos," he said, feeling his shoulders tighten with irritation as he recalled hearing that Verity had been climbing out of a window just moments before.

Foolish woman! She may have had far more than her pride hurt.

Not that it mattered to him. She was out of his life for good. He would no longer be plagued by her antics or her eyes. *Or her lips*, he thought distractedly.

Clearing his throat, he continued. "The intention was not to align herself with me, but to deflect the accusations of an unsavory foe."

The amusement fell from Snow's countenance like a sudden thaw. "Surely you cannot condone her actions."

"No," he responded carefully. "But a man is able to see another's perspective without adopting those practices, is he not?"

"*Mmm*," Snow grumbled but conceded with a nod and set his empty glass down on the table. Straightening, he stood in his usual eagle pose, talons hooked, wings at rest.

Magnus couldn't help but notice that he wasn't being invited to sit, to stay for dinner, or to see Miss Snow. The purpose of the appointment—whatever it may have been—was nearing an end.

Unsettled and trying to think of a way to move beyond what happened in Addlewick, he set his glass down as well and gestured to the enormous desk and wingback chair on the far side of the room. "Shall we move on to discussing the contract, then?"

"Eventually, I trust," Snow said. "However, I should like to wait a bit longer to ensure that nothing else crawls out of the woodwork. After all, this betrothal news took me by surprise. And I don't like surprises. They're usually flawed and require attention that I would rather put into making more money."

"The matter has been dealt with and concluded satisfactorily."

"Then another fortnight should not signify," the Button

King said, taking a heavy step toward the door in a way that brooked no misunderstanding on Magnus's part.

He was being escorted out, and he was no closer to marrying Miss Snow than he'd been a fortnight ago. In fact, his unplanned sojourn had set him back in more ways than he cared to think about at the moment.

Damn it all! A man with his pedigree shouldn't be having this problem. Snow should be begging him to marry his daughter and elevate her in society. Instead, *he* was on the verge of begging.

Everything depended on this marriage, and he was starting to suspect that Snow knew this. The man liked control even more than Magnus.

Searching his mind for a solution, he knew that reassurance was what a man like Snow required. And he could give him that.

At the door, he held out his hand. "There will be no more surprises. You can rely upon that."

"Then I look forward to our next meeting, Longhurst." Snow took his hand in a firm, meaty grip and Magnus left feeling more confident.

Of course, he didn't like the delay. But as long as nothing else went wrong, he should be engaged to Miss Snow the week after next.

Then the banns would have to be read, the marriage license obtained, the wedding, the contract and payment to secure the boat and the living for his brother, the repairs on the estate, hiring workers . . .

With the seemingly endless list of tasks awaiting him turning in his mind, and no hope for the smallest reprieve, he went home and strode directly to the study for one more nip of whisky. He needed something to take the edge off.

Lifting the decanter from the escritoire, he poured, absently wondering when was the last time he had ever been at ease. But just as he was about to convince himself that he'd been born feeling like a branch about to snap, he had a vision flash through his mind—a terrace at night, a sky full of stars overhead, and standing beside him was a woman with changeable violet-colored—

No, he thought. *Absurd.* A self-deprecating huff fogged the glass he held to his lips just before he took a hearty gulp.

His mind was overwhelmed, obviously. Of course, that might not have been the case if he'd been able to sleep at all. Instead, he'd been plagued by dreams of her every night. Lurid, uninhibited dreams where she matched his passion and welcomed his every feral desire.

It took supreme effort to shake off those dreams and manage his day with any sanity at all. He didn't know what was wrong with him. He was a man of sense and he knew there was nothing between them other than an unwelcome attraction.

Standing at the hearth, he propped one hand against the mantel while the other swirled the amber liquid in the glass. "It is time to forget about Verity Hartley."

"*Longhurst?*"

He spun on his heel at the startling sound of the familiar voice, then gaped at the figure standing in the doorway.

This wasn't happening, he thought with a hard blink. Verity wasn't there. And she most certainly couldn't have been wearing a ruffled lavender dressing down with one button unfastened at the white lace collar, her plaited hair draped over her shoulder, her brows arched in inquiry. He was having a vision. That was all.

And yet, after he blinked again, he knew he was awake.

Devil take it. He was actually losing his mind.

He watched as she stepped into the room, holding a book in one hand as her head tilted in question. "Long-hurst, did you hear me? I thought you called my name.

And why are you looking at me so strangely as if I were a ghost? Your mother did mention that I arrived with your grandmother this afternoon, did she not?"

Grandmother? What did she have to do with any of this?

He shook his head, trying to clear it. But it wasn't until he heard the sudden crack of the glass shattering against the floor, after it fell from his untended grasp, that he realized this wasn't a dream.

It was a nightmare.

Verity Hartley was here, and she could ruin all his plans.

Chapter Fifteen

VERITY RUSHED INTO Longhurst's study. She would like to have said that this was the first time today when a member of the Warring family had dropped something the instant they'd clapped eyes on her. Unfortunately, it wasn't.

Earlier, when Lady Broadbent ushered her into the parlor to meet her daughter, the Dowager Duchess of Longhurst let a porcelain vase slip through her fingers.

It had gone downhill from there.

To say that she was unwelcome beneath this roof was an understatement. But she had hoped that Magnus's greeting would have been a bit warmer, considering the fact that he'd kissed the stuffing out of her not too long ago.

Then again, he'd made no secret of the fact that he'd regretted it. And clearly, her arrival in Mayfair was the last thing he wanted, or expected.

She planned to have a chat with Lady Broadbent about bringing her all this way and never warning her own family.

Kneeling beside the hearth, Verity began gathering the shards of glass. He was doing the same and hadn't said a word. Well, that wasn't entirely true. He had muttered an expletive beneath his breath. But he hadn't said anything to her.

"It seems the cat I rescued that day has stolen your tongue," she quipped, attempting to lighten the dark mood that lurked between his furrowed brows. "Either that, or you are preparing to hurl a list of recriminations—"

She hissed as one of the shards sliced into her palm. But before she could investigate, he took hold of her wrist, opening her hand. She tried to draw back, but he wouldn't allow it, his grip firm and secure.

Even so, his inspection was incongruously gentle, the tender touch startling her far more than the puncture.

Eyes wide, she studied his bent head, his sloped brow, the hard, angular features set in concentration. A shadow of dark whiskers formed along the chiseled edge of his jaw and her fingertips tingled with curiosity, wondering what they would feel like.

"What are you doing here, Miss Hartley?" He growled the question, but his ministrations were careful as he pulled the sliver from her tender flesh. A bead of blood instantly welled to the surface.

She pressed her lips together against the sting. "I was getting a book."

"Not in this room. In *London*."

Still holding her hand captive, he withdrew a handkerchief and tenderly pressed against the wound. Then his gaze met hers. And there was more than expectation and impatience lingering in the flames reflected in the inky pupils.

But whatever warmth she might have seen, there was not a speck of welcome.

"Your grandmother called upon me to be her travel companion."

"You could have refused."

She arched a brow, her fingertips curling over his. "Have you ever tried to refuse her?"

"Fair point," he said. "And how did my mother receive you?"

"As expected, I suppose. I just hope you weren't too attached to the blue and white vase in the parlor." She glanced down to the broken glass in explanation.

He expelled a sardonic breath. "Grandmother's missive only mentioned that she would be traveling with a young woman of little consequence."

"Which is true enough." Verity had never been of much importance to anyone outside of her family.

He scoffed, turning her hand and wrapping the handkerchief around twice before tying the ends in a knot. "There you go again with your invented levels of honesty. A lie by omission is still a lie. There is no *true enough*. And she knows that as well as I do. She fully intended to surprise us with your arrival. Though, I cannot fathom what she thinks she might gain by her antics."

"You are far too cerebral. There is no great plot. And I'm certainly the last person that your grandmother would ever attempt to put in your path. Her ladyship knows full well of your intentions to marry Miss Snow. As far as I know, her primary desire is to ensure that your wife can hold her own in a battle of wits against her."

"I daresay, there are few who could, man or woman. Myself included," he said wryly. Then he paused for a breath before muttering crossly, "Well, there is little we can do about it now. The damage is done."

She fluttered her lashes. "Stop, please. You'll make me blush. Your hospitality is going straight to my head."

"Did you expect it to be any different?"

"No. I anticipated that our next meeting would be a close cousin to this—agonizingly awkward, but only with less broken glass and blood."

And absolutely no kissing involved, she thought. What had happened in Addlewick would forever stay in Addlewick.

Even though she didn't speak those words aloud, he

seemed to hear them because he locked eyes with her and shook his head once, slowly but decisively.

"There is nothing between us."

"I know." And yet, the weight of the *nothing* thickened the air between them as their gazes held.

Somewhere, in the back of her mind, she wondered if she would ever be able to look at him and not think about the way his lips moved over hers. Or how deliriously good it felt to be crushed in his embrace.

So she did the sensible thing and locked the door to that part of her mind.

He drew in a deep breath and stood, holding out his hand for her. She tentatively accepted, sliding her fingertips into his warm palm.

"Since you are here, there is no reason to confine yourself to this house." He let go the instant she gained her feet, then crossed the room in three strides. "Make the most of your time in London. Visit all the shops, galleries and wonders to your heart's content."

"In other words, be gone from your sight as much as possible?"

Standing behind his desk, he slanted her a look as if she should know the answer. "It is for the best."

She swallowed and nodded. But even though she agreed, she could still feel the heavy *nothing* between them. It was peering through the keyhole of the door she'd just locked.

Picking up her book, she turned to leave.

"And, Miss Hartley," he said, making her hesitate at the threshold, "proper young women do not traipse around the house in their nightclothes."

"I am completely covered from chin to heel, wearing both nightgown and formless dressing gown."

"That is not the point. It is a matter of decorum. One would never know that you are the daughter of a gentleman. You look like a wildling that has escaped from the country."

And just like that, her temper sparked. Must he always point out her flaws?

She seethed out a breath through her nostrils. Wildling, hmm? She jerked loose the violet ribbon that bound her hair and unwound the plait before ruffling her hands through the disheveled tangle until it resembled a lion's mane.

"I would say this is more like a wildling. Wouldn't you agree, Your Grace?"

He let his gaze travel over her before he returned his attention to his ledger. "And you have just proved my point."

She growled, took four stomping steps. Then hurled her ribbon in his direction and stalked off.

Chapter Sixteen

❧

$\mathcal{I}$N THE MORNING, Verity came downstairs to leave the handkerchief on his desk. She had rinsed out the blood—it was only the barest cut, after all—in the washbasin then left it to dry on the windowsill overnight.

The square of cambric was wrinkled but she was sure he would likely burn it or, at the very least, have it laundered a second time to ensure that anything feral was washed out of the fabric.

She walked toward the breakfast room, but stopped short at the vehement declaration of Longhurst's mother.

"I refuse to live beneath the same roof with any Hartley a moment longer."

"Then find other lodgings, Geraldine. I am the one who has let this town house for your use, after all," Lady Broadbent said with her usual frankness.

"Mother, this is not to be borne. It is because of her father that we are in this predicament."

"No, my dear. It is because your husband speculated wildly and often. Besides, it was proven at the trial that Hartley wasn't responsible. He was just as much a victim in the scheme as anyone else. After all, if the man had been sitting on a fortune, then he surely would have had Seasons for his daughters in order to have them advantageously married, and his son would have had no need to have become a merchant sailor."

It was all true, but Verity hated to have her family ordeal bandied about as if it were merely fodder over break-fast. That there weren't real people who'd suffered greatly for the years that followed.

"Well, Magnus has a theory regarding the sudden absence of that disreputable son."

Disreputable? Her brother was the most honorable and self-sacrificing of men! She knew if Longhurst were present, he surely wouldn't allow this discussion to continue. They had been friends, after all.

But no sooner had that thought arisen than she heard his voice with the others.

"The fact of the matter is that her presence here is not only unwelcome," he said, "but it comes at the worst possible time."

"Nonsense," his grandmother said. "I have given the matter a great deal of thought and I happen to know that this is the best course of action. She needs to be seen in London in order to quell any residual doubts. And I believe Mr. Snow must have some doubts, otherwise your betrothal to his daughter would already have been announced."

"Snow and I will discuss the matter again in a week," Longhurst admitted, his tone edged with frustration.

"There. You see? I was right," she said triumphantly. "Now, all we need to do is to make a concerted effort to show that Miss Hartley is not only completely over her youthful infatuation with you, but has decided to hunt for other marital prospects."

Verity balked at hearing this.

Lady Broadbent was planning to parade her around in front of the *ton* as the spinster who was looking for a husband? She would be a laughingstock!

She backed away from the room, her lungs cinching tight. The invitation to be a travel companion suddenly felt like a trap she couldn't escape. The dark paneling of the corridor began to close in on her. Her lips parted to draw in a breath, but her pinched throat refused to let enough air into her lungs.

She knew the first stages of one of her episodes enough to realize that she needed to step outside and *before* anyone came through the doorway and saw her gasping like a fish in a boat.

The butler stopped her at the doorway with a perplexed query. "Is Miss Hartley going out this morning?"

"Yes," she said, her voice strained. Seeing him move toward the coat tree, she gestured with a hurried nod as he reached for her pelisse. "Is there a park nearby?"

As he helped her into the garment, he relayed the location. However, before he handed over her hat, he offered advice that she really didn't want, or have time to hear. "I believe His Grace would prefer that you have a chaperone with you, miss. Perhaps one of the maids . . ."

There was a trace of disapproval in his tone, likely because he was thinking about how she hadn't traveled with a maid of her own. She could hardly have done so when she and her sisters shared one. And thinking about home and all the lovely grounds to walk made her lungs ache all the more.

"Thank you, Mr. Dodson. That won't be necessary."

She might have said more, but her need to be outside was far too great. In fact, she didn't even wait for him to open the door. Instead, she barged past him and headed out on her own.

Of course, the London air was far from fresh.

As she walked toward the park, her heart felt heavy. She had thought, after their week together and coming to know each other better—not to mention the kissing—that Longhurst would have come to her defense. Perhaps even tried to soothe the animosity his mother felt by explaining that Verity improved on further acquaintance.

Sure, she might have told a teensy lie that could potentially ruin the future of the Longhurst line, but was that so terrible?

She sighed. It was pretty terrible.

Drat. She couldn't even rally to her own defense. If only she hadn't told that lie. And yet, it wasn't just the big one, but all the little ones, too.

Hadn't Longhurst accused her of trying to make people like her by telling them what they wanted to hear? She hated to admit—*really* hated to admit it—but he'd been right.

So, she made a decision right there and then. No more lying from this moment forth. If anyone was going to like her, it would be for who she was, not for how she made them feel.

Then again, it would take far more than a few pretty words for Magnus's mother to like her. And there wasn't a reason to pretend otherwise.

She walked on with a determined stride.

Reaching the park, she felt her lungs expand on the aroma of green, the perfume of flowering trees, earth and grass. At last, she could breathe again.

Even though Mr. Dodson had caused her a pang of worry over leaving without a chaperone, it was still early by *ton* standards. Many people weren't even awake before ten. And further proof that she needn't worry was the fact that she saw that another woman was in the park without a chaperone.

She saw her down one of the forked paths. The woman wore a jaunty hat perched to one side of her inky coiffure. Dressed smartly in a green costume of the highest quality, she held a leash to walk her . . .

Verity squinted. Was that a . . . monkey?

The sight was so peculiar and unexpected that she found herself turning down that path in the hopes of meeting the pair. And yet, something compelled her to pause near the bench.

It was the surreptitious glance the young woman cast over her shoulder. Not because she saw Verity, who was still a distance away, but because she was looking for someone and, perhaps, making certain she wasn't being observed.

In the next instant, the woman was approached by a messenger in black livery. Their exchange was brief. A letter slyly passed between them. Then he moved on and she tucked the letter in her reticule.

However, as she was pulling the cord of the ruched opening, the monkey began to chatter and it dashed behind her skirts. Then the chatter turned to screeching as an elderly bearded gentleman with a clipped gait and a walking stick strolled by. He gave the pair a curious look but went on his way.

Just then, the monkey broke free of his leash and scrambled off in the opposite direction.

"*Sebastian!*" the young woman called out in alarm and dashed after him.

Without hesitation, Verity hurried down the forked path, hoping to intercept the monkey before he ventured out of the park and toward danger.

Unfortunately, spotting her charging after him did not help matters. His little black eyes widened and he clambered up the nearest tree.

The young woman came up beside her and raised her hand beseechingly. "Come down, Sebastian. No one is going to hurt you."

"Perhaps I should step away," Verity said, not wanting to interfere if she was the cause for the monkey's fright.

"No, indeed. I was not referring to you, but to the bearded—" Her words were abruptly cut off by the monkey's screeching, his agitation mounting as he climbed to a higher branch. The young woman dropped her hand and tapped her finger against the side of her mouth. "Oh dear. I should have known better than to speak it aloud. Sebastian is terribly afraid of b-e-a-r-d-s," she spelled, "because the man who had him before was a monster. Then, one day, this little creature followed a char woman into the factory and, much to my father's dismay, I fell in love with Sebastian at first sight."

Verity smiled, charmed by this stranger and glad that London wasn't full of people like Longhurst's mother. "I could climb up after him."

She was prepared for a gasp of shock at the suggestion.

Instead, she heard a hum of consideration. "Were I wearing the proper attire, I might do the same. Then again, it would be just my luck to have the story end up in the *Post.*"

"I know what you mean. A woman simply cannot climb a tree when she wants to without the risk of being caught."

"Further proof that society is filled with fogies and sobersides," the dark-haired woman nodded succinctly, amusement glinting in her eyes.

They exchanged a wry look and then laughed. The monkey chittered as well, drawing their attention.

They both returned to their attempts of coaxing him down from the limb. But he remained stubborn. The young woman was growing frustrated when he wouldn't even accept the biscuit she slipped out of her reticule.

Verity had the notion of using one of her bird calls. Something soothing, perhaps, like the coo of a mourning dove. Surprisingly, it worked. Entranced, Sebastian came down and wrapped his arms around her neck, pressing his dry little lips to her cheek.

"It seems as though you've made a friend. I'm Anna. Anna Snow, by the way."

Verity's eyes widened briefly. "And I'm Verity. Verity—"

"Miss Hartley!" a familiar, disapproving voice boomed. "It is unacceptable for you to be gallivanting around on your own. This is London, not the country and—"

Longhurst's diatribe ended abruptly as he saw the woman standing on the other side of the tree.

"Miss Snow." He doffed his hat. "Forgive me. I did not know you were here as well. Otherwise, I would have . . ."

"Subdued your ogreish nature?" Verity asked with a smile, batting her eyes.

He gave her a dark look in return. *If eyes could growl,* she thought . . .

But when she saw Miss Snow pale slightly, she realized that her quip sounded more like a castigation—probably because it was. The last thing she wanted was to have Longhurst's prediction that she would ruin everything come to fruition.

So, she amended with, "Though, I have it under authority that he is a rather pleasant and pragmatic fellow. It is only that I tend to bring out the worst in him, as you might imagine, given our family's history."

"Ah." Miss Snow looked at her with quick understanding. "So *you* are the Miss Hartley I've heard so much about."

Verity blushed with embarrassment. "I am she. However, I hope you will forgive me for being so foolish as to cause such an uproar. I never intended to lay claim to Longhurst. But I have this dreadful, sanctimonious neighbor and Longhurst's grandmother was visiting. Then, before I knew it, his name just sort of . . . slipped out. But, believe me, I have regretted it ever since."

Beside her, Longhurst's lips parted as if to interject his own opinion on the matter. Then he closed them again, choosing instead to expel an audible breath that suggested his regret far surpassed her own.

She arched a brow at him. He responded in kind, a muscle ticking along his jaw. She could practically see the list of castigations piling up on his tongue. And the minute they were alone, he would heap them on her head.

Yet, instead of having her ire sparked by the challenge in that glare, she felt the tug of a wry grin at the corner of her mouth at being able to interpret his unspoken dialogue.

The two of them could likely have an entire argument without uttering a single word.

Miss Snow's inquisitive gaze moved from her to Longhurst, and Verity wondered what she thought. Likely, that their mutual hatred was so palpable she speculated whether or not the two of them would make it a week before murdering each other.

"I, for one, am glad that it was his name that fell from your lips," Miss Snow said.

"*You are?*" Both Verity and Longhurst said in unison.

A beatific smile bloomed on the heiress's face as she reached out to squeeze Verity's hand. "Of course. Otherwise, Sebastian would still be in that tree and I would not have made a new friend. And I do hope that we can be friends, Miss Hartley."

Seeing only sincerity in her hazel eyes, Verity nodded. "I should like that very much."

"Splendid. Then you'll come to dinner this evening?" Then, as if an afterthought, she glanced up to Longhurst. "Both of you? That is, if you have no prior engagements."

"We do not," Longhurst said, speaking for both of them, which irked Verity to no end. Then he bowed. "I thank you for the most generous invitation. May I escort you home, Miss Snow?"

"Thank you, no. My carriage is just there, and my maid is waiting inside." She pointed with a gloved hand. Turning to go, she emitted a small gasp of alarm with Sebastian pulled the letter from her reticule and summarily flung it to the ground.

Longhurst bent to retrieve it. But Verity was faster.

She handed the folded missive over to its owner and saw something of relief glance across her countenance. And then, just as clearly, guilt.

Apparently, this was not a letter she wished for Longhurst to see.

Hmm . . . well, that was interesting. Her curiosity was sparked. But no, she told herself. She had interfered quite enough as it was. And, besides, it was none of her concern.

"Thank you, again." Miss Snow held her gaze, imploring.

Verity nodded in understanding. The letter and the person who delivered it were to remain a secret.

Longhurst led Verity back to his carriage, silent as the grave he likely wished to shove her in. Then he handed her inside.

Forgetting about her own wound, she hissed. He immediately shifted his hold to her elbow instead. But inside the carriage, he sat beside her and peeled off her glove with impatience before she had the chance to object.

She tried to jerk her hand away, but he held firm. "Hoping to see that it had festered overnight and my hand was black as pitch?"

"I've already summoned a surgeon to amputate at the wrist," he said without missing a beat, his warm breath tickling her palm. "A pity that I'll have to send him away. You seem to be healing nicely. Even so, you should take better care."

She slipped her hand free, covering it with the other. The accusation in his tone abraded the nerves that were still frayed from last night. "You're the one who manhandled me into the carriage."

"Which I would not have needed to do had you not left the house without a chaperone. Without even telling anyone."

"I told the butler." She hiked her chin. "Strange, but I did not hear you reprimand Miss Snow for being in the very same park."

"She is not my responsibility."

"Neither am I."

"You are living beneath my roof. She is not."

"Not yet. But that is the reason you are in town, is it not? To marry her?"

"Yes," he hissed and leaned closer. "Though I do not know why that information has any bearing on whether or not you are free to traipse about at will. There are any number of things that might have happened to you. And whether you like it or not, you are mine—"

He broke off, the word reverberating in the close confines.

Her lips parted on a soundless gasp and his gaze dropped to them. And in that brief but heated moment, the memory of their kisses—which, admittedly, were never too far away—seemed to blaze like a conflagration between them, warning them to take care or else be burned.

Drawing in a breath, she caught the pleasantly spicy fragrance of his shaving soap and the scent of freshly laundered linen, and the barest hint of lavender from the French milled soap by her wash basin. Though, with her body warmed by her brief walk, it seemed to take on a different aroma, the perfume more like wildflowers in a meadow.

Spice, linen and wildflowers. She saw his nostrils flare and wondered if he was thinking that their fragrances smelled good together, too.

Longhurst was the first to move. He straightened and raked a hand through his hair, making it stand on end.

She was so tempted to reach up, casual as you please, and set him back to rights. But he would only capture her wrist and give her a stern warning. And as he did, the pad of his thumb might aimlessly soothe her trampling pulse as it had done before. The thought made that fluttering place quicken as if begging to be touched, to be rubbed smooth like a worry stone.

"What I meant to say"—he cleared the hoarseness from his throat—"was that you are under the protection of my name while you are here. And I would be grateful if you would consider that before abandoning decorum and bringing another scandal to my doorstep."

"Well, that foils all my plans for the day." When she continued, she pretended to count a list of tasks on her fingers in order to keep her hands occupied. "Abandon every ounce of decorum by ten o'clock. Swing from the chandelier by three. Have scandal delivered to your doorstep by eight."

The Duke of Longhurst was not amused. If he clenched his jaw any harder, his teeth would crack.

She didn't know why she was goading him. After all, it was no secret that he wanted her to be anywhere else in the world but here. Wanted anyone else to be underneath his roof. And his reasons were justifiable. So there was no need to add more logs to this pyre.

The sensible part of Verity heaved out a great sigh of resignation. "Very well. I shall do my best to be out of your sight, and properly chaperoned, from this moment forth. Additionally, I will send my regrets to Miss Snow for this evening."

"You will do no such thing. It is already too late for that. At this very moment, Miss Snow is likely informing her father that you are here." He sat stiffly against the squabs, his fist wrapped around her glove. "And this is *before* I had the chance to tell him myself. Which was what I'd intended to do before Dobson informed me of your unaccompanied flight from the town house."

"You make me sound like an escaped prisoner. There will be times when I'll need to step out for a breath of air. Am I to ask your permission, oh, Magnus the Gaoler?"

She tried to keep her tone light, but there was worry behind the question. There were those occasional episodes that required her to have an egress to a place where she could catch her breath.

He turned his head to scrutinize her features as if he'd heard the faint tremor that she'd tried so hard to hide with a haughty laugh. Then he nodded. "You may enjoy the terrace and walled garden at your leisure. There is also a balcony attached to the family solar. I'll have my mother show you."

The mention of his mother instantly reminded her of the reason she'd left the house in the first place. Not only because she didn't want to be put on display in society as the oldest living debutante, but also because of the rebukes cast against her brother's character. It still bothered her that Magnus hadn't come to Truman's defense.

"May I ask you a question?"

He gave her a wary look but inclined his head.

She came directly to the point. "You and my brother were once friends, and I just want you to know that it hasn't been easy for him either, since the um . . . well . . . you know." She didn't say the word *scandal*. Then again, she didn't need to. It was always between them. "All Truman had ever wanted was to become an architect. And when he lost his position, it devastated him. He couldn't find a post anywhere. It was as if all of England was against him. He lost his friends and even the woman he was going to marry. He was left with nothing. So, he sold his house and lands and took the only opportunity he could and sailed away on a merchant ship."

"Why are you telling me this?" Longhurst was no longer looking at her but out the window instead.

"Because family is all I have. I do not have a title, a home of my own, a fortune or even the respect of my peers. I have my family. They are all I hold dear. And I would appreciate if you would try not to think too ill of them while I am a guest beneath your roof."

He was quiet for a long while, and she realized it was rather bold of her to demand anything of him. But then he surprised her by inclining his head.

It wasn't a solemn vow by any means, but she would take it.

As the carriage pulled to a stop in front of the town house, she reached over to extract her glove. He looked down as if he'd forgotten he held it, then released the kid leather at once.

"You should take better care of that cut," he grumbled. "I'll send a maid with some salve and fresh wrapping."

She expelled an exhausted sigh. "Longhurst, are you always this overbearing?"

He gave her a hard look that said he wasn't going to answer.

Verity put on her glove an instant before the footman brought out the step and opened the door. She was already on the pavement when she heard "Miss Hartley?" from within the carriage. And she turned back to Magnus, her brows lifting in inquiry.

"The answer is yes. Always."

If she didn't know that he was absolutely serious, she would have laughed. Then again, knowing that he was serious was likely the reason she caught herself smiling as she stepped through the town house door.

Chapter Seventeen

✣

ENTERING SNOW'S OFFICE that morning, Magnus knew that any ground he'd gained would hit a stumbling block when his future father-in-law learned of Miss Hartley's presence.

But before he could explain the situation, the Button King stood up from the throne chair behind his desk and leveled him with a glare. "My daughter just informed me that we are to have guests for dinner. I imagine that you are here to confirm that fact, and likely to try to explain the reason Miss Hartley is staying at your town house."

"Indeed, sir. Actually, I was just on my way to—"

"Don't bother. If there's one thing I detest, it's excuses. Excuses only make it seem as though you have something to hide. So let us simply cut to the marrow. Do you intend to marry this chit?"

"No."

"Then, do you plan to keep her as your mistress?"

"Certainly not." Magnus stiffened, his fists and jaw clenched in outrage. The very suggestion was a dishonor to Miss Hartley and his own family name. He'd never been spoken to in such a manner in all his life, not even in the last seven years that he'd spent knee-deep in dirt, working shoulder to shoulder with his men on the estate.

Snow issued a curt nod. "That's all I needed to know. Dinner is at eight."

And with that, he was dismissed.

∽≫◡

Hours later, at the end of the day, Magnus didn't know what to expect. Though, doubtlessly, there would be a chilly reception for himself and for Miss Hartley.

He had warned her of this earlier. In response, she'd assured him with a dubiously arched brow that she was quite familiar with being the recipient of unfounded animosity.

That brief interaction had been the only thing he'd trusted himself to say to her. After their rocky morning, he'd still wanted to rail at her for leaving the town house without a chaperone. She didn't know what dangers lurked in London. And the instant Dodson had informed him, Magnus had felt his blood run cold.

Finding her in the park had filled him with such relief, irritation and anger that all he'd wanted to do was shake her. In fact, he'd barely subdued the impulse before he saw Miss Snow standing there, too.

In that moment, he'd wondered if his life could possibly become more confoundedly complicated. He had a missing brother, a failing estate, a potentially irate future father-in-law who held Magnus's fate in his hands. His mother was furious with him. His grandmother was scheming against him. And worse, his future wife had invited his once-temporary fiancée to dinner.

It was far from ideal.

The tension he felt as he stepped across the threshold of Snow's town house that evening threatened to crush him into a shard of coal. He supposed it was for the best that his own mother had refused to come.

As the butler took their coats, Magnus glanced warily over to Miss Hartley. He'd been rather cross with her today and hoped she wasn't planning to retaliate by making him look like a fool.

Bollocks. He should have thought about that before. Then he might have tried *not* to be so cross with her. Or, at the very least, he could have told her she was pretty.

Though, after having spent the majority of the afternoon with his grandmother at the modiste, he had expected her to be dressed in a new frock at the height of fashion. But, to be honest, the simple apricot gown—the same one she'd worn to the village assembly—suited her. It drew the eye to the graceful lines of her bone structure. As did the way her hair was tamed into a chignon. She also wore a string of coral beads around her neck that rested delicately beneath the hollow of her throat. Her shoulders were straight, her bearing regal. Not even Snow, who demanded perfection in all things, could find fault with her.

Perhaps this evening wouldn't be the disaster that Magnus feared.

"How good to see you again, Miss Hartley," Miss Snow said with a smile as she swept across the marble foyer in a gown of white ruffles.

Extending her hand, she enveloped Verity's in an amiable clasp. They exchanged a few pleasantries, then Anna greeted Magnus in the same manner.

As he introduced her to his grandmother, he could not recall if Anna had ever been so at ease with him. She was usually quite shy and reserved. Though the reason must simply have been familiarity. Obviously, she was becoming accustomed to him. Which was a relief because he intended to propose at the end of next week. That would still leave time for the banns to be read, for the contracts to be signed and for the wedding to take place before Mr. Modine arrived in London.

She escorted them to the drawing room where her father was already waiting, a glass of whisky in hand.

Everyone who entered received the same shrewd appraisal as if they'd just been stamped off the line. His grandmother, dressed in dove gray, earned a nod of approval when she was introduced. Then those eagle eyes turned to the reason for this impromptu gathering.

Miss Snow was all smiles and eagerness as she made the introduction to her new *friend*. To which her father replied with a curt, "Miss Hartley."

For a moment, Magnus was tempted to stand beside Verity. He couldn't fathom why. It wasn't as though he imagined for an instant that she'd dissolve into tears at this chilly greeting. He'd seen her suffer through worse from those people in Addlewick. But, perhaps, he just didn't want her to feel alone.

As he was puzzling that random thought over, he saw her proud, stubborn chin jut out, the same way it did when she was vexed. He gritted his teeth, wishing that he would have warned her about Snow's demeanor and warned her against losing her temper.

"Mr. Snow," she said with a stiff curtsy. "You are very kind to have me here, and I'm so glad you didn't say something like 'It's a pleasure to make your acquaintance' or even a terribly droll '*Enchanter*.' After all, it is important to be true to one's own character, and it is clear that you would have rather avoided the association altogether."

Snow grumbled in response, his wiry brows dropping to a flat line.

Verity was undeterred and continued. "Not that I blame you. I too prefer to avoid unpleasant encounters when I am able. Regrettably, that is the very reason we are here . . ."

Magnus bit back a groan as Verity proceeded to recount the tale of her scaling down a wall of ivy and the lie she'd told to Miss Hunnicutt. He wanted to place his hand over her mouth. She was doing herself no favors. A man of Phineas Snow's no-nonsense disposition hadn't any desire to hear about her indecorous, uncontrolled exploits. He likely didn't want his daughter associating with her either.

And yet, by the time she finished, stating, "Well, you can imagine that I wished I'd set the dogs on her instead," the strangest thing happened.

Phineas Snow barked out a laugh. And by the rusty sound of it, he didn't do it very often. He gave her another appraising look, pursing his lips as if he'd found something good in this particular button. "I like you, Miss Hartley. I can see why Anna took an immediate shine to you. You're not false like so many others in your sphere. And you're not afraid to tell the truth even when it's hardly flattering. I admire that."

"Well, I wish you hadn't said that." She issued a resigned sigh. "Because now I am forced to admit that I had thought about leaping out of the carriage three times on the way here this evening."

"And what prevented you from doing so?" Miss Snow lifted her hand, her fingertips fanning out over her lips to shield a smile.

"Well, I wanted to visit with my new friend, of course," she said, then her shoulders lifted in an artless shrug. "And I also wanted to see if the vein, which has been present on Longhurst's forehead since this morning, would actually erupt."

All eyes turned to him and by sheer force of will he did not lift a hand to his forehead to investigate said vein.

The Button King hooted this time. Miss Snow gave in to a giggle, and so did his grandmother.

Magnus stood off to the side for a moment and tried to understand what had just occurred. The blustering man who'd never given him an inch of leeway or an ounce of praise for his own straightforward manner was suddenly eating out of her hand?

How had that happened?

His grandmother slipped her arm through his and whispered, "It appears as though Miss Hartley's frankness appeals to our host. And she has made a fast friend in Miss Snow as well. This should set your mind at ease."

"And why is that?"

"Because now you needn't be concerned with having her under your roof. And since Mr. Snow approves of her, there will be no reason to avoid each other at balls and parties. Isn't that simply splendid?"

Magnus felt as though a yoke had just been placed on his shoulders with large pails of stones hooked on either side. The ability to spend more time with her was the very last thing he wanted.

"Splendid," he muttered dryly.

ALL THINGS CONSIDERED, Verity thought the dinner went rather smoothly. She'd been so nervous when they'd arrived, fearing she'd do or say something truly embarrassing, that she wasn't going to speak at all.

However, it had been clear in the way that Longhurst held himself so stiffly that he had feared the same. Which was insulting, frankly, and became the very reason she'd decided to speak her mind.

It was so liberating!

Nevertheless she was thankful that Mr. Snow was not easily offended or else she might have ruined a budding friendship with his daughter.

As for Anna, she was a revelation. When Verity had first heard mention of Longhurst's heiress, she'd pictured someone quiet and unassuming. A biddable woman who would alter her own interests to align with his and never offer her own opinion.

The truth was, Anna had many interests that differed

from the duke's. His tended toward the agricultural, hers toward the industrial. She loved living in the city. He preferred the country.

She also had many ideas about improving production and working conditions at her father's factory . . . though neither of the men seemed to listen.

"Just so you know," Verity said as the two of them sat at a small table in the parlor, where they'd all gathered for cards after dinner, "I thought your notion of providing breaks for the workers during the day was inspired."

Miss Snow's lips spread into a smile over the fan of her piquet hand. "Thank you. I've also thought that we could provide tea, but I've kept that to myself. As you likely noticed, whenever I speak of the factory my father goes conveniently deaf." She rolled her eyes. "Oh, but he was more than delighted to answer all of Lady Broadbent's questions about his button empire."

"I noticed that as well. And the countess seemed quite the flirt after her second glass of wine," Verity whispered conspiratorially and earned a laugh as she laid a card, but lost the trick.

"I hope to be that bold when I'm her age. And she seems to be trouncing my father soundly at their game of loo." She slid a glance over to their table and lowered her voice. "By the by, thank you for not mentioning my letter. I never had a chance to explain."

"No explanation necessary. We're friends, are we not?"

She nodded without hesitation. "The letters aren't romantic. I'm not having an assignation, or anything of the sort. And I don't want you to think that it has something to do with Longhurst."

"Whyever would you imagine that would bother me?"

"Well, you were betrothed to him," Anna said as if that explained everything.

"Not really. It was only my outlandish fib."

"Perhaps at first. However, he told me that he actually did propose, out of honor."

"He . . . um"—Verity paused to swallow down a peculiar and sudden tightness in her throat—"mentioned that?"

Anna nodded, her expression sincere, kind even. "Therefore, I know there is a certain regard the two of you hold for each other. After all, a man who cared nothing for you would hardly feel compelled to pull me aside and express his concern for your comfort this evening."

Confused, she felt her brow pucker. "Longhurst expressed concern for me? That is highly unlikely."

"Oh, but it's true. As he escorted me to dinner, he mentioned that you might be a little"—she hemmed—"uncomfortable performing in front of others. And he was quite glad when I then suggested cards for our after-dinner entertainment instead of adjourning to the music room."

Verity didn't know what to say. That was rather thoughtful of Longhurst.

Then her suspicions flared. Would he actually show consideration for her? Hardly.

Doubtless, he assumed that she had never learned to play an instrument or couldn't carry a tune. She was almost tempted to call his bluff.

And yet, she hated performing far more than she hated his high-handed manner.

"I suppose that was rather kind of him," she admitted reluctantly, sliding a glance over to his table.

He laid a card and, as if sensing her attention, his gaze met hers.

The pulse on the side of her throat quickened for no reason whatsoever and she turned her attention back to her table just as Anna took the last trick and tallied the points.

"It looks like I win again."

At the other table, Mr. Snow grumbled something about being having been *looed*.

"Ah, Anna, my dear. I see that you are done. Perhaps you wouldn't mind taking my place here and winning back some of your inheritance that the countess has piled before her."

Lady Broadbent laughed, gathering ivory fish tokens in a heap.

"And Miss Hartley," he continued, "perhaps you would like to see my button collection?"

Desiring to be anywhere that Longhurst wasn't, she readily agreed.

Snow walked her down to his study and showed her a display case of ornate buttons. She did her best to express a fascination by inserting a "lovely" and an "exceptional craftsmanship" here and there. And they were remarkable, just not very interesting to her.

"Admirable effort," he said wryly, standing with his thumbs hooked into the open sleeves of his waistcoat. "However, I shall cut to the chase and tell you why I really asked you here. And I can see by the alertness in your gaze that you understand that this is a conversation best spoken away from the others."

His barrel chest expanded on a breath. "The moment I heard the rumor of that betrothal, I hired an investigator. You see, I remember that scheme your father was part of years ago."

"My father wasn't—" She stopped when he held up a hand and decided to hear him out before she gave him a piece of her mind.

"And for what had been such a public matter back then, it surprised me how much digging my investigator had to do to find out more information that went beyond Lord Underhill's trial. But I did," he said pointedly. "Find out, that is."

A sinking feeling settled in the pit of her stomach. And just outside the door, she could hear the unmistakable, purposeful stride of Longhurst approaching. She couldn't risk him overhearing. Her father would never forgive her.

"My family prefers not to speak of it. The entire ordeal was particularly painful to my father, as you might imagine."

Snow's forehead creased in a perplexed frown. "But if he—"

"His reasons are his own," she cut in, closing the matter for good just as Longhurst entered the room.

His gaze went from hers to their host's. "I was sent on an errand by my grandmother to see if you wished to try your luck—as she put it—once more, sir."

Snow chuckled. "The countess is positively bloodthirsty. But don't tell her I said that. She's formidable, that one." Then he looked directly at Verity as he said, "Besides, I think we've seen all the best buttons. Might as well return, eh, Miss Hartley?"

She agreed with a nod. And she hoped, for her father's sake, that the topic of their conversation would be buried once more.

It had been so terribly hard on him to carry the burden of guilt over the two men, his friends, who had died because of that scheme. She did not want the turmoil he had suffered through before to come back to haunt him again.

Chapter Eighteen

᠉

"*I* CANNOT THANK YOU enough for insisting that I accompany you this afternoon," Verity said the following day as she perused the drapers shop on Bond Street with Anna. "I was sure that Longhurst's mother was planning to lace my tea with arsenic if we were forced to breathe the same parlor air a moment longer."

Examining a length of orange bombazine, Anna smiled softly but shook her head. "Surely, it couldn't be that bad. I've always found Geraldine rather pleasant, in her own way."

"That is like saying Attila the Hun was quite a nice chap, in his own way, as long as you ignore all those murderous tendencies."

Her new friend laughed, earning a censorious glower from the pinched-nose clerk, who summed them up in a glance and summarily dismissed them with a sniff.

Anna sobered as they strolled aimlessly past the organdies and silks, and slid a sideways glance to the patrons who were staring at her and whispering behind cupped hands. "I'll never understand society, or why it is acceptable to laugh, but only at a certain volume. One may smile, but never too much. It's as though any display of sincerity is forbidden. Well, either that or everyone is afraid to show their teeth."

This time, Verity laughed, earning the same glower

and whispers. "Most definitely the latter. However, if it pleases you, I will show you my teeth as often as you like."

With that she flashed an overly broad grin.

Anna did the same, speaking through her smile. "Thank you ever so much."

And standing near a drab display of worsted wool, they both giggled.

They had become fast friends, even after Verity explained the reason behind the animosity between herself and Longhurst. Even after revealing to her that the Hartley name did not sit well in certain quarters. Anna had merely shrugged and said that her name didn't sit well in certain quarters either. And that was that. Neither their flaws nor family histories seemed to matter to either of them.

Of course, there was still one rather sticky wicket between them. *Longhurst.*

But Verity wasn't entirely certain how she felt about Anna and Longhurst. Oftentimes, she had found herself becoming overly cheerful and ebullient, hiding the fact that her stomach churned sourly at the sight of them together. Not that she was jealous, by any means. That would have been absurd. Completely and utterly absurd. So, *of course* it wasn't jealousy.

Although, if she could help it, she would much rather stay away from becoming the unwanted third party when they were together.

This afternoon, however, it couldn't have been prevented.

Longhurst had been in his study when Anna had arrived and he'd come out to greet her. And when she'd told him that she was on her way to Bond Street, he'd offered to escort her . . . before he realized she'd already invited Verity.

Then, once they were all inside the carriage, Anna had proceeded to invite her to the opera that evening. The very opera that Longhurst was taking her to.

Seated across the carriage, he had cut a look to Verity that warned her to think of an excuse to refuse.

But that was like a double-edged sword. On one hand, she would be able to spend more time with her friend, escape the seething civility from the dowager and finally see an opera.

On the other hand, she would be telling her friend a lie. And wasn't Longhurst forever harping on Verity about lying? And yet, when it was more convenient for him, he didn't seem to mind at all. At least, until their next tête-à-tête when he would invariably bring up her falsehood as a mark against her character. And so, with that last thought in mind, she had accepted.

Longhurst had said nothing, but the Pompeian vein had made another appearance.

Then, at the door of the drapers, he'd left them to shop while he'd walked on to the haberdashery, vowing to return to them in short order. And Verity hated that her pulse had leaped in anticipation at his promise.

Even now, she caught herself glancing to the door. Which was precisely when she saw the pinched-nose clerk sidle up to them and send a scathing look to where Anna was examining a length of golden silk.

"Might I be of service . . . ladies?" he asked, raking a condescending gaze over their simple spencers and day dresses.

The other patrons in the shop were all dressed at the height of fashion in fur-trimmed pelisses and feathered hats so large they could eclipse the moon. Anna had far more impressive garments in her wardrobe, but it was likely that she'd dressed in a way to ensure that her friend didn't feel out of place beside her. Because she also knew that Verity was still waiting for the modiste to finish her new gowns.

Her considerate nature would make her a fine duchess, and made Verity like her all the more. Which meant that, when Anna would invite her to the wedding breakfast, she would accept and be plagued by that *not jealousy* churning in her stomach during the whole of it. Drat it all.

As for the clerk, however, he didn't seem to like either of them.

"For your information," he continued, "it is customary to wait for assistance. We do not allow our patrons to paw the merchandise. So, unless you intend to buy that very costly silk, I would suggest you allow me to direct you to the printed cotton."

But before Anna could do more than release the fabric, another clerk bustled in through a door at the back of the shop. His eyes lit with recognition, and he hastily approached. "Miss Snow, how kind of you to grace our little shop once more. I do hope the black bombazine we sent to your father's factory was acceptable?"

"It was, thank you," she said, her cheeks coloring with embarrassment.

But as far as Verity was concerned, it was the first clerk who ought to have been embarrassed. Upon the instant of hearing her name, he immediately fell into fits of bowing, pandering and obsequious apologies. It was revolting.

Unable to stand by and watch her friend be treated in such a manner, Verity interjected, "I don't believe we'll require your services today. The selection is"—she cast an appraising look around the shop and wrinkled her nose—"too last Season."

The clerks gaped and began to mutter accusations at each other for not having shown her the new stock just in from Paris. While they attempted to win her over, Verity merely linked arms with Anna and they both strolled out of the shop, heads high.

"You were positively brilliant," Anna said with a laugh when they were out on the pavement and away from faces peering out from the shop-front window.

"And lying through my teeth," Verity confessed, glad that Longhurst hadn't been there. He'd never have let her live it down. "I have no idea what is *de rigueur*, but I was appalled by how they treated you. How can you stand it?"

She lifted her shoulders. "My father thinks that, because he has money, it has earned us a place in society. For some members, perhaps that is enough. But there are many, *many* others who would rather keep the classes separated by a brick wall, and my father and I are about as common as we can be. The only problem is, he doesn't see it. Whenever he is my chaperone and enters a room with all his bluster, ensuring that everyone knows just who he is, people act according to his design. As for me, I would much rather be surrounded by genuine people." She squeezed Verity's arm. "Like you."

"My parents have never been driven by money." Verity saw in Anna's expression that both she and Mr. Snow had known that already. "They always taught us that fortunes may come and go, but it is the heart that truly matters."

Uncannily, as the words left her lips, she caught sight of a familiar set of broad shoulders heading down the pavement in their direction. Even though he was a good distance away, Verity felt the organ beneath her breast skip a beat or two . . . or twenty.

"I agree." Anna's head tilted in an appraising smile. "Though, it's a pity that we cannot always control where our hearts may lead us, is it not?"

When her friend glanced from her to the approaching duke, Verity blanched.

In a sudden rush of panic and need to correct any misunderstanding, she said, "I would never let my heart lead me to where it didn't belong."

Her friend's eyes were soft with understanding. "I know you wouldn't. That is what makes you a true friend. But there are times when we cannot—"

Anna stopped abruptly when Verity stumbled. Or rather, when she was shoved from behind.

It happened so fast that Verity plowed directly into an older gentleman. He was so slight in build that she was sure they were both going to fall to the pavement.

Thankfully, she was wrong. They were tangled for a moment, long enough for her to see his wide eyes, curling gray mustachio and mile-high top hat. But by some miracle, they ended up keeping their feet and composure.

Well . . . almost.

Just as he was righting the angle of his hat, something fell out from underneath it. Something that gentlemen of a certain age and a certain baldness likely wouldn't want on display. At least, not when it wasn't properly affixed to his head.

Verity could only stare down at the toupee in shock. It had fallen upside down, looking as helpless as a turtle on its back. Just lying there, underbelly exposed for all the world to see. And with a glance, she saw that they were drawing a crowd of spectators.

She snapped out of it and quickly bent to pick it up, brushing off the dust and debris before she offered it to him as if she were holding it upon a coronation pillow. "I do believe this is yours, sir."

"Mine?" he asked, incredulous as he cemented his top hat in place. "I have no idea what you could mean."

"There's nothing to be ashamed of. It is actually a very fine piece. I've seen some that resemble a dead rat, but not this one." Her attempt to lessen an awkward moment fell flat.

The man snatched the toupee and shoved it under his arm as he cut a swath through the snickering crowd.

"It is a very fine piece," she called out once more as he climbed into his carriage.

Then a shadow fell over Verity. She looked up to see a muscle ticking along a rather hard jaw and a jagged vein about to erupt on a forehead.

The Duke of Longhurst was not amused.

ॐ

MAGNUS WAS SO incensed that he didn't trust himself to speak as he ushered the two women into the landau. Thankfully, Miss Snow gave the directions to his driver.

Yet, even as the carriage trundled down Bond Street, Magnus wasn't certain what part of the entire spectacle made him angrier. Was it the fact that Verity wasn't in the shop as agreed upon? The blame he felt for leaving her without an escort on the streets of London, all the while knowing her nature to fall into the most absurd situations? Or was it because he had seen the collision but had been too far away to intervene?

Across from him, Verity expelled a huff of embarrassed laughter. "Well, that was certainly awkward."

He shot a glare at her, his anger swiftly finding a target. "Is that all you have to say, Miss Hartley? Once again, you have made yourself an object of ridicule. There are times when I wonder if you have any sense of decorum at all."

"You needn't lecture me." She hiked her stubborn chin, her cheeks flushed, eyes flashing. "In fact, you should be pleased that I did not lie to that gentleman. I've been around costumes for my entire life and it was, indeed, a very fine toupee."

He spoke through gritted teeth. "Just because a statement may be true, doesn't mean one is required to air it in public."

"Should I have whispered in his ear, then?"

When she dared to bat her lashes innocently, he growled.

Damn it all, but that woman could try the patience of a monk. And he was no monk. In fact, all he wanted to do was take her by the—

He didn't finish the thought because he suddenly remembered Miss Snow sitting beside him. She seemed to be enjoying the spectacle, her gaze darting back and forth between them with great interest.

He ventured to regain his composure with a quick tug on his waistcoat. Clearing his throat, he attempted a more neutral tone. "There is nothing to be done about it now. Though, in the future, I should hope you would take better care to shield Miss Snow from any unfavorable on-dits that might end up in the newspaper."

Beside him, Anna issued a small laugh. "As far as I'm concerned, the newspapers may write whatever they wish, as they have always done. I lost interest in their tittle-tattle years ago." Then she drew in a hard breath and straightened her spine, her expression serious. "The only fact that bothers me is that someone pushed my friend, but no one seemed to have cared about the true culprit behind the ordeal."

"I'm sure it was an accident." Verity slid him a challenging glance. "After all, everyone else in society would have had decorum enough to offer an apology."

But Magnus knew differently. He had seen the entire episode clearly from his vantage point. And the collision might very well have appeared accidental . . . if not for the vicious delight he'd seen on Nell Hunnicutt's face the instant before she'd sauntered off in the opposite direction.

He was tempted to mention it. Yet, the more he thought about it, the more he felt his irritation mount. Or perhaps it wasn't irritation at all, but that damnable sense of protectiveness that overcame him whenever Verity was near. Somehow, he would rid himself of this madness.

Then again, the obvious solution was to ensure that he was never near her.

Unfortunately, he would have to endure the opera this evening, but tomorrow he would keep as far away from her as possible.

Or at least, that's what he planned . . . until Miss Snow was suddenly besieged by a terrible notion.

"I've just had a brilliant idea," she announced, sitting forward on the carriage bench and taking hold of Verity's hand. "You should be my chaperone!"

"What? *Me?*" Verity's uncertain gaze darted to Magnus.

Miss Snow continued. "It's perfect! You were already telling me that you didn't want to be paraded around town as if you were in search of a husband. And my father only accepts invitations to the most influential houses. But there's this ball I'd like to attend, along with a dozen other places, and having you with me instead of my father or my maid would be so much more fun. For both of us, I imagine. So, you can hardly refuse. What do you say? Will you be my chaperone?"

"Well, I don't know," Verity hemmed, looking at Magnus once more as if asking him to intervene.

Then Miss Snow turned to him. "Oh, I'm sure Longhurst doesn't mind. Do you, Longhurst? After all, the two of you are like old friends by this point, are you not?"

Magnus hated that his mind chose that moment to conjure the memory of that sweltering morning in the river. He wasn't sure he could consider anyone that he'd ever kissed that recklessly, that passionately as an *old friend.*

He was so distracted for a moment that he didn't even realize Anna had rested her hand on his sleeve. At least, not until he saw Verity's attention snared by the gesture before she quickly glanced away.

He saw her brow furrow and her hands clench around a fistful of skirts, but he didn't want to think about the reason.

Besides, there was nothing between them. They both knew it.

What mattered most was keeping his distance from her as much as possible. "The decision is not mine. However, Miss Hartley is here as a companion to my grandmother. So, perhaps . . ."

"Quite right," Verity interjected at once, turning to Miss Snow. "Lady Broadbent should, most definitely, be consulted. It is the proper thing to do. Of course, as your friend, I would be honored to accept this position. But I must speak with the countess before giving my answer."

And with that, Magnus held on to the small hope that this would not turn into a hell on earth.

Chapter Nineteen

❧

MUCH TO VERITY'S regret, Lady Broadbent was more than thrilled by the prospect of her playing chaperone to Miss Snow. She claimed to have been feeling pangs of guilt over the fact that she spent most of her time at the town house. So this was the perfect solution. At least, for *her*.

But as far as Verity was concerned, it was far from perfect.

She enjoyed the time spent with Anna, experiencing the sights and sounds of London. But the problem was, the memories she was creating would forever include Longhurst. Which was the last thing she wanted.

Not only that, but it was hardly enjoyable to be present for every carriage ride and conversation that her new friend had with the man who'd once kissed the stuffing out of her.

Nevertheless, she persevered and kept her attention on all the fun she was having.

The opera was a feast for her senses . . . as long as she didn't think about how breathtakingly handsome Magnus looked in yards of tailored black superfine, set off by a snow-white cravat against his swarthy skin.

The evening after that, the fireworks and music at Vauxhall were thrilling . . . as long as she chose to forget the moment when the sky had burst with light and color so bright that she caught sight of Magnus looking at her and not the display. It had made her stomach flip.

And yesterday's outing to Gunter's had been positively delicious . . . as long as she didn't think about the way her knee had brushed against his beneath the table, more than once. She couldn't even remember what flavor of ice cream she'd eaten.

What surprised her the most, however, was her unwarranted and unwanted fame.

She had feared that her last name would incite the scorn of society. But you give one compliment to a man on the quality of his toupee and, before you know it, suddenly you're a wit and people take notice of you. Whether you want them to or not.

And she, most fervently, did not.

A chaperone wasn't supposed to be surrounded by gentlemen. Sometimes they paid more attention to her than to her charge. It wasn't out of any desire for courtship, of course. They were simply waiting for her next bold observation.

Some were rather persistent, lining up the fellows in their coterie to be given a proper set-down for their evening's amusement. And when she politely declined, they had resorted to inviting her to dance.

Anna provided no assistance in this matter, but pestered her into accepting. And so, Verity did. Twice that evening.

Had she known that her continued foray into the realm of utter honesty would have such a consequence, she would have taken a vow of silence instead.

But the worst thing about being in London was Longhurst's growing—or should she say, *growling*—irritation at her.

Lately, it seemed to have reached its zenith.

He'd concealed it much better in Addlewick. Or, perhaps, his ongoing silence was his way of making an effort. She wasn't certain, but it was beginning to vex her.

Whenever he was waiting at the bottom of the stairs, before they left to meet Miss Snow, his impatient gaze would rake over her from head to toe and he would say nothing. Not a single word. Not about her appearance, her punctuality or even the weather. He simply looked at her with those dark eyes, barely surrounded by a sliver of burning amber as if he wanted to throttle her.

And she felt like an utter fool.

Ever since he'd kissed her in the river and she'd kissed him by the tree, she had convinced herself that, whenever he looked capable of throttling, it was actually kissing he had on his mind.

Clearly, she'd been wrong. And their kiss was likely just as he'd said—a mistake.

All in all, she felt that throughout her entire visit to London, Longhurst was making a point to prove that he wanted absolutely nothing to do with her.

This belief was further cemented by the fact that he was looming like a dark, glowering cloud and growled whenever anyone dared to approach. Fortunately, Anna asked if he wouldn't mind fetching her a glass of punch, leaving them to enjoy some of the evening.

Glad to have a moment alone with her friend, Verity looked out among the dancers. "The gowns are so much more vibrant than when I was first out. I'd only attended one ball, but everyone was dressed in the palest pastels. And our skirts did not have the volume to burst into bloom when we twirled."

She swished her own deep burgundy skirts and grinned.

Anna did the same with her ruffled blue gown. "Then I am the cornflower to your rose. And it would be a shame if you did not dance the waltz. Wouldn't you agree, Long-hurst?"

Verity closed her eyes, muttering *Drat!* beneath her breath. He was supposed to be fetching punch. Whyever did he have to be so efficient? Couldn't he have lingered at the refreshment table for the next hour or so? Now the comment made it seem as though she were begging for a partner.

"Indeed, I have no desire to dance. I was merely admiring the gowns," she interjected. "Besides, the waltz should be yours. The two of you."

She gestured to the pair of them and surreptitiously shook her head at Longhurst, silently warning, *Don't you dare play the gentleman.*

Unfortunately, whatever ability he'd once had to read her thoughts, and she his, was gone. Because, in the next moment, he handed Miss Snow her glass of punch and set the other down on a nearby pedestal.

He inclined his head, his palm extended. "Miss Hartley, would you do me the honor?"

Damn it all to Hades! If there was one thing worse than waltzing with a man who despised you, it was having him goaded into it.

Left without a choice, she gave him her hand as the orchestra struck a chord that sent a tremor through her.

Then off they went. There was no hesitation or misstep this time. But it was still awful because her body fit into the frame of his like a hand to a favorite glove. If she were of a romantic nature like her mother, she might have issued a soft sigh or thought how perfectly they moved, turning together on the dance floor.

Thankfully, she was sensible enough to know that it was his skill alone, his command of every movement that gave her a sense of floating around the ballroom like a downy feather caught in a whirlwind.

It wasn't romantic at all. Not in the least.

"Must you hold me so close?" she groused, trying not to enjoy the feeling of being in his arms again.

Though, it was almost impossible since her blood was

fizzing like champagne in her veins and her lungs were filled with clouds. He was such an exceptional dancer, and they really did move well together. She hated it.

He wasn't looking at her, but just above the braided twist of her hair, until she spoke. Then his gaze settled on hers and it was throttlingly dark. "This is the only way to save my toes."

She scoffed. "It was *one* time and I was taken off guard."

He pulled her a fraction closer, and dimly she wondered if he noticed her new gown or the way it clung to her torso as none of her older dresses had. Her corset was new as well, longer than the others she'd worn and with gusseted cups that lifted her breasts.

Yet, as his fingers flexed on the silk and his gaze dipped briefly to her bare shoulder, he said nothing of her appearance. He never did.

Well, except for that one time beside the river.

"Regardless," he said, "it is a man's duty to prepare for the worst."

"Which is precisely what you tell yourself before you look in the mirror each morning."

"Peering through my keyhole, are you? I'm not surprised. Everywhere I turn, you are always there. Never giving me a moment's peace."

"*Me?* I have been avoiding you like the plague."

"If these past days speak of your efforts, then the black death is surely upon me."

"As if I would wish to spend a single moment in your company when you treat me as though—" Hearing a catch in her voice, she broke off and averted her gaze. She refused to let him know that the daggers they'd been flinging at each other had hit the mark. "Oh, will this music ever end?"

And just then, it did.

She would wait to exhale with relief until after he was no longer at her side.

However, instead of returning her to Anna, he directed them through the open, linen-swathed doors leading to the terrace.

They weren't alone. The cool evening air had attracted a handful of couples to stand at the balustrade and stare up at the stars, so it wasn't at all scandalous. Additionally, the fact that she was a spinster and chaperone to his would-be fiancée would make any conversation between them draw little attention. It would likely be seen as a gentleman keeping a little old lady from slipping on the terrace stones.

But he walked with purpose. In fact, he didn't stop until he led her to the far end and around the side of the house that was eclipsed in shadow.

Then her breath caught when he took her by the shoulders and his head bent.

Was he going to kiss her? Was that the reason his eyes were so—

"This game you are playing must stop here," he said tersely.

She was confused by the low warning, and so was her body. His nearness made her heart quicken. Her bones softened, wanting to bend toward him. But his cold vehemence unsettled her stomach.

"I don't know what you mean."

"Come now, Verity. We both know you are far too clever to act oblivious. And it is unsuitable for a chaperone to lure a swarm of men around her like bees to a honeypot."

"*Lure.* How ridiculous you sound. You know very well I could do nothing of the sort."

"Stop pretending you have no idea how captivating

you are," he snarled and continued as if he hadn't just dissolved the ground from beneath her feet and stole the breath from her body. "I have a meeting with Mr. Snow at the end of the week to discuss my suit for his daughter. Do you think that will go in my favor with you constantly between us? Everywhere I turn, you are there. You're in my house, in my carriage, in my—"

Longhurst broke off at a glance to his hands on her shoulders. His fingers flexed and, for the barest instant, she felt herself being drawn closer.

Then he released her.

Befuddled by what he'd said and what—she imagined—he'd almost done, she teetered back on her heels. Yet, somehow, she managed to stay upright. Which was good because he had turned away, his attention on the darkness where the torchlight did not reach.

His shoulders were stiff, his form unforgiving. She saw the struggle within him, tension vibrating from him in waves that nearly made the darker part of him shimmer.

This was her fault, she knew. If not for her lie, he would be betrothed by now.

That was what he'd wanted all along. He certainly didn't need someone from a family he hated to interfere with his plans. And she had no doubt that he had considered every aspect of what a marriage to Anna would mean for himself, his family and for his bride.

Verity was in the way of all this. Not because she actually believed he thought she was beautiful. She had enough experience to the contrary to refute such a declaration made in the heat of the moment. No, indeed. He was just under a great deal of strain and—as he'd said—she was between him and what he wanted. Obviously, the words had been meant as an accusation, more cannon fodder for their constant argument.

Though, even with that understanding, she had to fight the urge to go to his side, to soothe him, to smooth her hands down the back of his nape and over his brow.

Somewhere along the way, she'd developed a fondness for this ill-tempered duke. *I am such an idiot.*

She expelled a heavy breath and clasped her hands. "I'll inform Anna that I will no longer be her chaperone, but I won't mention our conversation."

He nodded once. "And I'll spend more time at my club during the day."

"You're hardly home as it is."

"*Home?* It is not your home, Miss Hartley. Never forget that."

She swallowed thickly, feeling the strain of all this animosity collect in the back of her throat and sting the corners of her eyes. "Understood."

He escorted her back into the ballroom, just as a new dance was beginning.

Strange, but it had seemed as if a lifetime had flashed by out on the terrace. In truth, it was only a few minutes. And as they reached Anna's side, he bowed and asked her to dance. As if Verity wasn't even there.

Unable to watch them together, she slipped away to the retiring room, feeling fragile and in need of putting herself together.

Unfortunately, that would have to wait. Because the very last person she wanted to see found her just as she mounted the final stair and entered the corridor. The *Tick*.

This wasn't the first time they'd been invited to the same party. In fact, it seemed they were always forced to acknowledge each other with a tight smile.

Nell Hunnicutt, dressed in serpent green, sneered in her usual sour manner. "Why, if it isn't my *old* friend, Miss Hartley."

"Miss Hunnicutt," she said noticing the inflection, even

above the din of the orchestra playing directly below. But she refused to take the bait.

When she continued down the corridor, Nell snared her arm just as a maidservant passed by.

Verity would have jerked away but didn't want to make a scene. She had already caused enough of those to last a lifetime.

"I saw your waltz with the duke," the Tick said. "It was rather pathetic the way you clung to him, my dear. Is that why you became Miss Snow's friend, so that you could spend more time mooning over him? I certainly hope you don't actually think that you could ever compete with an heiress when you are just a poor, ill-bred country spinster with nothing to offer."

The insecurities that Verity had fought to control for most of her life suddenly seemed as if they'd jumped out of a locked trunk and were now parading naked around for all to see. But she refused to give Nell the satisfaction of knowing that she'd struck her target.

Instead, she drew in a slow, steadying breath and squared her shoulders. "Don't look now, but you are very close to being a country spinster yourself. And I have to wonder where all your admirers have gone. Wasn't it a knight, a viscount and a marquess all vying for your hand? What happened? Did they all go on holiday together?"

The Tick's eyes thinned with pure malice as she advanced on her, forcing Verity to take a step back. "I don't know if you're aware of it, but everyone is laughing at you. The most amusing part of it all is that you actually believe these members of the *haute ton* think you're a clever wit and that's why they are paying attention to you. And there you are, smiling through it all, completely oblivious."

It wasn't true. She told herself that it wasn't true. And yet, it was the word *oblivious*—the same word that Longhurst had just used a moment ago—that made her second-guess herself.

She wasn't even aware that Nell had backed her into a doorway until she was shoved.

Shocked, Verity stumbled back on a gasp. Then she tripped over something on the floor and fell flat on her bottom.

Stunned and smarting, she was about to unleash her outrage . . . just as a wealth of linens toppled down over her head.

No. Not a closet, she thought, batting the fabrics away.

She tried to right herself and scramble to her feet, but her limbs turned sluggish as cold dread sluiced through her veins.

When she heard the creak of the hinges, she looked up in time to see a malicious gleam in Nell's eyes. She swallowed thickly and tried to keep the rising panic from her voice. "Don't do this. Please. I'm beg—"

The door closed. And there was a tittering laugh on the other side. "Enjoy the rest of the ball, my dear."

Blindly, Verity scratched at the door, clawing at the handle just as the key turned in the lock.

Oh, how she hated closets. Her lungs cinched tight, making it hard to breathe.

"You're not going to panic, Verity," she said to herself, her voice frayed and panting, barely audible even to her own ears. "You're going to . . . knock on the door and that maidservant will come by . . . eventually . . . and let you out. There's nothing to be . . . afraid of."

And yet, as she knocked and knocked, rapping on the door until her knuckles ached, no one came. All she could hear was the swell of the music below as the orchestra played a lively country dance.

"Those aren't screams," she told herself. "Those are only violins."

But even though she was trying to be brave, the darkness threatened to close in on her, robbing her of rational thought. Suffocating her.

Then a sharp, haunting sound pierced the air. She was sure it wasn't just the violins.

The sound reminded her of the day, long ago, when all she could do was listen to her sister's screams on the other side of the door. And in that moment, she knew that the nightmare had won.

Chapter Twenty

～

$\mathcal{A}$FTER THEIR LENGTHY set, Magnus escorted Miss Snow from the dance floor.

Along the way, they witnessed a bit of tomfoolery with a crowd of cubs, barely old enough to shave, playfully passing a debutante's dance card between them as she squealed with delight. Her chaperone soon swooped in to bring the young bucks to heel and scold her charge.

Across the ballroom, one of the servants stood too close to the sconce and his wig caught fire. A nearby matron screamed at the top of her lungs, then summarily fainted on the spot. The stoic servant merely patted his head and immediately went to aid the woman, who already had a crowd gathered around her.

After a whiff of a vinaigrette, she was right as rain.

"Well, that was quite the commotion," Miss Snow said. "Thankfully, it seems all is well."

But Magnus was no longer paying attention. His gaze was sweeping the ballroom. "I don't see Miss Hartley, do you?"

"I thought she would be right here," she answered when he stopped near the archway leading up to the retiring chamber. It was where he last saw Verity and expected her to have been once more.

He was worried that he'd been too harsh on the terrace. Oh, who was he trying to fool? He knew he had been.

The only reason he'd danced with Verity was for the

chance to speak with her privately. He'd wanted to ask her plainly to stop being Miss Snow's chaperone. And yet, the instant he'd felt her in his arms, all his better intentions fled as his damnable desire flared.

Feeling like a prisoner to his own body, he'd become ill-tempered and readily foisted the blame onto her for his mood. He convinced himself that she'd been trying to make him jealous all week.

In the back of his mind, however, he knew that if he felt nothing of the sort, he never would have lashed out so churlishly.

Additionally, he knew that her friendship with Miss Snow was genuine. There was nothing conniving or scheming in it. They simply enjoyed one another's company.

The problem was all his own. And it was his own responsibility to deal with it.

But that didn't change the fact that he wanted—*needed*—Verity out of his life. For good.

"Perhaps, she is still upstairs." He received an alert glance from his companion, and realized too late that he'd just admitted to paying close attention to where she'd gone earlier.

She smiled softly. "I'll just be a minute."

He watched as she climbed the stairs, then turned his gaze to the ballroom once more, looking for each one of Miss Hartley's admirers and ensuring they were all present and accounted for.

They were. Which eased his mind marginally.

But his thoughts were so distracted that when he turned, he came face-to-face with Mrs. Hunnicutt and her daughter. He bit back an inner groan, wishing he'd seen the last of this pair. And then, recalling that day on the pavement, he had to rein in his temper and not demand Miss Hunnicutt to answer for her actions.

"Your Grace, what a pleasant surprise," the mother said with a simpering smile. "And here you are without a partner."

Before the woman could continue with an explanation on how available her own progeny was at that moment, he cut in with, "Actually, I am waiting for my partner, ma'am."

"Oh? And would that be Miss Snow or"—the daughter flashed a grin that slithered down his spine—"Miss Hartley?"

Magnus did not deign to respond. He simply inclined his head and turned toward the stairs.

Miss Snow appeared at once, her troubled expression causing a jolt of alarm to trample through him. "Longhurst, might I speak with you for a moment? Upstairs?"

Since it was frowned upon for a gentleman to step into the corridor of the ladies' retiring rooms, his alarm only amplified as he followed her without hesitation.

"One of the maids heard a sound from inside a closet," Miss Snow began. "She tried the door only to find it locked and the key missing. This occurred just as I passed by and, I cannot explain it, but a terrible feeling swept through me. So I knocked on the door and heard the most heart-wrenching sob answer. I am sure it is our friend. And I cannot disguise my worry for her welfare." At the top of the stairs, she laid a hand on his arm, though he wasn't sure if it was for her own comfort or his. "I have summoned the housekeeper, who holds a master key."

Was it worry or rage that caused his blood to rush like a thunderstorm in his ears?

He didn't know. But if Verity was in that closet, then someone had put her there.

The housekeeper arrived and opened the door with expedience. And there was Verity, hugging her knees to her chest.

Someone gasped. But his attention was solely on the figure huddled on the floor amidst a pile of linens.

Her skin was pale, cheeks tearstained. And her eyes—those unfathomable violet eyes that had once vexed him to no end—were now haunted, staring blindly ahead. Her knuckles were bloody as well. But her dress wasn't torn. So perhaps it had not been a man . . . And yet, he couldn't completely discount the possibility. As for her fingernails, they were all jagged and broken.

What monster had done this to her?

Lowering down, he approached her with care. "Miss Hartley?"

Verity startled at first, blinking back into awareness. Then, without warning, she launched herself at him, wrapping her arms around his neck, her face buried in his cravat. She broke on a juddering sob.

Her low keening cry made him want to commit murder for her. But all he could do was gather her close.

"Show me to your back stairs," he commanded over his shoulder. Lifting Verity in the cradle of his arms, he was careful to maneuver her through the opening without harm. "Tell no one."

The housekeeper and maid both nodded and showed him down the vacant hall, Miss Snow following close behind.

Moments later, he stepped into the carriage, shifting to situate her on the bench.

"Don't," Miss Snow implored, staying him with a beseeching look. "I think she has fallen asleep. I should hate to disturb her. If it wouldn't be too much trouble, could you continue to hold her?"

"Of course." He took the bench across from her with Verity still in his arms. It was no hardship to keep her there. In fact, he'd been reluctant to put her down at all, but that wasn't something he cared to think about.

As the carriage set off, a hundred questions tore through his mind, none of them having answers. It was difficult for him to do nothing. Until she awoke and told him who needed to be murdered, all he could do was wait.

It was enough to drive him to madness.

"I'm sure it wasn't a man," Miss Snow said gently. When he glanced at her in the lantern light, she offered a nod of reassurance and draped the carriage blanket over her friend. "The maid assured me that no gentlemen had been upstairs all evening, and that she knew this because she was bustling back and forth between the linen cupboard and the retiring chamber."

He nodded to placate her. However, he knew that a determined man was capable of anything. And there was no mistaking that something had happened to Verity to put her in this state.

Even in exhausted sleep, her breath still hitched occasionally, her body trembling, instinctively curling closer to his warmth. He would return to the house in the morning and question all the servants. Having a plan of action was the only thing to help quiet his own raging heart.

"I hate to leave her," Miss Snow said after a while, and Magnus wasn't even aware that the carriage had stopped in front of her father's town house. "But I have a feeling that she is in more capable hands. Thank you, Longhurst, for taking care of my friend."

As she reached over and touched his sleeve once more, he inclined his head. "I'll send word to you in the morning."

After the groomsmen handed her down and closed the door, Magnus did not resituate Verity so that she was on the bench beside him, but kept her on his lap. And when the carriage set off again, he lowered his head and pressed his lips to her hair, breathing in her scent.

A short while later, he felt her stir in his arms.

Drowsily, she blinked up at him, her eyes red-rimmed in the lantern light. "Longhurst? What are you doing here? Where am . . . ?" Her face paled with recollection.

His own blood turned to ice. "Who did this to you? Were you"—he swallowed—"harmed in any way?"

"No." She shook her head, having no idea the relief she'd just given him. "Not really. It was just a cruel joke, made all the worse by my childish fear of closets."

When she moved to hide her face in the cup of her hands, he gently stayed her. "You have nothing to be embarrassed about. And no one knows other than myself, Miss Snow and two servants from the household, none of whom will speak a word of this."

"The person who locked me in will likely crow over this until everyone knows."

"*Hmm*," he growled. He guessed who the culprit was at once. A wealth of fury, along with his own guilt for not having called out the villain days ago, swelled and seethed inside him.

"I plan to have a word with Miss Hunnicutt"—he saw the slight wince that confirmed his suspicion—"and her parents. I'll make sure that this is the last time she'll ever cause you trouble."

Verity searched his gaze for a moment. Then, almost belatedly, she seemed to realize her current position. Blushing, she shifted to move away from him.

But he shook his head, keeping her within the gentle protection of his arms. And when she put up no resistance, it seemed to soothe the frayed threads of his anger. "You have been here for the better part of an hour. There is no need to alter that now."

"Do you mean to tell me that Miss Snow saw all"—she gestured between them—"this?"

"Of course. In fact, she was the one who bade me to

continue to hold you in such a manner so that you could rest easier. She is concerned for you."

Verity sighed. "I will have to explain things to her. Assure her that I'm not a lunatic. I usually only suffer these on occasion and they are easily remedied with fresh air. But I think you were aware of them, at least in part."

"I saw the flash of panic in your eyes that morning I found you unchaperoned in the park," he admitted and she averted her face, her cheeks scarlet in the lamplight. Magnus never planned to go on, but to ease her embarrassment, he found himself offering more than he ever talked about before. "My father suffered similar attacks. Whereas yours require air to breathe, his caused him to retreat and lock himself away."

"That sounds awful," she said, meeting his gaze again.

"It was. He would stay in his rooms for days, sometimes weeks, refusing to come out. And, over time, the episodes weakened his heart. I would not want to see that happen to you," he added and with more force than he intended.

"Well, as long as I stay away from the wrong side of a locked closet door and avoid situations where I feel trapped, that shouldn't be a problem."

"When did this start?"

"Well, *someone* is quite the curious duke."

When her brow arched, he knew she was doing better. He likely could have set her down beside him. However, there was no reason to rush these things. "You don't have to speak of it, if that is your wish."

"I think you have a right to know after all the trouble I've put you through."

He made no comment, but waited with uncharacteristic patience, and was glad when she settled against him, her cheek resting, once more, a few inches above his heart.

"I was six years old. It began when my grandmother suffered a heart seizure in the garden, while she was watching my younger siblings play in the fountain pool. But when Honoria saw Grandmother collapse, she jumped out and fetched the nurse, who had stepped inside for a flannel to dry them off. And, from what I understand, everyone was so worried about Grandmother that they"—she paused, her breath stuttering as if she still couldn't get enough air and Magnus stroked a hand along her spine—"they weren't paying attention to little Ernest, still in the pool."

"Ernest?"

"He was Honoria's twin." There was a desolation in her voice when she spoke his name.

"I am sorry," Magnus said solemnly, wishing there was something more he could do. "I was not even aware that you had a younger brother."

"We don't really talk about him, though we probably should. He shouldn't be forgotten. But that was a devastating day for our family, as you might imagine."

He nodded with understanding, and yet . . . "Forgive me, but I'm still not certain why—"

"I went completely barmy this evening?" She attempted a self-deprecating laugh, but he could hear how embarrassed she was. "It's because of the closet. Which sounds completely idiotic when I say it aloud. But you might as well hear all of it.

"You see," she continued with patent resignation, "I had a governess who'd acted on the 'govern' aspect of her position to the letter. Whenever I strayed from her unspecified strictures of conduct, which tended to alter by the hour, she would lock me in the closet until I learned my lesson. It usually didn't last too long. At least, before Truman was sent to school. But one day—*that* day—no one came. And all I could hear were screams coming from outside. And still no one came."

His arms tightened around her. A sense of futility and a desire to comfort her were at war inside him, and he didn't know how to address this strange new emotion. All he knew was that he wished he could alter history for her.

"No one came for me until the next morning. I was embarrassed by the state I was in, humiliated by the stench coming from my clothes," she said, her voice breaking. "And when Miss Gundersen unlocked the door, she was livid. She scolded me as she scrubbed me clean, telling me that I should be thankful that she had found me, otherwise no one would have come for days and days because I was so easy to forget. She told me that no one else had been looking for me at all. And it wasn't until later that I learned what had happened."

But the damage had been done, he thought, hating that vile monster who'd had no business overseeing the care of children.

He lowered his chin to rest on her head and tried again to calm the erratic beating of his heart. "Where were your parents?"

This time, Verity didn't choose to linger in his arms.

Whipping aside the blanket, she bolted to the opposite bench, eyes flashing. "It wasn't their fault."

"I'm not suggesting it was."

She pointed her finger at him. "It was in your tone."

"I am only trying to understand. Isn't that what a sensible person would do?"

He knew his question would force her to answer, even if reluctantly.

Her shoulders twitched in a petulant shrug. "Before my father succeeded to the title, he and my mother traveled with a theatre group. We were primarily raised by our grandparents, along with a nurse, governess and tutor. Thea was not yet born. And even if my parents had been there, there's no way of knowing if anything would have been different."

"For you, it might have been," he said. "Had they been present for your childhood, perhaps your governess would not have gotten away with her actions for so long."

"I wouldn't have told them regardless, and for the same reason I never told my grandparents."

He stared across the carriage, incredulous. "Why the devil didn't you?"

"Because I didn't want to disappoint them and confess all the reasons that Miss Gundersen had to punish me. And before you judge me for that decision, I was a child."

"Damn it all, Verity. I wouldn't judge you for any of it."

She scoffed in disbelief. Then she sat back against the squabs, her arms crossed.

Frustrated, he sat back against the squabs as well, gritting his teeth. If he ever needed proof that he and Verity would never see eye to eye, it was there in the brittle silence that formed between them like a layer of thin ice over a shallow river.

"At least, tell me that your governess was sacked," he growled.

Chapter Twenty-One

※

AFTER THAT NIGHT, Verity decided to stay in her bed-chamber for a day or two. Or rather, on the balcony outside her bedchamber, for as long as possible without anyone spotting her. She still hated to be cooped up indoors.

Then a day or two turned into four. It was just too embarrassing to face Longhurst or Anna.

But on the fifth day, Lady Broadbent rapped on her door. "Miss Hartley, I've had enough, young lady."

And apparently, she had because she strolled right in, every other step punctuated by the tip of her cane thwacking against the floor.

Caught sneaking in through the window, Verity quickly smoothed her skirts and tried to look as sickly as she'd been pretending to be.

"You're coming with me to the museum," the countess announced without a by-your-leave. "Now. So put on a suitable frock. I like that green one with the buttons down the back. It's quite flattering on you."

It was also quite trim in the waist, accentuating the flare of her hips. With the gathers of fabric in the back, along with a slightly long train, it made her feel as if she had tail feathers. It was *trés à la mode* but she wasn't feeling altogether fashionable.

"I'm not certain I'm well enough." To prove it, Verity attempted a cough. But she was still dreadful at lying, because that only earned her an arched look.

Determined, the countess sifted through the wardrobe until she found the dress. Tossing it onto the bed, she turned to leave. "I'll send in your maid. In the meantime, snap out of your doldrums." Pausing at the door, she looked over her shoulder. "I don't know what happened, my dear. But, whatever it was, I know you can face it. You're no missish debutante, after all. And that's why I like you. So hop to it. Let's spend our afternoon looking at the work of dead painters and sculptors while we're still alive."

With the last statement, she tapped her cane against the floor, and Verity couldn't help but smile as she walked away.

Nevertheless, she didn't believe for a moment that her ladyship hadn't heard about the incident at the ball. People talked. That was just the way of things. Not that it mattered. It wasn't as though the closet had left her traumatized.

Well, not entirely.

There might have been a second or two when she'd imagined being locked in there overnight and not being found until morning. Completely forgotten. Until all of England heard about it. Then she would become a spectacle that everyone whispered about behind their cupped hands and fans, or tutted at with pity whenever she passed by. *"There she is. The spinster that was left behind. No one even noticed her absence."*

However, since she had survived the closet episodes in her life, in addition to living in the most meddlesome hamlet in all of England, she knew she could face whatever London doled out.

Whether she wanted to or not.

Lady Broadbent didn't know the real reason she'd been hiding herself away.

In fact, no one knew. Because no one else had been on the terrace when Longhurst had told her that he didn't want to see her anymore, and that she was ruining his life. Or something to that effect. She was paraphrasing.

But he'd made his point, nonetheless.

He wanted her to stay away from him and, for once, she agreed.

It was too confusing to be near him. How could he comfort her so tenderly and want nothing to do with her? Was it because of Miss Snow and his obligations? Or was it his lingering hatred for her family?

Whatever his reason, she wished they could at least be friends. She so wanted to be his friend. Her heart was desperate for it.

Before she left London, she would feel better knowing that he was living his life without harboring any hatred for her. Better still if he thought of her with a smile. Or thought of her at all.

As for Miss Snow, she hadn't been entirely honest in the missives they'd exchanged this week.

Verity found that it was much easier to lie on paper than in person. All week, she had written that she was unwell and unfit for callers. And it was because of the most foolish reason.

She was becoming jealous of her friend and of the life she would soon have. Which was absurd! Anna Snow was the kindest, wittiest, most generous soul and she deserved everything that was good in life. She deserved to be a duchess. Even if it killed Verity to watch it happen.

"*Ugh*," she muttered on an exhausted sigh. The countess was right. It was time to snap out of her doldrums.

∽୬৩

FROM BENEATH A wide-brimmed feathered hat, Lady Broadbent took one look at the lofty and imposing marble staircase and decided that she'd had enough of the British Museum for one afternoon.

"But don't let me stop you," she said, pursing her lips. "I'm going to have the driver take me to that little teahouse around the corner. You can join me there when you've finished."

Without waiting for a yea or nay, she struck the floor with the tip of her cane and walked to the door.

Verity didn't mind. She was actually glad to have a distraction from her constant tumultuous thoughts surrounding Longhurst. And she was determined to make at least one memory in London that didn't involve him.

She visited the Elgin Marbles first. Or was about to . . . until she saw a gentleman standing in front of the Parthenon Frieze and stopped at once.

It was none other than Baronet Reginald Kirby. Otherwise known as the man who'd left her on a bench in Hyde Park in the rain seven years ago.

She quickly turned on her heel.

It wasn't that she imagined he would remember her. He'd been far too concerned with himself and his own reputation to have given her a second thought over the years. But she fled because she didn't want to be reminded of just how forgettable she was. There was only so much trouncing one's ego could take.

So she went back out into the hall that overlooked the gallery below.

That was when she saw Longhurst. With Miss Snow, along with her maid that was trailing behind. And they were coming up the stairs. Drat!

Even though she'd gone most of this week without seeing him, she knew that, if he saw her there, he would either become cross with her all over again. Or worse, he'd look at her with pity because of how he'd found her. The image of her cowering in a closet was likely etched into his mind like a sad marble frieze.

Dithering for a moment, she looked left, then right,

then dashed across the tiled floor and slipped beneath a shadowy archway.

"Miss Hartley?" Anna called from the hall outside the partially closed door. "Strange. I was certain I just saw her."

"If so, then we're bound to see her," Longhurst added.

Standing just inside the oblong chamber, littered with the opened crates and pedestals of an unfinished exhibit, Verity heard the resignation in his voice. Her shoulders slumped.

It was worse than she'd suspected. He didn't want to see her at all.

"But what if she . . ." Anna continued, "is embarrassed about what happened and doesn't want to face us? I should hate to think that I did not do my part as a friend by assuring her of my affection. Would you mind, that is, if it isn't too much of a bother, helping me look for her? I'll go toward the exhibits at the far end and, perhaps, you could start here and we'll meet in the middle?"

"I am your servant, Miss Snow," he said.

The next thing Verity heard was the quick graceful patter of Anna's steps retreating.

Taking no chances, she slipped further into the room, her gaze fixed on the doorway. An unmistakably broad-shouldered shadow moved near the opening. Silently, she shuffled over to duck down behind a crate, in case he peered inside. But there was no doubt in her mind that the duke would put little effort into the search. It was clear she was the last person he would wish to find.

She waited in that hunched position for another minute, then two. Though, since she heard no footfalls coming her way, she stood . . . and came face-to-face with Longhurst.

A tiny shriek escaped her.

Embarrassed about being caught, she snapped at him. "Why are you sneaking up on me? And whatever are you doing here in the first place?"

"I could ask the same of you." He was standing between the crate and her path to freedom, and worse, he even took a step forward, which made her shuffle back toward the corner. "You must stop all this nonsense. I don't like it, all these days sequestering yourself in that bedchamber. You've been letting a moment of weakness run roughshod over you and I won't allow it a moment longer."

"I've been ill."

He took another step. "Don't even try to lie to me, Verity. I meant what I said. If you so much as refuse to come down to tea one more time, I will take that door off its hinges. I won't allow you to shut yourself away, or whatever game you were playing by hiding from me and Miss Snow just now."

"*Hiding?*" She issued a haughty *ha!* "I was merely exploring the . . . um . . ." She took a quick survey of the space in the dim light, trying to discern what room she might have been in. Seeing the swords and curious red armor she couldn't even hazard a guess. "Exhibit. Isn't it all so *fascina*—"

She broke off when—in the middle of making a sweeping gesture—her hand collided with a vase on the pedestal beside her.

Turning around swiftly, she grabbed it before it could crash to the floor. He rushed forward to do the same.

Then suddenly, his front was plastered to her back as he reached around her, his arms caging her in on either side as he secured the vase.

"I have it," they said at once. And then they both clarified in unison, "No. *I* have it."

All the strain must have broken something in Verity because she giggled. This was all so absurd. "Very well we both have it. But one of us is going to need to move."

"Since I have the stronger hands, you should slip out

from beneath me. There's no telling how much this thing would cost me if you broke it."

"If *I*—" She stopped on a grumble. As far as she was concerned, she wouldn't be in this predicament if he hadn't come to the museum in the first place. But she wasn't about to admit that he'd been right and she had been hiding from him. "Fine."

She tried to extricate herself from between the marble pedestal against her midriff and his solid form against her bottom, but something was wrong. She couldn't move more than an inch to the left or right. So she wiggled with more intent.

He hissed. "What seems to be the problem?"

"I think I might be caught," she said distracted by the hoarseness in his voice. Had she accidentally stepped on his foot? She lifted up to her tiptoes, just in case. But this had the unfortunate effect of causing her to teeter forward. Then to regain her balance she had to thrust her hips backward. He grunted on contact and she swiftly said, "Apologies. But I think my skirts are snagged on something."

"It's likely my watch fob. Here," he said abruptly and released the vase.

But she didn't have a firm hold on it and bobbled it in her grasp.

He lurched forward again, bending over her *and* bending her over the top of the pedestal. Well, this was rather . . . awkward.

His curse was low in her ear, his weight warm and solid along her back, bottom and thighs. He swallowed audibly. "Is it too heavy for you?"

She wet her lips, her breaths coming up short. "I don't mind."

"The vase, Verity. Is the vase too heavy for you? And be honest."

"Of course, I would be honest and tell you if I—" His growl of impatience cut her off. "Yes. It's too heavy. I only have it by my fingertips."

"Then reach back and try to unhook the fob from your skirts."

She nodded mutely and carefully let go of the vase.

When she did, she was forced to wiggle again in order to reach the place between them. She heard his quick intake of breath as her hand fanned out.

"That's *not* the watch fob," he said in a strangled voice.

Oh. *Ohhh.* The vision of her mother's sock puppet play suddenly swam to the forefront of her mind, but she shook her head to free herself from the thought. *And* the curiosity. This was hardly the time, after all.

Sliding her hand away—though she might have been a tad unhurried in her retreat—she located the fob.

The trouble became glaringly obvious. It was hooked on the buttons of her worsted skirt. And if the dratted thing wasn't so close fitting around her waist and hips, she might have been able to maneuver it out of the way.

As it was, it took a moment to finally unpin his fob and extricate herself.

When she did, he stood erect and lowered the vase to the pedestal. While his back was to her, she managed to untangle the mess and save the button. "Here is your watch fob."

"Set it down on the crate," he said without turning to take it from her outstretched hand.

"Are you so angry that you cannot even look at me?"

"No."

"Then it's because of me, isn't it? I know I was pathetic that night. A complete and utter mess. But I appreciate how kind you were. In fact, that's the reason I—"

"Damnation, Verity! I need a bloody moment," he growled, tossing a glance over his shoulder. Then he closed his eyes. "No. Don't look at me like that because then I will have to take you in my arms and hold you while I apologize for being such an arse. And I know I'm being an arse, but it is for the best."

She sniffed and thrust out her chin. "Fine. If you want to be surly, then you are better off alone."

It took effort, but she held her head high as she walked around the crate. And she waited until she slipped out the door before quickly swiping at the wetness gathering along the lower rims of her eyes.

Honestly, she didn't know why she let him affect her so. He'd made no secret of hating her from the very beginning.

It was just that, somewhere along the way, she had stopped hating him quite so much. And all this not hating him was making her heart ache.

Chapter Twenty-Two

❧

MAGNUS LEFT THE museum with Miss Snow. He stayed for tea at her father's house. But he was not much for conversation and didn't linger.

After sending a note that he wouldn't be home for dinner, he went to his club instead. He was in a mood for a darkly paneled room and a chair to brood in near the fire.

Tomorrow evening, he planned to meet again with Mr. Snow and come to an agreement. Then, by the end of the night, he would set a date for the wedding, contact Mr. Eugene, secure the post for his brother and ensure the longevity of the Longhurst legacy. That, after all, had been his primary objective from the beginning.

And yet, as he stared into the flames licking over the grate in the backgammon room, his thoughts turned again and again to the very woman he was trying to purge from his mind.

Of course, it didn't help that everything seemed to be conspiring against him.

At the tables in the same room, he overheard two gentlemen talking about horseflesh and Rotten Row. But all his mind conjured was himself racing on a towpath cut between tall grasses and the tree line, spurring his horse until Verity fell in a supple tangle of limbs into his arms.

Then someone else spoke of course fishing on the river. But any mention of that certain body of water flooded

Magnus with lush, forbidden memories that still haunted him every night.

Another man brought up waltzing at Almack's and Magnus growled in frustration. Then, when he heard a conversation about the latest exhibit at the museum, he gave up.

He'd had enough.

Something had to be done. He had far too much at stake to let any minor attraction stand in his way.

The problem was, there was something that kept pulling him to her time and time again. Some demented part of him that wanted to see the impish gleam in her eyes as she challenged him, to hear her thoughts and the honeyed sound of her voice . . .

It was driving him mad. And the fact that she'd been sequestering herself away made him livid.

She was far too strong to give in to such behavior, or allow someone as insignificant as Nell Hunnicutt to make her doubt herself for a single moment. If Verity had bothered to come out of her room, he would have told her just that and welcomed any argument she fired at him in return.

In the past week, there had been times when he couldn't sleep. And during those dangerous midnight hours, he'd been tempted to knock on her bedchamber door, if only to wake her, to talk to her, or say nothing at all. Something. Anything.

But Magnus never knocked. And he never would.

He left the club, disturbed by his thoughts.

In the carriage, he made the decision to send Miss Hartley back to Addlewick. That was the only solution. But the matter would have to wait until morning.

It was late by the time he came home. Even the servants had already retired, the sconces extinguished. The pressing stillness of night filled the quiet foyer. And in a room up a scant number of stairs, the woman who vexed him more than anyone he'd ever known, lay peacefully sleeping.

Damn. He needed a drink.

Striding down the corridor toward his study, he saw a glow of light shining on the floor and knew Dodson had left a fire in the grate for his return. And yet, he also saw a faint sliver of gold slipping through the crack in the library door across the hall.

His footsteps paused as something heavy dropped in his stomach, settling low with instinctive knowledge.

There was only one person who would be perusing the shelves at this hour.

He told himself to walk on. To leave the matter alone. She would be gone tomorrow. There was no reason to suffer through another encounter when his nerves were already so frayed.

And yet, he felt himself take a step in the wrong direction. Saw the way his hand shook as he reached for the door as though he'd already had too much to drink, when the opposite was true.

I'll simply take a quick look around the room, then I'll go, he reasoned. After all, it was his duty to ensure that all was well beneath this roof. He wouldn't have been able to sleep otherwise.

But the sight that greeted him went far from easing his mind.

He saw her high on the ladder with one foot on the rung, the other in the air. She had one hand on the rail, the other holding a chamberstick to illuminate the spines while she stretched like a circus performer on a trapeze and reached over as far as she could.

"Miss Hartley, what the blazes are you doing?"

Startled, she dropped the candle. It sputtered out on the way down, leaving the room lit only by embers.

He heard a *whoops* and then a *drat* before his eyes adjusted to the dim light and he saw her dangling from the ladder, her bare toes skating in the air beneath a white hem.

He stormed across the room in two strides, just as the ladder jolted into motion and she fell.

Thankfully, he was gaining experience with this particular female dangling from high places and he caught her handily.

Though, it likely wasn't the best decision to lower her to the floor so slowly, or to draw in a deep honeysuckle breath that momentarily addled his wits. So much so that he had to lean against the shelves for support.

Or rather, lean against *her* as she leaned against the shelves.

He should probably step away. And remind himself of all the reasons why it was a terrible idea to be this close to her.

"The ladder was stuck," she said looking up at him, her hands perched on his shoulders. "I was trying to jostle it into motion so that I wouldn't have to climb all the way down and move it in order to . . ." Her words trailed off as she studied him quizzically. "Surely, you couldn't be ready to throttle me over that."

He didn't bother to correct her. He just nodded as his gaze traveled from her eyes to her lips. "I think I could be."

Throttling sounded like a better idea than what he was actually thinking of doing.

"But it was hardly my fau—"

It was madness that drove him to kiss her, to silence her words, to feed the desperate hunger that had been gnawing at him for weeks.

He told himself, *Just this once, then I'll go.*

And he meant it, too.

But when she sighed into his mouth and twined her arms around his neck, with her unbound breasts pressed so tantalizingly against him, he thought one more kiss surely wouldn't hurt. It might even help him get her out of his system.

Needing to be rid of the Verity Hartley plague, he was thorough. He left no stone unturned, no humid recess unexplored.

He drank in all of her sounds, gorging himself on every mewl and purr. He even let her shove the coat from his shoulders. It freed him to hold her closer, to memorize every curve and cove until there would be nothing left to speculate over during his sleepless nights.

Once his curiosity was sated, he would be able to walk away.

But not yet.

Just a little longer, he told himself. *And I won't, absolutely will not, slide my hand along her ribcage to cup her full, lush breasts*—damn he was already doing it. *Well, I won't caress*—he cursed again as she thrust the perfect weight into his palm and made the most delicious needy sounds.

He was helpless to resist.

Nevertheless, he told himself as his lips coasted down her throat, *I will not unbutton her dressing gown. At least, not all the way. Very well, I'll just try not to notice the inviting, dusky peaks outlined through the thin cambric, or the enticing shadow of her sex. I'll only steal inside the dressing gown and hold her trembling body against mine.*

He groaned. She fit him as though her body were tailored to his form. Her soft valleys and coves fashioned to embrace his hard planes, to cradle the thick jutting length straining against his fall front.

Her silken sigh floated into his mouth. He could taste the anise tooth powder on her breath and a vision of her nightly ritual swam inside his mind: washing her face, brushing her teeth, plaiting her hair, removing her garments one by one until she stood naked in the moonlight. And oh, how he was jealous of the moonlight.

"Your heart is racing like mine," she whispered, her

lips trailing along his jaw. "So it isn't only throttling, after all. You do feel something for me, don't you?"

It was less of a question and more of a triumphant declaration as she boldly nipped his earlobe. The graze of her teeth on his flesh, combined with the teasing heat of her breath that swirled into the whorls of his ear, sent desire bolting through him, more intense than he'd ever known.

It let something loose inside of him. Something raw and feral.

An indecipherable sound rumbled in his throat as his hands delved into the untamed tresses that had escaped her plait. And this time, when he took her mouth, there wasn't any voice in his head telling him not to.

She had unleashed his desire, and he was lost to it.

Shifting his stance, he insinuated his thigh between hers, tasting her sweet gasp on his tongue. Then she hitched reflexively against him. The movement was like a siren's call, drawing his hands down her tapered waist, the flare of her hips, to the taut globes of her buttocks.

There was a wild, dazed look in her heavy-lidded eyes that he understood. So he gripped her and slid her higher, lifting her to her toes, urging her into a slow, methodical canter as he kissed her deeply.

And she kissed him back with equal fervor, riding his thigh, her hip rolling against the turgid length of his cock.

He felt like a beast as he tugged on the beribboned bow of her night rail, dragged down her bodice to expose her shoulders, then further down to reveal the creamy swells to the ember light. A grunt of satisfaction rumbled in his throat as he lifted the perfectly rounded weight and claimed the first rosy pebbled tip.

"*Magnus*," she rasped, her arms slipping free of her sleeves, hands threading in his hair as he suckled her ripe, tender flesh.

Urging her hips into a faster rhythm, he took her other

breast into his mouth, swirling his tongue around the ruched flesh, flicking the budded center before drawing her deeper. Her back arched, garbled pleas of pleasure tearing from her throat. And when her body shuddered on a choked cry, his mouth crushed hers, capturing the sound, devouring it.

She clung to him as his hips rocked against hers, drawing out every last ounce of carnal bliss until he nearly followed her over the edge. Then she sagged against him.

Panting, she rested her cheek above his hammering heart. "That was . . . some kiss. I finally understand . . . why Lady Content was always having convulsions around Lord Turgid."

Magnus didn't understand any of that. At the moment, he wasn't sure he knew what words were. But he was all too aware of her unbound and bared breasts, the impossible softness of her skin, the humid heat between her thighs, and the unquenched arousal still simmering in his blood.

As his fingertips traced along her sides and the delicate ladder of her spine, she stretched against him contentedly. And when she smiled up at him without the slightest degree of maidenly shyness, he knew he was too far gone to resist her.

He even reasoned that this was inevitable. Only, he'd been too stubborn to see it before.

This is the only way, he thought. The only way to get her out of his system. And she had to know it as well.

After all, she was too clever to think that this was an ordinary kiss. It was a prelude to more, much more. And he would show her with his mouth, his tongue, his fingers, his—

"I have to stop," someone said against the corner of her mouth. The voice sounded a lot like his own, but far too sensible. The untamed part of him didn't want to listen. And yet, he repeated himself along the column of her throat as he chased her purring response. "I have to stop."

Smoothing her hair away from her face, he knew he should let her go. But instead of doing that, he felt himself lean in. Felt the cushion of her lips give, surrender.

Against his better judgment, he kissed her again. Hitching her higher, he was rewarded—*tortured?*—by the faint tremors of aftershocks trampling through her.

Her hands splayed over his chest and glided up to his shoulders, his nape, fitting against his scalp. She stretched to take his lobe between her teeth, her heated breath tunneling erotically inside him. "But what if I don't want you to stop?"

Devil take it. He kissed her again.

This time, he lifted her off her feet and carried her to the sofa.

Magnus settled her beneath him, his will weak from lust. He was just a man, after all. Made of flesh and bone that desperately needed to be intimately acquainted with her flesh and bones.

He rocked against her and felt the welcoming yield of her body. Her face was flushed, her lids heavy, lips parted, plump and damp. Like him, she was passion drugged . . .

But she had no idea what she was doing.

That thought was the only thing that saved him.

He lifted off her at once and crossed the room, gripping the mantel with both hands.

"I'm not in control of myself, Verity. I need you to leave the room."

"But why?"

He hated the hurt in her voice as if she imagined he was rejecting her. That she wasn't everything he craved. But he couldn't risk telling her those things. They would only lead to more complications that he didn't need.

So, he decided to be blunt. "Because I've gone too far

and now I'm seconds away from taking your innocence on the library sofa."

"Oh," she said and he heard her swallow. "And you don't . . . desire me that way?"

"If only that were the problem. Quite the opposite, unfortunately."

She was quiet for a moment. So quiet that he was tempted to look back to see if she was still there.

However, the untamed animal that she had unleashed in him knew her precise location in the room. Her sweet honeysuckle scent reached out like curling fingers through the air, luring him. And if he decided to abandon all morals, he could reach her in two strides.

So he didn't dare look back.

"And you need to marry Miss Snow," Verity said with complete understanding, but there was still hurt in her voice.

He screwed his eyes shut against the truth and against the desire to soothe her. "I will marry Miss Snow."

A moment later, he heard the soft whisper of her steps on the rug and then the door opening and closing with a click.

But he continued to grip the mantel. The temptation to call her back, to follow her, was still far too strong. The intensity of it frightened him.

As his thoughts began to clear, he understood the reason. It wasn't only lust he felt for Verity. She kindled in him a deeper sentiment that was more than a desire to claim, but a need to protect and shelter her. And it was more of a problem than he ever imagined.

He would have to go away. That was the only answer. The only way to distance himself from the temptation to forget all about his duty.

Chapter Twenty-Three

WHEN VERITY WENT downstairs the following morning, she didn't find Magnus in the breakfast room. Nor did she find him in his study a few minutes later.

She suspected that he was planning to avoid her and spend the day at his club. But she would wait him out. No matter how long it took. They had too much to discuss after last night.

The memory of it still made her blush. She never knew she was capable of such raw, uninhibited passion. In those stolen moments, every ounce of sensibility was swept away on a torrent of desire. And she hadn't been alone.

By his own admission, the self-disciplined Duke of Longhurst had nearly lost control. Which meant that what happened in the river wasn't a mistake.

Now it was all too clear that there was something undeniably potent between them. She would dare him to deny it.

"If you are looking for my son, he has gone to settle a few estate matters," the duchess intoned from the doorway of his study.

Verity turned. She pasted on a genial smile, even though she was facing someone who looked as though she'd been fed lemons all her life. "Do you know when he plans to return?"

"Not for several days. Perhaps longer."

Why, that bloody coward, she thought, her fingernails biting into her palms. How dare he just leave without saying a word!

"I have always been able to rely on my son to do his duty for the family. He has never failed me or his brother, and he never will," the duchess continued.

Verity had heard her hostess mention Rowan Warring at dinner on several occasions, speaking of him as though he were a great adventurer, always traveling from one place to another. And yet, she recalled when her brother had said that he was something of a miscreant in school, winding up in one scrape after another, and that Magnus usually had to clean up his mess.

As for Magnus, he had not mentioned his brother to her. Which left her to wonder, "What does Mr. Warring have to do with Longhurst's duty?"

"You are rather outspoken, Miss Hartley. Although it is surely no concern of yours, the marriage of my eldest son will ensure a livelihood for my youngest. And he will finally have the life promised to him before your father destroyed us all."

The scowl Verity received was so full of loathing that she flinched, but she stood her ground. "Things are not always as they appear."

"In that, we differ in our opinions. It is of little consequence, however. In a few days, you will be leaving and you can hold fast to your own opinions. In Addlewick."

"Oh?" This was news to her.

Then the duchess smiled for the very first time. "Haven't you heard? My mother mentioned a desire to return to the comforts of her own home soon. I believe she is making the arrangements as we speak."

A few minutes later, in a bedchamber up one flight of stairs, the rumor was confirmed.

Verity stood beside Lady Broadbent's vanity as her

maid dressed her hair and relayed the information that she'd just heard.

"Alas, it is true," the countess said on a taut sigh. "I had hoped that my daughter and I could resolve our difference of opinion. But after learning of my grandson's departure this morning, I realize that my efforts have been for naught."

What did Longhurst's departure have to do with the countess and her daughter? And how did his brother factor in to his potential marriage to Miss Snow?

Verity didn't understand. At the moment, she was still reeling from the fact that he was gone. And apparently she would be leaving, too.

"Then, we are returning to Addlewick."

Lady Broadbent nodded in the oval mirror, her gaze soft and kind. "I'm afraid so, my dear."

But where did this leave her and Magnus? Was there even a her and Magnus?

Her brain tsked and she rolled her eyes with reproach. *Have you learned nothing in these twenty-six years?*

Her heart gave a hopeful thump. *You are still only five and twenty for another week. And he wouldn't have kissed you that way if he felt nothing for you.*

And yet, he had decided to leave London, to leave her without a word.

Stepping over to the window, she tried to ignore the hurt his rejection caused. But this was unlike the other times she'd been left alone, wondering what was wrong with her and why she wasn't enough.

But this time, she knew the answers.

First, she was a Hartley. Second, she was not an heiress. And, in the end, those two things were all that mattered to him.

In other words, whatever was between them, wasn't what he wanted.

"If you don't mind," she said, "I think I'll go for a walk in that little park around the corner."

"That sounds like a very sensible idea, my dear."

Not entirely sensible, Verity thought when she looked up at the dark clouds overhead as she entered the park. It looked like rain. The perfect weather to match her mood. And she wasn't carrying an umbrella.

Nevertheless, she was determined to escape that house and the reminders of the night before. But no sooner had that thought entered her mind, than she saw another reminder that she was trying to avoid. *Anna*.

It was too late to turn away. Her friend saw her and waved with alacrity, already striding her way with Sebastian in tow.

"Forgive me for hailing you, stranger. But I could have sworn you resemble my friend, Miss Hartley," she said with an arched look, her lips pursed into a pout. "At least, I had thought we were friends."

All at once, Verity felt so silly for the feelings of uncertainty she'd been harboring all week, and especially for the jealousy that would never amount to anything. It wasn't as though ruining her friendship with Anna was going to win Longhurst's affection.

Embarrassment washed over her from head to toe. "Of course we are friends, and I owe you an apology. I haven't been a very good one to you."

A melodious laugh was her answer and she was instantly crushed in Anna's embrace. "All is forgiven."

"That quickly?"

"I see what you mean. I should likely make you suffer in anguish because that is how we should treat each other, hmm?" She turned to her monkey who was busily munching on what looked to be a date. "What do you think, Sebastian? Shall we shun her, or forgive her?"

As if on command, Sebastian put the fruit in his mouth and clambered up Verity's side, wrapping his arms around her neck and settling against her like an infant.

"Well, I haven't been completely honest in my letters either . . ."

"Letters!" Anna announced, giving a startled look down to the watch pinned to her spencer. Then she handed the end of the leash to Verity. "Hold this for just a moment. I'll return directly."

As she watched, Anna strode briskly down the path and took a fork to greet that same messenger from before, on the day they had first met. An envelope passed between them and then, within a minute, she was back and looking rather sheepish.

"I feel as though I should explain," she said.

Considering all that Verity had withheld from her, she shook her head. "You don't have to."

"Oh, but I must. I've been keeping this a secret for so long that I'm about to burst." She darted a glance around them, then drew in a breath. "I've been writing letters to a man."

"Love letters?" Verity's voice lifted with no meager amount of hope.

"No. Nothing of the sort."

Anna continued without noticing her companion's sullen shoulders. Sebastian, on the other hand, thought Verity needed some cheer and offered the remainder of his date, pressing it to her lips. She declined.

Anna held up the letter. "This all began one day when I answered an advertisement in the newspaper. It said 'Seeking Trojan Rocking Horse' and left instructions to send a response to the editor. Well, since my father used to make rocking horses and toys of all sorts—beautiful, wondrous things—I answered. I wrote that I might not know of a *Trojan* rocking horse, but I was sure that there was a lovely rocking horse in the warehouse and that, perhaps, we could strike a bargain."

"You didn't."

"I did, indeed. And I know how shocking it is for a woman—an unmarried woman no less—to write a man she has never met, let alone engage in matters of business with him. But I couldn't resist the temptation." She leaned in to whisper. "And it has been going on for months, now."

Verity blinked. "Surely, the matter of the rocking horse has been concluded."

Her friend shifted nervously and fidgeted with the row of pearl buttons on the side of her glove. "It was. Then he asked why there were toys gathering dust in a warehouse. I told him that my father wasn't making them any longer, but that I wished he did because I had several ideas. And then the man wrote back and asked about my ideas. Mine. Can you believe it? Men usually only care about my fortune."

For Verity, it was her lack of fortune that a certain duke cared about, along with the scandal attached to her family name. But that still didn't give him the right to leave without a word!

"But over the course of these months," Anna continued, "this man has welcomed my advice. You see, he is planning to open a small shop that sells toys and other odds and ends. However, since he doesn't want his business to fail by trying to sell the wrong toys, he solicits my opinion."

"It must be nice to have someone trust you with his thoughts. To know the inner workings of his mind and the reasons he has for making his decisions," she grumbled.

"I suppose it is," Anna said with a distracted smile.

"And in all this time, you've never met?"

She shook her head. "This is merely business. And we

would still be exchanging letters through the editor of the paper, but he wasn't certain that he trusted the editor any longer and wanted to ensure my safety." A blush climbed to her cheeks. "So, one day, he sent a messenger to me here in this park. Which was odd because no one, at least not until I met you, knew that I always brought Sebastian here on Saturdays. For a monkey, he's quite particular about the parks he visits." She laughed.

A bemused smile touched Verity's lips. "But how did this man—"

"Mr. Dashing. Or, at least, that's the moniker he uses."

"Very well, then. How did Mr. Dashing know you would be here?"

"I asked him the same question and his response was rather mysterious. He said that he has eyes and ears all over the city."

"A toy shop owner?" Verity asked.

"I think it was merely a jest and he simply didn't want to admit that we had seen each other at the newspaper office at one time. Which leads me to wonder who he really is. Nevertheless, we also have a system of sorts. At the bottom of each page, he'll write the title of a book and I'll know that I can leave my letter to him between the covers when I visit the Temple of Muses. Isn't that clever?"

At the way her friend's eyes danced, Verity issued a hum of intrigue. "It seems as though you would like to meet him."

"Oh, I'm sure he is an old man. There is a formal manner in his writing. Besides," she said, her finger tracing the wax seal, "I've already scouted out the bookstore for hours and never saw anyone other than old men interested in the titles he always chooses." She tucked the letter into her reticule and drew the strings tight. "Although, I do plan to visit his shop, whenever he should open one."

By that time, Verity would be in Addlewick and her

friend would be married to Longhurst and living in the country. But she did not mention the observation aloud.

Anna took Sebastian in her arms and then walked with her, strolling side by side as if there weren't threatening clouds looming over them. "I am surprised Longhurst hasn't found you here, yet."

"His mother informed me that he has gone to the country to see to estate matters." *The coward.* She was back to being cross with him and hoped she would stay that way.

"Has he, indeed? Well, that is interesting, isn't it?"

"I do not see why. He does whatever he pleases in the moment and thinks nothing of it afterward, apparently."

"Well, he was supposed to meet with my father this evening. Then he sent a missive asking to postpone for a few days." Stopping on the path, Anna reached out and took hold of her hand, her demeanor kind and regal, and befitting that of a future duchess. "Verity, I want you to know that, no matter what occurs in the future, you will always have my friendship."

"And you will always have mine," Verity said without hesitation, and without considering that it would be an excruciating promise to keep on the day of Anna's wedding.

But she would keep her promise, no matter what.

It rained for the next three days.

When Verity wasn't playing backgammon with Lady Broadbent, pacing the floor by the terrace doors or annoying the duchess by having a caller who actually enjoyed her company, she was writing letters to her family.

Honest and heartfelt letters about missing home, but also about feeling as though she didn't have a home where she belonged.

She even wrote to Truman, all the while knowing that his reply was unlikely. His letters had become infrequent over these last years. In fact, one of the few she'd received had been in reference to Percival Culpepper and the humiliating event that she had relayed to her most trusted confidant.

Truman's response had been brief, ending with, "Never trust a man claiming to be a friend."

The sentiment was bitter and far from the wisdom he'd usually imparted. Like her, he was a mediator in the family, keeping the peace. He was protective, too. The ideal elder brother in so many ways. But she feared that his time away had altered him greatly.

She also wrote to her parents. Though, given the fact it was in the wee hours of the morning and she'd been at the mercy of her heart instead of her head, she probably shouldn't have sent it.

In the letter she had wished that they hadn't loved each other so much. It was their fault that she believed such a love was possible even for someone as flawed as herself.

She wrote to her sisters of her friendship with Anna and about her pet monkey, knowing that Thea, in particular, would enjoy reading about his antics. And she also mentioned that her friend would be marrying Longhurst. But she didn't tell them how she felt about that.

No. That was something too raw to be scratched onto a page with pen and ink.

As the rain fell in tiny silver beads against the glass, she sat in the window seat with her arms wrapped around her bent legs and her chin resting on her knees.

With her mind on her family, sitting in this position reminded her of the last time she spoke with her father.

It had been during the days following Longhurst's surprising kiss in the river, their strained conversation after and her subsequent confusion. To sort her thoughts, she'd stopped to sit beneath a grand oak tree on a hill, overlooking the grounds of Hartley Hall.

Other country estates hosted perfectly ordinary parks, manicured lawns or even walled gardens. Verity had always been rather envious when she'd walked the grounds of those houses.

But Hartley Hall had an amphitheater.

Also known as *the pit*, the theatre was part of a natural formation of hill and hollow, the escarpment carved into three tiers of demilune seating of moss and slate. Across from it stood a round stage of flagstone with a half circle of alabaster columns lining the back, along with curved ivy-enshrouded screens on either side. When seen from the top of the hill, the stage resembled a great eye, peering up from the bowels of the earth.

Her father had come up and sat beside her, legs crossed at the ankle as he'd surveyed the pit with a proud gleam in his eye. "I marvel every time I see this. It was your brother's first architectural feat. Proof that he will be great one day. Then again," he added, his voice turning somber, "he would already be great, if not for my own mistakes."

He'd blamed himself for the fact that Truman had been fired from the apprentice firm. And even though there had been many times that she wished he'd never had anything to do with the scandal, she also knew that there was nothing any of them could do to alter the past.

There had been no reason to make him feel worse than he already did. "You have done all you could to atone for them. More than anyone will ever know."

"If not for your brother's sacrifice, we would all still be floundering."

It was with the sale of Truman's land along with Father's hunting box that had provided them with the means to purchase railway stock at its infancy. Then, once the idea of train travel started gaining popularity and the stock prices climbed, they were able to sell a few shares to make other investments.

As they well knew, speculation was a risky venture. But desperation sometimes brings men to their knees and forces them to do whatever they must to make things right again.

Yet, because experience had taught them how dangerous it was to play such a game, they didn't speak of it outside the family. No one else would ever be involved. The risks were theirs and theirs alone.

Her father never forgot the high price of involving those who didn't understand the hazards. And, as part of his own penance, he made it a practice to make amends and give back all that he could before ever taking a shilling for himself.

"Though I do wish my son would come home," he'd said, staring out across the horizon. "Family is all we have. And it has been far too long since I've seen more than his penmanship."

"I miss him, too. And I hope he has earned enough to buy land and start building the house of his dreams, so that I may finally move on with the rest of my life."

"What do you mean?"

"Surely, you have not forgotten that I am to keep house for my brother?"

Her father had blinked in confusion, his head tilting to one side. "No, I have not forgotten your mention of it, years ago. However, I had thought the plan was forged because of Mr. Culpepper."

"Why does everyone think that I wanted to marry him?" She threw up her hands. "Was I going to, if he'd asked? Well, I might have done. But that's beside the point. And it doesn't mean I ever loved him."

"No Hartley ever marries without love."

"That's easy for you to say. You and Mother still look at each other as if your hearts are set ablaze whenever your eyes meet. Not everyone is that fortunate. Some of us are so pathetic that we have to invent our great romances out of thin air. We risk people laughing at us. But we hold on to the dream—no matter how fleeting—that someone might look at us and believe that we are more precious than any fortune."

His brows had inched higher. "I don't think I've heard you speak so adamantly."

"Well, you can blame Longhurst for that. With all the arguing we've done, the door that kept my internal thoughts at bay has been incinerated. I cannot seem to lock them in any longer."

The surprise in his expression had altered to one of understanding. But it wasn't until he brushed a hand across her cheek that she realized she'd let a few tears fall. "It always happens when you least expect it."

"What does?"

He'd shaken his head in dismissal. "I'm just glad you found your voice, at last."

Now, as she sat and stared out at the London rain, she realized what her father had meant. Her voice and her heart were one and the same. And Magnus had released them both.

Little good it did her, though. He needed to marry an heiress.

She pressed her forehead to the cool glass, her sigh turning the windowpane opaque just as a knock fell on the door.

"Beg pardon, miss, but there's a letter for you," the maid said, crossing the room with the salver in hand.

Verity picked up the missive and glanced quizzically at the lack of a return address. Eager to see who had sent it, she dismissed her with a "Thank you, Polly," and opened the letter straightaway.

My dearest daughter,

I have been a selfish old fool. For years, I thought only of my own pain and that of the people who had lost

*it all. As penance, I remained silent and took all the
blame leveled at me. I did not take into consideration
the lasting ramifications it would have on my children.
I suppose, I still saw each of you in just that way—as
children. But you have all grown up while I have been in
my own world. For that, I must beg your forgiveness.*

*I have come to London to make amends. However,
in order to do that, I must expose the true blackguard
responsible.*

A jolt of alarm speared through her. There were many
men who still held a grudge against him and who had
threatened him harm should he return to London.

*I am not writing to cause you alarm, but to inform you
of my whereabouts and prepare you for the possibility of
hearing rumor of my presence here. I know you are sensible
enough to understand that this is something I must do.*

*And with that said, I must ask you to do something
for me. Return home to Hartley Hall. I would be more at
ease knowing that you were with your mother. I will send
word there, when I have any to report.*

Until then . . .

> *Your adoring father,*
> *C. H.*

Verity read the letter thrice more, her alarm rising each
time. This did not seem like a letter to prepare for any
rumors. It seemed like a farewell.

Lowering the page, there were only two thoughts running through her mind—one, that there was no way in
Hades she was returning to Addlewick now; and two, that
she was tired of being the sensible one in the family.

Chapter Twenty-Four

꧜

Magnus stood in the study at his estate, staring out the window beyond the park and bosky creek to the expanse of muddied fields and ancient groves. These lands that were part of him were also infused with his own blood and his sweat, and would be passed down to his sons in the future.

He could still feel the calluses on his hands from digging the fence posts in the distance last summer. There was a jagged scar on his thumb from shingling the stable roof. And he was proud to say that there were a dozen more from toiling over these acres.

He had come here, not to admire his own labors, but to remind himself of all the reasons he was marrying Miss Snow. In addition to her wealth, she was also intelligent, pretty, kind and well-mannered. Any man would be fortunate to wed her.

It was a sound decision.

So why couldn't he push a poor, exasperating, willful and beautiful hoyden from his mind? Why couldn't he walk his grounds without wondering if she would like them, too, and if they were wild enough to suit her nature? Why couldn't he cross the threshold of these ancient halls without craving the scent of honeysuckle in the air? And how long would these musings plague him after he married Miss Snow?

Frustrated, he lifted his arm to rake a hand through his

hair. Then he stopped himself. What was he doing? He did not fidget. He did not dither. He faced matters head-on.

Then why the devil was he in the country when he should be making arrangements with Mr. Snow?

But Magnus knew the answer.

He was running away from temptation, like a coward.

He had no doubt that Verity knew this, too. She was probably cursing him to high heaven by now. And worse, he had left her with his mother.

There would be hell to pay from both of them when he returned. He actually caught himself grinning at the thought of being railed at by that ill-tempered, violet-eyed wildling.

However, his grin abruptly faded when he imagined facing her again after the liberties he'd taken. A gentleman did not seduce a gently bred woman he had no intention of marrying.

She would have every right to hate him after what he'd done. And yet, he did not regret those stolen moments in the library. They had been the most sublime torture he'd ever experienced.

Expelling a heavy breath, he turned from the window just as his secretary appeared in the doorway.

Victor Milo did not look like the typical gentleman's secretary with a pallid complexion and drawn features from staring at ledgers all day. Instead, he was stocky like a prizefighter with red hair, a tanned face—surprisingly without any freckles—and ears large enough to sail a ship. All that mattered was that he was good at his job.

Or, at least, he had been.

"You sent for me, sir?"

Magnus went to his desk and lifted the open ledger. "Can you explain this?"

A pair of ears turned from starboard to port as he shook his head after perusing the figures. "I cannot, sir.

It appears as though the clerks at your bank have made another error."

"Another error. In *my* favor," he said flatly. "Do you know how ridiculous and corrupt that sounds?" This had happened several times over the course of the last four years. In fact, he'd grown so suspicious that he'd requested two audits on his accounts. "I want a definitive answer this time. Money does not simply appear out of nowhere."

After all, if it appeared out of nowhere, then it could leave in the same manner. There was no trusting it. No telling what might happen in the future. And he hated having no control over his own fate.

"I'm certain the explanation is perfectly innocent, sir. Perhaps the deposits are a contribution from your brother."

Mr. Milo was spared a scathing response when the butler appeared in the doorway.

"Beg pardon, Your Grace," Mr. Hamish said, bearing a silver salver as he entered the room. "An urgent missive has just arrived from London by messenger."

Frowning, Magnus tore open the letter.

To the Duke of Longhurst,

   The man who orchestrated the swindle that killed your father has returned to London.

                              Signed,
                              A friend

At once, he lowered the page. "Is the messenger still here?"

"No, sir. He just bid me to deliver it posthaste."

Magnus stood. Making a swift decision, he tucked the letter into his pocket. "Ready my carriage. I'm returning to London without delay."

Hamish nodded and left.

Milo closed the ledger and held it with both hands as

if glad that the matter of inconsistencies was settled. But Magnus wasn't done with him yet.

He slipped the ledger out of his secretary's grasp. "I'm taking this with me. We will discuss my findings in the near future."

Without another word, he went up to his room to inform his valet.

Strange, but his thoughts were not on the message, the accounts or even the culprit he might finally confront in London. They were distracted by the knowledge that Verity was there, waiting to rail at him.

Begrudgingly, he noticed a lightness to his steps on the climb and a warm ache glowed in the center of his chest. It felt something like longing.

It wasn't that, of course. A man with a set plan of action ahead of him, a life of duty, would never bother with maudlin sentiment.

Besides, he was most likely going to put her father in gaol once he finally had his confession. And that would put an end to everything that never should have happened in the first place.

❧

VERITY DIDN'T WASTE any time. The instant she finished reading her father's letter, she leaped up from the window seat and scratched out a missive to send to Anna.

Slipping on a pair of shoes, she plucked the chestnut spencer from where it was draped over the back of a chair and dashed out the door, shoving her arms into the sleeves as she went.

"Miss Hartley, really," Geraldine Warring tutted with disapproval as they nearly collided in the hallway. "And you're not even dressed. Are you really going to visit your caller in that disheveled state?"

She stopped midsleeve. "I have a caller?"

"Indeed. Miss Snow is waiting in the parlor. Dressed appropriately, I might add," she groused even as she stepped forward and tugged the form-fitted sleeve up Verity's arm. Then she situated her collar before reaching up to tuck a wayward lock of hair in place. "I am sure your mother would not wish for you to be unkempt in public. Roxana was always admired wherever she went."

"I had forgotten that you and my mother were friends," Verity said thoughtfully, seeing a different, kinder side to the dowager for the first time. She wondered what the two of them were like before everything was lost to a swindler's scheme. Had they gossiped together? Laughed over tea and cake in the parlor?

Geraldine lowered her hands and retreated a step. A wistful sadness crept over her gaze before she looked down to tug on the cuffs of her sleeves. "That was long ago. And you shouldn't keep your guest waiting."

"Yes, ma'am."

Duly dismissed, Verity issued a hasty curtsy and walked toward the stairs. She passed Lady Broadbent as she was coming out of her own chamber and sent a cheerful "Good morning, my lady" to her.

Pausing on the landing to button her spencer, Verity heard the dowager say, "I do not know what you find so appealing in her, Mother. There's something altogether too untamed in her nature."

"Perhaps, she reminds me of myself when I was younger," the countess said. "Or, perhaps, she reminds me of my daughter who once went sea bathing without a stitch of clothes."

She scoffed. "I was a child. And besides, you let my brother go sea bathing without clothes. I didn't think it was fair that I had to wear that dreadful costume."

"What about that chariot race when you were eighteen, hmm?"

Verity stilled on her last button, grinning from ear to ear as she strained to listen to more scandalous exploits.

"Hush, Mother. Someone will hear you. And besides, I was . . ."

"You were a bit untamed, too. All the best of us are, my dear."

"I was nothing of the sort."

"When you get to be my age, you'll appreciate it more." Lady Broadbent sighed. "And I had so hoped that the trait would continue on in the family."

Family! The reminder caused Verity to hasten down the remaining steps. She entered the parlor at a run, startling Anna.

"Gracious, Verity! You gave me a fright. Why are you in such a rush?"

"Have you sent your letter, yet? The one to"—she had sense enough to lower her voice—"Mr. Dashing?"

Her friend squinted in confusion, her head tilting to one side. "I was about to this very morning. Why?"

"If he truly does have eyes and ears all over the city, I might require his assistance in finding my father," she said and proceeded to explain the situation, stressing the potential danger that could be awaiting her father. "Therefore, I must urge him not to do this."

Without hesitation, Anna reached into her reticule and withdrew the letter. Standing, she crossed the parlor toward the slender desk by the window as she spoke. "I'll add a note at the bottom and request that he send his answer—if he is even able to discover something—as soon as possible. Oh dear." She paused with the quill in hand.

"You don't have to do this." Verity came to her side at once. "In fact, it was wrong of me to ask it of you."

"Don't be silly. I *want* to do this. It's only that I don't know what address to give him. After all, we may be waiting for some time and we cannot stand about in the park all day."

"I hadn't thought of that. Perhaps, it would be better not to—" She stopped as Anna scratched the nib across the page.

"Too late. I've given him my father's address. Though, he likely already knows it, regardless."

Verity laid a hand over hers. "Are you certain?"

"I am more than certain," she said with a firm nod and an upward tilt to the corner of her mouth. "And perhaps this means that I will finally meet Mr. Dashing face-to-face."

When the ink dried, she folded and sealed the letter again. Then, together, they went to the Temple of Muses to slip it into the designated book.

They waited for the better part of the day and Verity nearly gave up hope. But just as they were considering a return to the bookstore to see if the letter had even been collected, a knock fell on the door.

It was the messenger with the news that her father was staying at the Ox & Lamb. And Verity knew exactly what she had to do.

Chapter Twenty-Five

❧

WHEN MAGNUS ARRIVED in London that evening, he wondered whose carriage was waiting in front of the town house. No sooner had he mounted the stairs and entered the foyer than he had his answer from Dodson.

He was not prepared to receive Miss Snow, however. His thoughts, since leaving his country estate, remained on Hartley *and* his eldest daughter.

Striding to the parlor, he had every intention of delivering an apology and explaining that he had no time to speak with anyone at the moment. At least, until he was greeted with the worried faces of Miss Snow, his grandmother *and* his mother.

It did not escape his notice that there was one person notably absent.

"Where is Miss Hartley?"

Miss Snow stepped forward, wringing her hands. "I was hoping she would have returned by now."

"What do you mean? Why is she not here?"

"I never should have let her go alone. But she insisted. And you know how stubborn and self-assured she can be."

He did, indeed. But that did not stop the impatience and alarm sprinting through him, tightening the muscles and tendons along his neck and shoulders. "Where did she go?"

"To find her father. Apparently, he'd sent her a note, stating that he was in London on a matter of business, but she was worried and asked for my assistance to find him."

"That man," his mother said beneath her breath. "He can never leave well enough alone. And now his daughter is off gallivanting around after him as if she had no more sense than her father."

"Geraldine, I am sure that Miss Hartley wouldn't do anything reckless."

Magnus heard the worry and doubt in his grandmother's voice, and he didn't bother to explain all the other wholly reckless things Verity had already done.

He wished he'd have throttled her when he had the chance. Wished he would have done a thousand things. But that point was moot. "Miss Snow, why did she think you would know how to find him?"

"Well, not me precisely. A friend of mine, of sorts. He knows how to find people. I don't know how he does it." She turned toward the writing desk then returned holding a missive. "This came addressed to you a short while ago. Forgive me, but I opened it without thinking. I thought I recognized the—"

"That's not Verity's handwriting," he said, paying no attention to what he'd revealed in that statement as he scanned the single line written on the page. An address. Turning the page over, there was only one name— *Longhurst*—in the same slanted scrawl of the letter he'd received at his estate.

He lifted his head and regarded Miss Snow. "And how do I meet this *friend* of yours?"

"That won't be possible, I'm afraid. Not even I have met him." After that confusing declaration, she proceeded to explain the nature of her acquaintance with a certain Mr. Dashing. Then she reached out and laid a fretful hand on his arm. "You have to help her. I would never forgive myself if anything happened."

If anything happened to her, he'd . . .

Magnus couldn't finish the thought. An icy wave of

dread washed over him. No solution came to him. His mind was blank. He simply couldn't imagine a world without that vexing creature in it.

"Fear not, Miss Snow," he heard his mother say when he turned to the door. "My son never fails when a task is set before him. He always does his duty."

And yet, for the first time in his life, he wasn't thinking about his duty to his family as he strode to his carriage. He was only thinking about Verity.

THIS COULDN'T BE *correct*, Verity thought as she looked at the abandoned building. There was no sign of anyone here.

She'd taken a hackney to this narrow lane, not far from the wharf. The blackened brick facade was covered in layers of sea salt and chimney smoke, the windows dark like vacant eyes. But this was the only chance she might have to find her father before it was too late. What else could she do but dare to enter?

So, under the gray shroud of twilight, she stole inside.

With the door open, there was just enough light for her to see a row of lanterns hanging from a hook. Most were empty of oil, the metal rusting through. A few held tapers, more than half gone, but there was just enough wick left in one of them to light it with the flint and steel hanging at the end by a thin rope.

All at once, a chill, briny breeze slammed the door shut behind her with a boom. Her startled shriek pierced the sudden stillness.

Her hands trembled as she lit the lantern. Holding it aloft, the wavering light revealed a vast, open space littered with paper, boxes and crates, with debris scattered about as if it had endured a frenzy of activity, much like the parlor rug after opening presents on Christmas Eve.

There was a separate room off to the side, lined with

a bank of interior box windows with a view of this larger area. Her careful footsteps echoed to the rafters. The corresponding delay of those hollow thumps made it seem as though she were being followed. And followed so closely that she should be able to feel the stalker's breath on the back of her neck.

She turned around to check, several times, but there was no one around.

Even so, her mind whispered:

> HERE LIES VERITY HARTLEY
> BELOVED DAUGHTER AND SISTER
> AND IDIOT WHO WENT INTO A DESERTED BUILDING
> BECAUSE A STRANGER TOLD HER TO

She swallowed. "Drat, you foolish girl. What have you gotten yourself into?"

"I'd say that's an excellent question," a voice growled from the doorway.

A strangled yawp left her. She whipped around, nearly sputtering the candle in the process. And then she saw him, dark and forbidding, and striding directly toward her.

"*Longhurst!*" She splayed a hand over her rabbiting heart. "You scared me half to death."

He stopped when they were toe-to-toe, his breathing erratic, his jaw clenched. "That saves me half the effort, then. Though, I'm not certain if I should strangle you or shake you to finish the job. Devil take it, Verity! Have you lost all sense?"

"I refuse to acknowledge that insult. You may keep your unsolicited opinions to yourself." She sniffed with indignation. And yet, as she held his fiery glare, she had to admit that she felt braver now that he was here. "If you have come to berate me, then you might as well leave. I have an errand to see to and you are only standing in my way."

"I'm not going anywhere without you."

Even though the words were spoken through gritted teeth, there was something about them that made her heart quicken . . .

Until she remembered that he *had* actually left her a few days ago!

She put one hand on her hip while the other held the lantern. "Oh? And yet, you can go wherever you please without so much as a by-your-leave. One minute, you're ravishing me in the library, and the next you're scampering off to your estate. What do you have to say for yourself?"

"I had to go. I have a duty to my family and you were making it too complicated."

"Well, you at least could have left me with a note. Instead, you left me with your mother." Who, as it turned out, wasn't altogether too terrible. But that was beside the point. Still holding fast to her pique, she squared her shoulders and turned toward the attached room. "And you aren't the only one with a fierce loyalty to family. I have a duty to mine as well."

"To what? To get yourself killed?"

She rolled her eyes as she stepped through the open doorway. Inside, she saw a drafting table in the center, a pair of desks against the wall and a row of open and untidy cupboards, still littered with paper and ledgers. There were even half bottles of ink, desiccated quills and pencil stubs. It was as if a stage were set, waiting for the workers to return to the production.

"I'm looking for my father. Which, I presume, you know. Otherwise, you wouldn't be here."

"And if you hadn't found him, but someone else altogether, what was your plan then, hmm? Use your family's gift and *talk* yourself out of danger?"

She didn't care for his tone. "You clearly were not paying attention to my acting ability. Regardless, that is why I brought this."

She lifted a cobalt-handled blade from her pocket with a measure of arrogance, her brow arched in challenge. His own brows flattened.

"A letter knife? Really?" Reaching out, he seized it from her hand and coasted his thumb along the edge. It didn't break the skin. In fact, it didn't even leave a mark. "It's about as sharp as a loaf of bread."

"So? It's pointy."

"Well, that makes *all* the difference. Any man will quickly surrender if he is threatened to be pricked to death!"

Not appreciating his sarcasm, she snatched her intimidating weapon back and stuffed it in her pocket. Spotting a set of stairs in the far corner, she marched toward them. "I've changed my mind. I'm no longer glad you found me. By the by, how did you? I purposely kept the address from Anna so she wouldn't follow."

"A missive arrived addressed to me."

"For you? That's rather mysterious," she murmured, lifting her skirt to set her foot on the first tread.

He stayed her with a hand surrounding her upper arm, and she hated the way her body reacted with a tingle of gooseflesh at his touch. "Which is why we will be leaving."

"Not before I check upstairs. My father might have been here earlier and I need to find out where he has gone before he does something foolish."

"Like father like daughter."

She shrugged out of his grasp. "He isn't guilty of the crime that you've accused him of."

"I know you want to believe that," Magnus said, his tone gentler. Something troubled crossed his expression. "And, for your sake, I wish it were true. But there is a reason that he's in London at this particular time and I'm trying to protect you from learning the truth."

"You don't know the truth, Magnus."

He took her hand, his gaze imploring in the lamplight. "I don't want to see you hurt."

She felt the honesty of his words warm her heart and her fingers threaded with his. She wished she could explain everything, but those weren't her secrets to tell. "Family is all I have. Even when we don't see eye to eye, they still mean the world to me. And I must do whatever I can to help my father, no matter the sacrifice."

"Believe me, I know about the sacrifices we make for the good of our family."

He sounded defeated, resigned. And as she gazed into his eyes, everything started to make sense. It wasn't only about duty for him. It was about family.

"Your mother told me about Rowan, and that you're doing your duty in order to ensure stability for him. Is that part of the reason you're marrying Miss Snow?" When his brow furrowed, she squeezed his hand. "I'm not judging you. After all, you and I are similar. Recent events notwithstanding, I'm usually the sensible one in the family. And those of us who are born with cooler heads and reasonable hearts are often called upon to make a sacrifice for those we love. We shield them and we safeguard them to the best of our abilities. That is why I know you will understand that I have to do this for my father."

Any gentleness in his countenance vanished beneath his swift glower. "No. We are leaving here this instant. No more arguing."

She jerked her hand free of his and marched up the stairs. "What gives you the right to tell me what to do? As you have so kindly reminded me, I am nothing more than an unwelcome guest beneath your roof. But that fact will be remedied in two days. Therefore, you are free to dismiss any notion that you are responsible for my welfare."

"That is where you are wrong. To my recollection, you never formally rejected my proposal. *Therefore*, we are still betrothed and you are very much my responsibility."

She nearly tripped.

Her lips parted on her next argument, but her mind was trying to remember everything she'd said that day by the river. The problem was, her wits had been rather scrambled and nothing had been clear in that moment, or ever since.

"I'm certain I did," she lied and stormed up the remaining stairs.

"You didn't."

"Well, I release you now. We are no longer betrothed."

"That doesn't count. One cannot make any formal declarations when one is angry."

"You just made that up!" At the top, she narrowed her eyes, finger pointed. "You are trying to create some arbitrary rule in order to control me."

"To keep you safe. There is a difference."

"Not from where I'm standing," she said, then turned and stalked down the narrow corridor and through the doorway on the far side.

He was hot on her heels, incensed. "You vex me to no end."

"Good!"

"You could drive a perfectly reasonable man to madness."

"Then I finally have a talent in which I can take immense pride."

"Damn it all, Verity! Do you think I wanted to lose my head over a woman like you?"

She gasped and spun around, her heart pausing midbeat. "Did you just admit to having—"

Longhurst didn't hear her. He was too preoccupied with his rant. "Spend every waking moment thinking of you? Even at my estate I couldn't escape you. Not to mention the dreams. Those bloody dreams. I hate what you've done to me!"

She was so busy staring at him in stunned stupefaction that she paid little attention to the way he slammed the door to punctuate the last sentence.

Not until a corresponding gust of air blew out the lantern and they were suddenly pitched into darkness.

Chapter Twenty-Six

❧

As the door shut, the closed space reverberated with the thunderclap. Whatever warm thoughts Verity might have had a moment ago, were gone.

All at once, she couldn't breathe.

Blindly, she tried to make it to the door, hands outstretched, feet shuffling over the debris-strewn floor. She stumbled over the lantern that had fallen from her slack fingertips. But before she toppled end over end, she was abruptly caught and held against a solid form.

Magnus.

She clung to him. "The door. Need . . . the door."

"It's right here," he said, his voice calm, soothing as he guided her a step, then two. "You're doing splendidly. We'll be out in a mere second."

She heard the hollow scrape of his callused hand sliding down the wood. The jostle of the latch. Felt his muscles flex to pull it open. But nothing happened. He jiggled the latch again, impatient this time. And again, his muscles flexed. Still nothing.

"What's wrong?"

"Nothing. I have it all under control," he said with taut reassurance as he made another attempt. The wood groaned. He cursed. "It appears to be . . . stuck."

"*Stuck?*" Her voice cracked as her throat constricted, lungs laboring.

He placed his hands on her shoulders, rolling his palms

in circles. "See here, wildling. You're going to be just fine. You're braver than you think. And you're not alone. I'm here. The door is a little warped, but—"

"*Warped?*" She was starting to sound like a parrot. A parrot of doom. Panic sluiced through her, her words tumbling out on a frayed breath. "We're trapped and we're never getting out of here because no one will even think to look for us, and it will be days upon days, weeks even, and they won't find our lifeless bodies until it's too late."

He pulled her close, his hands stroking her back in calming passes. "Shh . . . I won't let anything happen to you. I promise."

"How can you promise that? You didn't even come prepared to rescue me with anything other than your foul temper."

"I came with a pistol and a knife in my boot. A real knife, with sharp edges and everything."

"If you are trying to tease me out of my panic, you are doing terribly."

"I don't need to resort to tricks." His lips brushed against her temple. "Because we both know that you are already brave. Perhaps even too brave for your own good, for when it comes to others, you never hesitate to act. You climb trees to rescue cats. Save frightened monkeys. Refuse to put your friend in danger by dashing off to an undisclosed location in order to ensure your father's safety."

"This sounds suspiciously like a reprimand, only spoken softly," she said, her cheek resting against his chest.

"Hmm . . . perhaps." He pressed a kiss to the top of her head. "However, I have absolutely no doubt that if you came upon someone trapped behind a closed door that you wouldn't rest until you devised a way to free them. You told me yourself that the panic you suffered when you were a child and left in the closet was because you were afraid of what your family was suffering. In other words, you had wanted to be there. *For them*."

His words penetrated through years upon years of the baggage she'd carried with her from that day. And, the more she remembered and thought about it, she realized he made sense. It was always the sound of the screams that woke her from her nightmares of that day and the sense of being cut off from her family. Trapped. Isolated.

Of course, there were other aspects surrounding those frequent episodes in the closet, primarily the fear of everyone seeing her the way the governess had—flawed, imperfect and unworthy. Easily forgotten. She'd hated that most of all.

"You think I'm being silly, don't you? That I've conjured all this out of nothing?" She flushed with embarrassment and made a paltry attempt to squirm out of his embrace. But he held fast, refusing to let her go.

"No," he said, his tone serious, solemn. "Because I understand what it's like to be unable to control what is happening on the other side of a locked door."

With those words, she remembered what he'd said to her about his father having suffered bouts of panic. *He would stay in there for days, sometimes weeks, refusing to come out. And, over time, the episodes weakened his heart.*

She wrapped her arms around Magnus, pressing her lips to the center of his chest. "It must have been hard for you, not knowing how to help your father."

His arms tightened reflexively and he drew in a deep breath before he quietly said, "Unbearable."

The gravity of that single word filled the room and, with it, a deeper understanding of the man he came to be. They both knew what it was like to be cut off from someone they loved and filled with a sense of powerlessness. But he'd had the strength and determination to push through it, while she was still fighting against it.

As if he heard her thoughts, he lifted his hand, the crook of his finger settling beneath her chin, nudging her face up toward his. Even in the darkness, she could feel the intensity of his gaze.

"I admire your strength, Verity Hartley," he said and her breath caught. "That frightened little girl you once were has become a capable, intelligent, lovely and resilient young woman. I never want you to forget that."

With his arms around her, his body so solid and immovable, she should have felt blocked in, surrounded, entombed. And yet, as her fingers flexed over the cashmere of his waistcoat, her fears began to dissipate, little by little.

She felt stronger now. Strong enough to stand on her own.

But instead of standing apart from him, she huddled closer. Not because she was afraid, but because there was no other place she'd rather be than in his embrace. Whether they were trapped in a room, locked in a broom cupboard or buried in a cave near the center of the earth, she wanted to be just like this, with him.

She took a breath, his scent a comforting elixir that unfurled the tight band around her lungs. Relaxing against him, she slid her hands to his nape and drew his mouth down to hers.

He offered no resistance. And at the first familiar press, the rest of the world fell away. Then he angled her mouth beneath his and kissed her slowly, patiently, telling her warm and tender things without words.

Only then did she forget all about her panic. Only then did she feel truly brave. Only then, did she remember his angry declaration. And her heart lifted as if pushed by a whirlwind of air. In his arms, she could soar.

He was aware of all her flaws, the very worst of her. Yet, by some miracle, he cared for her. And as he held her so securely, cradling her cheek so tenderly, she'd felt as if nothing could possibly go wrong ever again as long as they stayed just like that.

"Why does it feel like I can only breathe when you're kissing me?" she asked on a contented sigh.

"Because you're stealing all the air from my lungs. You're killing me slowly, I hope you know," he said wryly, drawing her closer.

Their lips met again in the darkness. They were both smiling.

After a moment, she tsked. "Such a shame. How much longer until I'm kissing your corpse?"

"Heartless bit of baggage," he murmured, nuzzling a place beneath her jaw as she arched her neck for him.

"Fear not, I'll say something kind at your gravesite."

"Such as?"

"Oh, I don't know. Something along the lines of how impatient, controlling and maddening you are. And in spite of it all, I happened to fall in—"

She broke off as a sudden, sharp *boom* from below drew their collective attention. It was the front door slamming, the sound muffled and distant. But the reverberations through the floor at their feet caused them both to stiffen with alertness.

Their heads turned toward the office door.

There was a faint vertical sliver of light bleeding between the wood and warped frame. For a moment, neither one of them moved out of their embrace. But it was clear that they were no longer alone in the building.

It wasn't until they heard the echo of heavy footfalls and the muted murmur of conversation that they both seemed to recall their purpose.

And their feud.

She stepped apart at once, their differences lining up between them like bars of an iron gate. He thought her father was guilty of scheming and swindling his friends out of their money. She knew the painful truth.

But still, it surprised her when Magnus reached through the proverbial bars and took her hand in his.

"Whatever it is, we'll face it together."

Verity wasn't certain exactly what he meant. However, it sounded a lot like a promise. And she found herself holding her breath once more as she nodded and held on tightly.

Together, they went to the door.

She pulled with both hands wrapped around the latch, planting her feet as she bent at the waist, hoping the plump weight of her bottom would be of some use to her for once. She even grunted for good measure. But it was no use.

"Here," he said, placing the hilt of his dirk in her hand. "Wedge this through the seam while I pull."

Though it took a couple of tries, the door finally gave in a sudden *pop* of rending wood. They pried it open to reveal a faint glow of light coming from below and she practically fell out into the narrow corridor in her haste to be delivered from that enclosed space.

Verity took in a deep breath and felt his hand close over hers. She smiled up at him. "We did it."

"That we did," he said fondly, brushing away the clinging strands of hair from her cheek. Then he slipped the blade free from her grasp and his expression turned grave. "But it isn't over yet."

Chapter Twenty-Seven

FOLLOWING THE LIGHT, they quietly crept down the stairs, toward the murmur of indistinct voices.

Magnus didn't know who was waiting below. It might have been Hartley, the mysterious Mr. Dashing or anyone for that matter. But one thing was for certain, he wanted to get Verity away from there.

In order to do that, they would have to go through the office door and the main room without being seen.

Crouching down, they made it to the bank of smudged windows flanking the lower office door. In the lamplight that vacillated as the strangers walked, he could just make out two men—one was concealed by shadow, but the other had Hartley's familiar build and blond hair.

Damn. He didn't want Verity to witness the truth about her father. After all, it was a crushing blow to lose faith in a man you've looked up to. And he couldn't bear to see her hurt.

Things had changed between them. Not just upstairs a moment ago, but a gradual change that had begun since that very first day. He could no longer deny the feelings he had for her. But they left him torn, nonetheless. And he didn't know how to honor the duty to his family, *and* the duty to his heart. It seemed an insurmountable obstacle.

Wanting to shield her as long as possible, he turned her chin to face him and put a finger to his own lips. For once, she didn't argue. When she nodded, he wondered if things had altered within her as well. Or perhaps it was merely the result of the fright she'd suffered upstairs. No matter the reason, he would protect her.

They moved quickly, but silently through the doorway and into the larger room, staying low. With the shadows concealing them, they were able to duck behind the first crate.

"So this is the London office and machine works? Not nearly as impressive as the last one I toured seven years ago," Hartley said, his grand, resonant tone impossible to mistake.

Beside him, Verity shifted as if to stand, but he rested a hand on her shoulder, silently imploring her to keep out of sight. She rolled her eyes in acquiescence.

"That was Lord Underhill's preference, as you know," the other man said.

Magnus startled as he recognized the voice. Mr. Eugene. What was the engineer doing here? Why had he agreed to meet with Hartley? Unless . . . he was being recruited into playing a part in another scheme. But Magnus didn't think the younger man would willingly fall into the same trap as before. He hoped he was right.

"Mmm," Hartley murmured speculatively. "Though, I must say, it looks authentic with all these gears and tools lying about. And what's this fancy gadget?"

"It's a gauge to measure the gears."

"Is that right? And here, I thought it was used for drafting." He issued a self-deprecating chuckle. "My son has a sliding compass exactly like this at home. Then again, I'm not an engineer."

Safely ensconced in shadows, Magnus peered over the edge of the crate and frowned. Hartley was correct. The object was for drafting, not engineering. He'd learned that from studying with Hawk. And, beside him, Verity shook her head, mirroring his own confusion.

"M-my mistake. The dim lighting is playing tricks on my eyes. That must have been accidentally dropped by one of the previous workers."

"Of course. Any error would be easy to make in all this clutter"—Hartley issued a sweeping gesture of his arm as if on a stage—"with crates and bits of whatnot looking as though they were placed here randomly and scattered about without any real purpose. Additionally, I detect a bit of nerves in that stammer."

"Well, to tell you the truth, I was afraid to m-meet you. Lord Underhill told me about you, about how you orchestrated it all. I even think he w-was afraid of you. That's the reason he didn't s-say anything at his trial," he said, taking a clumsy step back.

Magnus tensed and a sick feeling churned in his stomach.

Until that moment, he didn't realize that he'd wanted Hartley to be innocent.

But more than that, he wanted him to be innocent for Verity's sake.

He saw her brow furrow as she watched the spectacle and closed his hand over hers in reassurance. He'd given her a promise, and he'd meant it. They were in this together.

Then her father suddenly laughed, startling them both. It was a belly-full sound that rang up to the rafters. "I thought I'd recognized a kindred spirit. Silver tongues, the two of us. Though, I cannot believe it took me this long to figure it out."

Eugene shifted from one foot to the other and adjusted the handle of his satchel. He was clearly nervous about the way Hartley was acting.

The baron began to pace in a strolling fashion and wagged his finger good-naturedly. "I must say, you're very good. This mild-mannered milksop character is a crafty disguise. The crooked spectacles. The ink-stained fingers. Toss in a few stammers for effect, and I can see why my old friend was deceived. He was clever. But he never understood actors."

"I d-don't know what you mean."

"Ah, go on and take your bow, man. You've played your part." Hartley's palms met in three hollow claps. Then stopped. "Unless, of course, you're trying to impress an unseen audience. Your friend up there, for example?"

Both Magnus and Verity jolted, looking high up toward the rafters where he pointed.

A figure cloaked in shadow stood on a narrow platform, which might have resembled a catwalk above a stage if not for the ropes and pulleys rigged for lifting heavy machinery.

And Magnus hated to admit that he was somewhat confused.

Until Mr. Eugene drew a pistol from his valise.

Then everything became fatally clear.

Verity's hand flew to her mouth to stifle her gasp. Magnus reflexively reached into his coat for his own pistol. His hand curved around the grip, his thumb resting on the crosshatched curve of the flintlock.

"So is your friend the one who orchestrated the scheme all those years ago? Or was it always just you whispering into Underhill's ear? You who even took us on a tour of a foundry in Birmingham and offices in Bristol so that it was too real to be a work of fiction?" Hartley asked. "Because it certainly is not the lumbering brute you hired to follow me this evening. I assume you're only using him as a last resort."

A cold chill slithered down Magnus's spine just as he heard hard footfalls closing in from behind. He hadn't been paying attention. His primary concern was Hartley. And Verity.

He turned. But before he could withdraw his pistol, a beefy hand descended in a swoop and Verity was jerked upright on a shriek, kicking and clawing.

The brute rendered her flailing fists useless with a single arm locked across her body as he tethered her to his side. "Drop the pistol or I'll snap 'er pretty neck."

Magnus didn't hesitate. He moved his finger away from the flintlock and lowered it to the ground. All the while, his gaze shifted to Verity, trying to reassure her. And yet, he'd never known true terror in his life until this moment.

"Let go of me, you big ox!" She lashed out again and again, but to no avail.

The brute, not bothered or inconvenienced in the least, carried Verity under his arm like a sack of potatoes as he grabbed the back of Magnus's collar and cravat in a choking grip. The feel of those fingers along his nape were like the hide of an elephant. No wonder he wasn't bothered by her scratching. He probably couldn't feel it.

Shoved from behind, Magnus was marched past the crate to where Mr. Eugene stood, holding Hartley at gunpoint.

"Well, well, well," Eugene said, casually folding his spectacles and slipping them into his pocket. Gone was his stammer and his obsequious manner, his disguise fading into the slashing shadows elongating his angular features. "It appears that neither of us came alone. Longhurst, this is an unfortunate surprise. But who is this charming hellion? A wayward doxy? No, her clothes are too fine. Longhurst's mistress? Or, wait, I think I see a resemblance." He tsked. "Hartley, did you bring your daughter to the docks? For shame. So many awful things can happen to a young woman when she's in the wrong place at the wrong time."

"You think I look young?" Verity asked at the same

time Magnus growled, "Touch her and you'll die," and the baron interjected, "I've never seen her before in my life."

Mr. Eugene tutted and shook his head. "Hartley, your prowess as an actor is slipping. I saw the fear in your eyes the instant she appeared. As for you, *Your Grace*, I thought you were days away from an heiress's marriage noose. We have a bargain, after all. And I'd been told you were a man of such high morals that you would sooner die than break a promise or shirk your familial duty." He heaved out a sigh. "But I guess we all have a price. And, apparently, Hartley's little anonymous gifts have swayed you."

Magnus kept his expression neutral, giving nothing away. And yet, as the statement filtered in through all the calculations he was making to disarm the brute and to free Verity while not getting shot by Eugene, he came to a startling realization.

Hartley was responsible for the peculiar banking errors in Magnus's favor.

He didn't know how he'd managed it, but he was fairly certain he knew why.

Right then, it didn't matter. His primary focus was to see Verity to safety. And the only way to do that would be to distract Mr. Eugene long enough for Magnus to take the brute out of the equation.

"I don't want anything to do with your blood money, Hartley!" he shouted, lurching forward with his arms outstretched, on the attack. The brute held fast to his collar, not letting him advance too far.

"It wasn't like that," Verity shouted. "He was only trying to set matters right for everyone. But he was never—"

"Hush, daughter. Longhurst is correct." Hartley looked at Magnus, his gaze steady as he offered a nod. "I was trying to ease my own guilt. I took the money from the sale of my hunting box and lands to buy stocks. And when they began to earn a pretty penny, I started the payments . . ."

As Hartley continued to explain, he put more and more emphasis on the money, on the railroad stock climbing and climbing. A glance at the rapt attention from Mr. Eugene revealed that the old silver tongue was working its magic.

It was now or never.

Magnus took a step back. As the grip on his coat slackened, he shrugged out of the garment and turned swiftly, twisting the coat around the brute's arm. Wasting no time, he raised his fist and punched the bully in the chin.

But on contact, pain juddered through his own knuckles to his wrist and down his arm. The brute barely staggered. But it was enough for Verity to wriggle free.

"Run," he commanded.

But he was too late.

The instant she found her footing, Mr. Eugene pounced. Lunging forward, he hooked an arm around her throat. The barrel of the pistol pressed to her temple.

Magnus went still. So did Hartley. And behind them, the brute took them both out at the knees. He shoved them low like dogs with a brutal, biting grip on their napes.

Eugene clucked his tongue. "As I was saying—clever, but not quite clever enough."

Magnus strained to lift his head to keep his gaze on Verity. She had her chin jutting out stubbornly.

He knew that look. He'd seen it the day she'd shoved him into the river. The *I'm going to do something that you won't like* look.

He narrowed his eyes with warning. This was no time to play. His heart drummed in a deafening panic as he glanced down and saw the letter knife concealed in her grasp. It was no weapon fit for a man with a gun!

Damn it all! He had to do something!

Though, unless they all worked together, Verity could be shot. And he wouldn't take that chance.

Thinking fast, Magnus said to Eugene, "Then, perhaps, you did not know what a good actor I am. In fact, I learned a good deal from the second act of Hartley's latest production, *A Mistake of Muses*."

His gaze briefly slid to Hartley and he received a nod of quick understanding.

As he continued, he reached back toward his boot. "You see, there was this man who thought he could come along and take what didn't belong to him. He was defeated."

"Don't skim over the best part, lad," Hartley interjected. "That was my shining moment."

"I will admit that the choreography was excellent. However, my attention was snared by the third muse—"

"I don't care about a stupid play!" Eugene railed. "I am going to take Miss Hartley out that door and drive away in my carriage. After a time, my colleagues will allow you to leave. But if you ever wish to see her again, you'll deposit the £12,000 that I was promised into my account."

Verity struggled against him, her face a purplish red from being choked. Lifting her free hand, she yanked down on his sleeve and drew in a gulp of air. "I am afraid you're missing the point."

And with that last word, she raised her other hand and drove the letter knife down toward Eugene's thigh.

In the same instant, Magnus slipped the dirk from his boot, and drove it down into the brute's foot, through leather, flesh and bone.

The man wailed and bent down to reach for the handle, just as Hartley reared up. With a mighty lurch like two rams squaring off, he struck the man's head with his own.

The brute staggered back.

Two steps away, Eugene yelled as Verity reared back to clock him on the chin with the crown of her head. His choke hold went slack and she scrambled away, running toward her father.

Hartley was delivering a blow to the brute, keeping him down. Verity wasn't going to let him finish. She tugged on her father's arm, pulling him away to make their escape. And Magnus was right behind them . . .

Until he heard the cock of the pistol.

The sound stopped him in his tracks. Slowly, he turned around. "You only have one shot."

"The way I see it," Eugene said, his face contorted in a grimace of pain, "you are my only real obstacle now. Clearly, you won't give me the money. But I'll find another way. I always do. And I don't need to kill a Hartley. Whatever they might say, no one will believe them. A duke, on the other hand . . ."

He raised his arm. The barrel aimed for the center of Magnus's chest.

Hartley shouted. Verity screamed, "No!"

And then a shot rang out.

Chapter Twenty-Eight

❧

MAGNUS JUST STOOD there as the sound of the gunshot rang in his ears. It was all happening so slowly, and he wondered when he would drop to his knees. When his vision would go dark. When his last breath and his last thought of Verity would fade from his body.

Across from him, Eugene's eyes widened with shock as if he couldn't believe he'd pulled the trigger either. But then his features twisted in agony. Jagged lines erupted on his face like a lightning storm. His firing arm fell slack, hanging limply at his side as the pistol fell to the floor with a dull thud.

Then a bloom of crimson saturated the pale blue of Eugene's waistcoat.

Magnus was confused. He looked down at his own waistcoat. Numbly patted the cashmere in search of a hole. But found nothing.

Out of the corner of his eye, he saw the shadowed figure dash away, a slight limp to his gait. Until that moment, he'd forgotten about their silent audience.

Had he shot Eugene by accident? Or had he saved Magnus's life?

"You idiot!" Verity whispered. Or rather, she shouted, only he couldn't hear properly at the moment. Everything sounded distorted as if he were under water. And for some reason, he imagined he heard a whistle blowing in the distance. But his focus was on the violet eyes in front of him and the pools gathering along the lower rims. "You were shot, you fool."

He shook his head, his hand covering the fist that she pressed against his heart. "I wasn't."

She arched a brow and whipped a handkerchief from his coat pocket. Then she pressed it to the top of his ear.

He winced. And the linen came back bloody.

He investigated the warm, sticky wound and, sure enough, he'd been shot. It seemed that part of his ear was missing, a crescent shaped sliver. Taking the handkerchief, he wiped the residue from his fingers, feeling rather lucky that it wasn't worse. "It's just a graze."

"I hate you." Shimmering tears rained down her cheeks in earnest as both fists came to lie on his chest.

He smoothed away the wet trails with his thumbs. "I know you do, wildling."

It was in his mind to lower his head and kiss her just then.

Unfortunately, his hearing started to return and he heard a throat clear behind him. And he turned to see Hartley, as four men in blue tailcoats and top hats rushed in to escort the prisoners away. One member of the police, who was stocky with bright red hair, big ears and who looked oddly familiar, stopped to shake Hartley's hand.

"Apologies for the delay, Lord Hartley. Though I see you handled it quite nicely. And Miss Hartley, it's good to see you again," he said with a bow and they both smiled at him warmly.

What was Magnus missing?

"Constable Milo," Hartley said. "I should like to introduce you to the Duke of Longhurst."

Milo? Magnus felt his brow furrow. That was the surname of his secretary. "By any chance are you related to one Victor Milo?"

"My big brother, Your Grace," he supplied. "We were

fortunate that Lord Hartley offered us a place to live years ago when our father, who was once in a theatre troop, was down on his luck. The baron helped us on our feet again and recommended a good post for my brother. Treated us like family, he did."

Magnus was forced to put all the pieces together and to see the truth for himself. It seemed impossible that Hartley wasn't the villain he had created in his mind all these years. And yet, with everything that had been revealed, it appeared that Hartley was far more like the man Magnus had once admired as a boy.

He shook his head in confusion. "If you weren't guilty, then why all the anonymous payments?"

Hartley's smile fell and sadness crept over his expression like a shadow. "My own arrogance caused pain to other people, to friends who were like family to me. A man's greatest duty is to his family. In that, I am certain you understand."

Magnus met Verity's fretful gaze and he offered a solemn nod. "I do, indeed."

❧

VERITY WAS RAILED at the instant her father entered the carriage behind her. "What do you mean by rushing into danger like that? I sent you that letter because I trusted you to be sensible. Where was your head? Do you have any idea what might have happened to you?"

Kidnapping and strangulation were the first answers that sprang to mind. However, she decided to keep her mouth closed.

She knew she'd been wrong. And yet . . . "What other choice did I have? Your note was rather ominous and I was afraid for you. Did you expect me to spend the night knitting my fingers in worry until I heard from you again?"

"Yes!" he declared as if that were the logical thing.

"Utterly foolish girl. Just wait until your mother learns of this . . ."

"And does she know why you are in town? And what might have happened to *you*?"

His chin jutted forward mulishly. "That is beside the point. And, perhaps, your mother doesn't need to know everything. I daresay if she found out, she'd likely murder us both."

"You should stay at the town house tonight, Hartley," Magnus interjected, and Verity didn't know if she was more surprised by this or by having had a gun against her temple. "After everything that you've been through, and knowing how much family means, I believe it would put your mind at ease to have the assurance of being near your daughter."

Her father fell silent for a moment. The truth was, he was likely shocked, too. But then he offered a nod of acceptance. "Thank you, lad. I would. Although, if you change your mind, I'd understand that, too."

"I won't change my mind." And with that, the matter was closed.

Then her father picked up the pitchfork and torch and resumed his rant at her.

But in the meantime, Magnus said nothing. He stared stoically out the dark window, his countenance shuttered.

Verity knew that look. It was his *I must not fail in the execution of my duty* look. And it broke her heart.

She knew that he was thinking about his family and the life promised for his brother. Discovering that Mr. Eugene had orchestrated not only this, but the first scheme that had taken nearly everything from him, must have been a crushing blow.

In addition, he was probably thinking about Anna and the dowry that the Longhurst estate needed.

Even though he might have declared a certain regard

for Verity in the heat of the moment, she had enough sense to understand that tender feelings didn't fill the family coffers.

As for herself, well, she wanted more than to vex a man to distraction.

After having been left and forgotten by others, she wanted to be a man's first thought in the morning and last thought at night. She wanted her existence to matter more than breathing. Well . . . perhaps not more than breathing. That might have been asking for too much.

And yet, was it? Her parents had that kind of love, after all. And if she was going to be loved by any man, then why not be the very air that he breathed? The one he could not live without? The one he would willingly overcome any obstacle for, just to be with her?

A sigh left her. She knew that some obstacles were simply too great.

Chapter Twenty-Nine

WHEN THE THREE of them entered the town house, a shocked silence fell over the foyer as the dowager, the countess and Miss Snow rushed forward. Then, in the time it took to draw a collective breath, more ranting began. Lady Broadbent and Anna joined forces against Verity.

Anna tearfully hugged her, then threatened to kill her if she ever did anything foolish like that again.

Lady Broadbent also embraced her, but withheld the death threat in favor of a fond pat to her cheek.

Magnus's mother stiffly acknowledged her father, then took one look at Verity's soot-covered skirts and ordered hot water for her bath. Without another word or even a meager "Welcome back. I'm glad you're not dead," she retired for the evening.

After everyone had said their piece, some more than others, the foyer gradually cleared.

Her father was shown to his own guest chamber, walking up beside the countess. In the meantime, Magnus moved to the door to escort Anna home. But when he passed Verity, he didn't say a word. He simply looked at her in that silent brooding way of his as if the world were breaking over his shoulders. And then he and Anna were gone.

Verity knew that any declarations they had made earlier needed to stay in that locked room. The tender feelings they shared did not belong in this reality. He was still a duke in need of a fortune, and she was still a penniless spinster. There was no future laid out for the two of them, no matter how much she wished otherwise.

Resigned to the truth, she went up the stairs with a heavy heart and leaden feet, weary and exhausted.

But hours later, she was still unable to fall asleep.

Clarity strikes a woman when faced with death, she supposed. And all she could think about was the sound of that pistol.

The instant the gun had been fired, she'd felt her own life end. Her heart had twisted into unbearable knots, wrenched into something unrecognizable as she had been able to do nothing more than stand helplessly by. Her hands had reached out. A scream ripped from her throat. And in the space of a single heartbeat, she had died a hundred times.

She was still shaking. The events of the night seemed almost as if they were a disturbing dream. A dream that someone else had experienced and she'd only heard a tale of it.

But it was real. It had happened. And she knew she wouldn't be able to sleep—possibly ever—unless she talked to Magnus.

She couldn't let it end like this. There was so much more she wanted to say. And she needed to understand his silence, let him rail at her, throttle her. Anything.

So, she slipped into her dressing gown and left her room.

Chamberstick in hand, she crept along the corridor and up the stairs and rapped lightly on his door. But there was no answer.

Wondering if, perhaps, he'd fallen asleep, she tried the door and found it unlocked. But when she peered inside, he wasn't there.

She frowned and went off in search of him.

Verity found him in his study, his head bent, shoulders hunched as he scribbled a fury of calculations in a ledger.

He was so absorbed that he didn't even notice when she stepped into the room.

"Longhurst?"

"Yes, Verity?" he answered at once without lifting his head. Apparently, he had noticed her. So then his continued coldness was for some other reason.

After everything they had been through this evening, she was fairly sure what that was. "Are you terribly angry with me for going to that building tonight?"

"If I'm to be honest, every time I think about it, I'm torn between wanting to commit murder and whether or not to have shackles fashioned for your ankles and wrists so that I can keep you exactly where you ought to be."

She nodded to herself, having thought as much. "Would you like to rail at me?"

"Later."

"Shall I wait here, then?" she asked wryly, padding closer to his desk.

He paused only to dip the nib into the ink pot, then continued writing. "If you like."

Absently, she picked up the cloth-covered tome resting on the corner and her mouth quirked. It was a book of plays. This was far from the reading material she would have expected from him. Then again, he wasn't finished. There was a scrap of folded paper peeking out from between the pages.

Curious, she opened the book. And nearly dropped it when she recognized the bookmark.

It was the missive she had sent to him, along with his coat.

She stared at the top of his bent head, a dozen thoughts running through her mind. "I cannot believe you kept my letter."

"Saving a cat, indeed," he muttered and dipped the nib again.

His disbelief still abraded her. "I really was, you know. It isn't as though I climb trees for my own amusement."

"I should hope not."

She huffed and tucked the paper against the margin once more, ready to close the book with a snap. But a flash of violet stopped her.

She opened the book wider and saw a slender ribbon nestled against the margin. It took her a moment. Then she recalled throwing it at him in this room. But no. It couldn't be. "Is this . . . my hair ribbon?"

"I believe so." He continued scribbling.

Her heart lifted in fluttering wingbeats. "And you kept it?"

"What else was I supposed to do with it?"

"Oh, I don't know. A dozen things," she said, wishing he would lift his gaze so she could read his expression.

In her mind, they were sharing a rather romantic moment. He had kept her letter and her ribbon. Which meant that, all this time, she wasn't the only one who'd felt this way.

And yet, he couldn't spare her a glance.

A frustrated breath left her. "Longhurst, what are you doing?"

"I'm calculating."

"I gathered that, what with all the numbers and such. But *what* are you calculating?"

He took another dab of ink and resumed. "How long it will be before we can marry."

Chapter Thirty

❧

THE DUKE OF Longhurst didn't dither. He was decisive and sure. And he believed that Verity knew this about him. So when she said nothing in response to his announcement, he assumed she was waiting for him to elaborate.

He checked over his figures and absently offered, "We can be married in seven years."

"Oh?" she asked, breathless. "And when did you make this decision?"

That was a good question. But the answer wasn't simple.

He couldn't pinpoint the precise moment when his attraction to her had grown into something deeper and undeniable. Though, if he really thought about it, he would have to admit to feeling a spark in that first conversation when she'd dared to suggest that his servants might spit in his tea.

He felt his mouth twitch at the memory.

"I've known for some time," he offered, matter-of-factly. The metal nib scratched along the page as he checked his column of figures. Dimly, he thought he heard the door closing. But he knew she was still in the room because he could see her out of the corner of his eye. "According to these calculations, my estate should be earning a tidy sum and I will be a far better prospect as a potential husband. As for the longevity of the dukedom and entailed properties, that will be left up to"—he stopped when a key dropped down onto the margin of his ledger and he looked up to see that she was unfastening the top button of her dressing gown—"our sons."

"Seven years, hmm?" she asked as she leaned her hip against his desk and slid the second pearl button free.

Instantly, saliva pooled beneath his tongue, his gaze transfixed on her deft fingers and the exposed column of her throat.

"Perhaps only five, if we're"—he swallowed as a third and fourth button came free—"economical."

"I love economy."

Though, waiting five long, agonizing years seemed like undue torment. He might very well go mad by then.

"Three years. No, two," he amended when the garment parted to reveal the pink ruffled confection underneath, and the white ribbon resting beneath the hollow of her throat. "Very well, one. One year."

"*If* we're economical."

"I will live on bread and water."

She gave the ribbon a single tug and slowly untied the bow at her neck. "Surely, you'll need something more to sustain you."

Damn. He'd wasted so much time scribbling in this ledger, when the answer was right in front of him. There was no need to calculate further, and no way that either of them could wait even one year.

Pushing back the chair, he stood in front of her. "You've made me waste a lot of ink, I hope you know."

"Are you going to rail at me now?" she asked with an impish grin.

"I'm afraid so," he said gravely. "All night long."

Then he slid a hand to her nape and captured her mouth.

Verity surrendered at once, lips parting, soft, eager. And as she wriggled closer, fitting her body against his, the shutters he'd kept tightly locked throughout their ordeal were suddenly opened.

He thought about the night—his desperation to find her, his overwhelming relief, his panic, his fear, his need for her—and he poured it all into that kiss.

Holding her face in both hands, he gave her every moment that he thought they might never have. And he took every moment that she had stolen from him as life without her had flashed before his eyes.

"When you kiss me," she said, panting, her harried breaths mingling with his own, "I feel like I could burst into flames."

He kissed her again, hungry and seeking. And she met him with her own fervency, clinging to him, her hands shoving beneath his coat in a mirror of his own impatience as his mouth skimmed down her throat.

"Fear not. I'll set my lips to every burning place. Like here." Magnus opened his mouth on her tender pulse. He wanted to taste every inch of her skin, bury himself deep inside her body, then stop time and live there for an eternity. Then he lowered her night rail, exposing pearl-colored flesh to the adoring glow of the candlelight. Lifting the weight to his lips, he whispered, "And here."

He took the dusky center with a slow, wet tug.

She gasped, her hands threading through his hair.

The tender scrape of her nails fueled his desire, heating his blood as it flooded his veins, descending to his cock in thick, heavy pulses.

Boldly, she arched closer, the heated juncture of her thighs cradling him with urgency. Verity was never shy with her passion. And her wild nature drew out the beast in him.

He groaned as he drew her nipple deeper into his mouth. Gripping her hips, he pulled flush and rocked against her. But it wasn't enough. He had to feel her, to touch her.

Lifting her to the edge of his desk, he stepped between her thighs, parting them. The hem of her gown ruckled higher and his gaze dipped to the fabric bunched between them, then to her bared breasts rising and falling with every breath.

Mine, he thought with a primitive hunger as he marveled at those pale, perfect orbs filling his swarthy hands. Her cheeks were rosy, her pupils dark beneath heavy lashes. "You are so beautiful."

Her breath caught just before his mouth took hers again. He wanted to feast on her, to be the flames that licked over her skin, that consumed her.

His hands charted a path over her body, gripping, fondling. He caressed the silken skin beneath the hem, trailing higher until, at last, he brushed her dampened curls. The dew coating his fingers before he even cupped her fevered flesh. She was so wet. There was no doubt in his mind that her passion matched his own.

A tremor of longing racked his body on a stuttered breath. "And what about here, my wildling? Are you burning here, too?"

A helpless whimper tore from her throat. He devoured the sound and roused another as he skated the tip of his finger along the swollen seam, then slipped between the slick folds.

"*Yes. There,*" she cried, eyes closed as she rained kisses over his face and jaw, his throat and lips. Frantic kisses. Then slow kisses that matched his leisurely circumnavigation until she was trembling so hard that it rattled the pot of ink.

She was so close already. He could feel the tightening of the little bud. How often had he thought of her shattering for him? Beneath him? Over him? He wanted it almost as much as she surely did. But he kept her on the precipice of rapture, building her desire with every teasing stroke, refusing to take her over the edge. Not yet.

He urged her to lie back on the bed of his open ledgers. His lips trailed down her body, pausing to lave and worship her lush, perfect breasts as she quivered with unslaked desire. He circled her entrance with the tip of one finger as he kissed and nibbled down her supple belly. Skirting his tongue around the rim of her navel, he nudged the snug opening.

Her flesh clamped tightly around his finger and lust coiled low in his gut the instant he edged inside, her slick sheath griping him like a fist.

Lust coiled low in his gut as he edged inside, her slick sheath gripping him like a fist. That first slow plunge left him shaken as her back arched on a soundless gasp. In and in, with every thrust his mouth moved lower, his hand inching her hem higher until he met with the triangle of golden silk.

"*So beautiful,*" he whispered, pausing to breathe in her scent. Heat and intoxicating musk filled his lungs, making his mouth water.

She lifted her head. Her cheeks flushed bright red as she looked down at him with a mixture of desire, curiosity and the barest amount of wariness.

"I'm afraid it can't be helped," he explained. "This is the only way to quench the flames."

He gave her no time to argue. His mouth opened over that honey-sweet juncture and he groaned in near ecstasy.

She issued a startled cry. Maidenly embarrassment drew her hands to his hair, nudging him away from these private curls. But as he rolled the flat of his tongue over her—*once, twice*—her nudge altered direction.

Magnus couldn't help it; he smiled against her. Damn, but he loved her untamed passion and he wanted to drink in every drop.

He had thought about this ever since she'd first tumbled into his arms. The desire only intensified when he saw her in the river, drenched from head to toe, her dress plastered to her body like tissue paper over a confection on a hot summer's day. Even then, he'd wanted his mouth on her, tasting, licking, sucking. And now he wanted to drown in the silken, honeyed taste of her.

She was more than a fantasy now, and he learned her body with every response, shiver and sigh. She set the pace for his exploration, gripping his hair, parting her thighs.

He growled hungrily, never wanting to stop. But as his finger sank into the dewy heat, her walls clamped tight. He knew she was too far gone. So he sealed his mouth over her and suckled the tender bud. Her back arched. And when she climaxed, a wash of sweet pleasure broke over his tongue in glorious waves.

He laved her with fervent hunger, chasing every tremor, tasting every drop deep inside her honeyed cove until her exultant cries nearly drove him over the edge, and he had to grip his cock in a tight fist to rein in his control.

When her last delicious shudder faded, he stood and gathered her limp and sated body in his arms. He held her frantic heartbeat against his own, nuzzling her neck, his nose buried in the sweet fragrance of her hair as her hips cradled his turgid length.

"I want to take you to my bedchamber," he rasped, nearly choking on unspent desire.

When she leaned back just far enough to look at him, he was afraid she would refuse. He could wait until they were married, of course . . . even if it killed him.

But then she fumbled for something on the desk and held up a key. With a grin, she said, "Don't forget this."

❧

VERITY HAD NEVER ascended a staircase so swiftly in all her life. Then again, she'd never been carried in Longhurst's arms either. But he was never one for patience.

She felt the same urgency. In fact, they were barely over the threshold of his bedchamber before he corralled her against the door and their mouths met, hungrily nibbling, tasting, their bodies pressing, gripping.

Would she ever get enough of him? Impossible. From the moment he'd first crushed his mouth to hers in the river, she had thought of little else. And with every kiss, he fed her fire and ambrosia, the burn so sweet it made her long for more.

How did people survive this torment? She thought it would ease, the closer she was to him. Instead, the gnawing ache inside her only intensified as her arms twined around his neck. Her unbound breasts felt heavy, her nipples taut and tender from his ardent ministrations.

She moved closer still until there was only the barest barrier of cambric and wool between them, then nearly groaned as her body fit perfectly to his. She wanted more of him. From the sound of his gruff grunt, the way his hands fisted the fabric of her nightclothes, and the hard shape pressed thickly between them, she knew he wanted her, too.

She liked the way that tumid part of him felt against her when she wriggled, hips against hips, trying to get closer still. Her heart began to race, the beats too fast to count as if a swarm of hummingbirds lived inside her chest. She might fly apart at any moment.

He deepened the kiss, his large hand curving around her nape, holding her precisely where he wanted her as his tongue plundered and twined with her own. He was driving her mad.

She suckled on his flesh, relishing his responding growl. Oh, how she loved that sound. Loved how it seemed to leave him without his control. Loved the way it vibrated through his entire body and into her own.

"I think you must be made of honey," he groaned, his mouth skimming along her jaw, down the column of her throat. "I cannot get enough of you."

A thrill tore through her as she arched her neck, hardly able to breathe as he laved the tender pulse, then raked his teeth down to the frilled collar of her nightdress.

"Then have all of me," she said. Or she might have begged.

He rose up, his hands threading in her hair as he gazed down at her with a powerful, unnamed emotion in his eyes and the clear intent to take her at her word. That look said he would, most definitely, have all of her. Then he cemented their bargain with another kiss, deeper still.

Long moments later, they were both panting, breaths filling each other's mouths. His hands roved over her body, learning every curve and hollow. Her own splayed possessively over his chest before she shoved at his coat, shucking it from his shoulders.

He let it drop to the floor as she unfastened the buttons of his waistcoat. They were both intent on one goal, but it was difficult to stay apart for any duration.

They collided again, his lips coasting from the tip of her shoulder and along her clavicle, drifting down aimlessly, sparking new sensations. And by the time he reached the tender peak of her breast, her back was arching in anticipation of his kiss.

But he teased her, his lips brushing softly against the warm underside as he charted a meandering course to the ruched, dusky center.

She gasped when his mouth finally closed over the aching peak.

Head falling back from the force of pleasure, she fisted her hands in the silky strands of his hair. He groaned and suckled her deeply into his mouth. A corresponding quickening pooled low in her womb, and she was writhing, her hips hitching against the hard jutting flesh between them.

Was it possible to die from pleasure? Her epitaph would be quite scandalous.

HERE LIES VERITY HARTLEY
A WANTON WOMAN WHO EXPIRED FROM . . .
OH . . . OH MY . . .

She lost the power of thought when Magnus gripped her bottom, pulling her flush, letting her feel all of him as he rocked against her with slow, wicked promise.

He whipped off her dressing gown and night rail, buttons scattering, some falling mutely onto the rug, others pinging against the hearth, as she stood wholly naked before him. And then he just stared, his eyes dark and hungry, his lips parted and damp from their kiss.

Verity didn't think she had an ounce of modesty left in her after such a scandalous kiss in his study. And yet, as his ardent gaze feasted on every pale curve and shadowy nook, she felt a wash of heat bloom on her skin from head to toe.

Shyly, she moved her arms to shield herself.

"No, don't," he said, his voice hoarse, raw. "You're even more exquisite than in my dreams."

A giddy breath filled her lungs. He'd told her earlier that he dreamed of her, but she didn't really believe it until now. "And what do I do in these dreams?"

He gave her a look that was so heated her knees melted.

He took a step closer and shored her against the length of his body. Delving his hands into her disheveled hair, he lifted the strands to the firelight. "There are so many things I've imagined doing with you, to you, for you . . . that I don't know where to start. I forget myself when I'm with you, and I lose control. You make me wild."

A shiver trampled through her at that raw admission, his voice hoarse and husky. But she wanted this. Wanted him. "Then be wild with me, Magnus."

In a swift dip, he swept her up into his arms. She let out a squeak of surprise, barely able to hold on as he strode across the room toward his massive four-poster bed. Then he sat her down on the edge of the mattress, took her hands and placed them on the waist of his trousers.

His chest rose and fell heavily as he looked down at her fingertips, waiting. Patient for the first time in his life. Was this one of the images from his dream?

Their gazes met. Held. And she could see the answer clearly. *Yes.* This and likely more.

But also, he was offering her the chance to be sure, telling her without words that, after this, there was no turning back.

He didn't know that she'd reached that point long before she entered his room. For her, this was the only solution. The only thing that brought any sense to her life.

Even so, her fingers were clumsy with the fastenings. And by the time she finished, his hands were shaking as he hooked his thumbs into the waist of his trousers to shuck out of them, leaving him standing in only his shirtsleeves. Then that garment was stripped away as well, whipped over his head to fall heedlessly to the floor.

As her gaze skimmed over him—all of him, from the ropey muscles of his shoulders, to the dark furring over his broad chest that tapered down over the abacus-like abdomen to a pair of lean hips, and—for the life of her, she couldn't recall what she'd just been thinking.

Her mind went blank as the vision before her eyes blotted out everything else.

This was no sock puppet.

His flesh was thick, rearing, dusky and dark, jutting

out proudly from a thatch of ebony curls, a jagged vein running down the considerable length.

"And just what do you intend to do with that," she asked—or croaked, rather—as she inched backward on the bed.

His grin was positively feral as his hungry eyes raked down her body. Then he prowled after her, his muscular shoulders rolling sinuously. "Wicked things."

Snatching her foot, he dragged her underneath him. She made a half-hearted attempt to escape, but ended up having her hands pinned to the mattress above her head.

Breathless and heart thumping, she grinned up at him. "You enjoy the chase, don't you? Beneath your gentleman's disguise, lurks a savage beast. Admit it."

He didn't answer. Instead, he remained poised over her, gazing intently in her eyes. Then he bent his head and kissed her softly, his exhale leaving his lungs without any rush as if to say *at last*.

Their frenzied hunger altered here in the quiet of his curtained bed, filling the spaces between each breath with a tender intensity that she never imagined the two of them—who were forever at each other's throats—would share. It seemed as though their passion was stripped bare, leaving their hearts naked and vulnerable. And soon the feeling enveloped them in long, slow kisses, where their mouths and clasped hands were the only parts of them that touched.

She never wanted to break this spell. But with every taste, she craved more, her body arching off the bed, seeking his. Then he moved over her slowly, cautiously, as if this were the careful taming of a wild spinster.

She nearly giggled at the thought, but then he lowered down, introducing her to the heat and weight and . . .

"*Oh*," she breathed.

He went still and looked down at her with concern. "Second thoughts? Because if you are uncertain . . . "

She shook her head. "It's just"—her greedy hands curved over his shoulders, her back arching—"skin against skin is so lovely. I just want to rub myself all over you."

His hips hitched reflexively and he growled against her mouth. "You're going to be the death of me."

He took her lips in a claiming, drugging kiss, settling between her thighs, giving her more of his weight. She welcomed it eagerly, urgently. Her hands rushed over his back as she wriggled beneath him, the crisp furring of his chest teasing and abrading her nipples.

But he was in no hurry. Instead, he caressed and gently fondled, getting her used to the feel of him as their legs entwined, hips undulating to music that was in the singing of their blood. As they kissed, they rolled together on the coverlet, back and forth, their bodies teasing and nudging.

She arched in welcome, cradling him, and he rocked against her, then withdrew. A familiar liquid throb made her ache for him.

"Please," she whispered, begged, her body strung tight and trembling, craving the pressure of his sex against hers.

And then at last, he was there nudging that tender throb. "What do you want? This?"

There was a wicked gleam in his eyes when he slid the length of his thick shaft against her. And an argument was poised on her lips just as he captured them with his own.

Then with excruciating slowness, he nudged inside her body . . . and she realized she might have been a little overconfident in her demands.

There was a definite sting, the burning from flesh stretching. A breath shuddered out of him. It fanned across her lips as she felt the slick walls of her body clamp tightly around him. She tensed, uncertain, her fingernails biting into his shoulders.

His kiss gentled as he slowly withdrew. There was something almost reverent in his gaze as he looked down at her. But his touch was decidedly sinful as he stroked and fondled, his caresses making her blood simmer. Then he nudged inside again, deeper this time, before he withdrew and repeated that same process.

Her body cinched around his invading flesh with every burning push, but he took his time. No longer the impatient duke, he seemed to revel in torturing her. He was diabolical.

He kissed her breasts, teasing her nipples into tender peaks as his clever hand stole between them, his finger drawing tiny circles beneath the hood of her sex until she was almost ready to shatter . . .

A huff of frustration left her and he had the nerve to smile against her lips. And when he nudged inside again, she bent her knees and pressed her inner thighs against his hips. He wasn't going to get away this time.

He kissed her, a boon for her efforts, a reward, perhaps. Then he drove in deep.

Swallowing down her cry, he held still and allowed her to adjust to his size while her body squeezed his flesh as if trying to expel him.

They were both panting again, open-mouthed and staring into each other's eyes. Without saying a word, they seemed to share an entire conversation about the creation of the universe and how it must have been formed for the sole purpose of this moment when they were finally one.

Then he let go of her hands and moved inside her in slow, languorous thrusts.

At first, she rebelled against this taming. The wildness in her nature wanted its rabid frenzy. And yet, as she eased into the gentle rocking rhythm, every thick slide, in and in and in, seemed to take her higher and higher toward a summit hidden in the deepest part of her.

Her breath quickened as he hooked an arm beneath her knee, opening her, lifting her as he sank all the way to the hilt. Something inside her jolted. Her body coiled tight on a gasp. She saw a glint of triumph in his brazier gaze just before he did that again. And again.

As he continued this sublime torture, her fingernails sank into his back, her neck arching and . . .

Suddenly, she tumbled over the edge on an endless rolling waves of rapture. It was like soaring through the heavens with wings outstretched. Stars burst behind her eyes as she clung to him, his name falling from her lips as he thrust deep into her quaking body, wringing out every ounce of pleasure before he issued a hoarse groan. Then on a choked groan, he jerked once, twice, filling her with spasms of molten heat.

He hunched over her, shielding her, his chest laboring, breaths panting as if he was wrung out too.

After a moment, he moved to lift away. But she held fast. "Stay inside me. I want to feel your heart beating with mine."

For once, he didn't argue.

"Come here, my little wildling," he crooned and turned them, still connected, until he was flat on his back, settling her against his chest, their hips locked. Pulling a corner of the coverlet over them, he caressed her back in gentle sweeps and she couldn't imagine how her life could be any better than this.

She must have dozed off because the next thing she knew, she was tucked against his side and he was gazing down at her with such primal satisfaction that it made her blush all over.

"You needn't look so smug." She lifted her hand to caress his cheek, the night stubble rasping against her palm.

He lowered his mouth to hers, a pleased grin lifting one corner of his mouth. "How could I not when I have just captured a wild creature, who lives in trees and rivers, and summarily tamed her?"

She nipped his bottom lip with her teeth, then playfully shoved him onto his back, her hair falling around them like a curtain. "You haven't tamed me. We live in the wilderness together now."

"That statement may be far truer than you know," he said wryly. But when her brow puckered in concern at his remark, he shook his head. "That was merely a jest. Do not worry. We will have all we need, I promise."

"But what about your estate and legacy? Your brother? And in case you haven't noticed, your mother hates me."

"As I mentioned earlier, it will take a few years, but the estate will be in good standing eventually. My brother will need to choose his own path. And, as for my mother, she will come around once you provide her with a grand-child to dote on." He slid his hand to her nape and drew her down to his mouth once more. "But this is really all that matters."

She was reluctant to believe him. At first.

Yet, as his kiss continued and her body started to thrum in low, liquid pulses, she gradually became convinced.

Breathless, she lifted her head and gazed down at him, her hand splayed over his thudding heart. The passion, tender affection and open honesty they shared truly was all that mattered. As long as they had that, they had everything.

Chapter Thirty-One

༄

HIS MOTHER WAS stunned into speechlessness. Magnus only hoped it would stay that way. Otherwise, he was fairly certain that shouting would be involved. Perhaps broken porcelain, as well.

He likely shouldn't have decided to tell her when she was inspecting the china in the dining room. Although, at least he had sense enough to dismiss the servants before he began.

Reaching forward, he eased the dinner plate from her inattentive grasp. "I realize the news might have come as a surprise. But I want to assure you that, in seven years' time, the estate will be far better off than it is now."

"But what about Miss Snow? I don't understand. Has she refused you?"

He decided to be blunt. "I did not propose to Miss Snow. I do not love her."

"I had a dowry when I went to your father. That is how marriage works for our class. Love comes later. Or fondness, at the very least."

A tender regard may have been there for a time between his parents. But he remembered the arguments, her constant disappointment in Father's inability to control his impulsive tendencies and to face the consequences of his actions, along with his pleas that she would simply understand that he was doing the best he could.

"I know this was not the ultimate goal originally set before me. However, I see nothing wrong with a man laboring on his own lands. To tell you the truth, I wouldn't know what to do with myself otherwise. It's a rewarding occupation to repair something with one's own hands, to expand one's mind toward methods of innovation. I would prefer to help my tenants, rather than sit across a desk from them and tell them to figure it out or else they'll lose their home."

His mother stared at him as if he were a stranger that had dropped down in front of her, speaking in a foreign tongue. "But what about your brother? Your duty to this family?"

"I am seeing to the duty of my family. It will simply take longer," he said, purposely directing the conversation away from Rowan.

All through Magnus's life, he had willingly shouldered the responsibility, not only as the heir, but acting in his father's stead. The roles of father and son were often turned on their heads and he had no one other than himself to rely on. For a time, his brother had commiserated with him, believing that he should have had a chance to live before he'd taken on the responsibilities of a duke. So Magnus had thought he'd had someone in his own family who understood.

But he'd been wrong. Every time—and there were many, many times—that Rowan had fallen into a scrape at school, or mischief abroad, gambling debts, drunkenness, recklessness . . . the list went on . . . Magnus would be called upon to settle matters.

Rowan had become a ne'er-do-well and rake, and everyone in the family loved him for it. No one considered for a single minute that the only reason he had the freedom to choose his own path—albeit a foolhardy one—was because of the sacrifices that Magnus made.

"And in the meantime," his mother said, "what about your brother's livelihood? The life he was promised?"

"What life was I promised, Mother?"

She blinked. "You are living it, of course. You are the Duke of Longhurst."

"And I have been since I was ten years old. But Father did not die until I was four and twenty. Someone should have told me to cram a good deal of life into those first ten years," he muttered dryly.

"I do not know what has gotten into you, Magnus. You've never been this unruly."

He smiled, thinking of Verity. "Perhaps it is the influence of Miss Hartley."

"That certainly does her no favors." Mother harrumphed and turned to leave the room.

"I disagree. I think she brings out the best in me." Seeing that his mother did not agree, he clasped her hand and gentled his tone, his gaze imploring. "Please make peace with my decision."

The finely wrinkled flesh around her eyes and lips compressed tight with strain. After a moment, she drew in a deep breath and nodded, squeezing his hand in return. Then she walked away. And that would have to be enough for now.

As he left the dining room and headed toward his study, he saw his mother in the corridor stop dead in her tracks as she came face-to-face with Lord Hartley. He opened his mouth to speak to her, but she turned abruptly on her heel and stormed down the servants' passage toward the kitchen instead.

Doubtless, the cook was about to have a surprisingly unpleasant visit.

❧

VERITY SNEAKED DOWN the servants' stairs, afraid she'd slept too long and had missed breakfast. But she was positively famished and hoped she could beg the cook for a cup of tea and a scone.

She had remained in Magnus's bedchamber until dawn, unable to leave his side.

They'd talked for hours. Or rather, they'd kissed and caressed for hours. However, there was some talking involved. Scandalous conversations such as him asking if the water he bathed her in was too cold, then offering to warm her with his mouth.

Afterward, she told him about the sock puppets while she explored Lord Turgid in greater depth. Magnus didn't mind her untutored kisses. In fact, he seemed to lose the power of speech the instant she suckled on his flesh, her tongue tasting salt and heat as he lost every last ounce of control, his back arching, his hands in her hair, and her name ripped from his lips.

Thoroughly spent, he had fallen asleep, his breaths shallow and even.

Knowing that she couldn't be found in his room, she'd left him with a kiss against his temple and her hand pressed to his heart. And in his ear, she whispered, "I love you."

He must have heard her, because a hum murmured on his lips as they'd curved in a smile.

Just thinking about all of it made Verity blush anew. She was certain that she must be glowing from within like a beacon, revealing her nighttime activities. So, the last thing she wanted to do was to run into his—

"Miss Hartley!" the dowager said with affront when they nearly collided at the bottom of the stairs.

"Oh. Pardon me, Your Grace. I was just on my way to . . . see if . . ."

At the instant scowl on her future mother-in-law's countenance, Verity's words trailed off and her appetite dissipated. That dark look made her want to run in the opposite direction. But that was probably something that a future duchess wouldn't do.

"My son has told me of his plans," Geraldine Warring

said, matter-of-factly. "You may have managed to beguile him, my dear. But do not think for one minute that his affection for you will last."

Verity squared her shoulders and stood her ground, needing to start off their relationship on equal footing. "I do not mean any disrespect, ma'am, but you are wrong. Your son and I are alike in mind and spirit. We share similar interests and are both of a sensible nature. Neither one of us has been beguiled. We see each other for who we are."

"There is no sense in his proposing to you. None at all. He is a duke. You are a penniless spinster. He is a man from a good, noble family. You are—"

"I will stop you there before you say something you will regret in the future," Verity interrupted. "The fact of the matter is, your son and I never intended to fall in love. But we have, nonetheless. And I have every faith that, one day, you will come to accept our union. Because I know the woman who raised him to be the man he is today did so with great love in her own heart and a desire for her son's happiness."

A scoff was her reply. "If you think that love is what matters most to my son then you are mistaken. He watched his own father shirk his duty and fritter away a fortune on whatever pleased him, leaving him to bear the brunt of all the consequences. He resented his father for that. And, no matter how much he professes to wanting you, he will come to resent you as well."

His mother was wrong, Verity knew it. He'd proven himself countless times that when he made a decision, he honored it. And last night, he had decided that whatever tensions might have been between their families did not matter as long as they loved each other.

Or, at least, she thought he loved her.

He'd never said the words. Then again, his actions spoke for him. So, of course, he loved her. Didn't he?

"He won't. That isn't the man he is," she declared, hiking her chin. "The past no longer matters to him. It is the future he cares about."

A look of pity crossed the older woman's countenance. "You don't know my son as well as you think you do. In the years to come, he will forget why he made this choice, and rue the day he did."

Verity wanted to argue the point, but Geraldine Warring walked away, the air turning cold in her wake.

"You're wrong," she said to the empty corridor, her throat tight as she chafed her hands along her arms to warm them.

Magnus wouldn't resent her. She knew he wouldn't. He'd made a plan, after all. Everything was settled. There would be financial strains, of course, but whatever they had to face, they would face it together. Side by side. She would never turn her back on him. And he would never turn his back on her, or leave her alone and—*she swallowed*—forgotten.

❧

MAGNUS LIFTED A hand to greet the baron as he approached. "Good morning, sir. I was hoping you might have a minute for a matter I would like to discuss."

Hartley looked steadily at him for a beat, his expression inscrutable. Then he nodded. "There's a matter I'd like to discuss with you as well."

Well, that sounded ominous and did nothing to tamp down an unprecedented rise of nerves. But Magnus led the way, regardless.

Once they were situated in his study, he broached the first topic weighing on his mind. "I want to apologize for my belief that you were behind the entire scheme. I should have been able to see the truth for myself," he said. "But I was so sure you were to blame."

"Don't be so hard on yourself, lad. Grief does that to us. If we do not let it out, the pain can poison us. As the bard said, 'Give sorrow words. The grief that does not speak/ Whispers the o'er-fraught heart, and bids it break.'"

Magnus swallowed down a rise of guilt at that particular quote from *Macbeth*. Instead of mourning his father, he had sought revenge. But perhaps it was time to bury the past, once and for all.

He nodded thoughtfully, grateful that Hartley was a generous and forgiving sort.

Then again, if Hartley knew that he'd spent a glorious night bedding his unmarried daughter, he might not have been so magnanimous.

In that instant, Magnus felt the need to shift from one foot to the other, to shrug his shoulders. But all he gave in to was the need to swallow.

Then again, if Hartley knew that he'd spent a glorious night bedding his unmarried daughter, he might not have been so magnanimous.

With a glance down to the desk between them, and the bed of open ledgers that had witnessed far more than calculations, Magnus surreptitiously tucked them away into the drawers.

"I've been thinking about last night," Hartley said as he sat.

Suddenly nervous, Magnus nearly fell into his own chair. "Last . . . night?"

"I'm sure you've been thinking about that other man, hidden in the shadows, too. After all, he saved your life."

"Yes, of course," Magnus replied, relieved.

Again, it entered his mind that he likely should have been more concerned about the fact that he'd narrowly escaped death. And yet, all he'd been able to think about was how close he'd been to losing Verity.

Although, prior to Verity entering his study last night, he had jotted down a few notes. He pulled them out now and scanned the few facts. "I believe he was the man who sent me the address of the building. Though I do not know about his business relationship with Mr. Eugene, the man apparently goes by the moniker of *Mr. Dashing*." Since he'd relayed the information about Miss Snow's friend last night, he saw no need to bring her involvement into the conversation. "Strangely enough, the name sounds familiar but I cannot think of the reason."

"Not strange at all, lad. It sounds familiar because you and Hawk were forever at war with Mr. Dashing. Don't you remember?"

At war with Mr. Dashing? And then it hit him.

All at once, he knew the real identity of the mysterious figure.

"Do you suppose . . . ?" Hartley mused, his brow puckered over the bridge of his nose.

Magnus looked at the scrap of paper. "I do, indeed. But that's a matter for later." He put the note in the drawer and closed it, realizing belatedly that he was stalling out of nervousness. Bloody hell, his palms were even sweating. "The reason I wanted to speak with you is regarding your daughter."

Hartley waited, refusing to fill in the gaps by saying something jovial and typical to his nature. Instead, he stared patiently with his elbows resting on the arms of the chair.

Magnus cleared his throat and straightened, tugging on the hem of his waistcoat.

"After careful consideration, I . . ." He trailed off, displeased with the start of that sentence. "You see, I've come to know your daughter over the course of these weeks and, well, it has occurred to me that we share a good deal of interests, in addition to common traits. She is the eldest female in her family, as you know, and I am mine. I mean, I'm the eldest male in my family."

He was running out of breath. Perspiration collected on his brow. Was it hot in here?

Hartley didn't seem affected at all. He barely twitched an eyebrow.

Magnus realized in that moment that he'd never sat across from someone and asked for something he wanted just for himself. Not for his family. Not for his lineage or estate. Just for him.

It was surprisingly difficult. He felt rather exposed, as if he were revealing the inner contents of his heart. It lay there, splayed open for study as if he were on a table in a surgery.

"Where was I?" he asked, mouth dry. "Ah, yes. I'm the eldest. And as the eldest I inherited a dukedom. But you know that already. More to the point, however, I should like to request . . . I mean, it would be my honor if you would . : . Oh, hang it all. I want to marry her. And I should like your blessing."

Hartley waited another beat—*two, three*—his face as impassive as a Sphinx. Then, suddenly he roared with laughter.

"Ah, lad. It was so fun to torture you. For a minute there, I thought I was going to have to loosen your cravat. Your face was turning a shade of purple I'd never seen." He stood and came around to the side of the desk, clapping Magnus on the shoulder as he stood as well. "Of course, you have my blessing. You have always been family."

The weight of the world seemed to pour out of Magnus's next breath as they shook hands. "Thank you, sir. I promise I'll be good to her."

"I know you will. And I don't want you to worry about that business with Truman and the apprenticeship. I understand, and it's all forgiven."

Verity suddenly appeared in the doorway, her lovely face furrowed with confusion. "What business with Truman and the apprenticeship?"

Magnus felt the weight of regret drop in his stomach like an anvil in a lake. Knowing her as he did now, and how much she loved her brother, he never would have hurt her for all the world. But there was no turning away from the truth.

He drew in a breath and went to her, cupping her shoulders, his thumbs making soothing circles. "I made certain that he was dismissed, and that he would have no further options along that vein."

She shrank back, stepping out of his reach, the betrayal in her eyes cutting him to the quick. "*You* were responsible?"

"I'm not proud of it. Especially now that I know the truth. It was wrong of me."

"Well, as long as you know that it is wrong now, then that changes everything, doesn't it?" She threw up her hands. "The last seven years of my brother's life don't matter. Seven years of him sailing on a merchant ship and barely coming home to visit. Seven years of him waiting to start his life."

"Verity," her father said, his tone consoling. "There's nothing to be done about it now. It's all in the past."

She stared at him as if he had also betrayed her. "You knew about this?"

Hartley nodded. "I thought Truman told you."

"No. He didn't." Her gaze hardened as it slid to Magnus. "But he once wrote to me, warning me to never trust a man who pretended to be a friend. Now I understand the reason. I feel like such a fool. I thought I knew you."

"You do know me," he said, and out of the corner of his eye, he saw Hartley exit the room to give them privacy. "And the most important thing is how we feel for each other."

"The worst of it is the hypocrisy of it all," she continued, ignoring him as she paced the study where just last night they were locked in an embrace. "From the beginning, you spoke to me about honor and honesty. And your words were so deeply ingrained, sincere in a way that made me believe that you were living for a greater purpose. As much as you vexed me, I admired you," she said, her voice threaded with accusation. "I saw you struggle with your hatred of my family and found nobility in your willingness to go along with my lie. I had been prepared for mockery, but instead I found a kinship with you. And when you left, I felt an absence I'd never known. I felt empty. Not only from missing you, but from something that was missing in myself that I had found with you." She shook her head. "You had challenged me to be more honest and honorable. You made me want to face matters bravely. You made me want to be better."

He swallowed, a sense of foreboding thick in his throat as he saw the brittle coldness enter those violet eyes that had been more like velvet mere hours ago.

"But all along, you were lying to me," she continued. "Every moment we spent together has been a lie, a lie of omission. All that time, you were harboring a secret. A vindictiveness in your nature. Something cold and callous."

When he saw the tears collect along the lower rims of her eyes, he felt a sharp lance of pain strike his heart. He reached out again. "Verity."

She took a step back, keeping her hands closed into fists at her sides. "You stole my brother's dream, his life and his sense of purpose."

"At the time, my father had just died and I thought that Hawk had been part of the scheme. I thought he was working with your father. You were all guilty in my mind," he admitted and saw her flinch. "But that was before."

"And you can justify turning your back on him as if

he didn't matter? Tell me, was it so easy to forget the man who had been your friend for so many years and leave him to suffer alone?"

He could see how this might play on her greatest fears and he wanted to reassure her. Reaching out, he took her hand, but she refused to unfurl her fingers.

"Verity, I would never leave you," he said softly, the pulse at her wrist fluttering like that of a skittish bird. "That was different. I am different."

"If you were in my place, would you accept someone's word on faith alone when all the evidence pointed to the contrary? Or would you require proof?" She slipped free. Then, stopping at the door, she said, "I cannot marry you. I release you from any responsibility."

Chapter Thirty-Two

✦

$\mathcal{H}$ARTLEY HALL WAS a bleak house in the rain, and it had been raining for the better part of the last three weeks since Verity's return.

And worse, on the very first fine day, she discovered that the cat was back. The last thing that she wanted was a reminder of Magnus and the day that he'd first noticed her.

The orange-spotted creature, who'd once manipulated her into thinking he needed rescuing, was currently eyeing the birdhouse garden with a decidedly ravenous look.

"Shoo! Shoo!" she called after the cat, waving her arms and watching as he scampered away, cutting through the fence and tall grasses. "Good riddance!"

Walking toward the row of birdhouses, she trilled her usual chickadee call. Well, perhaps not her usual. It didn't have the same lilt that it used to. But she left a row of crumbs on the gray stone bench, nonetheless.

As she walked on toward the path, she heard them chattering happily as if they hadn't a care in the world. She envied them.

She had far too much on her mind. However, to prevent those things from consuming her, she focused on other tasks.

In these past twenty-one days, she had had a birthday which made her all the more of a spinster. Had settled seventeen arguments between her sisters. Had exchanged a dozen letters with Miss Snow, who made no mention of Longhurst at all. Which was somewhat suspicious and Verity could guess the reason, but she preferred not to think about it.

She had also received twenty letters from Longhurst. But she returned them unopened. After all, letters didn't prove that a man had changed. Only actions could do that. She knew that, eventually, he would abandon his letter writing and that would confirm what she'd learned about his character.

Additionally, her courses had come, which meant there would be no forced wedding in her future. She was glad of that. Immensely glad.

Her walks by the river had resumed as well, even in the rain. In fact, sometimes she preferred walking in the rain. It nursed a need in her to have all the memories of him washed away.

She would have liked to pretend that she'd never met Longhurst. But that was childish, she supposed. So, she coldly faced the matter head-on and told herself that it just wasn't meant to be. And, in time, she would start to forget. Perhaps. After a very long time. Or sooner if she managed to get whacked on the head and develop amnesia.

She was sure she could talk Thea into walloping her with a broom. Her sister was quite cross at the moment because Verity refused to talk about all the sights and splendor of London.

There were only two things she had not done since her return—talk about London, and cry.

Anger was a far preferable feeling. It gave her a sense of control. She had power over her anger. She could keep it simmering or let it boil over. There was no one who could stop her.

So she let it simmer, the broth flavored with righteous indignation. Which was rather ironic, considering that

Longhurst likely felt the same way when he'd destroyed her brother's life. But at least she wasn't out to hurt anyone with her anger.

And to think, she had been honest for him!

Not that she was a liar by any means, but she had actually tried to make him see her in a better light. Thinking back now, she was positively disgusted by that fact.

What she really wanted was someone to accept her for the flawed, imperfect creature that she was. She wanted to be cherished. Perhaps even adored. And she wanted to feel safe in the knowledge that she was loved no matter what she did or who her family was.

That wasn't asking for too much, was it?

On a sigh, she climbed over the stile and made her way to the path.

Up ahead, she saw a figure approach and blushed the instant she recognized who it was.

Reverend Tobias.

"Ah, Miss Hartley," he said with a broad smile that drew attention to the attractive creases bracketing either side of his mouth. In the sunlight, his wavy hair looked like spun gold and his eyes were the blue of the sky that very day. "I saw you at church this past Sunday."

And I saw you naked, she thought, wondering if her cheeks were about to catch fire.

Pasting on a smile, she kept her gaze on his. "I saw you as well. You were the one standing at the pulpit."

He chuckled as if she were making a joke and not babbling like an idiot. She appreciated that.

"Yes, well, I'd tried to speak with you after church, but you dashed away," he said, and she pretended that she had no idea what he was talking about. "I gather you like walking and spending time in nature, which is the reason you are so quick."

She nodded. Then again, she could hardly deny it when, there they were, walking in nature . . . just like the day she'd seen him naked.

Drat! Why couldn't she stop thinking about that? It was like the confession was waiting on the tip of her tongue, demanding to be spit out.

She tried to swallow it down instead. "I do, indeed."

"I'll get right to the point. I ventured this way in hopes of meeting you. I wonder if, perhaps, you might allow me to accompany you on a walk."

"You want to walk with me? Not Honoria or Thea?"

His brow puckered as if her question made no sense. "With you. To tell you the truth, I had thought about asking when I'd first arrived. But then I heard about your betrothal, and refrained. Then when I learned of the subsequent end of your betrothal, I didn't want to put undue pressure on you."

"That was quite considerate of you," she said, dumbfounded.

"I hope that is in my favor, and you'll grant me the honor of calling on you this week."

He flashed another disarming grin. Those grooves in his lean cheeks were positively mesmerizing. And she found herself nodding before she even knew what she was doing.

"Excellent," he said. "Until then."

He turned. Verity should have simply let him go. But then something came over her.

She wasn't certain if it was nerves or the pressure of guilt weighing upon her but, all at once, she suddenly called out, "I saw you naked!"

Reverend Tobias looked over his shoulder and winked. "I know."

Then he walked away, and she never knew that confession could make a person want to swoon. Perhaps there was some intrinsic reward to honesty, after all.

And the best thing was, she didn't spend the rest of her

walk thinking about Magnus. Well, at least, not every step of the way. Just every three out of four.

It was progress.

She was moving forward with her life, and that was all that mattered.

∽◎∾

THE PAST THREE weeks had been hell on Magnus.

Not only had every single one of his letters to Verity been returned unopened, but he'd had to deal with his mother and her renewed matchmaking attempts. She was even more determined than ever.

In the meantime, he was working with police investigators on recuperating the stolen money. And he was on a personal mission to find Mr. Dashing.

He sought the assistance of Miss Snow. And after several outings, along with dinners at her father's house, he learned absolutely nothing. She refused to divulge her method of communication with Mr. Dashing.

Even though she had readily shared this information with Verity, she'd had a change of heart about embroiling the man in any further, potentially dangerous, ordeals. "I would never forgive myself if I allowed that kind, elderly gentleman to come to harm."

Yet, when Magnus had patiently reminded her of the fact that it had been Mr. Dashing who had shot the villain and could clearly take care of himself, she had still refused to assist him.

"If he was the man you saw," she'd said, "then he likely thought he was protecting me. I am the one who asked for the whereabouts of Baron Hartley, after all."

Magnus had not bothered to point out that a note had come addressed to him as well, knowing that it was a fruitless endeavor. Nothing could be gained from arguing with Miss Snow.

Fortunately, his mother happened to offer up a clue by revealing that she'd spotted the Button King's daughter at the Temple of Muses. Normally this would not incite his interest. However, when she mentioned this not just once, but twice in a single week, he was starting to wonder if, perhaps, Miss Snow's reason for visiting the shop was more than just a simple fondness for books.

So, Magnus decided to wait in a carriage near the shop on Finsbury Square to see what he might discover. Then, lo and behold, he saw a man on the pavement in a long coat and walking with a limp. Just like the man who'd been on the platform.

He followed. However, it was no elderly gentleman who spryly skirted around corners and disappeared out of thin air.

Magnus had met this man before. In fact, he knew him quite well.

It wasn't until later that week that they finally came face-to-face.

"So, the prodigal son has, indeed, returned," Magnus said pushing away from the stone facade around the corner from the bookshop.

Mr. Dashing stopped on the pavement, uttering a slew of curses under his breath. Angrily he asked, "Did she tell you where to find me?"

"No," he answered, instinctively knowing that he meant Miss Snow. "Mother did."

His younger brother shook his head in self-reproach. "Damn. I saw her the other day. And when she passed right by, I didn't think she recognized me."

Rowan's mouth pulled into a frown beneath the gray mustachio that reached all the way to his equally gray muttonchops. Though, considering that his brother was four years younger and still sported raven-black eyebrows beneath the low brim of his brown beaver hat, Magnus would have to say that it was a disguise. Which didn't surprise him. His brother's past dealings had often required clever camouflaging in order to extricate himself from trouble. But what was he involved in this time? There was no telling.

"She didn't," he said. "She was only too thrilled to mention that she'd run into Miss Snow twice in one week."

Those heavy brows lifted. "Ah. And how are her matchmaking attempts going?"

"Surprisingly successful," he said, dubious.

For some unknown reason, Mr. Snow was now pursuing him and quite persistently, too. The society pages were expecting a betrothal announcement any day.

"I take it this news does not please you."

Magnus looked down the street, searching aimlessly for something no longer within reach. "It pleases Mother for the time being."

"That's not what I asked," his brother said. They shared a stony look until Rowan glanced at his ear. "Not even going to thank me?"

He inclined his head gratefully. "What were you doing there that night?"

"Didn't you figure that out yet? No? I'm surprised. In the past, you were always two steps ahead of me."

"Not that it ever made a bit of difference. So, just tell me, hmm?" Magnus was too tired for games.

Rowan sketched a bow. "Well, in certain circles I go by the name of Mr. Modine, who made a fortune in scrap metal. I happened to let some information slip into Eugene's hands in order to whet his appetite. And he was more than interested in learning of a certain duke who would be marrying into a great fortune. So he took the bait, then proceeded to reel you in."

"And you would have let me marry Miss Snow, knowing all the while that I was doing it to secure a future for you?"

"Oh, get off your high horse. You were doing it for your own vanity. The ever-perfect Duke of Longhurst sacrifices himself on the altar for the sake of his family. Mother would have been so proud."

Magnus gritted his teeth. He was bloody tired of all that he'd done for his thankless brother. "And you knew Eugene's plan from the beginning."

"Knew it? Hell, I orchestrated it," Rowan said proudly. "Though, I'm sure your new papa-in-law would have padded your pockets. In fact, he still might. You haven't said."

"How long did you know about Eugene and his part in the swindle from seven years ago?" Magnus asked, keeping the conversation on track. But what he really wanted to know was how long his brother had known that Hartley was innocent.

Rowan shrugged in a manner that was reminiscent of their father. "I had a sense of it when I met him a year ago in America. The story he'd invented for himself didn't add up. And he was crafty, too. A good actor, just like Hartley had said."

A man rounded the corner, passing them on the pavement with a curious glance. Rowan leaned heavily on his cane, shoulders hunched. The man walked on by. But, not wanting to draw any more attention, they moved on.

Smoothing a hand down his whiskers, his brother continued in a low tone. "I was there to kill Hartley, too. That is, until I heard the truth. It was good of you to draw it out of him. You're not usually so . . . Oh, what's the word . . . *forgiving*. You seemed to have been offering him a chance to explain. I can only wonder at the reason."

If he was waiting for Magnus to offer up some profound insight, he was in for a long wait.

"Verity Hartley is brave, I'll grant her that," Rowan continued, not even bothering to pretend he wasn't watching his expression for any little flicker. "But I don't imagine Mother would ever forgive you if you didn't marry an heiress. She would make your bride's life . . . hmm . . . not entirely pleasant. That is, unless you happened to have a fortune of your own."

That sparked Magnus's attention. "Do you have a fortune, Rowan?"

"I'm this close to one." He held up his thumb and forefinger, pinching the air. "It's breathing down my neck as we speak."

Magnus heaved out a sigh. "Still speculating, I see."

"Still needing to control everything, I see," his brother countered. "I have a shilling in my pocket that says you've already calculated the number of years it will take before the accounts are in the clear." When that earned a growl, Rowan laughed. "When are you going to learn? You'll never get what you want if you don't take a risk."

"Father took enough risks for all of us, I think."

"There is a difference, brother. He couldn't stop himself. In some ways, he was always one decision away from total ruin." He paused in a moment of silence for the man who was good and kind, but troubled in so many ways. Then a wry smile touched his lips. "I still remember the time he'd danced around the family solar, taking me by the hands while chanting, 'We're going to have a silver mine. We're going to be rich as Croesus.'"

"The silver mine. Don't remind me," Magnus groaned.

Rowan's smile fell. "He felt just awful about that, you know, and how you were almost sent away from school. But all he ever wanted was for us to have security."

"Which we would've had if he'd just left well enough alone."

"'Well enough' isn't enough for everyone. Can you not forgive him for wanting more?" Rowan asked. "So he made a few mistakes. Haven't we all?"

It would have been the perfect opportunity to scoff and make a crack about how some men made more mistakes than could be counted. The old Magnus would have done just that.

But he could only think about his own, and what his inability to forgive had cost him. He realized that the blame that had driven him to lash out at Hawk all those years ago had actually been anger toward himself. If he hadn't judged his own father so harshly for every misstep, then he might have confided in Hawk. They might have worked through the problems that arose. Together. And his father wouldn't have suffered those episodes that had weakened his heart.

In that moment, he heard Verity's accusation in the back of his mind. *All that time, you were harboring a secret. A vindictiveness in your nature. Something cold and callous.*

Those words haunted him now, because he knew she'd been right. That had been the way he was seven years ago, and he would do anything he could to change the past. But he was not that man any longer.

"I know that Father did the best he could," he admitted.

Rowan's brows lifted in surprise. "I'm glad to hear you say that, brother, because I've just come up with a cracking good idea."

"No."

"You haven't even heard it, yet."

Magnus rubbed his temples and expelled a sigh. "Very well, then. What's your idea?"

"That we honor our father's last wish and create the Longhurst Empire." When Magnus closed his eyes, his brother continued. "Now, hear me out. We use your £1,000 that the police recovered."

"They haven't."

"Actually, they have. A certain constable will call on

you this afternoon. And don't ask me how I know about it, I just do. I know all sorts of things."

"And what if I have other intentions for the recovered funds?" Like paying back Baron Hartley, Magnus thought. "I don't suppose you'd be putting up any capital?"

Rowan chuckled as if the question were absurd. "Live a little, brother. It's like found money. What's the harm?"

"I could lose everything."

"That's why it's called a risk," his brother said. "And real risk takes bravery. It takes having nothing left to lose and wanting something more than you've ever wanted anything before."

Magnus didn't take chances. He erred on the side of caution and control. At least, he had until he'd met Verity. Then he'd thrown caution out the window, abandoned all control . . . and lost her anyway.

What he wanted was certainty. A clear path toward the future. Not a risk that would leave him in ruins.

Only a fool would ask his devil-may-care brother to tell him more about some half-baked plan.

Chapter Thirty-Three

❧

THE FOLLOWING WEEK, Hartley Hall was greeted by an unexpected visitor. And yet, *not* a visitor, but a long-lost brother.

"Truman!" The joyous cry rang through the house and was immediately followed by footsteps pattering from every direction.

But Mother was there first. Her tears were beautifully shed, flowing down her cheeks in an unending torrent no matter how many times Truman wiped them away with his thumbs.

He smiled sheepishly before he pulled her in for a hearty embrace. "It has been too long, I know. I meant to visit six months ago, but there was a storm that put us behind schedule."

The man in the foyer who had everyone blubbering over him was not the lean, scholarly brother Verity remembered. He had altered greatly, his skin nut-brown, his chestnut hair touched by the sun in streaks of molten gold around his forehead and temples. He was brawny now, his shoulders as broad as an ox.

"You have a scar," Honoria said with a frown as she traced the line on his face.

He shrugged, scrubbing a hand over the shadow of whiskers along his jaw. "Eh, what can I say? The other men were jealous that I was so pretty. But at least I'm not as ghastly as you."

It was his usual teasing and Honoria responded by sticking her tongue out at him and swatting his shoulder. But Verity saw something dark and haunted flicker across his gaze that told her of things he'd endured but had never written to her about.

She blamed that on Longhurst, too. "How long will you be home this time?"

He looked around at every expectant face, pausing to ruffle Thea's hair and to shake Father's hand. "I'm here to stay. Or rather, not as far from home. I'll be in London, once I find lodgings. You'll all be glad to know that I've been hired by an architectural firm. In fact, I received several offers." He looked directly at Verity. "They took me quite by surprise."

Oh, she just bet they did. And there was no question in her mind who was responsible.

Longhurst. Of all the nerve! Did he really imagine he could make amends so easily? A few letters cost him nothing. But the past seven years had cost her family far too much. She could not forgive him for that.

Clearly, Truman didn't know the truth behind this matter. At least, not yet. But as soon as she had the chance to speak to him alone, she would tell him everything.

Well . . . not *everything.* Nearly everything. Then again . . . perhaps she'd tell him just what he needed to know.

❧

LATE THAT NIGHT, they sat together on the great eye of the stage and looked up at the stars, the summer air warm and balmy. And in the heat, Verity's ire was starting to rise.

After telling her brother of the horrible thing that Longhurst had done by deliberately ruining his life, all Truman did was shrug his shoulders. Then he told her that he'd received a letter from Longhurst weeks ago, apologizing for his actions.

Trust Longhurst to do the honorable thing now, she groused to herself. But then it occurred to her that he would have had to mail the letter quite a while ago. Perhaps when she'd first arrived in London. Not that it mattered when he'd had his change of heart. It was far too late for him to make amends.

"Surely, you are not telling me that, after all he has done, you are willing to forgive him?"

Truman eased back on a pensive sigh, linking his hands behind his head, his long legs crossed at the ankle. "No. But I'd be a fool to refuse the job offer."

She eyed his relaxed pose with confusion. "I don't understand why you aren't shouting to the heavens at the injustice of it all. He took everything from you!"

"It's like lancing a festering wound, I think. All that's rotten is drawn out into the open. But then, what do you do with it? Try to hold on to it? Carry around that stinking putrescent mass? Or do you wash your hands of it while the wound scabs over?" The weariness in his voice was palpable, making her wonder again at all the things he'd been through. "Besides, it all happened so long ago. And, if I'm to be honest, I would have done the same in his position."

"You would have done no such thing. You are far above acting on revenge," she argued.

"Not actually," he said, that haunted look passing over his face in the moonlight. "Most men aren't, Verity. At least, not until they do something unforgiveable and are fortunate enough to have the chance to see the error of their ways. Guilt and regret are formidable tutors."

They sat in silence for a while, listening to the inquisitive hoot of an owl in the distance and the chirrup of crickets.

She thought about her own regrets. They seemed to be piling up like bricks, walling her in. "Even so, I would never forgive him."

"And yet, you love him," Truman said, startling her.

"And what makes you think that I—" She stopped when their gazes met. There was no fooling him. She eased down onto her back, too, their heads resting at an angle from each other. Her breath mingled with the night air. "If you read the society columns, then you'd know there was never anything real or honest between us. Nothing lasting. He's out nearly every night with Miss Snow. And if he wasn't interested in marrying her, he would have returned to his estate."

Or returned to me, she thought.

Her brother rolled up onto his elbow, concern on his countenance. It quickly hardened to steel and she knew that he'd discerned all that she hadn't told him. Even with so many years apart, he still saw too much. "Do I need to have a word with him? Shoot him or something?"

Her throat felt too raw at the moment to answer. So, she just shook her head.

He leaned over and kissed her forehead. "If you change your mind, just say the word."

❧

The following afternoon she returned from her perfectly pleasant walk with Reverend Tobias—*take that Longhurst!*—and went to the side garden to offer the nuts and berries she'd picked along the way to the birds.

But the instant she came close, she saw the cat.

She also saw feathers, nesting material, dried grasses, twigs and bits of ribbon strewn all over. Clapping her hands sharply, she chased the cat out of the garden. That blasted cat!

When she returned to the birdhouses, she surveyed the

damage. Then, much to her relief, she saw an egg lying in a thicket of grass. Perhaps she had come in time.

Kneeling down, she inspected it for any cracks but found none.

As luck would have it, Mr. Lawson strolled by on the path just beyond the garden, whistling a tune. He stopped, giving her an alert glance when she hailed him, then strode over to offer his assistance. He was always like that, willing to lend a hand. Even willing to dance with her at the assembly when she hadn't wanted Longhurst to think that no one else would.

But Bennet was skeptical when he stared down at the egg.

Removing his straw hat, he scratched a hand into the layers of dark hair and frowned. "Once a different scent is on that egg, the mother won't likely come back."

"I haven't touched it," Verity said, remembering when her grandfather had told her the same. In the springtime, he'd often said, *Don't meddle in the affairs of cats and birds, for cats cannot help their nature, and birds are skittish for good reason.* "I just cannot bring myself to turn my back on it."

He stared at her for a moment, then offered a nod.

Together, they gathered it into a makeshift nest. She even added a few feathers for warmth. Then she carried it, following him down to the stable yard where he fashioned a cage of sorts, with a nook below for warming stones, slats on the side to keep the cat out, but enough room for other birds to enter. That was Verity's idea. She wanted the mother bird to be free to come back.

He mounted it on a pole by the breakfast room window so that she could watch it each day and change the warming stones.

"Do you think it will be enough?" she asked after thanking him at least a hundred times.

He offered a kind smile. "I think you've done all you can, and more than most would do."

For the next few days, all she did was look after her little charge, still hoping that the mother and father bird would return to it. She had done everything right, wanting to ensure that this bird would not be alone. And, by the end of the week, she saw a tiny fissure on the shell.

She held her breath. The egg wobbled and her heart nearly exploded with happiness. It was hatching!

For hours and hours, she watched, waiting for the next crack in the shell. She alternated the warming stones in the nook beneath.

As time passed, Truman came to linger beside her for a while. Her sisters dropped by at different intervals, everyone waiting in anticipation for the hatchling to appear. Father tried to coax her away from the window, but she couldn't leave it.

But then more hours passed. She spent the night curled up on the window seat in the breakfast room.

Hearing the distant chatter of the birds roused her from sleep and she blinked, opening her eyes to the pale lavender light of predawn. At once, she hopped up and checked on the egg. Surely all the happy birdsong in the garden meant she would be greeted by the sight of a new hatchling.

But it was still just an egg. There were no additional fractures. No wobbling from within. And when her mother came up behind her and wrapped a shawl around her shoulders, Verity knew.

"Why didn't they come?" she asked bleakly. "I made sure not to touch it. So why didn't they come back for her? Help her break free?"

Mother smoothed a hand over Verity's hair. "You did everything you could. But it needed to be strong enough to peck through the shell and survive on its own."

"What if she's tired of being strong enough?" Her voice shook, her throat closing on raw emotion. And she slumped down onto the bench, her shoulders shaking.

It wasn't until she felt the dampness collecting on her skirt that she realized she was crying.

Her mother sat down beside her and gathered her in her arms, the comforting fragrance of lilac and vanilla orchid enveloping her.

"I don't understand it," Verity said. "How could all the others still be singing and chirruping? How could they go on with their lives? Don't they care at all?"

"What else can they do but continue on?" her mother asked in her soft, lilting drawl. "Would you rather see them sitting on a branch and staring desolately off in the distance?"

"Well, no. But I do think they should go after the cat, all at once, beaks at the ready."

"Would that undo what has already happened? No. Revenge is not the answer. Not for them, and not for you."

Verity lifted her head on a sniff, frowning. "What do you mean? I haven't done anything."

"Precisely." Her mother tucked a lock of hair behind her ear. "You have issued an attack of silent revenge against Longhurst, leaving him to grovel alone and to no one who will listen."

"He hurt my brother."

"But you're acting as though he hurt you instead."

"Well, he did," she declared, adamant. "Family is all we have. That is what you've taught each of us, isn't it?"

"Yes, but it was never a lesson to hide behind. And sometimes anger is a clever disguise for grief, and for fear." She smoothed the wetness from her cheeks, her gaze knowing. "So tell me, my darling girl, what are you really afraid of?"

She shook her head and swallowed thickly. "Nothing."

"Little finch, sometimes the way through the shell is to break it apart completely. Only then will you be able to feel the sunshine on your wings."

"I'm not afraid of anything."

Mother offered a patient smile. "Well, then I'm glad. If I were in your shoes, I likely would have already imagined how well he would have looked in the morning with a fresh shave and sitting at the breakfast table." She paused long enough to release a sigh as her gaze traveled to the empty chair beside Verity's. "I would have pictured him walking beside me through the garden, hand in hand, and seated at the dinner table across from me with the candle flames reflecting in his eyes as he looked at me with such warmth and tenderness that I felt the glow inside my own breast. And the way he—"

"Enough," Verity interrupted, feeling as though her ribs were about to break apart. "I know what you're doing. But I'm fine."

"Good."

Seeing the doubt in her mother's gaze, Verity tried to square her shoulders and hike her chin. But when her chin trembled, she shrugged stiffly. "Would it make you happy to hear that I've imagined all those things and then some? Breakfasting, dinners, rubbing salve into the calluses on his hands, nestling my head into the crook of his shoulder where it fits perfectly. I've thought about what it would be like to wake up beside him, to have his children, to hear his laugh as he carries our son on his shoulders. Believe me, Mother, there isn't anything I haven't thought of. But if he could turn his back on his best friend, then what would stop him from leaving . . . me?"

Her tirade stopped. Those words echoed off the painted walls, filling the room, pressing in, suffocating her. Tears clogged her throat. And the weight of grief crushing her ribs, forced her to face the truth.

"I'm afraid that I couldn't survive it if"—her voice cracked, a breath juddering into her lungs—"if he abandoned me, like I meant n-nothing to him."

If she thought she had been crying before, she was kidding herself.

This time she broke on a tidal wave of racking, throat-tearing sobs. She couldn't stop, even as her mother rocked her like an infant. Doubled over, she felt as though she were about to retch from the agony. But she could not rid herself of it. The unbearable ache was trapped inside her, along with the knowledge that she had lost the only man she would ever love because she had been too afraid to believe that he could ever truly love her in return.

And now, he had moved on with his life . . . without her.

Chapter Thirty-Four

❧

SHE NEVER INTENDED to stay in her bedchamber for the remainder of the week.

The first day took her by surprise when she discovered that she'd slept through the whole of it. And Mother was kind enough to send a tray of tea and cakes. But Verity had no appetite.

The second day was little better. She nibbled on the crusty top of a scone, then lay down and slept again.

By the third day, wrung out and listless, she barely managed to hobble across the room to the washstand before deciding that dressing and facing the world were about as appealing as the cold gruel and calf's-foot jelly that appeared on the tray from the kitchen.

Tea and cakes, it wasn't. Apparently, Mother was trying to scare her out of bed.

It didn't work. Staying beneath the coverlet was far more preferable to joining her family for an amusing game of charades after dinner, then witnessing her parents' flirtatious banter and heated looks, all the while knowing that such things were not in her own future.

She did manage to accomplish something, however.

As she stared up at the ceiling, with the rain pattering against the windowpanes, she came to a realization. She knew that the anger and righteous indignation that had been holding her together since leaving London were gone. They had only been masking her real fears.

Now there was nothing left but the knowledge that she had pushed Magnus away in order to save herself from potential misery. *And what a brilliant notion that had been. Throw in an apothecary with a bottle of poison and it might have been worthy of Shakespeare.*

Oh, but that wasn't even the worst of it.

One night, when everyone in the house was fast asleep, she awoke with an idea. *A letter*, she thought. A letter to Magnus where she poured out her heart and soul in four scribbled, tear-stained and nose-dribbled pages would surely set matters to right. And by the time he finished devouring every word, his own cheeks would be damp with longing. He'd leave for Addlewick at once, eager to gather her in his arms and profess his undying love, reminding her of the plan he'd forged in a ledger all those weeks ago.

It was the perfect dream.

But Magnus never came. She waited and waited, days falling into days without a word. Not even a letter.

Anna sent a letter, however. The contents of which confirmed that she and Longhurst had been dining together quite often. Her friend mentioned it because, peculiarly, Mr. Snow seemed to be the driving force, which left Anna confused.

But Verity couldn't provide her counsel. There was nothing she could say. Any words of congratulations would be a lie, and she had given up lying altogether. The consequences had been too heartbreaking.

By the end of the week, the rain lifted. It seemed as though the sun would stay for a spell.

Mother continued to send dreadful things from the kitchen. Her father and brother left for London to secure lodgings for Truman. Reverend Tobias sent her a bouquet of wildflowers. And life, no matter how unfair it seemed, was continuing onward.

Honoria rapped on her door several times and tried to coax her out of doors for a walk, but Verity was too tired. At least, she was . . . until Thea decided to camp outside her bedchamber and read aloud a play about a maudlin heroine who was smothered to death by her sisters in order to save them all from coming down with *the misery plague*.

Therefore, the following morning, Verity decided it was time to rejoin the living.

It was the sensible thing to do, after all. She'd lamented long enough. Not to mention, she was tired of looking at gruel and calf's-foot jelly.

So she cracked open her bedchamber door and stepped into the rest of her life.

The breakfast room, she noted, was suspiciously void of reading material. Honoria usually had her face buried in yesterday's scandal sheet. More times than not, Thea was scribbling in a notebook. And Mother often flipped through the pages of the *Ladies' Quarterly*. Today, her family was all cheerful smiles and happy chatter.

It felt as though she were walking into a stranger's house.

"You needn't worry," she told them as she ladled porridge into her bowl. "I'm not about to collapse into tears over the contents of a newspaper. I'm old enough to know when something is over and, besides, I've moved on."

Mother set the sugar cone and nippers in front of her. "Of course, dear. You've always been strong."

You are braver than you think, Magnus had once told her.

Yet after having read the recent scandal sheets, she knew that she had no choice to be anything but brave as she faced the rest of her lonely existence.

"There is also a letter for you. From Miss Snow," Honoria said with an encouraging smile as she held it out.

But Verity couldn't open it. She already knew what the contents would be. *A wedding invitation.* And thinking about Magnus standing at the altar, waiting for his bride to walk down the aisle, made the dam that held her tears at bay cause her throat to constrict painfully.

She couldn't eat a single bite. Laying down her spoon, she pushed away from the table. "I think I'll walk in the garden and check on the birdhouses."

Mother nodded with understanding. Thea sighed and liberated the notebook from her pocket. And Honoria said, "I'll join you."

Verity forced herself to venture outside instead of back to her bedchamber. She had to do something other than think about Magnus.

"You didn't have to join me, but I am glad for the company," she said to her sister as they stepped out into the warm sunshine. A breeze stirred up the fragrance of morning dew and sweet lilacs.

Honoria slid her arm into the crook of hers. "I know. I just missed talking to you."

"Oh? And what did you miss most of all, my utter un-originality or my boring nature?"

"You are hardly boring," she said with a scoff and a meaningful sideways glance to the newly repaired trellis.

Verity tried not to follow her gaze, but it proved impossible. The sight of fresh wooden rungs, golden beneath the bright shoots of tenacious curling ivy only reminded her of how it all began. And all that she'd lost.

She looked ahead, walking with purpose. "Simply because I'm determined to extricate myself from any theatrical production does not suddenly make me interesting like the rest of the Hartley family."

"But you are," Honoria insisted. "You may not be as vocal, but we all share the same passion to live a life with meaning and purpose. And you have an innate sensibility to bring peace to the chaos surrounding you. Not only that, but I've always envied your lethal stare."

"My *what*?"

"That superior look you have that makes men quake in their boots. When it is only Althea and me walking in the village, men tend to think . . . Oh, heaven only knows." She flitted her fingers in a noncommittal wave. "However, when you are there, all straight-backed and superior, they are forced to remember themselves and dutifully behave. I wish I had that power."

"You render men speechless with your beauty. Being the ugly duckling of the Hartley clan is hardly something to envy."

"*Ugly duckling*," Honoria repeated with a laugh as if it were a jest. Yet, when she studied her sister's face, she frowned. "Surely, it isn't possible that you actually believe that nonsense? Good gracious, you do! Please tell me this isn't about that day I returned from my brief Season and Percy followed me home like a lost puppy."

"Not everything is about Percival Culpepper!"

"Good, because Percy is an idiot. As for you, your beauty is something like this Queen Anne's lace," her sister said, trailing her fingertips over the delicate white blossoms that lined the stable yard. "Wild, and yet the most regal of the meadow flowers. Not to mention, the stems are quite stubbo— *Ouch!*" With a grin, she rubbed the underside of her arm where Verity pinched her. "It was a compliment."

"That flower you are comparing me to is hemlock. You've confused the two," she said and saw a mischievous gleam in her sister's eyes. "And don't you dare say that it is even more apt."

"Me? I would never." Honoria laughed and narrowly avoided another pinch. "Be that as it may, I've often thought that men were too intimidated to approach you.

They want to be the rulers. The power appeals to their fragile egos. But you would challenge them. It would take a man of great internal fortitude to stand by your side."

"Or a man who did not require an heiress's dowry," she said under her breath as her gaze drifted off in the distance.

"*Hmm* . . . There's that, too. But you deserve nothing less. I hope you know that."

Verity didn't respond. If Honoria's observations were meant to give her hope that she might fall in love again, she was wasting her breath.

Falling in love was like finally unlocking the latch of a cage door, spreading your wings and soaring high into the heavens . . . only to be shot by a hunter.

No, love wasn't for her. She would be fortunate to marry a man she could tolerate.

They strolled toward the stately oak at the top of the hill that overlooked the blooming gardens surrounding the dower house and the rolling green fields beyond it. A low rock wall bordered their lands and beyond that sat the lane in front of the Hunnicutt house.

Beneath the shaded canopy of leaves, they watched as a trunk-laden carriage trundled to their unpleasant neighbor's door. When the driver stopped and the footmen came to situate the step, Elaine Hunnicutt appeared, followed by her daughter.

Then Mr. Hunnicutt stepped out of the house to greet them and was instantly besieged by two irate women with their arms flailing in agitation, one of them shaking a rolled-up paper of some sort.

"I can hear their squawking all the way up here," Verity said.

"Nell is in a snit. Strange, she usually only gets that way when you are concerned."

"She does delight in tormenting me."

"Her jealousy is most vexing." Honoria glanced at her again. "Surely, you know she has forever been jealous of you? Come now, sister. She has never bothered to taunt Thea or me."

"Because both of you are too far out of her reach."

"No, you simpleton. It is because, with you, she sees a true adversary for any genuine eligible gentleman who might stumble upon Addle—" Honoria stopped. "Oh dear! She's pointing this way. Quick! Before she spots us!"

Verity was tugged to her knees behind a low outcropping of limestone, and when she looked at her sister, they both broke out in giggles. "You are an idiot."

"Takes one to know one," she said, draping her arms lazily around her neck in a fond embrace, their foreheads touching. "But I am glad you are my sister. Without you, I would likely start to believe my own tales of Viscount Vandemere."

"Well, you have been betrothed since infancy . . . or so you like to say."

Honoria pursed her lips. "It wasn't even my story in the beginning. It was our grandmother's, if you'll recall."

"And the silver tongue did not fall far from the tree."

Smiling, they sat together with their backs against the smooth, timeworn surface of rock. She was just about to ask her sister if she ever intended to tuck her fictional viscount away and look for a real husband when the cat suddenly appeared.

Verity stiffened, ready to shoo the orange-spotted villain. He sauntered casually up to them, as if merely on a stroll. Then the little beast plopped down beside her, rolled onto its side and began to purr.

She stared down at it, incredulous. "What do you think it wants?"

"I believe he's waiting for you to pet him," her sister answered, situating her skirts.

"Then he's in for a long wait."

"Oh, come now, Verity. He cannot control his nature any more than you or I can. He's just more honest about it. And perhaps, there's a small part of him that's trying to apologize for terrorizing your birds."

She slid the creature a skeptical glance. "Well, if he imagines we're going to be friends—"

"Oh! I almost forgot," Honoria interjected. "Speaking of friends, I brought your letter from Miss Snow. I saw that you left it behind. Though, I imagine you were simply in too much of a hurry to breathe the fresh air this morning?"

Verity saw the knowing look in her sister's face, but there was sympathy and understanding in her eyes. Everyone knew she'd been waiting for the news of the betrothal between Anna and the duke. And now the letter stared at her, daring her to be brave.

"I don't suppose avoiding the contents will make it any easier," she said, but didn't reach out to take it.

Her sister shook her head. "I can read it for you, if you like."

"No. I'll do it. I need to face this, after all."

"You don't have to do it alone. You never did, you know."

Verity felt the prick of tears at the corners of her eyes and she nodded. "Very well. I should like it if you stayed with me."

She cracked the seal on the letter. The breeze rustling through the leaves of the oak tree fell still as if it, too, were waiting in dreaded anticipation.

When she unfolded the letter, a newspaper clipping fell out, drifting to the grass between them with the bold headline drawing her attention: BUTTON KING RUINED.

The sisters gasped in unison.

Honoria was the first to pick it up. "'This venerable pa-

per learned that Phineas Snow, the aforementioned Button
King, was another victim of the Eugene Steamship Scandal. An anonymous report states that Snow had invested
heavily after Eugene approached him months ago. The
project was to become both a shipping empire of luxury
passenger steam vessels that would cross the Atlantic in
record time and a secret wedding present to the Duke of
L— and Snow's daughter. Reports state that Snow's in-
vestment was not among the assets recovered after the
investigation. He has lost the bulk of his fortune.'" She
lowered the clipping, her brow puckered in confusion.
"What does that mean? Is your friend no longer an heiress? Will she . . ."

Her sister didn't finish, but it was clear that she was
wondering if Anna would still marry Longhurst.

Stunned by the news, Verity wondered the same, her
hands shaking as she smoothed the unfolded letter against
her skirts.

"'Dearest Verity, Enclosed you'll find an article that
was never printed.'"

"*Never printed?*" Honoria interrupted. "I don't understand."

Verity held up a finger and continued. "'The contents
are all true, however. My father did, indeed, invest a great
sum with Mr. Eugene months ago. Apparently, he had
planned to surprise Longhurst with the news that they
would be partners during the signing of the'"—her voice
broke—"'betrothal contract.'"

She squeezed her eyes shut against the sting of incipi-
ent tears. It was done, she thought. There was no reason
to read the scandal sheets each day, waiting for the announcement.

Somehow this confirmation didn't make it any easier.

She wanted to hate Anna. But how could she hate her
friend? After all, Anna never asked to be an heiress. The

same way Verity never asked to be a spinster without a dowry. Of course, if she hadn't pushed Magnus away, then perhaps . . .

But there was no point in thinking about what might have been. She was too late.

Even after he'd gone to such lengths to amend the wrongs he'd done to her brother, she had refused to forgive him. Had returned each of his letters, unopened, shutting him out completely. And by doing so, she had ripped out her own heart.

A breeze rustled the leaves overhead and swept by to brush a lock of hair across her cheek, carrying away her heavy sigh.

"Keep reading," Honoria said, tucking that stray tendril behind her ear, her blue eyes filled with sympathy. "After all, she said her father *had planned to surprise Longhurst*, not that he did. Additionally, if Snow hadn't any fortune, then there could be no dowry. And if there was no dowry, there wouldn't be a marriage."

But what her sister did not know was that Magnus was a man of honor. He wouldn't leave Anna to suffer the scorn after having society believe she was set to be the next Duchess of Longhurst.

Verity drew in a deep breath and lifted the page. As she read, she absently stroked the cat's fur, its purring warmth pressed against her skirts. "'As you might imagine, the exorbitant amount of my dowry should have been the first to be absorbed in this calamity. However, my father wouldn't hear of it. He said he would start the business from the bottom up, as he had done before, and proclaimed that I would marry well, even if it was the last thing he ever did.'"

"*Blast*," Honoria muttered in defeat, slumping back against the rock as if it were her heart that had just been shattered again.

Verity managed to continue. "'The enclosed article arrived from my all-seeing friend, who stopped the editor from printing the story. In exchange, he requested an audience with my father. There is so much more to tell you in person. However, the long and short of it is, Mr. Dashing and my father are embarking on a business venture together! And that is all for now, but I cannot wait until I see you again. Until then, your dearest friend, Anna.'"

Verity lowered the page, trying to absorb the news instead of thinking about everything that had not been written.

"Surely, that isn't all," Honoria groused, stealing the letter to inspect it herself. "But there was nothing definitive about the . . ."

Her sister didn't finish. But the word *wedding* seemed to ring like a gong, nonetheless. Even the cat seemed to hear it, for he scampered off without a backward glance.

Blinking to clear away the dampness collecting along the lower rims of her eyes, Verity took the letter and folded the clipping back inside it with careful precision. "That's because there's nothing to tell that we don't already know."

Standing, they both dusted off their skirts, and began to walk down the hill toward the house.

"It won't be so bad," Honoria said, reaching out to squeeze Verity's hand and offer a reassuring smile. "We'll grow old together. I'll wear enormous hats and fringed shawls, and you'll carry a cane and glower at all the miscreants in town."

"Why do I have to be the one who glowers?"

"Well, you're already so good at—" She jumped to the side to evade Verity's pinch then stuck out her tongue.

Then the sound of a carriage rumbling down their drive drew their attention.

The driver was in a hurry, the wheels kicking up a

cloud of dust. From the stable yard, the dogs took off like a shot, tearing through the garden at a full gallop, and yawping excitedly when they reached the driveway.

Shielding her eyes from the sun, Verity watched as the driver stopped. Then, before the groomsman came to lower the step, Lady Broadbent threw open the door and practically vaulted out of the carriage at a run. She was in such a rush that she forgot her cane and a groomsman had to hasten after her.

"I wonder what all the fuss is about," Honoria said.

Verity caught sight of a paper in the countess's grasp and her own mind instantly ventured to what could only be the latest scandal sheet. She hated to think about the contents. Though, likely the news was something to the effect of: THE DUKE OF LONGHURST ENGAGED TO MISS SNOW.

Glumly, she lowered her hand, just as a high squeal came from inside the house.

"That was Mother, I'm sure of it," she said.

Honoria nodded. "Though she usually only makes that sound when Father attempts to toss her over his shoulder and carry her out of the room."

But with their father and brother in London, there had to have been another reason.

They both looked at each other, then lifted their skirts and ran the rest of the way to see what was the matter.

Chapter Thirty-Five

❧

$\mathcal{T}$HE INSTANT VERITY appeared in the morning room doorway, her mother swatted her with the newspaper. Then laughed. "I cannot believe you didn't tell me. Your own mother. But oh, what gloating I will do the next time I see Elaine Hunnicutt. Therefore, my darling girl, you are forgiven."

Her mother pressed a kiss to her cheek and Verity frowned, looking down at the paper. But before she could read it, Honoria snatched it. Then her eyes widened.

"Ah. Now I understand." She looked at Verity and tsked. "Poor you. If you had only been a better liar then none of this would have happened."

At the mention of her lying prowess, or lack thereof, a cold shiver of foreboding slithered down her spine. "And what is it that I have been accused of?"

"As if you didn't know," Lady Broadbent scoffed with a grin. Apparently, she was in on the joke with everyone else, but Verity still didn't have a clue.

She leaned over the back of the sofa to snatch the paper from Honoria, but Althea beat her to it.

Thea frowned. "Looks like there's been another speculation failure."

"Other side," Honoria singsonged as Mother and the countess were busily chatting over tea at the round table in the corner.

"I cannot believe it!" Thea huffed and glared at Verity

as she crumbled the paper and threw it on the Aubusson rug. "Why does no one tell me anything?"

She stormed past her and headed out the door.

Verity shook her head in exasperation. Her entire family had lost their minds.

Bending down, she picked up the paper and smoothed it out against the top of the camel back sofa.

The words *THE DUKE OF LONGHURST* stood out in bold on the first line. She expected the next line to read *ENGAGED*. Yet, as her hand moved over the page, she saw the word *ELOPED* instead.

Her heart plummeted to the ground. The organ must have dropped all the way to her knees because her legs refused to hold her up. She had to clutch the sofa's curved hump to stand upright.

He was married. It was over.

"But eloped?" she said to the room in disbelief. Why would he have eloped with Anna?

"I couldn't keep it a secret any longer," a low voice said from the doorway.

Startled, she whipped around, her head so dizzy she imagined she saw Magnus standing there. But that couldn't be true.

So she blinked to clear her vision. And yet, he was still standing there, holding his hat in his hands.

"*Longhurst?*"

"I couldn't keep it a secret any longer," he repeated and took a step into the room, his gaze never leaving hers. "But we both knew that the truth was bound to come out sooner or later."

Everyone was speaking in riddles today and she didn't understand. "The truth?"

Behind her, her mother laughed.

Magnus continued toward her, his eyes bright with something she didn't dare name. Not now. Not when it was too late. "The truth that we were married on Tuesday over a blacksmith's anvil."

"You were?"

"I was." He nodded, still holding her gaze. "And you were."

"*Me?*" She squeezed her eyes shut. Shook her head. This was some sort of dream, the kind where nothing made sense.

But then she felt the heat of him as he moved closer. Felt the brush of his breath against her cheek as he whispered, "You have to back me up on my lie, and then we'll be even."

Her eyes flew open to see copper irises, lit like brazier fires burning warmly. She felt the newspaper under her fingers and realized she hadn't finished reading all the way.

THE DUKE OF LONGHURST
ELOPED WITH
MISS VERITY HARTLEY

Her astonished gaze flew back to his. "I don't understand."

"Oh, I think you do," he challenged.

Her knees were shaking, but her heart seemed to lift and a tiny kernel of hope fluttered beneath her breast.

He'd told a lie. A whopping *big* lie.

The kind of lie that started a scandal.

"But what about your family? Your duty?"

"There are musts, wants and needs in every man's life. Such as, I must honor my duty as the Duke of Longhurst to king, country and family. And I want to live a good life, to have sons and daughters, and to live long enough to see the fruits of my labor blossom and ripen. But then, there is need." He took her hand. "At the core of my being, there is only one answer for this—I need Verity. Because I love Verity."

A breath fell out of her. "You do?"

"More than I can bear. Without you, nothing else matters." He brought her knuckles to his lips, and only then did she spot the purplish bruise around one eye.

She slipped her hand free and reached out to tenderly brush the swollen flesh. "Whatever happened?"

"Well, on my way here, I stopped to change horses at a coaching inn. By happenstance, your father and brother were there, too. Hawk and I had a chat, of sorts, and he"—his mouth curled ruefully—"welcomed me to the family."

"Then everything is settled between the two of you?"

"It will be," he said. "At least, it will when you give me your answer. So, will you, Verity?"

Her head was still spinning, trying to catch up with itself. "You mean, take part in your lie?"

He nodded again. "We'll have to be convincing, of course. Stay together for the next fifty years or so. Have a dozen children."

"A *dozen*?"

"There's really no other way to settle the score between us. After all, you did make me dance with Mrs. Horncastle."

Verity couldn't stop the laugh that bubbled up her throat. This was all so absurd, it had to be true. "I suppose it is only fair."

"Then come on," he said with a grin and tugged on her fingertips. "The carriage is waiting."

Lady Broadbent and Mother encouraged this by shooing them out of the morning room.

It wasn't until Verity stepped into the foyer that something occurred to her. "But what about your mother and my lack of fortune? That won't be an easy mountain to climb."

"You don't know the half of it," he said with an unconcerned chuckle. "Especially after I lost £1,000 on one of my brother's foolish speculations."

"That doesn't sound like you."

"I know, but I had to take the risk. It was the only chance I had of giving you, and our children, the life and future you deserve."

She stopped and faced him squarely. "I don't care about money. The only life I want is with you."

"And that's what I said to my mother when I told her that I was marrying you regardless."

"I imagine that went over well," she said dryly, even as her heart soared.

"Better than expected. In fact, she was actually in high spirits. Giddy, even." He nodded at her disbelieving expression. "Apparently, shortly before my announcement, a messenger arrived with the news that a silver mine, which my father invested in years ago, wasn't quite the disaster that it had seemed. But I'll tell you more about it on the way."

As they turned toward the door, Honoria called down from upstairs.

"Wait!" She glided swiftly down the steps, a valise in hand. Then she set it down and wrapped her arms around Verity. "I packed a few things for you. Lots of lace, you know, to keep you cool during all the sweltering evenings ahead."

Verity blushed. She was just about to thank her sister when the front door suddenly burst open.

Nell Hunnicutt charged in, waving her own copy of the scandal sheet. "This is all a lie. I know for a fact that you aren't married. I have it under good authority that you've been here, moping for weeks."

"I don't see that this is any concern of yours," Verity said, offering her best lethal stare.

But Nell was in a rant and nothing could stop her. "Your

Grace, I want you to know that I won't allow her family to get away with this. For your sake. In fact, I will be more than glad to let the world know that this was all a ruse and an attempt to trap you. I've known it from the beginning. She made it all up."

"Is that so?" Magnus asked. "Why don't we step into the parlor, and you can tell me all about it."

The Tick cast a triumphant grin over her shoulder at Verity when she took the arm of the duke and they walked across the foyer. "Well, it all started that day when . . ."

As she continued to explain, Verity watched as Magnus casually opened the door and gestured for her to precede him. Only it wasn't the parlor. It was the closet beneath the stairs. And Nell didn't even realize it until the door closed behind her.

"I think there's been a mistake, Your Grace," she said with a tittering laugh through the door. "But if this is about the ball, you must know that it was all in fun. Just a jest between old friends."

"Hmm . . . I still think you owe my wife an apology."

"She isn't your wife," the Tick hissed through the door. "There isn't any way that a spinster like her could ever snag a duke!"

"It appears there is a way," he said and turned the key in the lock. He gave it to Verity, who was tempted to take it all the way to Scotland.

Instead, she handed it to Honoria. "Promise you will open it the instant we leave."

"Of course." Honoria's expression was a mask of innocence, with an impish glint in her eyes as they headed toward the door.

Then, just as Verity crossed the threshold, she saw Reverend Tobias stepping beneath the portico. And he was carrying flowers.

"Ah, Miss Hartley. You are looking well, all bright eyes

and flushed cheeks. I thought, perhaps, you would join me for another . . . walk." He hesitated as Magnus came up beside her, his gaze drifted to the hand Magnus had on her valise and the other wrapped possessively around her waist. "Apparently, I have arrived too late."

His grin altered to one of chagrin as he handed her the bouquet.

Not knowing what to say, she offered, "Thank you."

As he walked away, she looked up at Magnus, who arched a dark brow. He arched a brow. She shrugged. "Well, you were out with Anna. Was I supposed to sit here all alone?"

"Clearly not," he groused, escorting her to their waiting carriage. "Is there anything you need to tell me?"

Before he handed her inside, she rose up on her toes and pressed her lips to his frown. "I should probably mention that you are the only man I have ever loved."

He grunted in approval and kissed her. "Now get in the carriage before anyone else arrives."

A throat cleared from near the other side of the carriage and they both turned to see a tall, handsome man dismounting from his horse.

"I don't mean to intrude," the stranger said, doffing his hat. "But is Miss Hartley at home?"

"Which one," Magnus growled, cinching her to his side.

"Miss Honoria Hartley."

Verity's head tilted. She didn't recognize this man as one of her sister's usual suitors. "Is she expecting you?"

"I should think so," he said, flashing a rakish grin. "I'm Viscount Vandemere."

She gasped, but before she could say a word, Magnus interjected, "Miss Hartley is inside."

The man inclined his head and walked past them.

"I need to tell my sister," Verity said, trying to slip out of Magnus's embrace.

He held fast. "She will be just fine. I've learned that the Hartley women are rather resourceful. So, get in the carriage."

She huffed, her hands perched on her hips. "Is this really how you're proposing to me?"

He kissed her stubborn chin, then her lips. And a few delicious moments later, he swept her off her feet and into the carriage without any further argument.

At least, for now.